ANN BRIDGE

PEKING PICNIC

WITH A NEW INTRODUCTION BY
KATE KELLAWAY

Virago

Published by VIRAGO PRESS Limited 1989
20–23 Mandela Street, Camden Town, London NW1 0HQ

First published in Great Britain by Chatto & Windus 1932
Copyright Ann Bridge 1932
Virago edition offset from Chatto & Windus 1948 edition

Introduction copyright © Kate Kellaway 1989

A CIP catalogue record for this book
is available from the British Library

Printed in Great Britain
by Cox and Wyman Ltd, Reading, Berks

To

Bridget, Jock, and Constance

and to

The Singing Kuniang

Herself

" All among the yellow fields the city stands, the walls keep watch, the gates lift up their heads, scorning the passage of the unregarded years, indifferent to affection or reproach, dead to remorse or hope. The Western Hills change their appearance thrice a day and put on once a year their transient green ; the lotus blooms, the willows turn to gold, and everywhere the splendour of the sun and frost is exercised. But all the pride and beauty of these things could not for long command or fortify a foreign heart, and so I went without regret back to the source of my beliefs and strength."

A Journey from Peking

Introduction

LAURA LEROY, heroine of *Peking Picnic*, is a diplomat's wife, a beauty and a lady of leisure. She moves languorously; is to be found, sitting slightly apart, reading letters from home; or leaning against cool marble contemplating Chinese cherry blossom; or with a cocktail in hand, charming her husband's colleagues. But languor and weariness are not to be confused with passivity or idleness. Nor is Laura, as you might suspect, a straightforward portrait of Ann Bridge.

There was nothing weary or idle about Ann Bridge: she produced twenty-six books in the forty-two years between 1932 when she published her first, and her death. They include three novels of North China; a novel about the Dalmatian coast (also used as a travel-guide); five historical, didactic and reportage novels on the Spanish Civil War, Albania, Turkey and Budapest; the "Julia" series, with its female-detective heroine, and four books of autobiography and family history.

Ann Bridge, like Laura, was a diplomat's wife and went in 1925, with her husband Owen O'Malley, to live in Peking where he had been appointed Counsellor in the Legation. A traditional rule of the Diplomatic Service precluded her from writing under her real name, Mary O'Malley. Bridge was taken from Bridge End, her house in Surrey; Ann was her middle name. In her partial autobiography *Facts and Fictions* she recalled: "People who knew we had been in China were constantly asking 'Who is Ann Bridge? Did you meet her in

Peking?' As one cannot very well meet oneself, I could truthfully say that I had not."

In 1929, at the age of forty, Ann Bridge started to write *Peking Picnic,* her first novel. After two traumatic years of illnesses and other difficulties following their return from China, the family was back at Bridge End, and in spite of the stresses she had gone through, Ann Bridge had reason to feel strong enough for anything. A year earlier, she and Owen had faced a crisis which was both personally distressing and publicly humiliating. To try to make a bit more money during the 1920s, Owen O'Malley had speculated in French francs. In what later became known as "the Francs Case" he was accused of making improper use of his official position for private gain and almost lost his position at the Foreign Office. He would certainly have done so had it not been for Ann Bridge who argued his case for him with the Whitehall establishment. She persuaded them that he had acted unwisely but not criminally and through the strength of her arguing as well as her arguments, he was exonerated. She wrote a book on the subject, *Permission to Resign,* but only decided to publish it three years before she died.

It is easy to see that her triumph must have been quite hard for her husband to take, and sad but telling to see how each wrote the other out of their account of the incident. Ann Bridge described:

> the exuberance with which I reported what was, in spite of the initial misery, a rather exhilarating experience for me. His Majesty's Government had made a wrong and cruel decision; with endless help from all sides, they were induced to reverse it. This does not happen every day; still less do common mortals have a hand in bringing it about.

In his autobiography *The Phantom Caravan* O'Malley said only that "it is certain that considerable efforts made in many quarters to secure a mitigation of the sentence had some effect".

Her daughters now refer to their mother as Bridge. "Bridge was a natural writer," says Jane O'Malley, her elder daughter. She used to write before breakfast, sitting in bed between the hours of seven and nine, with a cup of early-morning tea that must have got very cold before she was through. She began tentatively and would show *Peking Picnic* to friends demanding to know if it was a novel. Some of them said it wasn't but A.D. Peters, who became her agent, was impressed by it and fiercely determined that she should get a good deal. He placed the novel with Chatto & Windus and it appeared in 1932.

Peking Picnic rocketed Ann Bridge to fame. It was remarkable in that it achieved not only popular acclaim but also won over the most discriminating reviewers of the day. L.P. Hartley described the novel as "almost unmixed delight . . . It is pictorial and exciting and illuminating, and deserves comparison with that best novel of recent years *A Passage to India*". In the *Spectator* L.A.G. Strong praised *Peking Picnic* as "an unusual and beautiful first novel, which leaves one thinking long after one has put it down".

Gerald Gould too, for the *Observer*, hailed it as "a first novel of rare quality—beautiful, grave, humorous, exciting and wise", saying that it combined, "the thrilling narrative of external adventure with the sensitive interpretation of the fine shades in human relationships". He added that character, "as in real life, is allowed to grow on us, to reveal itself as astonishing while remaining consistent". It was, he concluded, "a model of delicate and exact writing".

Reviewers regretted that Laura Leroy was fictional, longing for her to step off the page and enliven their lives. Ellery Sedgwick, editor of the *Atlantic Monthly*, wrote of her defensively, almost as if justifying a slightly improper love affair:

> I am a man, and to me the incomparable asset of this book is the woman who will make it famous. Whether women will love Mrs Leroy I don't know, but men will vote for her—if the ballot is secret. Perhaps she is more desirable than admirable. Perhaps she is more satisfactory as a heroine than she would be as a wife. At any rate, here's to you, Laura Leroy!

She appealed to women every bit as much as to men and Ellery Sedgwick received several letters putting him right on the matter. Writing in the *Glasgow Evening News* J. B. Priestley praised *Peking Picnic* for its "fun", "poetry", and "sagacity" (quite a combination) and likewise recognised that if Laura was a personality then "obviously the author is a personality too".

But if Laura captivated reviewers, they were no less pleased by the characterisation of the maid Hubbard. Hubbard is no beauty but a great hit with the men, and although she is only the maid she knows more about the movements of warlords and Peking politics than all the diplomats put together. She was an exact portrait of Baker, Ann Bridge's maid, but, oddly, most reviewers seem to have taken it for granted that Hubbard must be an invention. English reviewers were enraptured, the Americans only a little less so. Some voiced tentative reservations about the aristocratic condescension of the author. But on both sides of the Atlantic there was discussion as to whether the word "brilliant" was superlative enough to describe the book. Ann Bridge couldn't believe her luck: "The reviewers were amazingly kind to *Peking Picnic*. I rubbed my eyes in astonishment, could this be my book that I'd been so tentative about?"

And there was another triumph. *Peking Picnic* had won the *Atlantic Monthly* fiction prize. The family were in dire financial straits and the £3,500 made Bridge weep with joy. She remembered:

> Poor Owen had had to deny himself many of his small pleasures, and even to sell our capital to meet those awful school bills; now with infinite pleasure, I wrote out a cheque "For one thousand pounds only", and took it down to him at breakfast.

Little Brown and Co., her Boston publishers, organised fancy promotions for the book, sending booksellers three-panel cut-outs of Chinese temples to put in their shop windows. Fan mail poured in. Collins' nursery wrote asking for the exact name of the white pine described in the novel. The nurseryman added his own compliment to the praise: "After reading the book I am not surprised that people want to plant a tree so beautifully described." The British Museum had a flood of visitors who came to see the Chinese picture The Earthly Paradise simply because of Ann Bridge's description of it in *Peking Picnic*.

Being the source of the family's income gave Ann Bridge both confidence and power—the freedom to be expansive, to tell her enthusiasms and to use her intelligence. She was, Jane O'Malley says, "a performer *par excellence*". This was her strength though it could be regarded as a flaw. She couldn't resist showing off, and, in a sense, the novels are themselves performances. Peking is theatrical: the crowd of cocktail drinkers are "like figures on a stage"; Laura Leroy's world shifts "like drop-scenes in the theatre".

"There is in Laura," Jane O'Malley says, "very much of what Bridge wanted to be. She was loving, generous, brave, but inclined to override and interfere and not always as intelligent about people as Laura. She had very strong opinions which she was quite sure were right."

Ann Bridge prided herself on inspiring confidences. Her letters written on board ship en route to China told of meeting a young man who was amazed by her manner: "it was completely new to him to meet people who were as frank, as drastic and as amused as the O'M's about the secret places of the heart". In the same letter, she also wrote, "I am getting to know the accent of the breaking heart." Sitting on deck late at night, their chairs side by side, she lectured the young man,

> on the text that loving people is *never* wasted—it's the loving that matters, and whether it eventuates in marriage or not is quite irrelevant. And that reality begins in the place where he sat in emptiness—especially if you are witty and play deck-quoits over it, and polish your sentences for middle-aged ladies (like me).

And like Bridge, everyone talks to Laura. Even Professor Vinstead, a dry Cambridge academic, confides in her. Yet though Laura entrances him with her conversation, the charm of *Peking Picnic* is the sense that she only confides in us. Bridge understood the art of conversation. Her gift is for dialogue of a critical, enthusiastic, sometimes intimate and always exacting nature. *Peking Picnic* is the equivalent of a challenging, sympathetic conversation.

Ann Bridge, by all accounts, was herself a terrific talker. "She was so brilliant, so enthusiastic in what she wanted to tell, that other people just couldn't get a word in edgeways," says her daughter. This power, which she retained to the end of her life, went with her engaging charm but was difficult for other people, and was the subject of many family jokes: when Ernie Bevin was Foreign Secretary, Bridge was sitting beside him at some party and burst into the conversation to put her own enthusiastic point of view, at which Bevin put out a restraining hand and said firmly, "Hush, I'm talking."

Laura is a woman of such extraordinary independence and strength of mind that she makes the men she encounters seem weak in comparison. She is every bit as much a diplomat as her husband. While he soaks in the bath, she has to soothe the ragged nerves of their guests. Ann Bridge's own view of the diplomatic world, like Laura's, was that it was "a job to be done", but while she enjoyed the scope it offered for her conversational gifts, her letters also tell of the strain of having to be circumspect to all kinds of difficult people and of "a lot of wearing my best clothes and putting my best social foot forward and thinking of amusing things to say". Sometimes the sham wearied her.

Peking Picnic did not exhaust Ann Bridge's desire to write about China although *The Ginger Griffin* and *Four-Part Setting* (published in 1934 and 1937) do not surpass her first attempt. But in all three novels Peking has a magical quality. Even its air may catch the unwary by surprise:

> The air of North China has this peculiar quality for causing nervous stimulation, which produces quite definite results . . . there comes a lightness, a nimbleness of mind and body, and a sort of emotional exaltation in which the most unusual behaviour seems positively normal and delightful.

So, for those not sipping cocktails on the terrace of a temple, or drinking tea with a dash of rum, or smoking cigarettes (at moments of crisis the question is always: "*Do* we have enough cigarettes?"), breathing the "white wine" air is likely to have an equally intoxicating effect. This heady atmosphere enhances our sense that characters may fall rapidly in and out of love and shift moods from despondency to elation and back again. Professor Vinstead, after several hundred pages of stimulation, arrives at his summary: "I suppose that *is* Peking." Mrs Leicester in *The Ginger Griffin* lets us know that, "Most girls who come to Peking leave it engaged, generally to the wrong man; and nearly all women leave Peking with a broken heart."

The politics of Peking in the 1920s were somewhat less intoxicating and were a bit of a picnic themselves. In 1911 or 1912, Sun Yat Sen and his reform party had proclaimed a republic. After the revolution Peking was much sought after—and much fought over—by competing politicians and warlords. The coming and going of generals was accepted as a fact of life: unsettling but not startling. "Nina's picnic was for the second time quite disastrously off", Ann Bridge writes. "This, for the party was the important feature of the military situation." However, the military situation turns out to be more than an inconvenience when, in the most exciting chapters of the novel, the picknickers are taken hostage.

In spite of this, Ann Bridge is more occupied by the appearance of Peking than with its history and she shows how familiarity dictates our perception of what is beautiful. Laura explains to Vinstead that at first she found China strange and arid, but that once accustomed to it and tutored into seeing its beauty, she knew that, when she returned to England, she would be homesick for it.

And Owen O'Malley wrote in *The Phantom Caravan* "The visitor from overseas is told that everyone reaches Peking in tears of disappointment and leaves it with tears of regret."

The pleasure for today's reader is in visiting a place that no longer exists. It is easy to arrive at the temple alongside Laura, to unpack with her, to see exactly where she sleeps. Although Peking itself may have changed beyond recognition, its details are preserved here along with the exact details of Laura's luggage. Laura has a special talent for making herself at home in her exotic surroundings and there is a particular delight in the domestic scene in which she unpacks her leather slippers, unusual red jacket and travelling washbasin with a leather lid, and makes her quarters at the temple not only habitable but faintly luxurious.

Laura Leroy is caught between China and England. As the first line of *Peking Picnic* explains—"To live in two different worlds at the same time is both difficult and disconcerting." This comes directly from Bridge's letters of the time. She wrote to a friend (28 Feb 1926):

> I suffered from a sort of divided consciousness, feeling that only half of me was on board [the ship outward bound to China] and that the main centre of my life lay miles behind me . . . I found the state of mind a disabling one and struggled against it.

In another letter, she complained that she felt "so uncomfortable . . . all in halves, half here and half at home; it is so hard to find anything which joins the two". This novel was what, eventually, fused them. And it is the tension between foreignness and familiarity that gives each its intensity. Owen O'Malley described the dislocation in the *Phantom Caravan*:

When we got home again to Bridge End, we felt we had got two worlds instead of one to live in. Short of going to the moon, we did not see how anyone in any other way could similarly enlarge their universe.

Ann Bridge had a sharp eye for detail. The descriptions of Peking itself are as delicate as a Chinese screen. Some of the portraits of the servants now have the quality of dated colonial snapshots. "The Chinese chauffeurs, in khaki-and-gold uniforms stood by their cars, spitting idly at the plum blossom in the Consul's flowerbeds." And, "Old Wang, the head *mafoo*, slippered softly back in to the stable yard . . . and pulling a very ancient kitchen chair out into the sun, sat down opposite his cherished pots of cactuses and lit a little black and silver pipe."

Among the Chinese, the servants were, of course, those whom Bridge knew best. In a letter (28 Feb 1926), she described lying in bed with a cold, and marvelled at the activity around her:

> One house coolie has been sweeping my room and another dusting it—No 1 in a long white coat, has brought me cocoa on a large silver tray and No 2 a couple of notes on a small one—while Baker, the maid has been fussing in and out wanting fresh orders for the amah and Chang, our private laundry man.

Her letters enthusiastically admired the Chinese, remarking that the children scarcely ever cried, that the women, although they often looked older than they were, had faces that were lined with contentment.

The disappointment of the novel is in its glancing characterisations of the Chinese themselves: "the usual overwhelming Chinese curiosity"; "their tendency to hysteria"; "the usual Chinese suddenness"; "as official as anything is official in China"; "Chinese servants always know everything"; "the Chinese are a perfectly rational people—the most rational on earth probably —so of course they aren't sentimentalists"; "the supreme characteristic of the Chinese is their inconsequence"; "I think they're the most lovable race on earth." *Peking Picnic* fails to escape from these generalisations, or to combine them. It is hard, too, to read now that, "A rickshaw is the most delightfully civilised form of locomotion", without flinching and sympathising with one of the picnickers, Miss Hande, the literal-minded American who gets a stern ticking-off for objecting to this mode of transport.

Miss Hande is a novelist, not entirely humourless, very keen on hygiene and human rights and very nationalistic herself. It is a plausible and amusing portrait and was inspired by a real American, a Miss Foot. Ann Bridge also makes merry with the Frenchman, Henri Delache. He is ludicrous, keen on the girls but not a true romantic. He pokes fun at the English for their singular way of allowing moonlight to promote kissing. But she is at her best when describing the English members of the party with their "profound English instinct for treating serious matters lightly".

"Understanding begins where familiarity leaves off," says Laura. In fact, Ann Bridge proves that the reverse is true. She has a vigorous gift for observation of other people, especially those of her own class and continually asks, directly or by implication, What makes people as they are? What makes them sympathetic or not?—It's when they show some sign of being really alive inside and aware of the things that move them, is one of her answers. It does well as a definition of Bridge's—and Laura's—ability. Another question which dominates the novel is, to what extent does place shape and influence our lives?—"No one has yet measured the pressure exercised on our moods and impulses in moments of tension by external things."

Ann Bridge was exceptionally receptive to natural beauty and never daunted by any landscape—however sublime. "The delicate, strange beauty of the whole landscape struck powerfully on her senses rousing her to an active delight." She was equally absorbed by female beauty, a judge and a deliberator on it. She was, in her daughter's phrase "calamitously beautiful" herself. This is confirmed by family photographs which show a woman of swan-like grace whose features have an imperious fascination. Her face recalls her definition of beauty in *Four-Part Setting* as "a special capacity for abandonment, masked by that silvery detachment".

Curiously Lilah, of *Peking Picnic*, although beautiful, was based on a very plain friend. In *Facts and Fictions* Bridge explained:

> I continually went over in the old Triumph to see a really *very* plain friend whose firm character and laconic speech were the foundations for Lilah—and discuss her activities; this precious creature was under no illusions about her looks, and gleefully told all her friends, "Mary Ann is putting me in her book, disguised as a beauty."

This explains why the description of Lilah has an idealised, radiant anonymity—"She was a massive glorious blonde, beautiful with a well-regulated beauty of snowy neck and shoulders, apple-blossom skin."

Judith, on the other hand, a portrait of greater exactitude and idiosyncracy, was modelled on a friend, Ursula Nettleship, and true to life: "The face was redeemed from ordinariness by rather fine light blue eyes, under brows much darker than her hair, which slanted almost upwards at the corners." At times this assessment can seem pitiless, written from the security of Bridge's own handsomeness:

> And glancing round the table she suddenly noticed Annette Ingersoll also watching Judith, with a curiously wistful expression on her pretty, inexpressive face—so much prettier than the English girl's, but so wholly without the life, the shooting play of expression from feature to feature which put Laura in mind of the flight of a swallow.

Ann Bridge's early novels are arguments about love and marriage; about both, she is tough and stoical. Bridge and Owen, says her daughter, could be seen as presenting, a strong argument against marriage.

> They fell in love, with a mind-blowing explosion, when Bridge was twenty-two, and were married for sixty-one of her eighty-four years. But they were profoundly ill-suited. In the face of life's difficulties she was a fighter. He was not.

In these novels, when romance comes to a married woman as it does to Laura in the unlikely shape of Vinstead, it is allowed to overwhelm but never overcome the characters. The heroines are not whisked off at the end in a state of transport. Love is rooted in pain and life in disappointment. In *Four-Part Setting* Rose, in spite of her unhappy marriage and her love for another, decides that duty must win the day, that marriage is too binding to break, and it seems now, reading with a modern eye, that this is a decision made through a kind of masochism, a decision to martyr the self for the sake of a greater good. Echoing Ann Bridge on board ship to Peking, Laura asks, "Can one stop people being hurt and had one better? In her experience all the richest and most valuable things were mixed up, somehow or other, with being hurt."

Peking Picnic contains a quotation from William Blake: "He who binds to himself a joy/Doth the winged life destroy?/He who kisses the joy as it flies/Lives in Eternity's sunrise." Ann Bridge tries heroically to make this her position—to win a kind of permanence by cheerfully waving the handkerchief at the right moment. Marriage is the joy which kills the winged life but to which the woman must all the same be bound.

Kate Kellaway, London, 1989

Chapter One

TO live in two different worlds at the same time is both difficult and disconcerting. Actually, of course, the body cannot be in China and in Oxfordshire simultaneously. But it can, and does, travel rapidly between the one place and the other, while the mind or the heart persists obstinately in lingering where the body is not, or in leaping ahead to the place whither the body is bound. The whole man—or perhaps chiefly the whole woman—is in such circumstances never completely anywhere.

"*La nef qui disjoint nos amours,*" cried Mary Stuart to France from the deck of the ship in which she sailed to Scotland:

> "*N'a 'cy de moy que la moictié.*
> *Une part te reste—elle est tienne . . .*"

And the lingering spirit, summoned back by some importunate demand on the attention, brings with it a host of pictures, of scenes complete with scents and sounds, which it intrudes at the most unsought moments, so that the images of both worlds shift and change before one like drop-scenes in a theatre. It is all most confusing and disabling, and so Mrs. Leroy found it.

She was sitting in the garden of a large house in the Tartar City. What she saw with her bodily eyes was a small goldfish-pond set in a miniature landscape of rocks and grottoes, against a background of pavilions with red pillars, painted eaves, and tent-like roofs of green tiles, over which the formal plumed tops of two

1

immense pines in the next courtyard showed black
against the light glittering sky. A band was playing in
one of the pavilions, a buffet was being served from
behind and depleted from in front in another; a short
stout lady and a tall thin man were receiving guests at
the top of a shallow flight of marble steps. Round the
grottoes people in light summer clothes sat, or shifted
to and fro; a high treble roar of voices hung over the
whole assembly; Chinese servants with sealed pale-green
faces, silent movements, and white coats with gold
sashes moved about handing ices, olives, cocktails and
caviare *croûtes* with serene dignity. She was, in fact, at
an At Home in the Scandinavian Legation. But she
was not really seeing any of it. Sitting back in her chair
under an oleander, for a moment alone, what she saw
with great clearness was a green field bordered with
youthful Scots pines, on which small white figures ran
about with happy cries. She heard the sound of wood
on leather and leather on wood, and treble voices
crying, "How's that?" and hurrahing eagerly if thinly.
And most clearly of all she saw one little flushed face,
broad of brow, with blue veins in the white temples
where the rough brown hair stuck damp to the skin, the
grey eyes set wide above the dumpy nose, which approached her with a shy entrancing smile and said,
"Might have been worse, Mummie, mightn't it?" as he
settled down on the grass at her feet. Oh, *so* clear—she
could see the little freckles on the white forehead and
the big ones on the bridge of that snub nose, and the
short broad hands, so absurdly strong for their size,
that twiddled at the binding of the cricket bat.

"Have one of this fellow's cocktails, Mrs. Leroy—he
seems to want you to," said a voice overhead.

Mrs. Leroy said, "No, I won't"—and then, "Yes, I
think I will"—before she looked up. The voice was

familiar; she knew that her line of vision would have to travel upwards through a considerable angle before it reached the drooping blond distinction of General Nevile's moustache and nose and eyelids, haloed by the green lining of a topi. She did, however, look up and smile, not insincerely—she liked the Military Attaché— as she took a cocktail from the tray proffered by the servant. The man bowed over the glasses and smiled brilliantly and furtively at her before he moved away.

"He seems to know you," observed the General, directing his monocle at the servant.

"Yes, it's my Number Three," said Mrs. Leroy. "I suppose he's a friend of the Knudsens' Number One."

"Look here," said General Nevile, "I know my wife is looking for you; may I see if I can find her?"

"Do," said Mrs. Leroy, and watched his tall thin figure move away, limping a little in his white ducks If she had hoped to remain alone, however, her hopes were frustrated—the German Counsellor came and clicked his heels before her and said that it was very hot; the Italian First Secretary kissed her hand and murmured that she looked deliciously cool; the Flemish Minister did likewise, and told her a funny story about their hostess in low, rapid and indistinct French; the Japanese Minister bowed very low and said that he regretted not to see her so distinguished husband in English which was monosyllabically correct. Mrs. Leroy said that her husband was engaged on business for the Minister—and she smiled as she said it, for he was, as she knew, at that moment in the farrier's shop at the American Legation, presiding over the shoeing of his own and Sir James Boggit's polo-ponies.

A very tall young man, exquisitely dressed, with an eyeglass in one of his extremely blue eyes, paused behind the Japanese Minister, and made an amiable grimace at Mrs. Leroy over the little man's head.

"Well, *au revoir*, Excellency," she said, winding up the interview deftly. "I shall give my husband your love. Good afternoon, Derek."

"*Good* afternoon, *ma chère*," said the young man, raising his hat and showing a head as black and curly as a spaniel's. "Where are your *Kuniangs*?"

"I sent them to the Summer Palace," said Mrs. Leroy, in her usual slow tones. "Miss Parke is going to tell them about the Empress Dowager. I thought it would amuse them more."

"I should think that highly probable," said Derek Fitzmaurice, sitting down beside her. "I should like to give a party for them next week," he went on. "Will they still be here?"

"Yes, they have another month here, you know," she said. "How nice of you, Derek."

"Would Thursday do?" he inquired. "Are you free then?"

"You don't mean *I'm* to come?" She spoke in dismay, or something like it.

"But of course—why not? Do come, my dear. There's going to be a really good film at the Chen-Kuang."

In Peking the cinema takes the place of the theatre, opera and concert-hall combined. None of these exist, and on the first night of a famous film the grand circle of the Chen-Kuang might be Covent Garden, so full is it of diamonds, *décolletages* and diplomatists.

Mrs. Leroy was not tempted, however.

"No," she said, "I'm busy all next week, I'm sure. But do have the Kuniangs—they will enjoy it. Our parties are very dull for them."

"I should have thought you would want them

chaperoned to my establishment," he said rather resentfully.

"Oh no—they can chaperon one another. Your establishment!" She gave a little laugh. "Don't have too many of your Russians that night."

"I'll tell you who I want to have," said the young man, leaning towards her confidentially. "Number Twenty-three! I've met her at last and she's an absolute peach. She really is *too* lovely."

"Which is Number Twenty-three? I've seen two or three of them about. Is it the tall one with an immense forelock and gold brocade, or the little one with a round face like a flower?"

"That's her!" he said enthusiastically. "I do want you to see her. She has the most comical mind. Isn't she lovely, Laura?"

"She is, most lovely—but I won't meet her at your house," said Mrs. Leroy slowly. "You really have very little sense, Derek. Concubines are going too far. Besides, you'll embroil us all with Li-Ching-Hui if you carry on publicly with his ladies. I don't think you ought to have her to the Legation at all—certainly not to meet the Kuniangs."

"Oh, very well." He looked rather crestfallen and cross.

"I don't mind meeting her casually and accidentally at tea at the Wagons-Lits," said Mrs. Leroy. "Indeed, I should like to. You can arrange that some time. I shall drift in and you can invite me to your table."

She said this not because she very much wanted to meet the beautiful concubine, but to smooth Fitzmaurice's ruffled feathers. He had taken off his hat, in the shade of the oleander, and again, as she looked at him, she thought how like he was to a disgruntled spaniel. How likeable he was really—there were genuine qualities underlying his exquisite appearance and his absurd pre-occupation with women. She thought his attitude to that side of life all wrong and quite fantastically silly, but she never tried to alter it. Looking at him now she quite forgot, as too often happened, that they were in the middle of a conversation, and let her mind run off by itself. She always tried to conceal from him the embarrassments in which his confidences about his various loves sometimes involved her, and she wondered now if she need have been so short with him about Number Twenty-three. Yes; someone had to tell him these things. Fitzmaurice was rather *mal vu* by most of the Legation ladies, and responded by treating them with a marked lack of that polite attentiveness which is supposed to be their due from young secretaries. On her, on the contrary, he conferred almost too much of his confidence; he had the run of her house, and what was more costly, of her leisure and attention. "Still, why should they bar him and cold-shoulder him?" she reflected. As usual her thoughts flew to Tim at the same time, how he would one day be grown up and almost certainly extravagant and silly in some way; she revolted in advance against the way the married women in some remote place overseas would probably treat him. "Why do we give ourselves such airs, merely because we are older, and have scrounged some wretched man as a husband?" she thought, frowning a little. "Age has no merit, unless we make it lovely and wise." "Unless age brings charity," she thought, "it brings very little; so much that is best goes with youth."

And she went on reflecting about youth and age. But though she bracketed herself so definitely with the elderly, to look at her no one would have taken Mrs. Leroy for even her age, which was thirty-seven. Very long, very thin, very dark, she leant back in her chair in the easy attitude of a strong and supple body, which no skill in corseting can counterfeit or replace. Her dark brows were still drawn a little together above her grey eyes, an expression of contempt for the behaviour of *T'ai-t'ais* (married women) compressed her thin unreddened lips. Fitzmaurice watched her. He was accustomed to her vague fits and did not object. He knew it was useless to try any more to make her come to his party, and that he was "planted with the Kuni-angs," as he would have expressed it—but his feathers *were* smoothed.

"Hullo! who's that?" he asked suddenly. An excessively tall, very pretty girl, with an exquisite figure, had appeared from round a small pagoda, and stood, her white dress patterned with the moving zigzag shadows of bamboo leaves, at a little distance among the crowd.

"Oh, that's Little Annette, Nina Nevile's niece," said Mrs. Leroy.

"Annette who?—or Annette what?" asked Fitzmaurice, sticking his eyeglass in more firmly, the better to examine her.

"I can't remember," said Mrs. Leroy. "Yes, Ingersoll—anyhow she's staying with them." At this moment the young woman in question caught sight of Mrs. Leroy, and her rather impassive face brightened into a smile as she moved towards her. "Why, hullo, Mrs. Leroy!" she exclaimed; "aren't you cool there in the shade!"

"Sit down and be cool too," said Mrs. Leroy. "Let me introduce Mr. Fitzmaurice, of our Legation."

"Why, I'd love to sit," the girl answered, shaking hands with Fitzmaurice with an absent-minded "Pleased to meet you!" "but I have to ride with the La Tours. Have you seen Nina? She's making inquiries for you."

"No, but I daresay I shall, if I go on sitting here," said Mrs. Leroy.

The girl broke into a laugh.

"Dear Mrs. Leroy, isn't that English?" she exclaimed. All her remarks were made in the same high soft voice, pretty and colourless. "Why, if I heard someone was wanting me I should be all around after them."

"Well then, go 'all around' now with Mr. Fitzmaurice, and bring Nina here if you find her," said Mrs. Leroy.

"I will—if you will?" to Fitzmaurice, with the little automatic glance of coquetry which seems to be as much a part of the female American's social equipment as a frock. Fitzmaurice expressed himself as delighted, and they moved off together, a few notes of the high voice informing Mrs. Leroy from a distance that Little Annette considered her to be "the *love*liest woman in Peking." "How *incredible* Americans are, really," she murmured, but paused, remembering how fond she was of Nina, who was also an American. And Little Annette's beauty and simplicity had a certain charm. "She looks full of life," she thought, and was wandering back to her interrupted meditation on youth when she was again interrupted. An At Home is not a good place for meditation.

This time it really was Nina. A little fairy of a woman, with a blond head, Parisian chic, and a queer irregular Hogarth face—broad mouth, run-away nose, wide-set eyes—darted upon her from behind. "Dearest Laura, *here* you are!"

"My dear, I told you she was here as soon as I found you," observed General Nevile, taking off his topi and fanning himself with it. "Yes—I'll have one of those," to a servant who paused with another tray of cocktails. "You, Nina?"

"Most certainly yes! You have one too, Laura—you'll need it."

"Why?" said Mrs. Leroy, taking the cocktail and lighting a cigarette in a long ivory holder.

"Well—to dispose you favourably! Now listen—I've got a plan, and you must say Yes. We want you to come to Chieh T'ai Ssu with us next week-end."

"Oh, I don't think I can," said Mrs. Leroy, in her most languid voice. "I'm frightfully busy, you know." Her first impulse was always to say No to any projected engagement. "I don't see how I can get away." She sipped her cocktail. "What's the party?" she inquired, after a moment.

"Well, will she come, Nina? Have you persuaded her?" inquired a crisp clear voice, which conformed regrettably to the adjective "melodious." A short fair man in riding-clothes, with the most completely military figure and appearance it is possible to imagine, had come up to the group under the oleander, and stood darting bright bird-like glances of inquiry from face to face.

"Mrs. Leroy hasn't really heard what it's all about yet," said the General, pulling his moustache gloomily.

"Why, we have this Professor coming to-morrow," said Mrs. Nevile, "and we must do something about him. I thought we would take him to the hills for the week-end and give him a real Peking picnic. So there would be him, and we two, and you, and Touchy here (the military man saluted), and perhaps Henri."

"Laura, you must come," said the man referred to as Touchy. "Chieh T'ai Ssu will be like Heaven now with all the fruit-blossom out. And there's a moon—think of moonlight on the terrace, and the white pine!"

"Well, I don't know—I might manage it," said Mrs. Leroy. "Is that all? And what is your Professor?"

"Oh, he's just some learned man from England—the Minister has been told about him, and he's planted us with him," said Mrs. Nevile airily. "He's inquiring into something, like they do."

"It's Vinstead of Cambridge," said General Nevile, who, after twelve years of marriage, was still troubled by his wife's inaccuracies. "He has one of those travelling Fellowships, and has come out to study Oriental psychology. It's a semi-official thing in this case, but Sir James looked him up in *Who's Who*, and when he saw the names of his books"—a smile appeared for a moment under the General's moustache, making his lean gloomy face suddenly charming—"he said he thought 'the felloh had better stay with someone who could talk to him,' so he has turned him over to us."

Mrs. Leroy laughed out loud.

"Is that complimentary?" inquired the General, fixing his eyeglass on her.

"Very, I should say!" she said, still laughing. "I must have him and Sir James to dine and hear them talk to one another."

"But will you come and talk to him at Chieh T'ai Ssu? That's the point," said the General.

"Yes, and Miss Hande—Big Annette," said Nina Nevile. "She *will* talk to you, Laura, and she's such a bad mixer."

"Is Miss Hande coming too, then?" Mrs. Leroy inquired.

"Why yes—I must take her. And Little Annette—didn't I say so?"

"No, you didn't, my dear," said the General. "Now you know the worst, Mrs. Leroy; will you come?"

It was characteristic of General Nevile that in a society which dealt almost exclusively in Christian names, he should have continued to call the woman whom, except his wife, he knew best, and perhaps liked most, by her formal prefix. It belonged to his rather Edwardian

character and appearance to do this, and Mrs. Leroy
liked it, if only for that reason. She marvelled perpetually at the tendency of Peking Society, as of other
small societies, to invent and use nicknames, and had
formed a theory that it was because they seemed somehow to give the impression of a larger number of people.
Major La Touche, for instance, who was now standing
in front of her, measuring the distance between the top
of his riding-boots and the bottom of his drill jacket on
his riding-whip with great care and persistence, had two
perfectly good names. You could call him Major La
Touche, or you could call him James; you might even
call him Jim; but no one ever called him anything but
Touchy, which was not in the least appropriate to his
character. Then there was this business of the Annettes.
They were not related; they were not alike. Miss Anna
Hande, who had been referred to as Big Annette, was
a middle-aged and eminent American novelist (in her
own country she was called "the American Hardy")—if
anything she was small of stature, and a most uncompromising subject for a nickname. But just because she
happened to be visiting the Neviles in Peking at the
same time as Annette Ingersoll, Nina's niece, she had
to be, it appeared, "Big Annette," while the immensely
tall Miss Ingersoll became, with equal incongruity,
"Little Annette." Mrs. Leroy used the current nicknames, like everyone else, but they added to the sense
of theatricality which sometimes overcame her. At that
moment, for instance, she saw the figures about her,
spattered with the irregular starry shadows of the
oleander leaves—the General, standing, because his
lame leg made it too much trouble to lower himself
into any seat for a short time; his wife in a chair, her hat,
which she had pulled off, on her lap, showing her
childish waved yellow head, sipping her cocktail;

Major La Touche, now, his foot on the tub of the
oleander, measuring his riding-boot with his whip—like
figures on a stage; they seemed to her, in the subdued
wavering light, against the background of fantastic
architecture and shifting crowd, with the music from
the band spraying over them, completely unreal, arti-
ficial presentations of types. She listened, as to a stage
dialogue, to the chatter exchanged between Mrs. Nevile
and La Touche, and almost started when she heard
herself again addressed.

"Well, Laura, you'll come, will you?"

Mrs. Leroy roused herself with sudden decision. "If
I come," she said, "I must bring my Kuniangs."

Chapter Two

IN Mandarin the word *kuniang* denotes an unmarried girl of rank—literally, a virgin. Mrs. Leroy's announcement that she must bring her virgins with her to Chieh T'ai Ssu produced a sort of pause.

"My dear, that will make us the most terrific crowd of women," said Mrs. Nevile. "Two, four—six! and only four men."

"Does that matter?" said Mrs. Leroy. "Why not four men?"

"Why men at all, eh?" said General Nevile, twinkling unexpectedly.

"No, I like there to be men," said Laura calmly, "only I don't see why they need fit, except at dinner."

"Dear Laura—the Singing Kuniang by all means—but the other? Couldn't she have a rest-cure or a headache?" urged Major La Touche.

"Yes, Laura—do bring the singing one," said Mrs. Nevile. "We'll make her sing by moonlight; it will be lovely. But *must* you bring the other one?"

"How disagreeable you all are about poor Lilah," said Mrs. Leroy, with unruffled calm. "I won't leave her out. What is the matter with her?"

"The grave, the temple, the tomb!" ejaculated La Touche rapidly, "none of them is more silent."

"Well, you can look at her while you listen to Judith," said Mrs. Leroy. "She's worth looking at."

"Not the *animated* bust, anyhow," murmured La Touche.

"Oh, do be quiet, Touchy, and let us get on with plans," said Nina Nevile. "Very well, Laura darling— we must have you, and if I bring my Kuniangs, it's only fair you should bring yours, I suppose. Though if anyone is a worse mixer than Big Annette," she sighed, "I must say it is your Beauty. But look, Laura—can you bring an extra man or two?"

"Do you mean Henry?" asked Mrs. Leroy. "Because if so I should say No. Vol. Two is well on its way just now."

Henry Leroy was Commercial and Oriental Attaché to the British Legation in Peking. His official duties were onerous in spasms: as when civil war approached the capital more nearly than usual, or when a fresh *Tuchun* (war-lord) captured or purchased the city from a rival, and produced a change of government. But at other times they left him with a sufficiency of leisure, which he filled with polo and Oriental studies. He wrote books, and very good books too, on Chinese Linguistics and Chinese Commercial History, on one of which he was now engaged. Laura Leroy was interested in his official work, and aware of his very considerable local importance—as an inconspicuous, silent, but quite essential cog in the great diplomatic machine; she was also, secretly, very proud of his scholarship. She was intelligent enough to appreciate at their proper worth the books which, at longish intervals, appeared over his name, each one in turn creating its quiet stir of approbation among the experts. She appeared to accept quite naturally, and without the smallest resentment, the fact that these occupations left her husband with very little time or attention to spare for her or her interests; that she had to carry on their social life practically singlehanded and fill in any leisure of her own as best she might. She was much too wise to attempt to share in

any way in his labours; she spoke Peking colloquial
Chinese fluently, and had a sufficiency of Mandarin at
command for social purposes, but she was no sinologue,
and could only read a bare two or three thousand
characters—accomplishments which she rated very low.
She did not, indeed, set a very high value on herself or
any of her activities—an attitude which leaves one
peculiarly free to assess other values. It was perhaps to
an obscure sense of this freedom about her, of unuttered
judgments based on a secret independence—the sense
almost of a hidden and incorruptible tribunal—that she
owed her peculiar position in the small world of Peking.
Not very prominent, not very young, not excessively
beautiful, and not in the least ambitious, she was nevertheless quietly important to it in a way that other women
who were all these things were not. Nobody ever
troubled to formulate the reasons for this except perhaps
Touchy; and he was an exception, knew it, and wisely
held his peace. There can be few places in the world
where Matthew Arnold's dictum, that "ideas cannot be
too much prized in and for themselves—cannot be too
much lived with" would find a more hollow echo than
in the European society of Peking. Touchy read this
sentence out to Laura Leroy one day, not very long
after his arrival, as a sort of test. "Who said that?" she
asked; and when he had told her, "What a sensible
man!" she said, and that was all. At the time Touchy
was a little disappointed; but afterwards, when he got to
know Laura better, he felt that the answer was both
adequate and characteristic. He realised presently that
she agreed profoundly with Matthew Arnold, and he
sometimes wondered what she did with her ideas. He,
for his part, liked to use ideas as currency, and he
experienced all the discomfort of a sort of enforced intellectual moratorium in a place where they had so

little value. But Laura, though her intellectual finances were obviously of the soundest—positively, he said to himself, on a gold basis—never seemed to court interchange particularly; if you could nobble her quietly she would give you a high rate of exchange, but she never looked for a market, so to speak. Yes, it was, Touchy had long since decided, probably these large gold reserves, this sense of things left unsaid, rather than anything she said or did in particular, which caused Laura Leroy to be admired, valued, yes, and a little feared as she was. There were those who said, not wholly without reason, that she was a prig. But there was nothing overtly peculiar about her; she conformed smoothly, if a little indifferently, to the *milieu* in which she found herself. Touchy also took off his hat, among other things, to her skilful and unobtrusive protection of Henry's leisure and labours. As now. "Vol. Two," she said, "is well on its way," and that disposed of Henry as far as Chieh T'ai Ssu was concerned.

"No, I'm too modest to hope for Henry," said Nina, "but can't you bring someone else?"

"I'll see—though I can't think why we want all these men," said Laura. "Yes—I can bring Derek, of course."

On her way home Mrs. Leroy reviewed the situation. The car was at the Summer Palace with the Kuniangs, so she took a ricksha from the crowd which thronged the narrow *hut'ung* among the waiting motors, the coolies squatting in the deep slate-coloured dust, gossiping and smoking American cigarettes, till the appearance of a possible fare galvanised them into activity. Then they arose and hurried forward between their brass-topped shafts, jostling one another vigorously and shouting, "Want-not-want?" in a deafening chorus.

A ricksha is the most delightfully civilised form of locomotion. Seated in a well-sprung bath-chair, the passenger bowls along on pneumatic tyres at a surprising speed; he is alone, for it only holds one; his view is unimpeded by anything but the lowered head and shoulders of the trotting coolie; the air fans his face gently, and there is nothing to prevent his holding up a sunshade in comfort. The only drawback is that in order to reach any objective unfamiliar to the coolie he must know not only the way thither, but the points of the compass *en route* as well, for the Chinese do not use left and right as directions, but north, south, and so on. "*Wang tung!*" (turn east!) you cry at a corner, or "*Wang 'pei!*" (turn north!) (Which is also, if you come to think of it, both a more civilised and a more intellectual way of giving directions than our own.) However, the British Legation is known to all ricksha coolies, so Mrs. Leroy merely said, "*Ying-Kuo Fu!*" and sat back in peace to consider.

On the whole she was inclined not to regret having agreed to join Nina's picnic. It was true that the party would be large to the point of unwieldiness—at the last moment Mrs. Nevile had invited Henri Delache, a young Frenchman, who had a camp bed of his own, and could therefore be included without disturbing what Touchy called "the flea-bag ratio" of the party—and sufficiently ill-assorted to call for a certain amount of social effort and perseverance on somebody's part; but Mrs. Leroy hoped and intended that the somebody should be for the most part either Touchy, who was indefatigable and good-natured, or Nina. In any case they would all have to rub along somehow, and it would be a nice outing for the Kuniangs. Mrs. Leroy had a certain amount of conscience about entertaining her two nieces. The children of an elder step-sister, they were near enough to her own age not to require elaborate taking care of, but she did want them to have a good

time in Peking. She knew them really very little. For
the last eight years now she had been in China, most of
the time, and when she did go home she was usually too
much absorbed in Tim and Sarah, their holidays and
their clothes and their amusements and arrangements,
to have much leisure for anything else. It was terrible
how fast time flew then. She seized the moments,
grasped them, held on to them with an almost physical
intensity—but they slipped by like water, flowed past,
sank away, and were gone; and she was left staring after
two trains which had swallowed up those two small
funny faces. She never seemed to have time, even, to see
how the faces had altered from last year, let alone the
funny minds behind the funny faces—though she used
to look and look till her eyes ached. Oh, she knew all
about not seizing the wingèd joy, she used to tell herself
almost angrily—but what would Blake have said if *his*
joy had lived in England and he in Peking, and he'd
had it for two months, two short, short months once a
year, or not even that? Once a year, an operation
without an anaesthetic—and then staring after two
trains! Tim, thank Heaven, was too small to mind
much—he still, right up to the last, wanted to study the
makes of engines from the platform, and would fidget
about like a fish on the end of a line, his hand in her
foolish idiotic hand which so liked to feel the small
strength of his, when he caught sight of his little companions. But Sarah—Sarah with her untidiness, her
inky fingers and furry hair, her bleak sincerity, savage
contempts and loyal burning affection—Sarah, whose
jokes became more acid, and her good-night hugs more
strained and long, the last two days—there were no
engines for her. How was one to *bear* her short staccato
remarks, indifferent or snappish, the last morning?—
and at the station, the ferocious frowns with which she

winked away moisture, the last helpless, sudden trembling of her lips before her brusque dive into the carriage? It was hard to make "eternity's sunrise" out of them.

Anyhow, these things had prevented her from cultivating her nieces, and now she found herself with two grown-up young women whom she hardly knew on her hands for a couple of months. On the whole she was inclined to like them. Judith was the easiest; Mrs. Leroy suspected Judith of being rather a warrior. She was not very pretty—pretty in some moods and some frocks, but that was all—so she had had, presumably, to do something about it. What she had done about it was to train for a singer, in a thorough-paced and professional way, and with considerable success, judging by her voice. She was also intelligent and pleasantly enthusiastic—she had jumped at the chance of going to the Summer Palace with old Miss Parke; she would probably jump at going to Chieh T'ai Ssu. Lilah, on the other hand, never jumped at anything. She was a massive glorious blonde, beautiful with a well-regulated beauty of snowy neck and shoulders, apple-blossom skin, and golden hair which she had not shingled. But her beauty had apparently prevented her from feeling the necessity of doing—or, indeed, saying—much about anything. She dressed very well in a slightly grandiose way—much better than Judith, who was inclined to be gipsyfied about clothes and treated her rather moderate complexion with scornful neglect. But her expression was neutral almost to the point of sulkiness, and her capacity for silence almost illimitable. Never had Laura seen anyone make less contribution to the general social give-and-take, or less response to the efforts of others. She had watched, even in the short time they had been with her, person after person, lured by Lilah's loveliness,

moving cheerfully up to the attack, and after a little
while falling back baffled and disgruntled. She had a
mental picture of Lilah passing leisurely through the
East on her way out, like some Indian Goddess (in-
fluenced by Greek art, of course) with monumental im-
passivity, receiving the garlands and the obeisances, but
giving no sign to her worshippers. She rather thought
Judith must have got some fun out of watching this—
she already credited Judith with getting quite a lot of
fun out of watching things; but just what Lilah got out
of it she did not know. And yet she was clearly not
stupid. It was a puzzle.

Wrapped in these thoughts, she was borne rapidly
homewards. She was too familiar with the dirty sordid
streets to be struck any more by the peculiarity of a whole
city of one-storey houses; by the teeming yellow faces,
the dust and squalor, the innumerable donkeys; but as
her ricksha crossed the Ta Ch'ang An Chieh, the great
street running along the north side of the Legation
Quarter, she turned her head to look at the Forbidden
City. That was a sight on which, after all these years,
she could never look unmoved. One behind the other,
the great red gateways stood up in the evening light like
immense double-decker Noah's Arks, roofed in golden
tiles, above the high crimson walls. Close at hand, on
the right, showed the silvery green of the saecular thujas
round the Temple of the Ancestors—the "sunny spots
of greenery," of Xanadu, planted, legend says, by
Kublai Khan. The egrets had come back after their
winter absence, and their white shapes showed among
the ancient trees, their harsh cries filled the air above
the clang of trams and the blasts of motor-horns. Change-
less matchless beauty, holding the eyes and the mind,
as beauty does! She remembered her first sight of it,
on the evening of their arrival in Peking. Henry had

taken her arm and led her, tired and stiff and discouraged with unpacking, with the allocation of rooms,
the dispersal of blankets and linen and silver to various
household destinations, out into the icy dusk. They
went through the West Gate of the Legation, across the
glacis outside the Quarter, and found themselves
presently in a red-walled avenue a hundred yards wide,
stretching down on their left to the immense green-tiled
gate-tower of the Ch'ien-mên, stretching up on their
right to the red and golden Noah's Arks, with gleams of
white marble at their base. "There!" said Henry.
They looked. "It's the eighth Wonder of the World," he
said. And she had gone back to the house with him,
partly reconciled to a place of exile which held such
breath-taking beauty.

"*Ying-Kuo-fu!*" said the coolie suddenly, and dumped
down the shafts. Mrs. Leroy, accustomed to this manœuvre, was not pitched out. "Go in, go in!" she saïd,
waving her hand towards the squat ugly grey gateway
of the Legation. The coolie resumed his shafts and
trotted obediently through it, past the sentry on the left,
past the Constable's lodge with the grey parrot on the
right, past the painted scarlet-pillared *T'ing'rhs* of the
Minister's house. The Legation compound was dotted
with good-sized bungalows and a few larger houses;
there were open spaces which would later be grass, there
were trees and flowering shrubs and office-y-looking
buildings in a network of well-kept roads. "Turn south!"
said Mrs. Leroy at a cross-road. "Turn west!" a few
yards further on. The ricksha bowled up a curved
gravel sweep between thickets of sweet-scented yellow
briars, and stopped before a large well-built house. She
was at home.

Chapter Three

STANDING in the cool polished hall of her house, Mrs. Leroy called "*Lai!*" A servant in white appeared. "Give money that man," she said in Chinese, pointing towards the door. The servant bowed and went. Mrs. Leroy threw off her hat and sat down on a sofa, and began to read through a pile of notes which had accumulated during the afternoon on a silver tray near the inner door. When the servant returned, "Great-Man back-come-not?" she inquired. The servant answered that the Great Man had come back, and now ride pony with No. 2 Envoy, by which communication Mrs. Leroy knew that her husband was out riding with the Counsellor, Grant-Howard. She next inquired as to her nieces' whereabouts. Niu, who like all Chinese upper servants made it his business to be minutely informed about the doings of the whole household, was prompt and clear. The Virgins had returned in the gas-cart (motor)—the one Virgin was in her room, the Enormous Virgin (the servants' name for the massive Lilah) was walking with the Third Envoy. Laura was pleased. Derek must have nipped home from the Knudsens' and carried Lilah off for a walk—a rather enterprising move. She refused a cocktail which Niu told her was waiting, and bade him tell Ho Kuniang (Hubbard, her maid) to get a bath ready—what she actually said was, "Want bath"; then gathering up her notes she went into her own sitting-room to write a few answers before dinner.

The Leroys' was one of the three or four English-built

houses in the Legation—that is to say it had an upstairs as well as a downstairs, while the servants had quarters of their own in a roomy compound outside. The room in which Mrs. Leroy now sat had a southern aspect, and was somewhat darkened by the shadow of the *p'êng* which ran along the whole south side of the house. A *p'êng* is an ingenious contrivance for keeping houses cool in summer, common in Peking; it consists of a sort of extension of the roof made of straw matting, thrown out at roof level and supported on poles, which keeps the sunny side of the house perpetually in shadow, but permits a free movement of air below it. *P'êngs* are put up at the beginning of the summer and removed in autumn; it was fully early for one, but Henry Leroy had a theory that to keep a house cool you must never let it get hot—so his *p'êng* was always erected a fortnight or more before other people's. Sitting down before a large writing-table of the G.H.F. (Government Heavy Furniture) type, supplied by the Office of Works, Mrs. Leroy wrote rapidly, from time to time consulting a large red note-book labelled "Engagements," and scribbling a word or two in another book bound in blue, throwing the notes as she finished them on to the floor at her side. She had nearly finished when the door opened; she looked up and saw Judith Milne poised at the threshold.

"Come in, Judith," she said.

"Oh, not if you're busy, Laura."

"No, I've just finished," said Mrs. Leroy. "Come and tell me how you got on while I log these up."

"It was *mar*vellous!" began Judith eagerly, coming forward as she spoke and perching on the arm of a sofa close to the writing-table. "Miss Parke is a wonder! Fancy her having lived there like that." She went on describing her day at the Summer Palace while Mrs. Leroy collected her notes off the floor, took a third book labelled "Chits" in gold lettering, and began to write in it the names of the recipients under the day's date, looking up at Judith now and then, with a nod or a laugh, as she did so.

Judith Milne was only medium tall, but she had a strong elastic figure, like a boy's, and extremely pretty shapely feet, legs and hands. Her hair was *cendré* fair, and curled by itself; she wore it shingled, rather long, so that her face was always framed in a pale fuzzy halo. The face was redeemed from ordinariness by rather fine light-blue eyes, under brows much darker than her hair, which slanted almost upwards at the corners; there was something about this slant of the brows and the winged cut-away line of her nostrils that reminded Laura of one of the Michelangelo youths at the corners of the Sistine Chapel. She talked fast and headlong, tumbling out her sentences and interrupting herself with little burbles of laughter—there was a sort of warm vibration of enthusiasm in her voice when she was excited, which made it very nice to listen to. She ended her recital as she began—it was a marvellous place, they had had a marvellous day, it was terribly good of Laura to have arranged it. "Miss Parke, of course, simply *made* it. I *am* sorry for people who go to the Summer Palace without her to tell them about the Empress Dowager's picnics." There was always at least one word in italics in each of Judith's sentences.

Mrs. Leroy had by this time finished entering her notes in the chit-book, and rang the bell. Niu appeared; she handed him the book and the notes, and said something to him in Chinese. "Understand, understand!" he replied briefly, and went out.

"I think that's such a *killing* way of carrying on one's correspondence," said Judith, looking after the man. 'Do you never post letters?"

"Not to people in Peking," replied Laura. "It's much quicker to send the chit-coolie."

Judith was idly handling the things on the writing-table. "Profit and loss account," she read out, holding up the book bound in blue, in which Laura had been making entries as she wrote her notes. "What on earth is this?"

Laura smiled. "Lunches and dinners given and received," she said. "They are all written up in that, and when I am giving a party I can turn anyone up and see at once what I owe them, and work them off. I balance it once a quarter or so and start afresh."

Judith Milne turned the leaves thoughtfully, and then looked at Laura. "I think it's rather frightful," she said.

"Why?" asked Laura, interested.

"It seems so horrible to run one's entertaining like a bank," the girl said slowly. "Making friendship a sort of business. Don't you *want* to see any of these people?"

"Some of them," said Mrs. Leroy.

"Then why do you have the ones you don't want to see?" persisted Judith, still looking at the book. "Mrs. Brownlow," she read out. "That's that awful fat woman who's so badly made up, with the husband who was screwed the other night at the hotel, isn't it? She looks like a barmaid. You can't want to see her *or* him, ever."

"She *was* a barmaid," said Mrs. Leroy coolly, "and I don't want to see her very much, though there are plenty of people in Peking who are duller and less kind than Mother Brownlow. But he represents a big British commercial interest, and one must be civil to them."

"But can't you be civil to people without having them to dinner?" asked Judith, still studying the blue book, horror at the number of meals the Brownlows were asked to clearly visible on her face. "It seems so awfully insincere!" She paused. "It isn't *like* you, Laura!" she burst out.

"It isn't *like* anyone," Laura answered, wondering what idea the girl had been forming of her. "It's just part of the job. This entertaining is simply a system."

"Well, I call it a rotten system," said Judith. "Such a fearful waste of time. One never sees enough of the people one *really* wants to see—one never gets to know *anyone* well enough. And to spend ages feeding people who bore you seems to me simply crazy."

Laura was more interested than ever. "I agree with you that as a life it would be crazy," she said. "But as I keep telling you, it's a job."

"But why is it part of the job?" said Judith. "Does it help Uncle Henry, for instance, to dine with duds?"

Laura laughed out. "Not exactly," she answered. "Yes, indirectly it does. Look here—every one in Peking is here to transact business of some sort with someone or other—we are, the colleagues are, the business people are. And in practice it's been found that business is transacted more easily between people who know one another socially than between those who only meet officially. Hence the system." She rose and took the book from Judith and put it in a drawer. "And hence that book," she added. "One may as well be efficient about things. Come on—we ought to go and dress."

"No—wait a moment, Laura," said Judith. "Surely all this must make people very insincere?"

"Perhaps it does," said Laura a little wearily. "I think sincerity is often very much over-rated, though."

"Laura! What *do* you mean?" Judith began. But she was interrupted by the entrance of Niu, with the information that the Big Envoy wished to strike electric talk with the Great Man. Mrs. Leroy went towards the door.

"The Minister is on the telephone," she said as she went. "I must go."

On her way upstairs—"I'm so sorry, Sir James," Judith heard Laura's voice, "Henry is out riding with Mr. Grant-Howard. Shall I send him across when he comes in?"

Sir James was perturbed. His Counsellor was out, his Commercial and Oriental Attaché was out. "I can't even get that felloh Fitzmaurice," he complained. Laura's voice became very soothing. "Aren't you dining with the Schuylers too?" she said. "Well, then, won't you come across when you're dressed and have a cocktail and talk to Henry quietly here, and we can all go on together. Do—I'll make you one of your special ones."

Sir James was soothed. He thought perhaps he would. That would be delightful, Laura said—in about half an hour? She hoped it wasn't anything tiresome? Oh, that felloh Tu—there was a telegram from that felloh at what's-its-name, a jumpy felloh, seemed to think he was on the move again. "Your husband'll know what it's all worth," said Sir James. "Half an hour, then."

In Laura's room Hubbard, the maid, waited with a face registering resignation. "This is the second bath I've drawn you, madam. I hope it won't be cold."

"Run in some more hot, Hubbard," said Laura.

"I've put the gold dress out for you, madam," Hubbard went on, moving towards the bathroom.

"No—I'll wear the black lace," said Laura.

"You wore the black lace the last time you was at the American Legation, madam," said Hubbard reprovingly.

"Oh, did I? Very well, the gold then," said Laura indifferently, as the maid left the room.

A few moments later Mrs. Leroy plunged into her bath, found it boiling hot, and blessed her servant.

Hubbard was an undersized skinny little woman, the wrong side of forty, with a sallow complexion, beady black eyes, and tightly frizzed black hair; she was, as Henry Leroy often said, much uglier than sin. But she was also from Laura's point of view a jewel. It was not only that she sewed like an angel, and could *really* copy French frocks—that usually legendary accomplishment; it was not only that she always remembered, as now, what frock her mistress had worn where, and ruled the wash-man and the house-coolies with a rod of iron and three words of Chinese; nor that every garment, shoe, and stocking flourished like a living entity under her skilled care. These things were much. But in all the eight years they had spent in China together Mrs. Leroy had never seen her maid frightened, and never known her go sick. Her mincing gentility concealed a highly adventurous spirit, and her plain little person housed, most improbably, a raging and successful coquette. None of the young and pretty maids and nurses of the Legation had a tithe of her success—she simply walked through the hearts of the British and American Legation Guards. And though she grumbled like any Tommy, baths were always hot, and cigarette-cases always filled, and clothes and handkerchiefs always scented. Happy the woman who lights on such a maid; happier still the one who, like Mrs. Leroy, contrives to inspire in such a paragon an unexpressed devotion.

"So we're likely to have another war then, madam," remarked Hubbard conversationally, as she put on her mistress's shoes and fastened her suspenders, while Laura, before the mirror, dealt rather perfunctorily with her face.

"Oh, are we?" said Laura. "Who with this time, Hubbard?"

"Well, the boys were saying at the 'Y' this afternoon

that one of these Doojoons, as they call them, was
setting out to attack Peking," replied Hubbard. "Doo,
I think they said his name was; though I can't make
much of these names after all these years, and that's a
fact."

Laura, remembering the Minister's words, smiled to
herself. It would not be the first time that Hubbard had
proved to be at least as well informed as anyone in the
Legation. The Y.M.C.A. was a mine of information.

"Well, that will make your—what, sixth siege, Hubbard?" she said cheerfully.

"*Seventh*, madam," replied Hubbard, with modest
pride.

"Where is he supposed to be coming from?" Mrs.
Leroy went on, hoping for more.

"Well, madam, Howard, one of the Marines at the
American Legation, has a friend in the Posts at a place
called Why Lie? so he says—though it seems a funny
name," said Hubbard, with a discreet giggle; "and
Howard has been wanting to go on leaf to Tientsin, to
see a friend, you understand, when the weather should
be warmer. So he asked this friend to tip him one in
good time, if there should be any trouble up that way,
so that he could make his arrangements before leaf was
stopped. And he had a telegram to-day about this Doo,
or whatever his name is. He must be quite a personage,"
Hubbard went on, "for Howard's friend said he had a
hundred thousand men with him. He seems to live near
Why Lie? Shall you wear your pearls, madam?"

"No, diamonds with the gold," said Laura.

"So Howard put in for his leaf after tiffin," Hubbard
continued, clasping the diamonds round her mistress's
neck, "and he's going on the 7.30 to-night—gone,
I should say," she added, with a glance at the
clock.

"Well done, Howard!" said Laura laughing. "Was the Bridge good at the Y.M.C.A., Hubbard?"

"Mahjong it was to-day, madam, and rather a poor table," said Hubbard critically. "Shall you take a fan, madam? I've put out the gold."

"No, the jade—and jade bag too. Change over my things—sorry, Hubbard," said Mrs. Leroy. "Bring them down with my cloak."

Before going downstairs she went to her husband's room. Sounds of splashing through the half-open door of the bathroom beyond told her that he had returned. She sat down on a settee at the foot of the bed, and they talked through the door. It was the quiet, rather desultory commentary on the day that people who know one another's lives well exchange almost mechanically— but miss if they do not get it. She heard that the shoeing had been successful, and the ride too—Grant-Howard had bought the cross-bred, and might buy the roan as well. Then it was her turn. She reported the Kuniangs' successful outing at the Summer Palace, and told her husband of the arrangements for Nina's week-end picnic. "We go on Friday—Nina's doing the food and Touchy the drinks. I thought of taking Niu and Number Three to wait—you can manage with Li, can't you? And one of the coolies for beds and washing up? I think it's rather a good plan."

To her surprise Henry didn't. "What an ass Nevile is!" he growled through the door. "Trust the Military Attaché for ignoring movements of troops! He must have heard about Wang."

"What about Wang?" Laura asked—she had expected another name, and was surprised.

"Oh, he's made some new combination, and has paid off three battalions—so he says. Paid off!" he snorted. "We all know what that means. 'Returning honest peasants to civil life,' he said in his manifesto. Letting the bandit return to his banditry, I should call it."

"But, Henry, Wang is *miles* away, surely," his wife expostulated. "Right off beyond Hsiao Wu T'ai Shan. That can't affect us at Chieh T'ai Ssu."

"Oh, can't it?" grumbled Leroy's voice. "The Hills will be swarming with *T'ao-pings* (deserters, leaderless soldiers) now for weeks—pure-bred brigands resuming their normal avocation, without any pay, and fully armed. These fellows always get away with their rifles. I call it a rotten plan."

"Oh, well, we shall have to see," said Laura pacifically. "It may turn out to be a rumour, mayn't it? Anyhow, we shall be a large party, and close home, and we can always chuck it at the last minute. By the way," she went on, prudently changing the subject, "the Minister is coming round before dinner—he wants to see you."

"What does *he* want?" asked Leroy, still from his bath. He was a large man, and believed in prolonged soakings after exercise for keeping down weight.

"Oh, he's had a telegram that fussed him—something about Tu Yu-jen," said Laura. "You and G.-H. and Derek were all out, and he seemed to be stewing, so I told him to come over and have a cocktail later on, and see you. It was you he really wanted," she added, diplomatically—and truthfully.

"Well, keep him in play, there's a good creature," groaned Henry. "Out of this bath I don't get for another ten minutes, not for twenty Ministers."

"Right—I'll go down and see to him," said Mrs. Leroy.

"And look here, Laura!" her husband called after her.

"Yes?" She turned at the door.

"Did you say it was Vinstead, the *Psychology of Neutrality* man, who's going to Nina's?"

"Yes," said Laura again.

"Well, book him for dinner one night, quietly, as soon as you can. I want to talk to him."

"All right—can-do!" she said, and went out.

Chapter Four

THE Minister had not arrived when Mrs. Leroy got down. She made the cocktails rather perfunctorily, while Niu stood looking on in disapprobation. To use his own words, "I before-time bar-room man"; he was an expert on drinks and felt that he lost a certain amount of "face" if his employers mixed their own. What did the *T'ai-t'ai* (lady) know about a *mixwine* (cocktail) that he did not? He did not say any of this, but Laura knew it perfectly well and ignored it; in a way she rather enjoyed scoring off Niu, who was as tyrannical as any old family butler in England, and much more subtle and persistent in his methods of attaining his ends. She told him of the week-end arrangements: luggage and beds for three to be at Chieh T'ai Ssu at four on Friday. Niu repeated all the orders with additions and corrections of his own—Laura crossed these out, verbally, inexorably. Once a Chinese servant understands—or rather agrees to carry out—orders, he will do so perfectly, but his contempt for the mentality of foreign devils is so engrained that it is usually some time before this stage of agreement is reached. He can always think of some new and more ingenious combination of his own, which he will employ unless ruthlessly prevented. But at last, "Understand, understand," said Niu again, and left the room.

Mrs. Leroy moved over to the open French window and stepped through it on to the broad tiled verandah outside. Tubs of oleanders stood all along its outer edge, chairs and rugs and tables furnished it like a

33

room; between the oleanders white stocks and wallflowers in shallow pots made it gay and formal at once.
She stood looking out over her garden. Two tall thick
plantations of fragrant evergreen thujas screened it on
both sides—the further end was blocked by some big
trees just coming into leaf, through which showed a high
and forbidding grey wall, stuck with glass at the top,
and over it the huge gloomy buildings of the Soviet
Embassy. Most of the garden was lawn, but now only
a few thin spikes of green showed above the brown earth
and flattened matted leaves of last year's grass. A low
stone parapet, on which stood pots of wallflowers,
separated the lower garden from the upper one. A week
ago an avenue of lilacs had sprung up in the night along
the path across the lawn—dug out from the underground
pit where they had spent the winter and sunk, tubs and
all, in the turf. Their sweetness came in waves now on
her face as she walked towards the upper garden, where
gnarled ancient trees and bushes of flowering cherry and
plum held out on black fantastic branches their annual
miracle of pink and rose-red blossom. Here there were
stone seats, and groups of trees for shade, and a pergola—
a little mystery and a little secrecy, such as a garden
should have. The air was full of the scent of the yellow
briars round the house, and mixed with it other scents—
wood-smoke and Chinese cooking and Chinese sanitation and donkey-dung—the intimate penetrating Peking
smell, which is like the smell of no other city on earth.
Laura smelt it with positive pleasure—its strength, in
the warm dusk, meant that spring was fully come, and
the baking splendours of a Chinese summer on the way.
In the snowless winter of cold sunshine and frost and
tearing winds the smell of Peking suffers a strange
diminution, and dwindles to a mere ghost.

She wandered over to a group of tamarisks, whose

boughs wore a faint bloom of pale green and pale rose, transparent and tenuous as chiffon, and sat down on a bench below the leaning trunks. The air was as full of sounds as of smells. Even in the quiet Legation garden the confused noise of the city reached her, but it was a different quality of sound from the roar of traffic in a European city, the muffled drumming of soft feet on unpaved earth—bare or slippered human feet, the pads of camels, the light tapping of the small unshod feet of donkeys. In this low murmur other sounds stood out sharply, like loud notes in soft music—the hoot of a distant motor-horn, the ringing of tram-bells, a scream of a steam-whistle and sounds of shunting from the railway-station just outside the city wall. She could hear, too, innumerable cries from the streets outside—but strange cries, with another note in the voices; now and then in the distance crackers were let off with a noise like revolver shots. There were small noises near at hand as well; a Peking crow barked now and then from over by the stables; she could hear the creak of the shadoof as the gardener hauled up water from the well, and a sort of crackling sound as his colleague rolled back the straw *lienzas* off the conservatory, now that the sun had set. The hoopees had just come back, and tripped about the lawn with their little running steps, fluting low isolated notes. Suddenly out of the sky came a faint winging of music, as from small harps overhead—she looked up and saw a flight of birds wheeling over the house. It was that loveliest of Chinese inventions, the small pipes bound to the pinion-feathers of pigeons, so that the birds cannot fly without creating this aethereal music. Who would not love and honour a race which could devise a thing like that? she thought, as she watched the birds wheeling to and fro, up and down, in the air above her. The glare had gone, and one or two

faint stars pricked the blue—a blue so pale that it was
almost grey. The light could not lie more tenderly in
the upper reaches of the sky above an English garden—
not even above the garden at Garsover. And with the
thought she was there. Her two worlds met for a moment
under the sky that arched over both, and then that
distant one invaded the present and blotted it out. She
was in that garden, muffled so deep in trees, sheltered
so by its grey stone walls, watching the wagtails tripping
about the green deep turf between the flower-beds
outside the old yellow house. The lawn stretched up,
up, up to the great horse-chestnut, under which daffodils
swung in the light air over the place whence the crocuses
and aconites had just departed. She saw Grandpère
going to and fro along the terrace walk, shuffling a little,
his silver head bent in meditation, a volume of Kant
sticking out of his pocket, a volume of Inge clasped in his
hands behind his back. She saw Grandmamma come
out on to the steps, a stiff spare figure in black, and walk
along the flags with a sort of ungainly sprightliness to
the door in the wall. Jasmine was wreathing in the arch
over it, smothering the delicate Italian carving wrought
in the pale Oxfordshire stone; Grandmamma was going
up to Evensong, and the sound of the bells came down
over the hill. A steady stream of rooks flowed over the
garden, going home to roost at Chislehampton in the
woods above the river; and from every corner of the
smothering shrubberies rang the evening anthem of the
blackbirds, carrying the air in a whole symphony of
lesser song. How deep the peace was, there, after a long
English day, empty of people and soaked in books—long
solid stretches of work or reading, which she herself
interrupted as she chose: to drive into Oxford to see
Rachel or Richard, or to buy another book, to walk
over to Stadham to see Arnold or Frances.

The thought of that quiet English day brought her back to her day now ending. There was peace in Peking too, among the sounds of the Tartar City, but what of her day? Looking back she saw it as a protracted little bustle about little things—clothes and notes and comings and goings and people and interruptions and more clothes and more notes. Clothes and notes—that was really the bulk of her life. Yes, and cocktails—clothes and notes and cocktails! Probably Judith was right about its being a silly system. Still, she thought a little wearily, she could not alter it, and she switched off on to thinking about Judith. The girl had shown something like passion about wasting time on people to whom one was indifferent—"One never gets to know *anyone* well enough!" she had said. Judith had opened a corner of her mind to her, and Mrs. Leroy was interested in what she found inside. She felt that she had probably been a little lazy herself, or she might have found her way into Judith's mind sooner. She had been providing her two nieces with adequate and suitable entertainment, but with half her mind elsewhere, as usual. That was how one dealt with everybody and everything in this divided life of hers! Incompetent! she thought, and rather more conscious of weariness, resolved to do better.

A movement close by made her focus her eyes on something more immediate than the pale plume of one tamarisk bough against the sky at which, unconsciously, she had been staring with great concentration. Glancing towards the sound, she saw Derek Fitzmaurice's figure emerge from the thicket of plum-blossom, now becoming ghostly in the dusk—he came and sat down beside her.

"La Belle Laure all alone!" he observed.

"Has the Minister come?" asked Laura, glancing at her watch.

"I don't know—I came round by the garden," replied

Fitzmaurice. "I saw your dress shining up here, so I came along." He had an incurable habit of using any means of ingress to the house rather than the front door. "I've been for a walk on the Wall with the Beauty," he went on.

"So I heard."

"Who told you?" he asked, rather quickly.

"Niu, of course."

"Old brute!" grunted Derek. "He brought me the wrong girl. I asked him for Judith. I wish you'd have a boy who speaks English, Laura."

"Well, did you have a nice walk?" asked Laura pacifically.

"As a matter of fact, we did," said Fitzmaurice. "She's rather a character, you know, when you get her going."

"Do you mean to say you *did* get her going?"

"Oh, yes, in a way. She makes rather supreme remarks about people—not many, but rather supreme." He paused. "She said you were like a wise lily," he added, and turned on her to watch the effect.

"Goodness!" said Laura. "What an extraordinary thing to say!"

"Yes, wasn't it? But she was much more extraordinary afterwards," pursued Derek. "I said wise, yes, but that you weren't like a lily, they were white and cold and—er, so forth—and she said, 'Their sweetness draws all the world to them, and they have golden hearts.'"

"God bless my soul!" exclaimed Laura, and stopped, too startled to say more.

"Yes, isn't it?" said Derek. "It's a golden sentence. And true, *ma chère*. I wish I'd thought of it myself. Then she was quite supreme," he went on, "about poor old James." (This disrespectful allusion was to the Minister.) "She said, 'He reminds me of a parson's cob out hunting.

I shouldn't think he ever got over any obstacle without at least three people urging him from behind.' That's very good, you know."

"It's masterly!" said Laura. "What a marvel you are, though, Derek, to have opened these flood-gates! Poor Sir James! The parson's cob! It's perfect."

"So is the wise lily!" he said, smiling at her.

"*Most* extraordinary!" went on Laura, not paying the smallest attention to him. "Who would have believed it?" She was really startled at this sudden manifestation of mental activity on Lilah's part. Within the last hour light had been thrown on both her nieces: Judith with her passion to *know* people, and now Lilah's apparent capacity for learning a great deal about them merely by observation. And she was touched, inevitably, by the "wise lily."

"Come indoors!" she said to Derek. "Sir James must be there by this time." Derek jibbed. "No, you must come. There's a telegram, and Henry may not be down yet."

Fitzmaurice followed her faintly glimmering gold figure obediently across the lawn.

They found Sir James in the drawing-room. All that thought, care, and the personal attention of himself and an excellent valet could do for Sir James's appearance was done; but in spite of immaculate suits and shirts and shoes he remained a rather undistinguished presence, rubicund of face, short and stocky of figure—a cob, in fact, elderly and well-groomed. Henry was not there. Laura apologised for him—"But here is Mr. Fitzmaurice, Sir James, and Henry will be down in a moment. Now have a cocktail. Perhaps you and Mr. Fitzmaurice would like to have a look at the telegram together?"

Sir James displayed his usual mixture of the affable and the irritable. "Oh, don't go, Mrs. Henry," he said, taking his cocktail. "That's a new dress, isn't it? I congratulate you!" He raised his glass and drank to her. "I don't know where *you've* been for the last four hours, my boy," he went on, turning to Fitzmaurice, "but not in your Chancery. Not a soul there but the cipher clerks the whole blessed afternoon! Bad, you know. This telegram arrived—no one to deal with it."

"I'm extremely sorry, sir," said Fitzmaurice. "I went to the Knudsens' At Home. I heard none of the Legation staff were going, and as it was for the Crown Prince I thought one of us at least had better show up. Of course I was wrong."

Sir James grunted. He himself had clean forgotten the Crown Prince and had gone off to play golf. Fitzmaurice was a past-master of the accusatory apology, as he had often found to his cost in the past. The afternoon was best left alone.

"Well, you had better look at this now," he said, extracting a folded paper with some trouble from the breast pocket of his tightly fitting dress-suit. He smoothed it out, on a small table beside him. "Read it out—Mrs. Henry will forgive us."

Fitzmaurice, with the expression of bored loathing which the mere sight of a telegram engenders in Heads of Chanceries, took up the paper and read aloud in a slightly sick tone:

"It is rumoured here that Tu Yu-Jen is concentrating troops secretly in hills west of (four words undecipherable) stop. Objective said to be Peking stop. Strength estimated at 200,000 stop. Stodart."

"H'm," he said, handing it back to his chief. "Another *Kuominchün* push, I suppose. They said Tu was going to write poems in Moscow, but he seems to have thought better of it."

"Stodart is that temporary felloh at Taiyuan, isn't

he?" observed Sir James. "Rather an alarmist felloh, I consider."

"He only says it's a rumour," said Fitzmaurice. "But if you'll excuse me, sir, I think I had better slip across to the Chancery and have a go at this telegram. Our Mr. Deering has left the yolk out of the egg. What we want to know is where—if at all—Mr. Tu is concentrating. And that is just what we don't know—on this."

"Yes, do, my boy," said Sir James.

"I think you'll find Tu is somewhere near Huai Lai," observed Mrs. Leroy, from the corner of the sofa where she was sitting back and smoking quietly, her eyes on the darkening garden. The two men turned and stared at her.

"Dear lady, how *do* you know that?" inquired Sir James.

"Huai Lai! Cripes! that's pretty close home!" exclaimed Fitzmaurice. "Two hundred thousand men is a goodish crowd too. I wonder if Li will clear out, or try to hold this place. He hasn't got sixty thousand, according to the M.A."

"I think Tu's numbers must have grown on the way to Taiyuan," said Laura. "It's a long way from Huai Lai. The local version gives him a hundred thousand, and I expect you can halve that."

"But where did *you* get this information, Mrs. Henry?" persisted the Minister.

"It came in a telegram from Huai Lai this morning," said Laura. "Not to me, of course. But I rather think it's reliable." She smiled at the Minister. "Dear Sir James, you must allow me my little private intelligence service, you know!"

"Well, it's all very irregular!" said Sir James, only half mollified. "This is a most irregular country." He walked up and down, gnawing at his small reddish moustache; Laura began to fear an explosion, and wished Henry would come. The trouble in which Henry's ablutions involved her! She hinted that Mr. Fitzmaurice might perhaps go as he had suggested and see what he could make of the telegram—then they would have the *official* version. Sir James agreed, and Laura breathed more freely when Derek had taken himself off. Sir James had no great love for this particular subordinate, a state of affairs which Derek did nothing that he could help to remedy.

"Casual! Casual!" he muttered now, as he walked up and down; "the boy's far too casual. It won't do in this job." He went on gnawing and muttering as he walked, a sure sign of mental discomfort. The state of Sir James's moustache was used as a sort of political barometer by the observant. If it was drooping, worn, and frayed it was a sure indicator of trouble. Touchy used to say that during a crisis which occurred soon after his arrival there was hardly a hair left in it.

Laura understood the Minister's discomposure. China is a trying place for all European diplomatists, and especially so for those of the type of Sir James Boggit. It is, as he said, a most irregular country. Humour, flexibility, and the very casualness he deplored in Fitzmaurice are essential qualities, if not to success, at least to a quiet life, out there. Sir James lacked them. He had a certain humour of a puckish sort, but he too seldom extended it to the affairs of his mission. What he liked was regular conditions, and a consistent policy to carry out—the sort of steady-going diplomacy which enables a Minister to say in almost every dispatch, "I repeated to His Excellency what I had said to him last week . . ." or *vice versa*. He could almost never say this in China. No one in the Wai Chiao Pu (the Chinese Foreign Office) ever said the same thing to him twice running, and there was seldom the same Excellency for him to address himself to for many weeks on end. In the first six months after his arrival he had been in charge of certain negotiations connected with loans, and had had to deal, in that period, with four different Finance Ministers. One after another, for various excellent political or private reasons, they had betaken themselves, "with their spittoons and their concubines" in the classic phrase, to the Wagons-Lits Hotel in the Legation Quarter, *en route* for private life in a foreign Concession or abroad. Two different war-lords had held the capital and erected transient Governments since he came, and now it looked as if a third were about to unseat the present incumbent. It was all most unsettling, and made a consistent policy very hard to carry out.

Mrs. Leroy knew, but did not share Sir James's views on a consistent policy in China. As a wise and experienced foreigner once expressed it to her: "The best policy in the world will be wrong in China, Madame, if it is consistent, just *because* it is consistent. To-day you must use the bludgeon, to-morrow you offer the gift. You must not have a policy—you must send a man you trust to act *à discrétion,* who will choose the appropriate inconsistency for each emergency as it arises." But Sir James had not grasped this great truth. He lacked what the Leroys called "comme-ci-comme-ça-ness." They had coined the phrase on a visit to a Treaty Port during a prolonged and rather dangerous crisis. They found the British Concession practically abandoned and under guard, the Russian a ruin, the Japanese an armed camp, bristling with barbed wire and machine-guns. Business took them to the French Consulate. In the French Concession tennis parties were in full swing, nurses and babies were strolling about, while Chinese wandered in and out freely. They asked the Consul how he was getting on. He raised his shoulders—"*Comme-ci, comme-ça!*" Did he have no trouble with the Chinese? "*O, comme-ci, comme-ça!* Sometimes, yes." He placed no guards, he left the place open? "*O, comme-ci, comme-ça!* at times yes, he placed a guard—and at other times, no." "*Il faut se ficher un peu de ces bonhommes-là!*" he added. Henry Leroy left full of admiration for the wisdom and flexibility of the little provincial Frenchman, who had grasped the needs of the situation so completely and met them with such skilful suppleness.

All this passed through Laura's mind as she watched the Minister gnawing and muttering his way up and down her high pale drawing-room. She saw that he was tired, worried, and thoroughly discomposed, and she was sorry. There was an importunate strain in her character which persisted obstinately in infusing an element of humanity into the most unpromising relationships. Under its influence she rose now from her sofa, advanced upon Sir James, and took him firmly by the arm.

"The latest orders from the Higher Command," she said gaily, "are that His Britannic Majesty's Minister Plenipotentiary and Envoy Extraordinary sits down in that chair and has another cocktail."

There is still magic in formulas; who can doubt it? Those titles have a soothing sound in the ears of him who bears them, whether he knows it or not. Sir James obeyed, and smiled as he obeyed. Mrs. Leroy strove further to persuade him to "*se ficher un peu de ces bonhommes-là.*" "Half the time," she urged, "these rumours come to nothing."

She persevered in her efforts till she saw the Minister gradually brighten considerably. Presently she looked at the clock.

"Sir James, if we aren't to be late we ought to go. I

think Henry must be dead!" She rang the bell. Niu appeared. "Gas-cart come?" she inquired. "Has come!" responded Niu. "The car's there," Laura went on. "We'd better go; I'll order the ricksha for him." She spoke rapidly in Chinese to Niu and moved towards the door. As Niu opened it they heard Henry Leroy's voice booming from the hall, "Well, you young women, you're looking very glorious!"

"Oh, he's there!" she said, relieved.

A cold draught from the hall caught the door as they went out; it slammed behind them. In the deepening dusk the room was left deserted. The glowing Fantin-Latour over the mantelpiece, and the one or two Riches and Arnold-Forsters on the walls looked down on the formal chintzes, the Kabiristan rugs, and the Queen Anne tallboy and escritoire which made Mrs. Leroy's drawing-room so English, and so unusual in Peking. There was not a single Chinese thing in it except the earthenware bowls in which freesias stood blooming everywhere. Their scent contended now with the fading smell of the cocktails from the emptied glasses—as the night wind blew in through the open French windows it conquered, and at last had the room to itself.

Chapter Five

THE Knudsens' At Home was on a Monday. Between one and half-past on the following Friday cars began to assemble under the trees at the edge of the big grass square in the British Legation. The Leroys' saloon stood up near their house, with suit-cases strapped on the back. Further down was the Neviles' big tourer, somewhat piled with luggage, and further on still a rather decayed Sports Buick belonging to Touchy. The Chinese chauffeurs, in khaki-and-gold uniforms, stood by their cars, spitting idly at the plum-blossom in the Consul's flower-beds, or giving a final polish to the nickel-work and the big green and white Legation number-plates with old pieces of Wolsey underclothing, hoarded for this purpose under the driving-seat. Servants in white gowns came and went, bringing various objects—Li appeared laden with rucksacks; Fitzmaurice's boy came flapping round the square with a *Tchilumchi*, which he placed in Laura's car. Little groups of servants were visible in all directions, gathered at the entrances to their several compounds, staring and laughing, all animated by the usual overwhelming Chinese curiosity. Down by the Legation Chapel, Jumbo, the old head-coolie, a superb rhomboid of a man, six feet high and five feet broad, aired his notable pigtail and his glorious six-inch grin on the steps of the little bell-tower among a knot of his minions; on the stable drive Wang, the old head *mafoo*, stood more discreetly under a bush, one eye cocked on the proceedings in the square, the other on his stable courtyard—a strong contrast to Jumbo with

46

his spare slight figure in black velvet slippers, jodhpurs, and stable jacket, his shaven head and dreamy ascetic face. There was a feeling of tension and excitement in the air such as the Chinese, with their tendency to hysteria, contrive to infuse into the simplest occasions which show any features out of the ordinary. Presently Derek Fitzmaurice emerged from his house and strolled across the square, tall and slight in his khaki shorts and shirt of tropical drill, and up the drive to the Leroys' house.

"*T'ai-t'ai!*" he said briefly to the servant. His Chinese was as scanty and as bad as possible; he always used very few words, and those usually incorrectly, but he prided himself a good deal on what he did know.

Li made some fluent reply which he could not follow and showed him into Laura's sitting-room. She was not there. He wandered coolly into Henry's study—he was not there either. He tried a cast back across the hall into the drawing-room—the scent of the freesias filled it as before, but no other living presence disturbed its rather bare and spacious grace. He was turning back into the hall when he met Lilah Milne.

"Hullo!" said she abruptly, and nothing else.

"Well, are we really going?" asked Fitzmaurice.

"No one seems to know," said Lilah indifferently.

"Where's Laura?"

"No one seems to know that either." She walked past him rather aimlessly and out on to the verandah, and sat down in an arm-chair. Derek followed her, fretted.

"Where's Leroy?" he next inquired.

"He went over to the Minister a few minutes ago," said Lilah. "There's been another telegram, I think. General Nevile came in and they went off together."

"Cripes! That looks as though the show was off."

Lilah said nothing at all. She picked up *La Chine en*

Folie from a wicker table beside her and began to turn the leaves idly.

"Well, I shall try to get hold of Laura," muttered Derek impatiently, and took himself off to the Neviles', hoping to find her there.

But Mrs. Leroy was not at the Neviles'. She was sitting in an obscure corner of the Grant-Howards' garden, under the sullen creeper-clad wall of the septic tank, and, a writing-pad on her knee, she was finishing a letter to Sarah. She had hidden herself deliberately. This place was one of her favourite funk-holes, screened by a group of thujas and a mammoth rubbish-heap; here she was for the moment out of the way of the discussion and fussification about the start, and if in the end she did contribute a little more to the delay, already immense, there was just a chance that the mail would be in before they left, and she would have her letters to take with her.

She had been running over in her mind the happenings of the last few days, choosing what should amuse Sarah. At dinner on Monday night they had found the American Legation seething with excitement, the alarm already given, and "leaf" stopped. "But Hubbard says Howard did get off to Tientsin, with just fifteen minutes to spare!" According to Dr. Schuyler's information, Wang and Tu, the two rival war lords, had formed an alliance and were marching together on the capital; as a result of this news Nina's picnic was pronounced to be off.

On Tuesday, however, with the usual Chinese suddenness, all the rumours were declared to be false. Confidence prevailed, and Nina sent chits triumphantly to every one to say that the picnic was on again. But late on Tuesday night, when the Leroys returned from a ball at the French Legation, Niu met them at the door with the announcement that an Englishman was waiting to see the Great Man in the drawing-room, and Henry, grumbling and disgusted, had sought out this unseasonable visitor, who paid calls at 1.30 a.m. It proved to be a certain ex-missionary, now, like most ex-missionaries, employed in some highly lucrative business, and well known for the paternal officiousness with which he endeavoured to "keep the Legation on the right track, you know. Outsiders sometimes see most of the game." This *cliché*, seldom off his lips, had earned him the appellation of "the Outsider," to which indeed he was entitled on other grounds. The Outsider, in hushed tones, and with an "are-we-observed?" manner, now informed Leroy that he had learned from most reliable sources that the situation was very grave, very grave indeed—Tu was moving rapidly against Peking and would cut the Nankou railway by dawn at latest; Li was preparing to evacuate the city already. "I have that from Yang Po Chih's nephew." Henry, growling, had suggested that breakfast-time would show soon enough how much there was in it all, and that the Legation could neither keep Li *in* Peking, nor Tu out, in any case; he had refused point-blank to arouse the Minister to give him this information, as the Outsider suggested. But he went to bed somewhat disquieted. Yang Po Chih was Li's most trusted *chung-jen*, or middle-man, who negotiated his victories and defeats by the sale or purchase of generals and Army-Corps, and the Outsider was known to have his own means of securing trustworthy information.

Wednesday morning brought partial confirmation of his report. The Leroys, going at 7 a.m. for their usual ride on the glacis, the wide open space which surrounds the Legation Quarter on three sides, had noticed, as they galloped up the cinder-track beside the polo-ground, an unusual amount of traffic pouring through the Hatamên gateway. Peking carts, handcarts, wheelbarrows and donkeys, all piled with household effects to capsizing point, told their own dismal and familiar tale of refugees hurrying into the city before the approach of an army. By breakfast-time a siege was pronounced to be imminent, as officially as anything ever is official in China. By 11 a.m. the city gates were closed, and the stream of refugees and their effects dammed back. But all day long there continued to flow into the Legation Quarter a lesser stream of rickshas containing the valuables of wealthy Chinese, each little group of three or four followed by one in which sat the wealthy Chinese himself, imperturbable in black brocade and little black satin cap, coming to supervise personally the deposit of his more precious possessions in the strong-rooms of one of the European Banks, or in the cellars of the German photographer or the Swiss coiffeur. The Kuniangs, who had planned an expedition to the Yuan-Ming-Yuan, the old ruined Summer Palace, for that particular day, were thrilled to find themselves forcibly enclosed in a walled city by massive gates guarded by armed men; Judith had insisted on driving to the P'ing Tze Mên to see if it were really shut, and returned almost incoherent with italics on finding that it was. Even Lilah had displayed a measure of interest in the constant procession of the wealthy Chinese and their belongings through the half-closed bullet-proof gates of the Quarter.

And the evening had afforded the Kuniangs a further thrill. The Paraguayan Minister was holding ·a re-ception in the Wagons-Lits Hotel, the large European building just inside the Water-gate, which competes with the Hôtel de Pékin, without the Quarter, for the patronage of foreigner and Chinese alike. On occasions such as this the Wagons-Lits wins hands down, as far as the Chinese are concerned. The big gaudy brightly lit lounge was swarming with them when the Leroys' party arrived. Elegant little ladies with the coiffure and gestures of ivory statuettes were sipping tea or *crème de menthe* in every corner; stouter and more matronly figures in brocade sat on sofas and called to their offspring in low voices; as for the children, they were everywhere—running in the corridors, playing on the stairs, poking their round black heads and bright mask-like faces into every corner, including the ladies' lavatories. Henry Leroy pointed out the Minister of Finance and the Minister of Justice to the Milnes—the Cabinet had apparently taken refuge more or less *en bloc* in the hotel. "Because no Chinese troops are allowed to enter the Quarter," he explained in answer to Judith's inquiries. "They're perfectly safe in here." "How nice for them to have a Legation Quarter to come to!" said Lilah cheerfully, gazing round on the sanctuary-seeking politicians and their families, who were preparing to sleep, according to Touchy, in the bathrooms and billiard-room, and even along the corridors on the upper floors. And Laura had laughed low and suddenly. Perhaps the real use of the presence of Europeans in Peking was to afford shelter to *embusqués* Chinese. Anyhow, of one thing there could be no doubt—Nina's picnic was, for the second time, quite disastrously off. This, for the party, was the really important feature of the military situation.

The next day, however, had produced another of those sudden changes of the political scene which in China are so common that they cease to be startling, though they remain bewildering. An entirely new alignment of forces had apparently taken place in the night, and fresh alliances and combinations sprang up like mushrooms in the dew. Tu and Li, it was now reported, had formed a telegraphic alliance; Tu was moving against Wang and not against Peking; Li, instead of evacuating the capital, was remaining there to greet his victorious brother-in-arms when the campaign should be over. The city gates were re-opened, the politicians and their families emerged from the bathrooms of the Wagons-Lits Hotel, and by cocktail time, in spite of Henry Leroy's disapproval, the picnic was once more on.

But Hubbard at dressing-time had supplied a footnote to the *couleur de rose* official bulletins. "The boys were saying at the 'Y' this afternoon, madam, that this alliance business is all my-eye." "Oh, really, Hubbard. Why is that?" "Why, madam, as far as I can make it out, this Lee has put it about as a bluff, like, so that he can keep the railways open, and go on getting money, and then make a quiet get-away to Tientsin. And this Doo—the boys don't trust him. They say he means business, and will have Peking yet." "But Hubbard," Laura had said, pondering this gloomy view while she plied the powder-puff, "the Chinese themselves believe there won't be a siege—they've opened the gates and are going on just as usual." "Ah, and so they may," replied Hubbard darkly. "They'll swallow anything if there's enough of it, as the saying goes. Saying's believing, not seeing, with these people, seemingly. What scent shall you wear to-night, madam?"

All this uncertainty and to-ing and fro-ing, as Lilah called it, had made the worst possible preparation for any expedition, in Laura's view. Before such an undertaking, if it is to succeed, the participants should keep as much apart as possible until the actual start. But on this occasion they had all seen a quite intolerable amount of one another. At almost every party, in the interval between its inception and the day of departure, they had

drawn together, as by some fatality, to discuss the pros
and cons, the chances of success and the fears of failure.
And when they were not meeting in public, they had
been running round to one another's houses to ask for
the latest news. But one feature of interest had emerged
for Mrs. Leroy—the sudden and unexpected growth of
her acquaintance with Little Annette.

It began, literally, by accident. On the Tuesday after
the Knudsens' At Home, when rumours were stilled and
all was peace, a party had ridden out under Touchy's
auspices to the Marco Polo Bridge, about eight miles
from Peking. It was getting late for cross-country
riding; the spring planting was beginning, and there
was no more galloping slap across the dusty cold fields
from landmark to landmark—to a red-walled tomb, a
temple, a dark patch of wood marking some burial plot.
But Touchy, who relieved the monotony of his duties
as Commandant of the Legation Guard by the more
onerous and exciting ones of Joint Master of the Drag-
Hunt, knew the country like the inside of his pocket,
and led them by devious ways of his own—now along
narrow sunk roads, from which only their heads projected as they rode along, now across an open sandy
patch, still free for an inspiriting gallop, till they reached
the long high-backed bridge spanning the Hun-ho. It
was a hot soft April day—the brilliant light poured over
the flat brown landscape, on which the coloured walls
of temples and tombs, and the dark masses of grave-yard
trees, detached themselves with great vividness; and all
the way the sharp outline of the Western Hills kept them
company on the right, like a bright pink and lavender-
coloured back-cloth hung on the sky. They had ridden
up on to the arc of the bridge between the Chippendale-
looking panels of the carved stone parapets, topped at
intervals with those little green effigies of beasts which

amused Marco Polo so much that he counted them in
1263, when he rode across this same bridge into Ch'ang-
tu, or Xanadu, the old Peking. The General handed
out this piece of information for the benefit of Judith
and Little Annette. "I expect the traffic then looked
much as it does now," he added. "This road is still the
start of the great trade-route to Tibet." Small hooded
carts with solid wheels creaked up the slopes of the
bridge, drawn by mules or shaggy ponies; strings of
donkeys with laden panniers tripped over the huge
steep paving-slabs on their neat unshod feet, urged on
by men with rough faces and wild clothes; now and then
a group of Tibetans, in flapping green and yellow garments, strode past, their wrinkled faces much more
typically Mongolian than the Chinese. Long files of
camels were fording the river a little above the bridge,
moving with the curious slow rhythm that suggests a
waltz in every leg, lifting their strange supercilious heads
in a timeless challenge to distances and deserts and little
weariable man, treading stones or sand or water with
the same aloof indifference.

As the party turned homewards and passed through the
dirty tiny broken-walled town which holds the bridge-
head, Mrs. Leroy called out, "Have we time for the
Red Temple, Touchy?" La Touche, a little ahead, did
not hear, but Annette Ingersoll, who happened to be
riding behind with Mrs. Leroy, was at once consumed
with a desire to see something more. "What is it? Can't
we go to it?"

"It's just a little temple on the river bank," replied
Laura. "There's nothing to see, but it stands rather
beautifully, and I like it."

"Oh, do let's go, Mrs. Leroy," the girl said urgently.

Laura looked at her watch, and then at her companion's pony. "What's that horse you're on?" she

asked. "Po Chih? Oh, all right—we'll go and look at it and catch the others up. He's fast."

They turned to the left, and cantered upstream along a stony sandy flat beside the river. The hills were now ahead of them. The sort of track they followed presently skirted the foot of a high bank which gradually hid the stream from their view. "Let him out!" called Mrs. Leroy, and put her grey into a gallop. Annette thought it rather unsafe to ride at that speed over ground pock-marked with pot-holes and heaps of stones, but did as she was bidden. With wind and sand and hair in her eyes, trying to see her way and to hold on to Po Chih, who pulled, she was aware of nothing else till they slackened speed. "Up here!" said Mrs. Leroy, and led the way up a slope of rough wiry yellow turf. Annette expected to fall off backwards, the ground was so steep, but Po Chih scrambled up like a monkey, and breathless and excited she found herself at their goal.

The Red Temple does indeed stand beautifully, even dramatically, perched like a crow's nest on the high bank above the river. Behind it the ground falls steeply to the flat along which they had ridden; in front it drops at once to the river bed. The Hun-ho at this point makes a wide sweep southwards after its straight run out from the mountains, and the bank on which they stood was revetted with blocks of stone to control the summer fury of the stream. For it is not in the dry cold winter, but in the summer rains that the rivers of North China rage like unchained beasts, sweeping out with sudden violence from their lairs in the hills to carry destruction over the plain. The Hun-ho had eaten its way into the narrow ridge till now there were only a few feet of soil between the carved marble gate of the little temple and the crumbling edge of the drop. Standing there, their bridles over their arms, they had almost the sense of being poised in space above the world, looking out over it. And what a view! Upstream and down, in the distance, the river-bed broadened out into wide pale stretches of sand, which the wind was lifting in great smoky clouds, lit up by the westering sun till they shone like some celestial conflagration. In front of them were the hills, near enough now to cease to be a painted curtain—it was possible to look into them, and see the bony structure of ridge and hollow and sharp-walled valley on the nearer slopes, and the agitated perspective of the sea of tossing crests behind. But the magical thing was the sense of being lifted up into the heart of light and the power of the free wind. The battered and weather-stained walls of the temple, the twisted and misshapen tree or two which rose above them, bore witness to the wind's power. The long pale stems of dead grasses and the bare twigs of bushes whipped and scrabbled at the faded red plaster of the walls, making little worn patches; the sharp cutting sand lay drifted in little heaps in the angles of their carved marble footings.

"The first time I brought Sarah here she said this temple reminded her of a very poor humble Saint, who found himself lifted half-way to Heaven," said Mrs. Leroy suddenly.

"Why, what a wonderful comment!" said Annette. "Who is Sarah, Mrs. Leroy?"

"Sarah is my daughter."

"I haven't met her yet, have I? I'd love to," said Annette.

"You won't meet her—she's in England, at school," said Mrs. Leroy briefly, and the girl saw her face change from the bright musing look with which she had gazed at the view. The older woman turned and walked a few paces away along the ridge, leading her horse;

Annette saw her take out her handkerchief and realised swiftly that Sarah was not a case for her usual bright interest. That the thought of her child should move to tears a grown woman—a woman, moreover, whom she had felt to be rather peculiarly *hautaine* and self-contained—was something new in her experience, and stirred her to a sudden warmth of feeling. But when she turned round Mrs. Leroy spoke with business-like abruptness. "Now we must hurry, Miss Ingersoll. We'll lead them down the bank."

They slithered down the bristly turf, mounted, and set off at a canter, not along the track by which they had come, but cutting across country at an angle to it, to bring them back into their road home beyond the bridge-head. The waste and open flat gave place presently to small sandy clearings, separated from one another by low loose-growing rows of wind-swept tamarisks. Galloping through a gap in one of these, "Look out!" screamed Laura suddenly. Annette saw the grey make a spring, but she was too close behind to turn or stop, and Po Chih, never much of a jumper, saw too late the deep-dug pit which yawned beyond the gap. He gathered himself together and had a shot at it, half-landed, stumbled, and rolled over in the deep soft sand, pitching his rider ahead of him.

Chapter Six

THE long walk home afforded opportunity for a good many things. Po Chih was badly lame; Annette Ingersoll, though stiff and shaken, not much the worse once the sand was removed from her eyes, ears and mouth. She rode the grey, and Laura walked, leading Po Chih. She was not pleased with herself. It had been stupid and careless to take an inexperienced rider galloping across country like that—she ought to have stuck to the others and not yielded to the sudden impulse to go and look at her beloved Red Temple. It was a place for which she had a particular affection, partly for its own sake, partly because Sarah had loved it so much. It was full of memories of Sarah—Sarah scrambling up the steep bank, hardy and skilful, on her pony; Sarah climbing the wall to enter the temple and coming back with descriptions of the shrine within; of the March day when they found the great tuft of purple pasque-flowers growing half-way down the river-face, and Sarah would go and pick them. So now to come to the Red Temple was for Mrs. Leroy almost to catch sight of Sarah, to get a brief draught of that for which she was perpetually athirst, and she had yielded to the temptation. Ashamed of her habitual self-indulgence, ashamed of General Nevile's polo-pony disastrously lamed, she turned with an impulse of penitence to lightening the long road home, as far as might be, for her young companion. And Annette Ingersoll, shaken by her fall and still warmed by the recollection of Mrs. Leroy's changed face and brusque

58

movement at the mention of her child, forgot the slight awe in which she had stood of her, and fairly let herself go in return.

Mrs. Leroy found out a lot in the next two hours. Miss Ingersoll, it appeared, was a young woman of considerable culture and ambition. She knew Russian, and read Gogol and Pushkin in their native tongue; she had lived a good deal in Rome, and spoke Italian fluently. Mrs. Leroy could not follow her into the realms of untranslated Russian, but they compared notes on Italian literature and she was surprised by the girl's knowledge of some of its lesser-known treasures, such as the minor poets of the court of Frederick II. Annette's ambition was to write a history of the novel in all countries, from its earliest beginnings! Culture thus beguiled the way to Pa-mao-ch'ang, the sort of suburb of villas and temples outside Peking near the race-course. "If we don't find anyone at the Minister's villa we must telephone for the car," said Mrs. Leroy as they approached it; "the gates will be shut by the time we get there, and I haven't got a pass."

'A pass?" queried Little Annette.

Laura explained that the city gates were always shut at 7.30, and that without a pass it was literally impossible to get in. But on reaching the Great Mound, the acacia-plumed hillock on which Sir James Boggit's country-house stood, they saw Touchy's Buick standing below the wall, while his chauffeur and a couple of grooms were gambling quietly, squatting in the deep sand by the roadside. As they drove back in the car the girl had turned to Mrs. Leroy and proffered a request with a sort of shy animation: would Mrs. Leroy mind if she asked to be called Annette and not Miss Ingersoll? In her then mood of penitence Laura would have agreed to anything; she had taken one glance at the girl's pale face, darkened under the eyes, and had called her Annette on the spot.

They continued to meet. Next day, on that Wednesday of alarms and no excursions, Mrs. Leroy and the Kuniangs, walking with Derek Fitzmaurice on the City Wall, ran into Miss Ingersoll and Henri Delache. They joined forces—not too much to Henri's delight, Laura fancied—and Annette at once walked with her, talking with the intimacy of old acquaintance. She liked the girl more and more; there was a warmth, a simplicity and an eagerness about her which was more than mere American brightness. Acting on an impulse which surprised herself, Mrs. Leroy had invited her to ride next day at the Temple of Heaven, and they had spent an hour or two cantering round the untidy park, half wild spinney, half open space, which surrounds it. They had, of course, talked all the time—but the better she got to know Little Annette the more Laura Leroy was surprised at the odd combination in her of so much culture with such a curious, almost babyish, flatness and unperceptiveness about people. She had her little *clichés*, which she used with no discrimination at all. Women were "the greatest dear" or "a lovely person," or "terribly clever," or "terribly chic"—men were also "the greatest dears," "perfectly lovely men," or merely "quaint," or—in Henry's case—"terribly learned." (Laura suspected that Henry was really also "quaint" as well.) It was not shyness, for she had ceased to be shy; she was most ready to pour out her impressions of people and things—it was, Laura came to believe, really that she only saw people in the flat, like cardboard dolls to which labels could be pinned. Her experience of life, she decided, was so far wholly literary; she was discerning enough about the standard figures of fiction, but almost myopic about real people and the actualities of daily life. She had no idea of how to set about getting to know people properly, and no genuine curiosity to impel her to learn; her technique was simply her bright diffused enthusiasm and an affectionate disposition; her only criterion, how much she liked them. "She's quite intelligent, but simply asleep as far as reality is concerned," she told Derek. Derek had been prosecuting his acquaintance with Judith with considerable energy during the same period—or else Judith had been prosecuting her acquaintance with him, Laura was not quite sure which; but she could not help contrasting in her mind Annette Ingersoll's methods with those of her niece. Judith was far from being asleep as regarded reality or anything else. Things move fast in Peking, and Laura had watched with interest but without surprise the rapid growth of her intimacy with Fitzmaurice in the last few days. In her dealings with him, as indeed with every one, Judith showed a sort of valiant curiosity, a determination to understand people and motives, and to face facts. She could be disconcertingly direct.

"Is he an absolute rotter? I can't make out," she had asked suddenly, when Derek's name was mentioned.

"Oh, no, he's not an absolute rotter," Laura had replied unhesitatingly—and then she had paused, a little bothered. There were plenty of people who would, and did, consider that that was just what Derek was. And she realised that her words might be taken as a sort of guarantee by her niece. She hastened to qualify them. "Yes, I suppose some people would say that he was."

"But *you* don't think so?" Judith pressed her.

"No, I don't. I see that he behaves very much like one in some ways, but I don't believe he is really. There's something too real in the middle of him. And he is affectionate, and can be honest."

That had satisfied Judith, who had gone off, a meditative look on her Michelangelo face. Very much to Laura's surprise Lilah had uttered on the subject too. "Where is Judith?" Mrs. Leroy had asked, coming in from her ride at the Temple of Heaven with Miss Ingersoll, and finding Lilah alone, extended in a chaise-longue on the verandah, languid and lovely.

"Gone for a walk with Mr. Fitzmaurice," Lilah answered, putting down her book and looking up at her aunt. "They're rather progressive, those two, aren't they?" she added.

Laura assented.

"I shouldn't wonder if Master Derek has met his match this time," Lilah went on, with a sort of sleepy amusement on her lovely face.

"Yes—if his being so much more experienced doesn't put her at a disadvantage," said Laura, glad to voice her secret anxiety to someone, especially to the person who knew Judith best.

"Oh, no, that's all right," said Lilah, with languid confidence. "Because she fights with real weapons, and he's only using sham ones."

Laura looked at her niece with increased respect for this remark which she drawled out so casually. She found herself pondering on it afterwards. But what if Derek ever took to fighting with real weapons? Ah, well then, of course, he would have ceased to be what he now was, so the problem would anyhow be different.

She had been running over all this in her mind, sitting under the septic tank after early lunch on Friday. Much of it had *not* gone into her letter to Sarah. She was just about to finish that off, and close it for the post, when a fluttering of white appeared through the thujas in front. Mrs. Leroy kept very still—she must on no account give away her hiding-place. But the white approached inexorably, and in a moment Li stood in front of her, impassive and respectful. He knew her corner all right—Chinese servants always know everything! Laura almost laughed.

"*Yao shen-ma?*" (What do you want?) she said.

The Ping Ying T'i Tu (the Commandant of the Guard) was at the house and wanted the *T'ai-t'ai.* Laura rose and went in, Li flapping across the garden behind her with undiminished respectfulness.

The General as well as Touchy awaited her on the verandah.

"It's all right—we're off," Touchy hailed her across the lawn.

"Are you all ready?" asked General Nevile in a slightly comminatory tone, looking inquiringly at her drill jodhpurs and loose silk shirt.

"Yes," said Mrs. Leroy, picking up a soft felt hat from a chair on the verandah and cramming it on to her thick dark shingle. "What about the telegram? Was it anything?" she asked in her turn.

"It was only from home. The Tass Agency has been improving on these latest rumours, as usual, and Parliament has got into a fuss about the missionaries." ("Also as usual!" interjected Touchy.) "So they telegraphed for more information and sent some general instructions," pursued the General, looking gloomily amused, "in case of emergency."

"Can't you imagine the papers at home!" said Touchy, absently measuring an oleander with the polo-stick, shorn of its mallet, which he carried as a walking-stick. "Dangerous situation in China!"

"If Mrs. Leroy is really ready we ought to start," observed the General.

"Yes, come on, Laura."

Laura made some vague excuse about a handkerchief,

and vanished. She was determined to see if the mail
was really in. Striding upstairs, she met Hubbard on the
landing. The maid was carrying a fan and had a drill
jacket over her arm.

"Is the mail in, Hubbard?"

"Yes, madam. I thought you would want your
letters, so I've put them in your pocket." She tapped the
jacket. "And I've filled your large travelling-case—and
matches—and two handkerchiefs. And here's your fan."

"Oh, bless you, Hubbard!" Laura exclaimed, putting
on the coat. "There's a letter for Miss Sarah in a block
on the verandah," she went on over her shoulder, as the
maid straightened her collar and gave little professional
pulls and pats to the coat, which was loose, much worn,
and of a comfortable shapelessness—a hopeless garment
from Hubbard's point of view. "Put it in an envelope
and see that it goes."

"Yes, madam. Do you think you shall want anything
else, madam?"

"No, that's the lot, thank you, Hubbard. Good-bye!"
She turned to go.

"Should you mind if I go out this week-end, madam?
If I should be invited?"

"No, of course not—go by all means."

"Thank you, madam. I hope you'll have a pleasant
time, and not get mixed up with that Doo or his lot,"
she added, with a demure giggle. "I don't like what I
hear of him at the 'Y.'"

On the square Mrs. Leroy saw the whole party assembled in a group round the cars, and she found time as
she approached to be amused by the variety of their
costumes. La Touche and the General were military
and correct in riding-dress; Derek was in shorts; Henri
Delache, however, was content to picnic in grey flannel
trousers, brown boots, and a small Trilby hat. This

young man had the high fresh colour and premature
baldness of many Frenchmen; his inquiring up-tilted
nose and weak, rather prominent eyes combined to give
an air at once of impertinence and sophistication to his
smooth round face. Nina's Professor stood a little apart
—tallish, thinnish, youngish for a professor, Laura
thought; there was no colour at all except freckliness
about him; his light suit would not have been amiss in
Bond Street. Someone had lent him a topi, which he
was examining rather gingerly, turning it about in his
hands. Suddenly he put it on his head, and his face
wrinkled into a quick pleasing grin, presumably at himself—it was gone in an instant, but it inspired Laura with
a certain confidence. The ladies of the party showed an
equal disparity in dress. Judith Milne, like her aunt,
wore cotton jodhpurs and a shirt; with a silk handkerchief knotted round her throat and a broad-brimmed
hat, she looked like an operatic cowboy. Mrs. Nevile
was in shorts—an impossible dress for most women, but
admirably becoming to her perfect little figure; eager
and businesslike, she moved about like a diminutive
Boy Scout, directing operations. But Miss Hande, short,
thin, dark and sensible, had imported New York into
Peking complete with one of those neat little travelling-
suits, beloved of American women, a "shirt-waist," and
a small close hat. The novelist and the Professor matched
one another in their urban trimness.

"Our intellectuals are very tidy," murmured Laura
to Derek, as she approached the group.

"My God! I don't think much of Nina's Professor,"
returned Derek in the same tone. "He looks like a slice
of galantine! I'm sure there's a layer of jelly between
him and his suit."

"Oh, nonsense! I think he looks rather nice."

"My dear Laura! At last 'ere you are!" exclaimed

Delache, coming up to Mrs. Leroy and taking her hand in both of his. "*On vous a découverte à la fin. J'avais cru*——" he leant forward and whispered something into her ear which made her laugh and redden in spite of herself.

"Oh, shut up, Henri!" she said impatiently. "*Il faut respecter la jeunesse!*" she added, with a glance at the Kuniangs.

"*Mais, ma chère,*" protested Delache, opening his hands, "you know that with *jeunes filles* I am always perfectly *correc*'."

He was interrupted by Mrs. Nevile, who came up to them with the Professor in tow. "My dear, they've found you at last! Let me introduce Professor Vinstead to you." Laura and the Professor shook hands. "Now we must really be off. It's terribly late. Shang and the donkeys were to be at the ferry at two, and it's a quarter before this minute. We shan't be there till three as it is."

"Nina, let us get this ferry business exactly right," said La Touche, also coming up. "It's not to Men-t'ou-kou we go, but to Moyu—is that it?"

"No, *not* to Moyu—to the Mo-shih-k'ou Ferry," said Mrs. Nevile. "But I'll lead you and you can all follow on."

Touchy saluted.

"Laura," Mrs. Nevile went on, "don't you think we should divide up a little? I thought if you would take Miss Hande, I would borrow Miss Lilah from you."

"Yes, rather," Laura agreed absently. Her letters were burning a hole in her pocket, and she was thinking of when and how she could read them; she realised too late that to exchange Miss Hande for Lilah in her own car would make it more difficult to devour them *en route*.

"I shall have a nice restful time as a gooseberry!"

murmured La Touche to Nina Nevile, glancing at Miss Ingersoll and Henri Delache, who even in these disjointed moments of departure were engaged in a promising and—judging by their faces—highly enjoyable *tête-à-tête*. The American girl showed an unusual animation which was highly becoming to her.

"So will Laura and Big Annette, I should say," returned Mrs. Nevile. "Look at Mr. Fitzmaurice! I've never seen him so taken up with anyone respectable before."

"Oh dear!—two pairs of sweethearts in one party," groaned Touchy in dismay. "Nina, my dear, you'll have a lot to answer for."

"Come on—we simply must start," said Mrs. Nevile, disregarding him.

At last they did all stop saying, "We must start," and, somehow, started. They piled themselves in, and the three cars, freighted with luggage, bodies, and who knows what secret cargo of private preoccupations, hopes, fears and expectations, ground up the gravel of the road and swung off out of the square, past the dispensary, the electric light plant, the pumping station and all the other hideous accessories of the Legation—past the *manège*, with its battered turf and *kaoliang* fences for jumping, with low barrack buildings opposite, and finally past Touchy's bungalow near the West Gate. The sentry, seeing many cars approaching, stiffened to attention, thinking one might be the Minister's—found that none was, refrained from saluting, and then saw, too late, that the second contained his commanding officer. When they had passed he continued his march to and fro, stumping his heavy English boots in the white dust, thinly patterned with the shadows of the budding mimosa boughs. The Legation servants returned from their points of vantage to their various compounds, there to sleep on the pantry shelves and floor till tea; Jumbo left the belfry steps and lit another Lucky Strike cigarette; Old Wang, the head *mafoo*, slippered softly back into the stable-yard, scolded a few of his minions, and then, pulling a very ancient kitchen chair out into the sun, sat down opposite his cherished pot of cactuses and lit a little black and silver pipe. In the Chancery, behind the lowered *lienzas*, the unhappy Mr. Deering wrestled with a cipher book and the Minister's remarks to the Foreign Office about the safety of missionaries; a typewriter, driven by one of the ladies commonly referred to as The Fairies, clattered monotonously in the heat from an adjoining room; in the *T'ing-ch'ai's* office next door Mr. Chun sorted the mail of the smaller Legation fry, his spectacles perched precariously on his yellow nose as he studied each address. Over at the Minister's house Sir James had ordered coffee in the inner courtyard, and now, his short bulk disposed in a garden chair, a cigar between his lips, he settled himself for a brief rest after the labours of the morning, before the labours of polo to come. Everything was most irregular, and that felloh Leroy— excellent felloh, of course—had been worrying him about this jaunt of the M.A.'s missis. But the heat was soothing, and there would be polo later with some very decent fellohs. The usual gentle afternoon coma descended on the Legation, and it descended also on Sir James.

Chapter Seven

MISS ANNA HANDE, the novelist, had not come to Peking in search of local colour; she was much too intelligent and conscientious to do anything of the sort. She had come to see one of the greatest wonders of the world, and to pay a visit to her friend, Mrs. Nevile. But like all novelists she had something of the journalistic mind; she liked to see everything, and to understand what she saw. As the party drove out now her lorgnette was kept perpetually above her long, distinguished nose, helping her short-sighted but intelligent eyes to observations and deductions. They left the city by the Shun-chi-mên, the most westerly of the three gates in the South Wall. Outside it the car passed a level-crossing and a bridge, and now swung suddenly to the right through a narrow alley and proceeded to skirt the bank of the canal which lies outside the wall of the Tartar City. The road was merely a wide rutted waste of dust several inches deep, out of which the trunks of trees rose irregularly. To the right lay the canal, in whose filthy waters both men and women were hopefully washing clothes, or dipping up pointed wicker buckets of water for domestic purposes; on the left was a raw bank of earth with a few buildings perched at intervals along the top of it. A mixture of smells of more than usual fearfulness and virulence hung in the air— Miss Hande and Judith Milne put handkerchiefs to their noses involuntarily and simultaneously. As the car lurched and bounded over the ruts, bumps and hollows, Derek amused himself by an endeavour to discompose

69

Miss Hande's hygienic American mind. He pointed out to her two dark discoloured streams which oozed and trickled down the bank and into the canal, the effluents from a slaughter-house and a manure factory respectively.

"That is where your ice comes from," he told her, pointing to the canal. Miss Hande shuddered incredulously.

"It's a fact. In winter it freezes solid, and they cut the top off in blocks and bury it up there." He waved his hand towards an empty bit of ground above the bank. "No, not just there—that's a criminals' graveyard; it drains into the canal too—a little further on. Then in summer the ice has a joyful resurrection—unlike the criminals. Look—they're getting some out now."

In fact, from a straw-filled quarry-like hollow up the bank a coolie emerged, carrying a large block of ice slung from a shoulder-yoke. He trotted down the bank with it, and then paused to light a cigarette. The ice was dumped in the dust, and the coolie sat on it; being Chinese he spat, and spat on his cargo. Miss Hande watched with a sort of horrified fascination. Derek laughed.

"The boys keep the fish on that, and probably put it in the cocktails, if you aren't careful," he said cheerfully. "They've no ideas of sanitation or infection or anything."

"I wonder you aren't all dead," said Miss Hande, looking distressfully at Laura.

"It is rather a struggle to keep alive, for the housekeeper," Laura admitted. "I taught my cook never to put fish or anything directly *on* the ice, and then one day I found that his way of keeping the milk cool was to stand the bottles up against the block and wrap a dirty old sack over the lot, so that it dripped nicely into them." She laughed too.

"But isn't there a very great deal of illness?" asked Miss Hande.

"There's a good deal of death!" said Derek grimly. "You don't get ill in Peking—you die; in about forty-eight hours, as a rule. Only last month——" he told a ghastly story of the lovely young wife of a foreign consul, who had been well and brilliant at a dinner-party one evening, rushed to hospital at 5 a.m. the next morning, and dead by lunch-time the following day.

"Well, it's most distressing," observed Miss Hande. "And yet Peking seems to have such a marvellous climate."

"It has," said Mrs. Leroy. "It isn't the climate that kills you as a rule—it's dirt—dirt and indifference."

"That's why the Foreign Office schedules it as a healthy post!" observed Derek.

"Well, I can't help it!" burst out Judith. "I *like* to be in a place where people do things in the way that seems good to them, and don't care a *hoot* about germs, and aren't all sanitary and tidy and *hideous*, but dirty and beautiful."

"I said you were a gipsy!" remarked Fitzmaurice, letting his eyes rest on the girl in a way that made her blush.

The car at this point lurched up a steep slope, and swung precariously round a blind corner between high walls, and they found themselves before another gate in yet another city wall. It should be explained that on the south the Chinese City encloses the Tartar City, like a double box; they had left the Tartar City by the Shun-chi-mên, and were now about to leave the Chinese City by the Hsi-pien-mên. Being the outer gate, it was strongly guarded by soldiers with fixed bayonets, in soiled grey cotton uniforms, wearing pink calico armlets on the left arm. Derek (who was playing up rather well,

Mrs. Leroy thought) explained to Miss Hande that all Chinese armies wear the same uniform, and that the troops of the various war-lords are only distinguished from one another by these armlets, of different colours. "It's very convenient and economical, because when they change sides all they have to do is to change armlets," he told her.

"Then whose are the pink armlets?" inquired Miss Hande.

"Li-Ch'ing-hui, the Marshal's, who's got Peking now."

They had paused before the gateway to let through a convoy of long solid-wheeled carts, laden with sacks of grain and flour, which were creaking up the steep cobbled slope and through the vaulted archway, their teams of mules and oxen straining painfully at the loads. Many of the beasts were sickeningly galled under their clumsy harness, and Judith exclaimed with pity and horror at the sight, "How can they treat animals so cruelly?"

"It isn't cruelty," said Fitzmaurice, "they treat animals just as they treat themselves. Look at that chap!"

Another cart came into view at the moment, drawn by a mixed team of two oxen, a donkey, and a huge coolie who, glistening with sweat, the muscles standing out under his bronzed skin, strained at the rope across his breast and shoulder. Where it passed he, too, was galled to the collar-bone.

"He doesn't care, and he doesn't expect the mule to mind," pursued Derek. "They're quite accustomed to it. You must remember that the principal draught animal in Peking is still man."

"You don't say so!" exclaimed Miss Hande, startled. The intensity of her expression when she heard something striking almost gave one the impression that she was scribbling rapidly in a notebook, though in fact

her hands were still occupied, one with her lorgnette
and the other with a handkerchief. Though the odours
of the canal were left behind, the fumes of garlic from
the soldiers filled the enclosed space by the gateway
with an almost visible cloud.

"Of course he is. What carries practically the entire
human traffic? Rickshas. And quite half the goods
traffic is borne on shoulder-yokes and wheeled in hand-
barrows, inside the city. Dirt and beauty have their
seamy side!" he said, grinning at Judith.

"Well, what you tell me is very interesting," observed
Miss Hande. "It raises a very curious prahblem."

"What?" Laura felt bound to ask.

"Why, isn't it strange that a people of such ancient
civilisation, of so much culture and such exalted ideas
as the Chinese, should tahlerate the use of human
beings for the work of beasts? Doesn't it strike you as
shocking?" she said, turning to Laura.

"No, it doesn't," said Laura flatly. "I don't think
hauling a cart or pulling a ricksha is nearly as unhealthy
as being a stoker on a liner, nor as dangerous as coal-
mining, and it's certainly far less demoralising than
leaning against a wall all day and drawing the dole. It
isn't really strange, either," she went on, getting wound
up, as she sometimes did; "the Chinese are a perfectly
rational people—the most rational on earth, probably—
so of course they aren't sentimentalists."

"How do you mean, Laura?" asked Judith.

"I mean that they don't talk about the dignity of
labour, and then constantly go on strike; they *are* the
dignity of labour. There is greater poverty here than
anywhere else in the world, but somehow no squalor.
Look at your human beast of burden!" she said to Miss
Hande. The cart had passed through the gateway and
halted for a rest inside it. As the car moved forward

they saw the coolie stretch his superb limbs, freed for a moment from the rope, and turn with a cheerful grin to exchange a joke with the soldiers. His hairless polished torso was modelled with the perfection of a god's; his movements were full of grace and natural dignity; his broad face, no longer contorted with the terrific strain of hauling, shone with contentment and easy humour. "Have you ever seen a stoker?" Laura asked, turning to Miss Hande, as the car passed through the gate.

The gates of walled cities have caught man's imagination from the time when King Solomon compared the nose of his beloved to the tower which looked towards Damascus. or King David bade the gates of Jerusalem lift up their heads that the King of Glory might come in. There is a splendid formality about the sharp line of masonry where the city ends at stroke, and the open country spreads up to its very foot; the gates are the breaches in this line, sluices through which the life of the fields pours in to nourish the life of the town. A glamour of past events hangs about them—the lifted heads of the gates have looked on the entrances of kings and the exits of armies; they are grey with the dust of departures on great journeys, their outlines have been caressed from afar by the glad eyes of return. This interior thrill, this sense of the past, is intensified in a city such as Peking, where past and present meet; where the city's daily food still pours in, on donkeys' backs, on ancient carts and on shoulder-yokes, through the grey gateways beneath their mighty towers; where the motors of golfers and race-goers mingle their dust with that stirred up by the feet of long files of camels, coming in as they have come for centuries laden with coal from the hills, or with who knows what strange burden of silks or carpets or furs, from Tibet and from beyond the Gobi Desert.

Outside the Hsi-pien-mên a stretch of green and stagnant water lies at the Wall's very foot. A file of camels had been halted to drink there on its way into the city, and the strange creatures were stooping their heads to the water, and raising them to swallow, with that same clumsy and compelling rhythm which they show in walking. Thick furry brown felt reached to their knees like plus-fours, and clothed most of their bodies; from it their spindly shanks, improbable swan necks and double humps emerged bare and grey. These winter coats were moulting in patches, but camel's-hair is valuable, and the loose bits were looped up and tied on with odds and ends of string, which gave to each a curiously disordered appearance, as of a badly done-up brown paper parcel. Yet their matchless dignity and timeless beauty of outline triumphed over this disability; philosophers in rags, they drank slowly, taking their time, while the drivers squatted on the muddy margin of the canal, smoking and exchanging news with the vegetable-sellers who were washing their salads, cabbages and neat bundles of garlic, in the filthy water, before taking them in to the market. But when Derek hastened to point this out to Miss Hande, she seemed for once oblivious to hygiene, hypnotised by the beauty of the scene at the gateway—the drinking camels, the blue-clad drivers, the green and creamy piles of vegetables, and over all the grey and silent line of the wall, reflected in the water.

They drove on, now, along a sandy road raised three or four feet above the surrounding country, which was brown, flat and densely cultivated. Here and there a line of tall willows, showing a filmy green, was reflected in the still waters of some canal, breaking the monotony of the fawn-coloured soil. At a dangerous speed they overhauled a line of curious-looking wicker carts, which

creaked along in the dust ahead of them; their peculiar
shape attracted Miss Hande's attention, and she asked
what they contained.

"They're *fu-carts*," Derek told her, with malicious
pleasure.

"What are *fu-carts*?" asked Judith.

"It's sewage, going out from the city to be put on the
land—those vegetables you saw at the gate were grown
on it."

Miss Hande's intensity of expression returned.

"Solemn fact," Derek assured her. "The Chinese are
much too practical to waste good manure. That's why
there's no sanitation in Peking—or any other city. A
contractor not long ago paid six thousand pounds for
the sole rights over the night-soil from the International
Concession at Shanghai for one year alone."

"You don't tell me so!" exclaimed Miss Hande.
"Why, that's thirty thousand dollars! Surely," she
paused delicately, "*it* can't be worth that sum?"

"That was for manufacture and sale, of course," said
Derek. "It would be sent up-country to agricultural
districts."

"But I don't see how you can *export* sewage," objected
Judith, who was every bit as curious as Miss Hande, and
had no nice feelings at all; "it's such sloppy stuff to
cart about."

"They dry it and turn it into bricks, neat as anything,"
said Derek. "I'll take you to see a manure factory one
day—there's that one we passed by the canal. It's most
interesting."

Laura watched Miss Hande with amusement. She
longed to ask her whether she felt that the use of human
manure for agriculture was also inconsistent with the
"ancient culture and exalted ideas" of the Chinese,
and constituted another "prahblem." She was prepared

to like the novelist, but all the same she was aware of
the faint irritation with which Americans nearly always
inspired her. "They won't use their eyes," she thought,
"it's always the same. They want uplift, and uplift
they've got to have; facts must take their chance. And
it must be their idea of what is uplifting too. They're so
deafened with the clamour of their own synthetic idealism
that they can't hear any of the funny little tones of
reality." "She'll waste her time here," she thought,
"like all the rest of them—she's come to look for exalted
ideas, and she'll get them all right—American ideas of
Chinese ideas. But she'll learn nothing about China."
She listened to her companions again. The road was
approaching a railway embankment at a long angle;
a train, consisting of Pullmans and sleeping-cars, was
drawn up beside the permanent way. It was overflowing
with Chinese soldiers who, in various stages of undress,
were cooking, washing, eating and hanging their under-
wear out of the windows. The former splendours of the
coaches, the blue paint and gilding, showed signs of
decay—battered and dirty, festooned with filthy rags,
they resembled some street of fine houses turned into a
slum. Derek was explaining that this was the famous
Blue Train, the Pullman express which used to run
between Pukow and Tientsin, but which now served as
a barracks for some of Li's men. "It was bought on
borrowed money and hasn't been paid for yet—it never
will be now, of course."

"But why do they use it for this, instead of running
it?" asked Judith.

"Oh, that's just their way of doing things," replied
Derek. "It was briganded down the line some time
back, and all the passengers turned out in their night
things; then Li got hold of it, and has stuck to it ever
since."

"But surely the railway company could get the Government to make him hand it back?" said Miss Hande.

"Li *is* the Government up here," said Derek; "no one can make war-lords do anything."

"Well, it seems extremely uneconomic," observed Miss Hande.

Some distance further on, the car left the road, such as it was, leading to Paomachang and the race-course, and turned northwards along a track still rougher and narrower, which continued for a mile or more till it joined another road leading westward to the golf course. Near the junction of the two roads stood a building enclosed by high walls; along the wall which faced the roads was scrawled in letters five feet high— "GOD DAMN BRITISHERS, GET OUT THIS ROAD." Miss Hande's lorgnette was at once in action, but she politely refrained from any comment, being in a carful of god-damn Britishers. Judith, however, burst out with, "Gracious! What's that for?" Derek explained that some enterprising Chinese students had put it there during "the fuss in '25—when we had the strike and all that."

"Why how *very* disagreeable," said Miss Hande. "Can't you get it removed, now?"

"Oh, we wouldn't have it taken away for anything," said Derek. "The Chinese lost more face over that than over anything that's happened up here for years. I believe Henry has it secretly painted up once a year to keep it fresh, doesn't he?" turning to Laura. She merely smiled, and shook her head.

Miss Hande's notebook expression reappeared in full strength.

"Now please do explain, Mr. Fitzmaurice. Why should you British wish to preserve that unpleasant inscription? I should feel horribly every time I looked at it."

"Oh, no," said Derek. "It's a tremendous asset. It's the Chinese who feel horribly every time they look at it. You see out here good manners really count, and that's a very ill-bred notice, so they're frightfully ashamed of it. If some Minister starts to get—fresh, don't you call it?— all you have to do is to bring him along here for a picnic or a game of golf, where he'll see that. He sees *we* don't mind, and he simply withers. It's most useful."

This was obviously a very new point of view to Miss Hande, and a rather disturbing one. She turned to Laura. "Don't you find it painful to live among people who don't feel cordially to you? I should think it was most trying."

"They respect us," said Laura. "As much as they respect any foreigners, that is. I don't attach very much importance to being liked."

"Now isn't that strange?" said Miss Hande. "Of course, our people live on such wonderful terms with the Chinese, with all our intercourse; and having no Concessions helps to keep our relations very cordial. So it's rather difficult for us to understand your viewpoint."

This reference to the old old controversy, the smug American complacency about having no Concessions in China, while trading freely from those of the British, who incur most of the odium, irritated Laura. She had an almost overwhelming impulse to ask Miss Hande if she knew the pidgin-English name for Americans in the Treaty Ports—"second-chop Englishmen" (chop meaning quality). She restrained herself, and took up the argument in a more dignified manner.

"The Oriental mind is very hard to understand, Miss Hande. We have been on the job longer than you, and with more responsibility, and we know that the cordiality you value so much doesn't necessarily include either respect or affection." She paused. "In fact, it may have to be bought at a price that we are not always prepared to pay."

She paused again. She did not say, "They don't really dislike us either; no American who ever lived has been loved and respected by the Chinese as Gordon was, or Hart, or Jordan, or has done a tithe as much for them." She did not say either, "We don't buy our popularity, we let it take care of itself." She refrained from all this, and watched Miss Hande's face. There, looming up, she was sure that she saw an impending disquisition on the brilliant American effort in the Philippines, as an example to less favoured races of how to deal with Orientals. She had heard this so often; just now she felt that she could not bear it, and hastened to dispose of it in advance.

"Your problem in the Philippines," she went on, "isn't really comparable. They're a flimsy race compared to the Chinese, or to the peoples of India, and there isn't the massiveness of a great traditional civilisation behind them."

"And anyhow they're such a flea-bite, aren't they?" said Derek amiably, coming unexpectedly to her aid.

Miss Hande looked from one to the other, disconcerted and silenced. The Philippines, the one big American gun in Oriental affairs, which she had duly intended to fire—Laura was quite right—had been let off at half-cock, dismissed with a friendliness more wounding than hostility as a flea-bite, and a flimsy flea-bite at that. And this cool tall Englishwoman, leaning back beside her in the car with her quite unconscious air of rather arrogant distinction, nearly beautiful in spite of her shabby riding clothes, nearly lovable in spite of her avowed indifference to being liked, was a puzzling subject to Miss Hande.

She wished to like her; she already respected her intelligence, in spite of what seemed to the American her perverse and reactionary point of view about the Chinese. Her patronage about the Philippines was irritating, but to give Miss Hande her due, intellectual detachment generally triumphed in her over the emotions, and she was as much interested as irritated. She would gladly have continued the discussion, but Mr. Fitzmaurice was now rattling away to the Milne girl, and Mrs. Leroy sitting with half-closed eyes. Miss Hande had recourse to her lorgnette. The car passed through the gateway of a small town straddled across the road—its high brick walls, of the prevailing brown, stretched out on either side, broken and ruinous, into the fields, with crumbling towers at the corners. The unpaved street was swarming with people in the bright blue cotton clothes which are such a feature of the Chinese countryside; there was an air of disturbance and excitement about the crowd. Mrs. Leroy roused herself and looked out. On the right they approached a temple, with dark trees and golden roofs showing over a high white and scarlet wall. Little stumpy China ponies, not more than twelve hands high, with long shaggy coats like teddy bears, were tethered in scores along the wall, and the courtyard within was teeming with the grey uniforms of soldiers.

"Look at that, Derek!" said Mrs. Leroy suddenly—they all started a little at the tone of her voice. Derek's eyes followed hers to the soldiers.

"By Jove!" he said, "that looks like business, doesn't it?"

Miss Hande's and Judith's "What?" came as one word.

"Look at their armlets."

They looked. Whereas the soldiers at the City gate

had worn a pink armlet on the left arm, these men wore two armlets, an orange one on the right arm as well as the pink on the left.

"The orange is Tu, isn't it? I can't remember."

"Yes, it's Tu's. I wonder how soon they expect him?"

"Prepared for all emergencies, you see!" said Derek gaily to the two newcomers. "Whichever side they find themselves on, they're ready."

As the car bounced on its way in clouds of suffocating dust the perpetual scene of the North China plain unrolled itself before them. On their left rose Pa-Pao Shan, a golden hill on a landscape the colour of brown paper; in the distance spindly trees shaped themselves as patterns in blue lace on the skyline. Once, on a parallel track, they saw a file of camels half a mile long, stencilled brown on the brown horizon, like a moving colonnade—high, slow, unceasing. The hills rose nearer and clearer ahead of them, till they could see the dark smears of green where the woods of thuja and juniper ran up into the hollows. Now that they had left the golf course behind at Pa-Pao Shan the road degenerated out of all resemblance to anything of its name; large stones the size of footballs were scattered over its surface, and several times they had to skid down off it and make detours through the fields below to avoid ditches a couple of feet deep, dug across it from side to side. These ditches aroused Judith's curiosity, and Derek explained that they were dug by the peasants to block traffic. "They may be for the foreign devils, or they may be for Mr. Tu's guns."

"These are pretty new," observed Laura, inspecting one carefully. "I expect they're for Tu."

Without warning they found themselves again among houses, in a straggling village, where a brisk buying and selling was going on on both sides of the rough strip of dust which served for a street. At a crossways they turned to the left down a narrow alley between high walls, and emerged into the open fields. They drove on now along a mere single footpath, following the tracks of the other cars in the ploughed earth on both sides of it. A hill with ruins on the top towered steeply above them on the right; it ended in a high yellow bluff. Swinging abruptly round the foot of this they saw before them a wide river between empty sandy banks; on the nearer bank, modern and incongruous, stood the two cars, their late occupants grouped aimlessly round them. As the saloon pulled up Mrs. Nevile hurried towards them with a tragic face.

"The donkeys haven't come!" she announced.

Chapter Eight

IT was really very hard on Nina. Disaster had over-taken her picnic at the outset. Here were eleven people and their luggage planted on a river-bank, with eight miles of rough walking still between them and their destination, and no transport of any kind. They gathered in groups to discuss the situation. How had she ordered the donkeys, Touchy wanted to know?

"Mr. Lin ordered them for me"—Nina's soft voice was almost a wail—"the *T'ing-ch'ai* at the American Legation. That nice Shang was to bring them from Pa-ta-Ch'u."

"Oh, yes—I know Shang. He isn't the sort of man to fail you, I should have thought."

"He's failed her this time, anyhow," was the General's gloomy comment. He had perched himself rather gingerly on a steep slab of yellow rock at the foot of the bluff, and gazed with disfavour on the scene about him—the narrow strip of sandy stony bank between the hill and river, the brown and swirling waters in front.

"Do you think he can have come and gone? We're awfully late," was Touchy's next suggestion.

"The ferrymen would know that," said Laura, glancing upstream to where a large clumsy boat lay moored to the bank some two hundred yards from where they stood.

"Oh, yes. William, do go and talk to them and find out. Go with him, Laura—you're both so good at Chinese."

The General raised himself stiffly from his slab, and

84

limped off beside Mrs. Leroy; except for his stiffness and her grace their two tall figures, both in khaki riding-clothes, looked curiously alike, as Derek pointed out to Judith. From a distance the others watched their colloquy with the ferrymen. It was loud and extremely prolonged, as conversations with Chinese country-people invariably are. You must first convince them that you, a foreign devil, are talking Chinese at all—a long and difficult process, best achieved by repeating some simple and well-known phrase over and over again, very fast and very loud, till it catches their ear as familiar. You have next to satisfy their curiosity as to who you are and what your business is. Hopeless to attempt to cut out this preliminary! Leading the most monotonous of lives, without posts, without papers and without books, their one mental interest and sustenance is that derived from the spoken word. A stranger is a blessing; a Chinese-speaking foreigner a gold-mine. No peasant will contemplate for a moment so much as telling you your way until he knows where you come from and *why* you wish to reach your objective.

The General and Mrs. Leroy, familiar with this peculiarity, furnished the three Charons who sprawled in the ferry-boat with much and varied information in reply to their questions. He was Hsing Nei and she Li T'ai-t'ai (the Chinese versions of their names), both of the *Ying-Kuo-fu* (British Legation). No, the others were *not* all *Ying-Kuo-jen* (English)—some were *Mei-Kuo-jen* (Americans), and one was even a *Fa-Kuo-jen* (French-man). Certainly they had come from Peking, and they were going up to Chieh T'ai Ssu. For pleasure, and for three days. They agreed politely that at Chieh T'ai Ssu it was *hen hao* (very fine). Then they tackled the question of donkeys. Ten donkeys, from Pa-ta-Ch'u— had they been there? The ferrymen repeated all the

questions several times, with additional questions of their
own, but it was finally established beyond doubt that
Shang and his team had not been at Mo-shih-k'ou
Ferry that day.

With this news General Nevile and Mrs. Leroy returned to the others. The party was already slightly
disintegrated. Henri Delache and Little Annette had
strolled off down the river; Derek and Judith Milne had
scrambled some distance up the bluff and established
themselves in a minute patch of shade beneath a small
and solitary thuja which clung, stunted and scraggy,
to the face of the cliff. It was very hot. The sun beat
right into the hollow of the hill-side, and there was not
a scrap of shade anywhere except under the thuja up on
the rocks. The stones and soil of the narrow track
between the bluff and the river were hot to the feet,
and uninviting to sit upon, stained and discoloured with
the passing of beasts from the ferry. It was very still—if
now and then a light puff of air struck on their faces, it
was like the hot breath from a kiln. Miss Hande was
sitting on her suit-case, surveying the river through her
lorgnette from under her painted paper sunshade;
Lilah Milne was attending to her face under hers; the
Professor was leaning against the cliff with a wilted
collar, unaffectedly mopping his brow; Touchy was
measuring a boulder with his polo-stick. There was
already over the party a silence, and an isolation of its
members each within his own discomfort, which boded
ill for the future. After some further consultation it was
decided to send for donkeys from Mo-shih-k'ou, the
village they had passed, less than a mile away. "The
chauffeurs can order them, of course," said Nina.

But on turning to execute this plan it was found that
the cars had gone! The suit-cases, the *tchilumchis*, the
rucksacks sat like an inanimate picnic party on the bare

sand among the wheel-ruts, but the cars had departed. After a fresh conversation with the ferrymen the youngest Charon was persuaded to go to Mo-shih-k'ou and to bring back ten donkeys; he stood out for an exorbitant rate for men and asses in advance, with a prudent eye to his own future commission on the deal. Our travellers were, however, not in a position to haggle seriously, and having cut down his demands by a mere half, let him go. More than an hour, on the most optimistic computation, must elapse before his return, and there was nothing for it but to settle down to wait, and make themselves as comfortable as circumstances permitted.

This was Laura's opportunity. While La Touche and the General arranged suit-cases as seats for the ladies, and the Professor fiddled with the stops of a very elaborate camera, she wandered off to read her letters. Beyond the ferry the bluff shelved down steeply into the water; scrambling over the loose slabby rocks and between low thorny plants, she settled down on a little promontory with her back against a big block. Her firm body, soaked with the heat of many Chinese summers, felt no discomfort from the strong sun—tilting the broad brim of her felt hat unbecomingly over her eyes, she lit a cigarette, pulled out her packet of letters, and was immediately ten thousand miles away. A single kite wheeled, mewing at intervals, in the hot blue overhead— she did not hear it. Crickets shrilled ecstatically among the still-withered plants between the rocks; small lizards ran among the stones or paused, spread-eagled on the hot yellow surfaces for a motionless moment, moving nothing but their winking diamond eyes—she never heeded them. By Tim's untidy and disjointed script, by Sarah's ragged and yet somehow cultivated scrawl, she was transported into the green and chilly heart of England—to damp playing-fields under grey skies, to

bare and draughty class-rooms and play-rooms, full of
a din of young voices, and, with the advent of the Easter
holidays, to Garsover. They would be there now. Sarah
would hang out of her window of a morning to watch
the shafts of sunlight striking through the blue hollows
of the chestnut across the lawn, and to spy for hedge-
hogs' tracks in the white dew; Tim would run out before
breakfast to find the holes left by the hammer-strokes
of the green woodpecker's beak (which he had observed
when he should have been in his bath) driven into the
rough turf on the slope where the daffodils grew so
thickly. He would come in to breakfast, late, and be
sent by Grandmamma to change his shoes—Grandpapa
would scold Grandmamma, in his absence, for scolding
him, and when he returned Grandmamma would load
his plate with kidneys and his cup with cream to make
up. There they would sit round the long table in the
panelled room, the two brown heads intent on their
own secret ploys and purposes, the two silver heads
brooding over the brown ones, hanging on their words
and looks with the touching and tender humility of old
age. And when the children, fidgety with inaction, tried
to slip away—"Grannie and Grandpère are always
such an *eternity* over meals," wailed Sarah's letter—she
knew how the old man would lean out from his chair
to catch one or the other by the arm as they passed,
draw them to him and murmur, "My child, what can I
do for you?" Footfalls in the passages, voices in the
garden, shouts in the paddock above the thud of horses'
hoofs—she could hear them all, loudly clearly. No
wonder that the shrill vibrant whirring of the crickets,
the far mewing of that one kite, a wheeling speck in the
hot blue above the yellow hill, could not reach her ears.

Will you tell me, you philosophers, where in those
moments *was* Laura Leroy? In her long relaxed body,

resting on the sun-baked rocks above the Hun-ho? Or in the rooms and gardens of that manor-house in Oxfordshire, where her spirit followed after and watched her children? If you tell me that she was certainly in China, then you make the seat of reality the body— would you wish to say that? And yet if she was in England, who was it that the Professor saw when he presently scrambled round the promontory, in search of a picture for his camera? He saw a woman sitting under a rock with a lapful of letters, staring straight before her, the marks of tears on her face. He saw her, and he had a strong wish to speak to her, for her face was sensitive and intelligent, and he was cruelly bored. But he must have seen too that she was not really there—though her eyes looked towards him, looked at his face, he could not get into her eyes, within a few yards of her as he was; for her, *he* was not there. Professor Vinstead, being a psychologist, may have known the answer about reality— anyhow he scrambled back as quietly as he could by the way he had come, leaving his word, whatever it was, unspoken, and rejoined the others.

It became hotter than ever. The heat off the sun-warmed rocks seemed to strike the air in a series of vibrations, made audible in the shrill persistent voices of the crickets. Every one grew restless. Derek and Judith climbed down from their patch of shade, cramped and stiff, to stretch their legs on level ground. There was no sign of the donkeys. It was Lilah who made the suggestion that they might be cooler if they crossed to the other bank, away from the heated hill-side. Any change was welcome, and the idea was applauded; they could, in any case, save time by getting the luggage across. The ferrymen, Derek, and Touchy, carted the suit-cases and knapsacks along the steep little path to the boat. This was an extremely Stone Age looking affair, with square sloping ends and a flat bottom; a stout post, standing mast-like at one end, carried the steel hawser which crossed the river from bank to bank. It was all rather dirty and smelt of donkeys; they seated themselves cautiously on the low sides and began their voyage. Half-way across, "Why, we've left Laura behind!" exclaimed Mrs. Nevile. "Has anyone seen her?"

"She's up there on the rocks, reading," Vinstead replied. "We need not disturb her, need we, as we aren't going on?"

Something in the words or tone made Mrs. Nevile look at him with some attention. Why should he not want Laura disturbed? He hadn't spoken three words to her! But he gave no further explanation; his face, lean, lined, intellectual and somehow sympathetic in spite of the dry Cambridge precision of his expression and manner, returned her glance with a sort of friendly blankness as he made some remark about the boat. As they drew further across they could see Mrs. Leroy's figure, her dark hat and pale shirt making a sharp patch of brown and white on the yellow hill-side. Touchy hailed her with a yell, shattering the sunny silence—the patch never moved or stirred. "She's in one of her dreams, I expect," said Lilah in her flat drawling tone. "Leave her alone." It was La Touche who stared this time. He was not accustomed to having young women use the categorical imperative to him with quite such casual abruptness; still less did he relish being told how to behave to Mrs. Leroy. In a world which they both found rather alien and arid in many ways, Touchy had always felt that he had more in common with Laura than most people; it had been his pleasure and his secret pride to understand her rather well, to raid her capital of ideas and make her put them into currency;

in an unobtrusive way he had been the Member for Mrs. Leroy, so to speak. It had all been as unsentimental as it was in Touchy's character to be with any woman. In a society where flirtations were almost *de rigueur* and liaisons as common as tea-parties, Mrs. Leroy preserved a graceful discretion in her personal conduct, in spite of a rather haughty freedom of ideas and speech. She gave the impression that she behaved as she did from fastidious personal choice rather than from principle, which possibly accounted for her attraction for admitted rakes like Derek and Henri Delache.

Touchy, therefore, looked at Miss Milne with some disfavour. He had not liked her from the start. He liked at least a little subtlety, and she was not subtle— her beauty was aggressive, her silence was aggressive, and when she *did* speak it appeared that her speech was aggressive too. Even her plan for crossing the river proved not to be so good after all. The further bank, when they had disembarked on it, was low and muddy, and offered nothing at all, not even heated rocks, to sit upon; except for the damp foreshore every foot of soil was cultivated— dusty, hot and neat. Its full disagreeableness had just been established when Touchy raised a sudden cry, "Corn in Egypt! There are the asses!"

Indeed, round the corner of the bluff across the river some little grey forms were seen moving towards the ferry, escorted by blue-clad drivers. Leaving the luggage on the shore the party joyfully boarded the boat once more, and ferried back across the stream to meet them. But even as they approached the bluff a chill of disillusionment came over their hopes. There were only four donkeys! And from the prolonged and almost passionate discussion which ensued between the General, the ferrymen and the donkey-boys it emerged inexorably that they were all booked—booked completely and finally for some *Wai-kuo-jen* (foreigner) who was coming later.

The morale of the party was still further shattered by this fresh blow. Miss Hande had not spoken for nearly an hour—nor had Lilah, except for her remark to Touchy. Judith and Little Annette and their attendant swains alone showed any trace of animation or enjoyment. It was Judith who suggested that they should at least accompany the unknown foreigner's asses to the further bank again, because she "liked going in the boat." The others, for lack of anything better to do, acceded to her suggestion—at least, as Touchy remarked when they once more swung out into the current, they were getting plenty of yachting! It was cooler on the water, too, and when the foreigner's donkeys had been disembarked the ferrymen were easily persuaded, for about threepence, to pole them out into midstream and keep them there, swinging easily in the brown current below the hawser, pending the arrival of their transport.

From her perch on the promontory Mrs. Leroy saw them swinging there. She had come out of what Lilah called "her dream," the profound and trance-like absorption in the other half of her life into which her letters had plunged her, and was once more awake to the present world. Her eyes rested with pleasure on the scene before her. Beyond the river a wide stretch of alluvial flat ran up into the hills, brown and level, curiously sprinkled with young isolated poplars whose round fluffy tops resembled puffs of green shrapnel loose in the air, so inconspicuous were their straight slender boles. On her right the hot yellow outline of the bluff, curving round, cut off this view with theatrical abruptness; downstream, on her left, wide sand-flats, glittering like water in the heat, gave place gradually to the dusty distances of the Peking plain—she could just see, far

away, the outline of the Red Temple on its ridge above
the river. Behind the green puffs of shrapnel rose the
hills, lavender, pink, creamy, grey, with sinister black
smears where the coal seams ran out on to the face,
sharply coloured even in the distance under the pouring
glittering brilliance of the intense light, detailed beyond
European belief in the desiccating clearness of the bone-
dry air of Central Asia. The delicate strange beauty of
the whole landscape struck powerfully on her senses,
rousing her to an active delight. What was the quality
in this Chinese scene which so moved her, she wondered?
She remembered with curious distinctness the distress
she had felt during the first months of her sojourn in
Peking at the sheer unfamiliarity of the face of Nature.
Her mind, accustomed to draw nourishment from the
well-known scenes of England, the great elms standing
round the quiet fields, the broad sweep of distant downs,
the white roads winding over de Wint-like skylines,
dotted with rick and barn, to the huddle of red village
roofs, had ranged eagerly, vainly, over the Chinese
country-side, finding no resting-place. She remembered
how alien at first had seemed these dusty flat fields, un-
marked by hedge or tree, and the prevailing brown
tone of the landscape; how unnatural the sharpness of
outlines in crystal-dry air, the vivid colour of far-off
mountain shapes—till her very spirit had sickened for
green, for the touch of dew, for the soft aqueous blue of
distances in a moist climate. The stylised formal beauty
of it she had seen at once—what had been lacking was
beauty in familiarity, the richness of association entwined
with sights and scents, going back through the quiet
swing of the seasons to the enormous days and tiny
pleasures of childhood; going back deeper and further
still, blood of her English blood and bone of her English
bone, to the very roots of life. Cut off from all that,

planted down in a life as strange as the world she looked
upon, she had wilted within like an uprooted plant.
She could still remember her own astonishment at the
depth of her distress, at finding how much the spirit
depends for its strength on the changing but familiar
beauty without, the face of the earth, the changeful
face of the sky. But gradually the alien beauty of China
had awakened its own response in her, and now this
scene too, under the blazing untempered light, had
power to nourish her spirit. The eastern changes of the
seasons, the sudden swing and rush from brown earth
to a high waving sea of green, the autumn gold of
willows, the pictures of Chinese country life—spring
tillage, the blindfold oxen treading out the grain on the
round threshing-floors, the patient gathering of the
stumps of maize and *kaoling* for fuel as winter approached, had the comfort of familiarity, brought their
own sense of stability and strength.

What is it, she pondered, shifting her seat on the
yellow rock, and sending the lizards shooting away with
her movement—what *is* this sustenance that we draw
from scenery? Why does the spirit live so much through
the eye? Two lines of Robert Bridges came into her
mind:

"Man's happiness, his flaunting honeyed flower of soul
   Is his loving response to the wealth of Nature."

Yes, it is the "loving response," she thought—that there
must be, to nourish the flower of the soul; and until one
learned to make that response to an alien nature, the
spirit withered. But now——! She stretched out her
arms, exulting in her solitude; in the fierce heat of the
sun, striking through the skin deep into muscle and
sinew, in her sense of companionship with that heated

landscape, so fiercely illuminated. She could see the peasants in the fields across the river, sharp notes of blue on the brown earth, and her mind followed them. "It *is* different here, all the same," she thought. "At home we have our own roots in the life of the soil; when I see men ploughing in Oxfordshire I know that I am part of their life, as they are of mine. None of us can say that out here. We have no roots in the life of this soil—we're like cactuses, feeding on air." Her thoughts drifted on, following this theme and that—to people at home, to Aubrey, whose letter lay in her pocket. Presently she saw the ferry-boat pull in towards the nearer shore; it disappeared under the yellow foreground of rock, and she forgot about it. She went on thinking of Aubrey, recently gone to take up a Fellowship at Clare. A moment later, over the yellow rocks, the Professor's head appeared suddenly within a few feet of her. He sat down, took off his topi, wiped his forehead, and looked at her with friendliness on his face. "What are you thinking about?" he asked abruptly.

"Cambridge," said Mrs. Leroy.

Chapter Nine

PROFESSOR VINSTEAD had not climbed the rocks to offer Mrs. Leroy a penny for her thoughts. He had volunteered to summon her down to a consultation. The temporary lessee of the four donkeys had turned up, and proved to be the Iberian Minister, also bound for Chieh T'ai Ssu—a tall heavy man, with ingratiating manners and tight yellow kid boots. He immediately placed one donkey at the disposal of the ladies; the quantity of luggage which accompanied him made Judith doubt if he ought to spare even one, and his boots quite clearly precluded the possibility of his walking eight miles. Mrs. Nevile was becoming anxious to get on to Chieh T'ai Ssu somehow, to see whether the beds and food, sent out in advance with the servants, had shared the unknown fate of Shang and the donkeys. She and General Nevile had also observed the portent of the double armlets worn by the soldiers at the road-side temple, and this indication of military unrest made them slightly uneasy. On the other hand, it was essential that someone should wait to escort the luggage when the Mo-shih-k'ou donkeys should arrive. It was decided that one party should push on—the young people and Touchy walking, Lilah Milne and Mrs. Nevile taking turns on the Iberian's ass; while the General, whose lameness made the distance impossible for him, and Miss Hande, who was no walker, should wait for the ass-team. Laura agreed to remain to keep Miss Hande company, and the Professor, rather to their surprise, decided to wait too.

The luggage party, seated in the boat, watched the advance-guard receding into the distance across the flat open country—Judith and Derek striding ahead, Lilah looking more like a Hindu goddess than ever, perched under her sunshade on the minute ass; Henri Delache, his Trilby at a jaunty angle, squiring Miss Ingersoll assiduously. The General fixed his monocle on them with a certain glum amusement.

"That fellow Delache!" he at length ejaculated.

"What of him?" inquired Miss Hande, surprised.

"Elegant!" He threw an ironic contempt into the word.

"He struck me as rather an interesting type," observed Miss Hande.

"He's a regular Frenchman—carries that *boulevardier* air with him wherever he goes; but I'm not sure that I think it particularly interesting."

"Why, not in itself—but it's surely only a superficial aspect," pursued Miss Hande, her lorgnette also fixed on the now distant figures. "He seems to be very much attracted by Miss Ingersoll," she went on. "I hope he's a desirable personality. She's such a wonderful character.

"I know nothing of his personality," said General Nevile briefly. "You must ask Mrs. Leroy here about that. She makes friends with all the rips."

The Professor, at this last statement, turned and looked at Mrs. Leroy with some attention. She had taken off her hat, in spite of the sun; her long thin face, with the minimum of make-up and framed in her dark hair, wore a look of almost sibylline meditation as she sat trailing her fingers in the water. She had not in the least the air of a person who specialised in rips. If she heard what the General said, which seemed doubtful, she paid no attention whatever.

"Mrs. Leroy, Miss Hande wants a character sketch of Master Delache," said the General, hoping for some distraction.

Laura looked up. "Henri?" she said. "He's very French."

"Yes, we see that; but Miss Hande wants to know if he's worthy of Little Annette," said the General, with his usual Edwardian chuckle.

The words, "Do you mean as a lover or as a husband?" sprang to Laura's lips, but she did not say them, reflecting that the Professor looked as if he might be a little prim, and that she had already treated Miss Hande rather roughly in the car. She had herself speculated a good deal about Henri and Little Annette in the last few days uncertain whether this were merely one of his usual flirtations or something more important. Henri Delache was a thorough and serious-minded devotee of the *vie amoureuse*, but interspersed his major activities with a number of minor flirtations on what he was pleased to call the English Model—they were, so to speak, the intellectual side of the thing, and he said that they kept his hand in for Englishwomen. "*C'est un fait singulier, et d'ailleurs assez rigolo*, but you must think always that we admire your mind as well as your body, you English-women, or you are not satisfied," he said once to Laura. "*Mais ça n'a rien à faire!*" It was the more *rigolo*, according to Henri, because Englishwomen were physi-cally superb—"*c'est inouï, leurs torses!—ces muscles!—on dirait des déesses grecques*"—and intellectually on the whole rather dull, without subtlety and therefore without mental attraction. "*Et l'idée qu'elles se font de l'amour, ma chère! C'est d'une banalité qui frise l'imbécillité!*" All the same, he valued his experiences with Americans and Englishwomen for a particular thrill afforded him by their physical self-control. "*Quand vous avez possédé une femme la veille, et elle fait semblant de ne pas vous reconnaître ou à peine—c'est excitant, cela!*" This was a unique feature, Henri declared, not elsewhere observable, "*même parmi les Russes.*" However, among the multitude of his affairs Laura had never yet seen Henri Delache make love or anything like it to a marriageable girl, and she wondered a good deal what he was up to.

None of these reflections, however, would be very suitable or helpful to Miss Hande.

"Henri is affectionate," she said thoughtfully, "and considerate, and very sensible. And rather rich," she added.

"Does he care about intellectual things?" Miss Hande pursued. "Annette Ingersoll is a real intellectual type."

"Most Frenchmen are intellectual, aren't they?" said Laura a little impatiently. She was secretly convinced that Henri would probably consider Miss Ingersoll's rather jejune intellectuality to be "*d'une banalité qui frise l'imbécillité*"—as indeed she did herself. Whatever else he admired in her, it wasn't that! He might conceivably be caught by the glow of her youth, by her bright enthusiasm, her warm affectionate happiness—much more probably by her lovely elastic figure; but he would have the minimum of respect for the History of the Novel in all Ages, unless she was much mistaken.

"The French are so different to us, don't you think?" she went on, feeling her responsibility for Miss Hande rather acutely. "They like to keep their minds sharp and bright, like scissors, and to use them for snipping up ideas into patterns, instead of using them like big soft brushes to paint rather large vague pictures, as we do." ("Oh, damn!" she said to herself, "now I'm prosing.")

But the Professor gave a little sudden cough of

laughter. "That is a very good psychological observation," he said.

Laura turned to him, delighted with this opportunity of relinquishing the subject of Henri Delache, and made some civil inquiries as to his progress in his Oriental researches. Professor Vinstead expanded a little. The Chinese were going to be very baffling—perhaps the most baffling race on earth, psychologically. One would have to tackle it from the linguistic end, he thought, to do any good. "I hope your husband will help to put me on the right track—his books are most remarkable."

Laura said that Henry would be delighted, and duly booked the Professor for dinner on the night after their return from the picnic.

"His knowledge of the Chinese must be very exceptional; he writes of them with so much understanding," pursued the Professor.

"He loves them, of course—and they really do like and trust him."

"And you—what do you make of them"?

"I think they're the most lovable race on earth," said Laura simply. She saw Miss Hande give a stifled gasp, and laughed. "Does that surprise you?"

"Why, your comments on the way out didn't lead me to feel that you *loved* the Chinese," said Miss Hande mildly.

"Because I don't idealise them? But you can't understand anything you idealise, because then you are looking at your picture of the thing, and not the thing itself. The Chinese are frightfully well worth understanding; they have some marvellous qualities, but they have a lot of most peculiar characteristics as well, and you must recognise the whole lot to get them right. Isn't that true?" she appealed to the Professor.

"Perfectly true," he said emphatically. "One must

drop all preconceptions in approaching another race, if one is to get anywhere. Those rough generalised pictures that one nation forms of another are always caricatures or distortions, and if one makes them a basis for observations, he is put wrong from the start."

"No one has suffered from that more than the Chinese," remarked the General unexpectedly. "Europe still thinks of them as a race of lascivious intellectuals, wearing pigtails and smoking opium, with kite-flying and murdering Europeans as their chief recreations. In America," he turned to Miss Hande, "you vary it a little, I fancy, and think of them as high-minded philosophers to a man, engaged in meditating on the ideal existence when they aren't being murdered by the brutal whites." He chuckled again.

"And what is the truth?" inquired Miss Hande.

"Oh, I don't pretend to know them," said the General. "But I suppose eighty per cent. of them can't afford opium, for one thing, and they're not all intellectuals, for another. A hospital fellow here told me that a very high percentage of the coolie class are practically cretinous, only use about two hundred words all their lives. And their murders are generally due to pure hysteria, or done for money. But they're frightfully good fellows, on the whole—amiable and merry, and thundering workers, and much more honest in their way than either Europeans *or* Americans," he concluded, with his gloomy grin.

"Surely their religion is very lofty?" said Miss Hande.

"Well, you will be able to form some opinion of that for yourself over the week-end," he said. "Chieh T'ai Ssu is one of their most famous temples—in fact it's a sort of Cuddesdon, a theological college where they make the priests for half North China."

"You don't say so!" Miss Hande was enchanted with

the prospect, and so was the Professor. But Chinese religion was interrupted by the advent, at last, of the donkey team from Mo-shih-k'ou. The little grey beasts were ferried across the river, the luggage fastened to the pack-saddles; the General hoisted himself on to one small ass, Miss Hande with her parasol took her seat on another, and the long straggling train set off.

Laura and the Professor walked. The Mo-shih-k'ou ferry is an unimportant one, used mostly for light peasant traffic, and nothing in the nature of even a Chinese main road approaches it. They followed a number of small wandering paths which skirted the fields, or led along the banks of the irrigation channels which watered them, frequently crossing these on narrow rickety wooden bridges of one or two rough planks, without handrails. There was as yet no roadside vegetation, no grass nor flowers—only light splashes of shade from the round-topped poplars to alter the appearance of the brown path, though where an early crop was coming through the fields showed pale spears of green. Peasants in blue raked and hoed in the fields about them; those nearest the track ceased their work to hail the donkey-train with a hoarse, "*Shang na'erh?*" (Where to?) The donkey-boys yelled back, "*Shang Chieh T'ai Ssu!*" and furnished further particulars at the tops of their voices, "Foreigners from Peking," and so on, which were received with appreciative grunts and Ahs!—and then the whole business, question and answer, was repeated by their hearers to remoter groups, and by them to others further off still, till an area of some miles was filled with the details of their advent. This semaphore system amused the Professor very much when Mrs. Leroy translated the exchanges for him. At one point they came to another arm of the Hun-ho, wide and shallow, without bridge or ferry; the donkey-boys halted and urgently invited Mrs. Leroy and Professor Vinstead to mount two of the animals. The Professor, with a glance at his neat trousers, did so, and was carried across, holding his long legs out almost horizontally to keep them clear of the water, in close imitation of the General, who was fording just in front; but on looking round he saw that Mrs. Leroy, like the donkey-boys, splashed unconcernedly through, jodhpurs and all, and like them emerged on the further bank wet to the knees.

"It makes one cooler—I like it," she said in answer to his astonished protest.

When he left his donkey and rejoined her, "Will you tell me a little about all these people?" he said, as they walked on together. "A large party of strangers is so confusing unless one can get the hang of them to some extent."

"Which of them interest you? Who do you want to hear about?"

He looked at her a little inquiringly, at this rather bald question, but there was a tone of reassurance in his voice as he answered, "Well, primarily the General, the Frenchman, and that beautiful Miss Something—but really I want a *catalogue raisonné* of the lot."

"Very well, you shall—but it's clever of you to spot those three, especially Lilah."

"Is that the beauty? She interests me particularly," he said, "because her face and her character seem to be totally at variance. Her appearance is so peculiarly luscious, and yet her speech, what there is of it, is as pawky as a Lowland Scot's. Beautiful people nearly always act up to their part; she doesn't. Who is she, and why is she here?"

"She's my niece," said Laura, smiling in her turn at his bluntness, "and so is Judith, the other one. They're here simply on a visit—seeing the world."

"Oh, then you can really tell me about her, if she's your niece. Good!"

"That's just what I can't." She explained that she had hardly known the Milnes before they arrived in Peking; ending up with, "And now I'm really beginning to get interested in them."

"Aren't you always interested in people?" the Professor asked.

"No—far from it; only in some." She flipped a horse-fly off her knee as she spoke.

"What is it that makes you interested in the 'some'? Do you know?" he asked, watching with a sort of fascination the flies swarming round the damp legs of her jodhpurs, on which the dust was settling and drying.

"Yes, I think so. It's when they show some sign of being really alive inside, and aware of the things that move them. So many people seem to live almost mechanically."

"Oh, it's consciousness you value, is it?"

"Yes—if that's the word. I think it's the quality which puts most reality into people's relations with one another. Don't you value it?" She stooped and smote at yet another horse-fly.

"In relationships, certainly; for purposes of study the very unconscious people are more valuable."

"Oh, well, you'll be able to make a study of Annette Ingersoll," said Laura gaily; "she's as unconscious as anyone can be."

"The American girl? Oh yes. Is she engaged to the Frenchman?"

"We don't know," said Laura. "Miss Hande seems to think she may be before we get home again."

"The real intellectual type," murmured the Professor, to Laura's delight. "Tell me about the Frenchman," he went on. "Is he really a friend of yours? And why does the General call him a rip?"

"Yes, I know Henri very well indeed." She paused. "General Nevile calls him a rip because he makes his love-affairs the main business of his life—he's as serious about them as an Englishman might be about polo."

The Professor received this with charming calm. "It's the French national sport, of course," he said, "and they are generally very intelligent and amusing about it."

"Henri is very intelligent and amusing about it," said Laura thoughtlessly; and then she blushed. Her remark might lead anyone to suppose that she had experience of Henri's practice as well as of his theory; but why blush, even if she had? she thought angrily—it was no business of the Professor's, in any case. The Professor, however, took it in the right spirit.

"Now is he conscious or unconscious, would you say?"

"I can't quite make that apply to foreigners," she said; "at least not to the French. I think they're the hardest people in the world for us to understand. Take Monsieur Delache, for instance. I know him really well. He's as analytical, as aware of himself, as anyone can possibly be in some directions—but there's a whole world, familiar to Englishmen, which he never enters." She stopped, trying to find words to express what this world was. It was worth while, she already felt, to put forward a tenuous or a sketchy idea to Professor Vinstead. She experienced a little pang of pleasure at the sudden ease and freedom of their intercourse, so unlike the talk she was accustomed to in Peking; it was the way one talked at home, in rooms in Oxford or Cambridge, or during walks along muddy English lanes and field-paths. She felt that it was unfettered and free, an honest attempt to express honest opinions, instead of the parrying of empty gallantries, or the smooth emission of nicely measured platitudes, carefully calculated to give away nothing at all to anybody, which make up so large a part of diplomatic conversation. So she might have talked to Aubrey, in the days before their speech became burdened, like a thunder-cloud, with undischarged emotion—so she had talked to him later, in the days when emotion had been laid aside. Momentarily she bathed in the freedom, swam in it, glad as a child released from the cramp and stuffiness of a desk in a schoolroom.

The Professor had to jog her mind about the world Frenchmen do not enter—what was it? Would it be the sense of pathos? she hazarded. He reminded her of Flaubert's old servant with the parrot.

"Yes, but how rare that is. Look at the pitilessness of most of it! De Maupassant, Stendhal, Anatole France! Do you *know L'Histoire comique*? It's a racial thing, of course, and I'm trying to get at it. They have *panache*, tragedy, most exquisite comedy—but no pity."

"What you said in the boat about their minds and ours was very true, I thought—is that what you mean?"

"Partly. I think of Frenchmen," said Mrs. Leroy, "as the clerks in God's Office. They're clever, and shrewd, and busy—they nose out everything, and assess everything, and their card-indexing system is simply perfect. But the great Englishmen—like Shakespeare and Bridges—and the great Germans, have minds more like God himself—patient, brooding, tender. And though the bulk of us are not like that, we can understand it, and it's the sort of thing we sympathise with and like."

The Professor laughed. "It looks as if the world Frenchmen didn't enter was the Kingdom of Heaven," he said drily.

"I think they're extremely good companions for us,

but I don't think they're easy to marry," was Laura's final pronouncement.

"Not if they card-index their emotions, certainly."

"But that's exactly what they do do," said Laura, thinking again of Henri's confidences.

"Well, the Frenchman is conscious, then, though Heaven is closed to him; and his young woman isn't. Now tell me," he went on, "about the other couple. Did you say she was your niece too? And is she engaged to that young Irishman?"

"No, no—how you harp on engagements!" said Laura, amused. "They're just 'walking out,' as the villagers call it."

"What is he, by the way?"

"He's First Secretary in the Legation—Head of the Chancery, if you know what that is."

"Not in the least—but please don't tell me, I shouldn't understand. Diplomacy is a sealed book to me."

"You ought to open it, and make a study of the psychology of Ministers," said Laura, thinking of Sir James Boggit. "There's lots of material here." She laughed, a rather pleasing soft gurgle.

"Impossible. History shows that they conform to no known laws. Their aberrations are positively Freudian!" he said, turning to her with an engaging grin. "I'm much more interested in your niece and her young man. He seems very attractive, in spite of all that manner; but rather immature, isn't he, for her? She strikes me as unusually balanced and aware of things."

"There must *be* something in psychology," said Laura, startled by his perspicacity. "I believe you are right, but you've been very quick. Most of us are still thinking that she is at a disadvantage because of her inexperience. He—well, he *isn't* inexperienced."

"Oh, he's another of the General's rips, is he?"

Professor Vinstead looked amused. "Well, I back the lady, all the same. Surely you agree that she is fully conscious?"

"Judith? Oh dear, yes. She's absolutely awake to everything."

"Awake is really better. Well, the young man isn't properly awake, in your sense, is he, in spite of his experiences? Haven't you noticed that people who specialise in sexual adventures are often curiously in-expert or immature about other things? We don't always realise it, because they assume a sort of false sophistication—they give themselves all the airs of being *the Real-politikers*. And they get away with it, nine times out of ten, because so many people are too timid to be *Real-politikers* about sex, and so have a sort of furtive admiration for them."

"People aren't like that out here," said Laura de-cidedly. "Half of them are always having liaisons, and the other half are pretending that they have them. But generally speaking I think what you say is true."

"Too close a preoccupation with sex has a curiously muffling effect on the faculties, especially in older people," pursued the Professor. "It's very like alcohol in its action. A little stimulates the higher centres, and pro-duces a heightened intensity of everything—perception, response, creative power. The function of sex in the domain of the intellect is really as purely creative as in the physical kingdom. But too much of it, like too much alcohol, slows everything down, blankets it. It's a dangerous drug, and has its addicts."

Mrs. Leroy watched her companion at intervals while he talked. Prim wasn't exactly the word for him, certainly, but she wondered a little how much he knew about it all, except clinically. She was moved to ask if he didn't think too little sex in a lifetime as bad as too much?

"Oh, worse, much worse. Except, of course, for a few spiritual geniuses, who are probably abnormal, anyhow. The normal healthy thing is to take it in one's stride in youth; get it into proportion and leave it there. There may be later manifestations, of course."

"And those? What about them?" asked Laura, almost blinded by the sudden intensity of her recollection of Aubrey.

"I think they should be dealt with drastically," said the Professor. "In oneself——"

The end of his sentence was lost. Round the corner of a wall at the entrance to a village they ran slap into the ass-train, huddled into a confused mass; the narrow alley-like street beyond was completely blocked by a company of Chinese soldiers, passing down towards them. Mrs. Leroy and the Professor backed against the wall to let them pass. The men marched in twos and threes, anyhow, with gay paper umbrellas slung at their backs; their rifles were lashed together in bundles and tied to the pack-saddles of several donkeys who trotted in their midst. Two machine-guns on mules brought up the rear. The men's armlets were neither pink nor yellow, but scarlet. When they had passed, the General, who had dismounted, limped over to Laura.

"See that?"

"Yes—Wang's men. They're some of the three battalions, I suppose."

"Don't much like it," said the General. "I wonder how many there are about. *They* aren't being paid off— see the guns? Well, let's get on."

They passed through the village. The street, not more than five feet wide, was sunk to half a man's height between broad earthen parapets, on which the houses stood; these parapets swarmed with men, women and children, standing and sitting, on a level with the

passers-by and almost within touching distance. Many
of the children lay listlessly in the dust, or in their
mothers' laps, their hands and faces, as well as those of
some of the adults, hideously covered with a dark purple
eruption, from which pus oozed in places.

"Good heavens! What is the matter with them?"
exclaimed the Professor in horror.

"Black smallpox," said Laura. "Walk as fast as you
can and don't let them touch you." For some of the
unfortunates stretched out their hands for alms as the
travellers passed. "Keep your mouth shut too," she
added.

In silence they passed through the nightmare village.
When they emerged at the further end the Professor
drew a deep breath.

"What a horrible sight!"

"You know they think smallpox very lucky," said
Laura. "They call it the *hua-ping*, the flower illness."

"Is there much mortality from it?"

"Not as much as you might expect, among the
Chinese themselves; Europeans don't usually recover,
though—it's a very virulent form," said Mrs. Leroy
tranquilly.

The Professor shuddered slightly. Perhaps he thought
smallpox and armed men a curious prelude to a picnic;
perhaps he was meditating on the psychology of pleasure.
But his face wore an expression of considerable concentration as he walked on towards Chieh T'ai Ssu.

Chapter Ten

CHIEH T'AI SSU, the Monastery of the Platform of Vows, stands on a sort of natural terrace just below the crest of one of the ridges running down from the Western Hills towards the Peking plain, flanking the valley of the Hun-ho on the south. Its innumerable courts, pavilions, shrines and terraces stretch up the hillside, one above another, connected by paved walks and broad flights of marble steps, scattered irregularly in all directions at all sorts of levels; diversified by trees springing from the stone pavements, by rocky landscapes and grottoes in corners, by little pagodas, by Drum Towers and Bell Towers, and by vast bronze incense-burners—the whole beautiful confusion, covering several acres and containing as many souls as an English village, enclosed within a high wall which follows its irregular outline over the contours of the steep stony slopes. Men in bright flower-blue cassocks, with blue trousers tucked into high white gaiter boots, wander about its shade-splashed walks and disappear through its unexpected doorways; grey-robed priests tend its latticed shrines, filling the courts with the perfume of incense, beat its vast resonant drums and its musical gongs; or stand in dreamy meditation, rosary in hand, beside its carved marble balustrades. It is a great religious foundation in being, in full and serene activity. Here the monastic life of a thousand years·ago, painstakingly dug up and described by travellers like Hédin and Stein in the ruined temples of the Central Asian wastes, is unrolled before the Western eyes of the week-end visitor from

Peking, breathing, actual, undecaying—the past wells
up into the present in a timeless continuity, unchanging,
quiet, with the still perfection of the figures on some
Greek vase.

Nothing is stranger to the newcomer to China than this
custom of Temple authorities of throwing open their
sacred precincts to European visitors. A courtyard,
or two, or three, according to their needs, is let off to each
party, and there with their beds, food, chairs and servants they establish themselves for a day or two. But
they are not confined to their hired apartments—freely
they stroll about the terraces, among the shrines and
pavilions, where the wealth and tribute of centuries is
accumulated in buildings, in treasures, of a stylised
beauty and a formal grace peculiarly Chinese, saluted
with grave courtesy as they go by the black-robed monks.
And in and around the whole temple, in spring, the
fruit-blossom flows like a tide, surging up in waves of
exquisite pale colour against the ancient walls, springing
like flowery fountains in the paved courtyards. More
than one of the party, that night, was to fall asleep
with sprays of peach-blossom shadowed between him
and the stars, and to wake with fallen petals on his face.
Strange magic of the blossoming tree—ancient wisdom
that brings in the spring to worship within its holy
places! It is not easy to escape these wholly; all did not
wholly escape. There is no cause for wonder if in that
place, and then, some bonds of thought and custom
were loosened, some curtains of the soul drawn back—
if eyes were opened, if vision for a moment gleamed, and
ardour sprang in pursuit.

Chieh T'ai Ssu is approached from below by a paved
road, winding up and round the curves and hollows of
the hill, crossing the beds of torrents on beautifully-
arched bridges, and protected always on the valley side

by a plastered parapet. On leaving the smallpox village the General's little party turned to the left, crossed a stream near a broken high-backed bridge, and began the ascent of this road. For the first time for nearly eight miles they walked in shade, for they were close in under the hill now, and the ridge cut off the sun. And immediately the fruit-blossom was about them. All over the brown hill-side, on narrow stone-built terraces and wherever the slope would hold a little soil, stood the trees, so irregularly and in such profusion as to suggest a natural growth—the pink of almond-flower, the deeper pink of apricot, the phlox-like greenish white of pear-blossom. But with no green carpet, pied with daisies, below them; straight from the brown soil, an incredible flowering from the still naked earth. North China, with its rainless snowless winter, knows no spring as Europe knows it—only the deeply-rooted plants and trees can come to life. Later the thunder-storms of early summer revive the parched world, covering the hills with a rank un-nourishing verdure, but in spring the flowering trees carry the torch of re-birth alone. Unbelievable, the shock of this beauty— the delicately-shaped perfection of flower of rose and paler rose and white, against the unrelieved fawn-coloured background. It is easy, here, to see why the Chinese have painted their masterpieces of flowers on backgrounds of brown silk—even Nature, in China, is a consummate artist, and with a sure hand has shown the way in which that race of consummate artists has followed, to produce a beauty unknown to the Western world. If you want to get some idea of the road to Chieh T'ai Ssu, go to the British Museum and look at the Chinese paintings—above all at the "Earthly Para-dise." But fill its air with a delicate scent, hardly more than a freshness, and yet more; and break its silence with the loud sweet notes of hidden babblers among bare wayside bushes, and with the tapping and scraping of the small feet of donkeys on steep cobbles. And because that picture is one of the supreme masterpieces of the world, and because Art carries truth like an arrow or a pang, you shall perhaps come to some knowledge of a Chinese spring, one of the rarest perfections ever permitted itself by the rejoicing spirit of creation.

A little silenced by this loveliness, or possibly by heat and fatigue, the party proceeded up the road. At a curve they were overtaken by two young monks, shaven-headed, in faded blue clothes, carrying rosaries of little carved brown beads; they paused just ahead of the party to look over the parapet into the blossom-filled hollow below, and as they moved on again the rosary of one caught against a projecting tile and broke, scattering the beads in all directions. With a cry of distress the young monk stooped to gather them up, but they rolled insidiously away and downhill, along the little channels between the cobble-stones. His face, beautiful and spiritual, with the expression of natural mysticism sometimes seen amongst the Chinese, wore a look almost of anguish as he pursued the beads. Mrs. Leroy stooped and began to pick them up—the Professor, after a moment's hesitation, did likewise. When they were reassembled the young monk sat down where he was in the road and counted them over in his blue lap; beaming, he thrust them into a little pouch in the belt under his cassock, rose, and addressed Mrs. Leroy and her companion. The Professor watched, unable to understand; he saw the youth put out a long-nailed finger and point to Laura's neck. She smiled and shook her head as she answered. Bowing, the two monks strode on, moving fast and easily up the steep road in their string-soled slippers, and were lost to view round a flowery curve.

"What was he asking you?" the Professor inquired.

"He wanted to know if my pearls were a rosary too." She smiled as she touched the string at her neck. Professor Vinstead had noticed the pearls under her shirt and had thought them a very odd combination with jodhpurs. "Don't they mind our touching their rosaries? I should have thought they would have done," he observed.

"Not a bit, as a rule—they have very little sensitiveness about such things. They must *have* feelings of religious reverence, I suppose, but they are so different to European ones that they are quite unrecognisable by us. They treat their own sacred objects with extraordinary casualness. It's quite common in country temples to find maize and millet stored in the main shrine, and strings of onions hung round the images to dry."

Professor Vinstead was struck by this aspect of Oriental psychology. The General, however, took a different view of the small episode.

"I thought it was supposed to be very bad joss to touch a bonze's belongings, Mrs. Leroy," he called from his ass. "You and the Professor had better look out."

"He looked such a very saintly bonze," said Miss Hande. "I don't feel he'll bring them any harm."

"Well, *I* wouldn't do it," said the General.

"We didn't touch them in anger or mockery," said Laura.

"And you think Buddha takes motives into account?"

"Probably. I shall be sorry if I've let you in for bad joss," said Laura, turning to the Professor with a smile; "but that's a European superstition, and I don't think they're valid out here."

"We're in the same boat, anyhow," said Vinstead.

He found himself drawing an obscure comfort from that thought, among a number of disquieting recollections— the smallpox in the village below, the soldiers with machine-guns, the obviously disturbed state of the country. The possible forms of "bad joss" seemed very numerous—it was most peculiar, the indifferent way in which all these people went casually about among them, taking their pleasure as if in the most complete and suburban security. He found himself feeling a slight irritation at their irrationality—and then his irritation turned against himself. It must be the sun, confound it! —*he* to be having superstitious forebodings, because he had touched a few inanimate beads belonging to a harmless Chinaman! He strove to throw off his depression, and prepared to talk again to Mrs. Leroy, with whom alone, among all these strangers, he felt that he had established a little link of intimacy. But Mrs. Leroy was now walking beside Miss Hande's donkey, deeply engaged in conversation; they were talking about the Chinese again, and Mrs. Leroy was, so she alleged, preaching a sermon. "My dear Miss Hande, it's really a duty for people like you, writers of reputation, to understand them as well as you can. But you simply *must* scrap all your theories about them, and just open your eyes and ears and see what you get. The soul of a people isn't in the writings of its publicists. That's the mistake you Americans always make; you accept the written statements, and shut your eyes to the facts before you. It's the little common everyday things that teach one about another race—get familiar with them. Remember, understanding begins where familiarity leaves off."

"Who said that?" interrupted Vinstead, struck by the phrase.

"I did! I do! I'm doing a fearful lot of saying, amn't I?" she said, smiling at Miss Hande.

"Well, I think you've given us some very valuable indications for racial study," replied the novelist; "but they're not easy to carry out in a short visit."

"No, but then one *can* only learn very little on a short visit, can't one? One can't theorise after it, that's certain," said Mrs. Leroy, turning aside to break a branch from an almond tree, with which she proceeded to switch the flies from Miss Hande's ass. Nina's boy was always so slack—he ought to have given Miss Hande a fly-switch. "But one can report small visible facts accurately," she proceeded, switching away; "and that's far better than any number of inaccurate theories."

At a turn of the road a flat-topped gateway rose before them. They passed through it into a sloping courtyard, where donkeys stood tied to tall trees, and piles of fodder, coal-dust and luggage lay about in confusion. The General and Miss Hande dismounted; the donkey-boys began to unload the asses. Niu appeared, and was given some instructions in Chinese. "Come on," said General Nevile, and limping stiffly ahead led the way, beneath flat-topped pillared *p'ailous* and across other courts, till passing through a final doorway he turned to his companions with, "Here we are at last."

Hot, dusty and weary, they found themselves at one end of an immense flagged terrace, broad as an English High Street and apparently nearly a quarter of a mile long, where the evening air moved coolly round the boles of the huge conifers which rose here and there from the pavement. On the left they were vaguely aware of great pavilions with scarlet pillars and painted eaves, rising above marble steps; on the right the terrace was bounded by a carved marble balustrade, with nothing beyond it but space, and sky, and through blossoming tree-tops a distant view of the mountains

beyond the Hun-ho. They strolled along it, cooled by
the delicious freshness, soothed by the space and peace
and dignity of their surroundings, and the indefinable
sense of achievement which lies at the end of all journeys.
At the further end, under the shadow of an immense
stone pine with a leaning trunk, two tables stood,
gleaming cheerfully with white linen; Touchy arose
from a pile of cushions close by, dropped his book, and
advanced upon them with the cocktail-shaker. It was
delicious to sink down into a cushion, and stretch out
hot and dusty feet before one—Touchy was an artist,
and his drink at the moment tasted like nectar. It was
still something of a surprise to the Professor to find
himself drinking cocktails at all with any frequency—to
be drinking them in such a scene gave him a sense of
being on some stage, acting a part not his own. With
the idle and unconscious absorption of fatigue he watched
Touchy measuring the top of the cocktail-shaker against
its squat bulk, up and down, up and down, while he and
the General exchanged the details of their journeys. The
walkers had met some soldiers too, but theirs had worn
no armlets at all, showing that they were deserters—
T'ao-pings, or masterless soldiers—a piece of news at
which the General frowned.

"Touchy, Miss Hande and I want to know where we
live," said Laura at length.

"Oh, but my dear, of course! Come on—you too, sir;
and you, Professor. We're all in the same courtyard this
time—one of the big ones."

Their quarters had the merit of beauty if not of con-
venience. A square paved courtyard sixty yards across,
with buildings round three sides of it and a wall with a
door on the fourth; in the centre a carved marble well-
head under a group of peach trees in full bloom. On the
further side to that by which they entered a flight of

marble steps led up to an imposing pavilion, whose projecting painted eaves, supported on scarlet pillars, made a sort of loggia along the whole of its latticed front—the side buildings, also with tiled roofs and latticed paper windows, but without loggias, stood, like it, on a sort of raised stone terrace a few feet above the court. Here and there a strangely-shaped roof of fluted sea-green or golden tiles showed over the tops of the pavilions; from somewhere out of sight rose two great pines, whose trunks, flushed pink in the evening light, carried their black plumy tops a hundred feet clear into the sun-gilt air. Touchy led them to the loggiaed pavilion. "Here you are—ladies on the left, men on the right."

Laura and Miss Hande stepped left and entered a latticed door. They found themselves in a largish room with plastered walls and a stone floor covered with rush matting; all across one side of it stretched a shallow brick platform some eighteen inches high and several feet in depth, built out from the wall—the *k'ang*, or bed. There was no furniture at all, but the servants had set up the ladies' six camp-beds in this apartment, and deposited a selection of luggage on each. In the dim yellowish light which entered through the paper lattices they observed Lilah Milne, a mirror and some pots of stuff perched before her on the edge of the *k'ang*, kneeling on the floor and attending to her face. A tin wash-basin stood close by. Laura looked upon it all with disfavour— she walked to the door, put out her head and called, "*Lai!*" Niu appeared, in spotless white, as usual. There was no room here, Laura said—six *T'ai-t'ais* could not sleep in one room. Niu explained that there was no other place, "*Mei-yu fah-tzu!*" (it can't be helped) he said resignedly. Laura was quite determined that it should be helped, and that speedily; she was not going to sleep and wash for three days crammed up in a room with five other women. She pointed across the court to the buildings on the left, "There is what?"

There, it seemed, was the Son of the Kitchen and the servant-men. She pointed to the right, "There is what?"

Niu began to stammer. There, it appeared, was no man, but it was a not-good place. "What-not-good?" "Not clean!" said Niu unhappily. "Give see!" Laura strode across to the smaller pavilion and examined it. A door in the centre opened into a fair-sized room, with two lesser rooms leading out of it, both with *k'angs*. It was dusty and unswept, but not unduly dirty. "Make clean!" said Laura briefly. Niu poured out a flood of explanation, guiltily. He knew quite well that he should have prepared more rooms. It was not that the servant-men had not wished to make plenty of room for the *T'ai-t'ais*, but that place was an extremely not-good place—there were (here Niu displayed a thoroughly sound bit of psychology) rats!

Psychology was wasted on Laura. She scorned the rats. *Kaoliang* brooms were fetched, the small pavilion was swept out, straw matting laid on the *k'angs* and floors of the inner rooms, and in ten minutes Laura's bed and luggage and *tchilumchi* were installed in one, and Lilah at her invitation had her bed moved across too and placed in the other. "What about Judith?"

"She'll sleep out, if I know her," said Lilah.

"Then we'd better get her bed moved out from there, anyhow," Laura said, and commanded it to be placed in the central chamber of the new pavilion. Miss Hande's grateful relief at these dispositions was obvious if unexpressed. Then Mrs. Leroy went into her room to wash and unpack, calling aloud to space in general for *k'ai shui* (hot water) as she did so.

In the dimly-lighted chamber she set to work with a practised hand to arrange her few effects. The *tchilumchi*, an enamel basin with a leather cover, was emptied of its collection of toilet articles and set ready on the *k'ang* to receive the hot water (which space in general duly produced in a tin jug). Taking a couple of nails from her trouser pocket she drove them into the wall with a brickbat picked up in the courtyard, and hung her pocket mirror on one and her towel on the other. Her spare clothing was placed under the pillow of her camp bed to heighten it, and the camp bed itself shoved up close against the *k'ang*, so that the latter served as a bed-table, on which her book, chocolate, a box of cigarettes and a candle stuck in a tin saucer were neatly arranged. In a few minutes the room had taken on a curiously inhabited appearance. While she washed and put on a clean shirt, Lilah strolled in and surveyed her arrangements silently, as usual.

"Did you have a nice ride up?" Laura asked, shaking Houbigant powder over her arms and neck.

"M-m—yes. How neat you are!" said Lilah, sitting down on a vacant space on the *k'ang*. This remark seemed to call for no reply, and Laura made none, but sat down on the bed to wash and powder her feet before putting on a pair of scarlet leather travelling-slippers.

"Where is everybody? Are they all all right?" she next inquired.

"They all sort of scattered when we got here. Our two lots of lovers are very much all right, I should say!" said Lilah, taking one of Laura's cigarettes and lighting it with her air of rather sleepy amusement. "Properly boiling up. They all seemed to need to hold hands to cross those little plank bridges as we came along, and the last I saw of Master Henri and Little Annette up here was sitting in one of those little corner pagodas,

telling one another's fortunes by palmistry!" She
laughed. "And Judith and Derek were drinking cocktails on the steps of one of those temple affairs and talking
about religion. Have you noticed, Laura, how religion
nearly always comes in at the beginning of love affairs?"

"No, I hadn't." But on thinking it over she at once
saw that this, like most of Lilah's observations, was
accurate enough.

"Oh yes, it does. It's a serious symptom," said Lilah,
who was in an unusually conversational mood.

"I don't think it will be much good for Little Annette
to talk to Henri about religion," said Laura, absently
uttering her thoughts aloud, while she pulled out from
under her pillow a scarlet embroidered jacket and put
it on.

"Not it! I say, how superb you look in that jacket
affair! Laura," the girl went on, with a sudden change
of tone, "I suppose Mrs. N. can look *after* that Annette
child all right? Because I don't think she can look after
herself a bit."

"What do you mean?" said Laura.

"Oh, I don't mean stop her being seduced," replied
Lilah, with her usual flat calm. "I imagine she has just
wits enough for that herself. I mean stop her being too
much hurt. I should think the surface she presents to
that young man just now is pretty tender, and I can't
imagine his understanding that in the least. You look
at her face at dinner. She's coming alive suddenly—
just to-day, just up here, really—like an Iris Stylosa
opening in a warm room."

"*Can* one stop people being hurt? And had one
better?" Laura asked this question more of herself than
of Lilah. In her experience all the richest and most
valuable things were mixed up, somehow or other, with
being hurt. Sooner or later everything that was nice

hurt as well: love-affairs hurt (like the devil); marriage
hurt; children hurt—she half shut her eyes at the thought
of children, as if to shut out Tim and Sarah and the intolerable pain of separation from them. And directly
from being hurt, it seemed to her, sprang all the qualities
she valued most, in others or in herself—courage; a
measure of insight, and self-knowledge; and the secret
sense of strength, of the indestructibility of the human
spirit in the face of disasters, which is the most precious
possession of all. All these things could only be had at
a price, and cash in advance at that—the price of being
hurt, again and again, and sometimes almost to the
point of extinction. Happiness—she thought of Bridges—
was the flaunting honeyed *flower* of the soul; but the root
was pain, and the twin fruits knowledge and strength.
She thought again of Little Annette; it was difficult to
set her in any relation to this bleak doctrine. And it
struck her with sudden force—how cunningly the life of
man is arranged! If pain were not so indissolubly bound
up with all the joys he pursues, who would seek it or
reap its fruits?

But Lilah, watching her with steady blue eyes, said,
"Perhaps one can't. And perhaps some grown-up
people one had better not. But if you can help it you
don't let a downy chicken be hurt, Laura, or a kitten
when its tail is still triangular. And she's like that."
And out she went, very definite somehow in spite of her
beauty and the trailing shawl that she had thrown
over her frock. Laura merely stopped to fill her cigarette-
case, and then followed her.

A few minutes later Professor Vinstead also left his
room and strolled out on to the terrace. The evening
light laid a deeper brilliance on everything it touched.
The valley below was in shadow now, blue and clear;
the terrace was in shadow too, but the green and golden

roofs of some of the great shrines behind it caught the last sun like jewels, and the hills away across the river glowed with an astonishing enamelled vividness in clear tones of amethyst and rose and topaz. The near end of the terrace was closed by a high wall with tiled eaves—over it rose an immense white pine, its snowy trunk and branches shining among the great trusses of dark-green needles. The white pine is the most improbable of trees —too good to be true; it is impossible to believe at first that some ingenious Chinese has not sandpapered its smooth trunk and boughs, and then given it several coats of whitewash. The Professor pushed open a door in the wall and walked through. An inner terrace, narrower and more secluded, lay beyond. The flag-stones of the nearer end were uneven from the thrust of the roots of the great tree, whose white trunk rose shining from the pavement—further on was a memorial tablet standing next to a small yellow fir; somehow the clipped and twisted tree had almost the same formality and permanence as the inscribed marble on its square carved pediment. Rising above the edge of the terrace stood a little pagoda, octagonal in shape; from each angle of its fluted stone frills hung a small bronze bell. He leant over the marble balustrade and reaching out, hit one of the bells lightly to set it in motion—it rang with a thin small note as it swung to and fro. At the extreme end of this inner terrace a little turret projected from the wall for several feet, roofed with a tiled cupola supported on small stone pillars, and approached by two or three steps. The Professor saw that its pillared openings would command a view of the terrace front, and make a wonderful frame for pictures of the valley and the further hill-sides beyond, now spread out above the balustrade; with an eye to possible photographs on the morrow he moved towards it. But at the doorway he paused. The pillars framed, indeed, the picture he had foreseen—the coloured outline of the shining hills bisecting the level line of the plain, all in a glory of late light—but they framed another picture as well. In one of the openings stood Mrs. Leroy, in her scarlet slippers and bizarre crimson jacket—as he watched she leant over the parapet and plucked a spray of blossom from a tree which bloomed high against the wall. She bent her head to smell the spray, and stood again, holding it, looking out at the view. So framed in the pillared opening, outlined against the sky and the hills, with flowers in her hands and an air of meditation on her grave face, she reminded him of some North Italian Madonna, set in a porticoed building on the slope of the Alps. The unexpected picture struck strangely on Vinstead's heart, as though someone had dealt him a soft blow. Something made her turn her head and look at him. "Don't move," he said involuntarily.

"Why?" she said, but she did not move. Nor did she smile, but her gravity was not unfriendly. Vinstead could not have answered her question for his life—he had spoken without thought or intention. For most of us certain places mean one person, and he may have had an obscure foreknowledge that for him Chieh T'ai Ssu was to mean, ultimately, Laura Leroy. He certainly wanted to *see* her there, as she stood, thoroughly. We all know occasionally this need to stamp a particular image on the mind, even though at the time we may not recognise its source. In a moment, a little self-consciously, he said something about a photograph to-morrow. "So difficult to get the right figure for architecture." A whistle sounded—Touchy's signal. "I believe that means that dinner is ready," he added.

"All right—I'll come. Don't wait." She turned back for a last look at the view, still pondering over Lilah's remarks about Little Annette—troubled by them. "But who can stop lovers loving, *here*?" she thought, smelling her spray of flowers. She turned to go, assuming that the Professor had gone, and dreading another messenger —people were always pursuing Mrs. Leroy for the meals which she forgot.

But the Professor had waited.

Chapter Eleven

WHEN Professor Vinstead was first told by the Neviles that he was to go to the Hills on a week-end picnic, his mind had immediately conjured up those rather unpleasing visions of sandwiches, sardines, and ruined coffee in thermos flasks with which the word is usually associated in English minds, prolonged over three painful days and nights. It was, therefore, with some surprise that he found himself sitting down at a table correctly spread with linen, glass, and a profusion of silver, being offered sherry by one white-robed manservant, and clear soup with a pigeon's egg in it by another. How such things were produced in the heart of the hills, twenty miles from anywhere, was a mystery with which his mind, dulled by fatigue and hours spent in the open air, refused to grapple for the moment. It was sufficiently astonishing to be dining in such a place. The tables were set under the stone pine with the leaning trunk, and commanded the immense vista of the terrace, with the narrowing perspective of the marble balustrade along one side, and hints of great shrines on the other. A monk in black was pacing slowly to and fro in the distance, grave and dignified; another European party was dining on a raised platform a little way off, and their voices rose on the air, mingled now and then with a deep distant note of drums and gongs, booming from somewhere out of sight. As broiled cray-fish with Hollandaise sauce succeeded the soup, and white wine the sherry, the Professor turned his attention from his surroundings to his companions. Mrs. Nevile,

sparkling and animated, was alternately inquiring after
his comfort and exchanging laughing insults with La
Touche, who accused her of having captured the affec-
tions of the Iberian Minister. Judith Milne was pouring
out italics to the General, her sister and Miss Hande
(living up to their several reputations) were eating their
dinner in silence; Fitzmaurice was rather quiet, looking
now at Judith, to-night definitely in one of her pretty
moods, and now, almost inquiringly, at Mrs. Leroy, who
was telling Henri and Miss Ingersoll about Niu's mis-
deeds in the matter of the pavilion. About the time of
the advent of grilled chicken à l'Américaine (with
Russian salad) the conversation was suddenly dominated
by rats.

"But, my dear Laura, you will not sleep in this room
if 'e says there are rats? *Quelle horreur!*" Henri's high
voice rose, shrill with protest, above the others.

Laura, eating her chicken, said she didn't believe there
were any—they were an invention of Niu's to exculpate
himself.

"A *few* rats do no harm to anyone," said the General
calmly. "They have to reach three figures before they
are dangerous."

"But, my *dear* William," protested Nina, horrified at
this further threat to the peace and prosperity of her
already much-tried party, "no one has ever seen rats
even in *one* figure up here, so why theorise in that horrible
manner? I assure you"—she turned anxiously to Miss
Hande and the Professor—"there *really* never are any."

"Perhaps the rats will be our bad joss," said Vinstead
to Laura, smiling—but the small smile was like a gesture
of intimacy, and it did not escape Nina. She seized
thankfully, however, on the bad joss as an escape from
the more menacing subject, and the bonze and his
beads swamped the rats at one end of the tables, though

Henri at the other was heard declaring stubbornly, "I shall 'ave my bed carried outside—I 'ate rats."

After the *macédoine* of fruit and cream *mousse* came coffee and liqueurs. The servants placed red-shaded candles on the tables, which lit up the faces round them with a shadowy glow, touching off outlines and hollows and accentuating the play of expression as in a screen photograph. Mrs. Leroy leant back and studied the ones in which she was most interested at the moment. Little Annette—Lilah was quite right; there was a delicate warmth, an unfolding, an almost visible bloom of happiness on her face, for all her little conventional tricks of smiles and movements of the head—something unprotected, childish, touching. Henri's face, on the other hand, gave away nothing but what he chose—he was being gallant and extravagant, and was obviously willing to appear so—that was all you could see. She looked at the other couple. Judith was very much "on her day," that was clear; her cloudy fair hair was pushed off her forehead with an even more windswept air than usual; there was colour in her face, and some fresh emphasis about the always decisive lines of her eyebrows and nostrils—something assured, triumphant, almost warrior-like in her whole aspect. "*Être aimée embellit beaucoup!*" Touchy whispered to Laura, following her glance. She smiled, but without answering, and looked at Derek. With his shining spaniel's head and brilliant blue eyes he looked healthy and animated, as always, but his face in repose had a look of inquiry, almost of strain. Laura studied him covertly. So Tim perhaps would one day look, when he was in a stew over some young woman—if it *was* Judith he was stewing over; and she wondered with affectionate concentration just how that was bothering him. How could she teach Tim about life so that he would grow up honest, unafraid and above all responsible? Derek's irresponsibility was his trouble. "Casual! Casual!" she thought, remembering Sir James, and laughed out loud, suddenly. They all looked at her, but Derek, at whom she was looking, caught her eye and held it in a sort of appeal. As they rose from the tables he moved round to her, but Mrs. Nevile was ahead of him—slipping her arm into Laura's, she claimed her for a stroll with, "I simply haven't *seen* you to-day."

As they walked along the terrace in the dusk, "Well, how do you think it's going?" Nina asked.

"Oh, rather well—don't you?"

"Why yes—I think so. How do you and the Professor get on?"

"Oh, very well—he's nice," said Laura emphatically.

"You're just wonderful with learned men!" said Nina admiringly. "I think it really looks as if Henri and Little Annette might get engaged on this trip," she went on complacently.

"Nina, do you think that's all right? I'm rather bothered about her," said Laura.

"My dear, he's a wonderful *parti* if he does decide to marry, and he's most charming."

"I daresay, but you know what Henri is. I'm afraid of his making her unhappy."

"But I really think he's serious this time," Nina Nevile protested.

"All the worse if he is, I should say," said Laura brusquely. "She'll almost certainly be miserable if she marries him."

"Oh, American women are very good at international marriages," said Nina airily. "They're adaptable, and they know how to keep their end up." She laughed a little consciously. "We're much better at that than you are, my dear."

They had turned in their walk and were approaching the tables again. The servants were clearing them, and some of the party still lingered under the leaning pine, smoking on the cushions. As Mrs. Leroy and Mrs. Nevile came up, Touchy rose to consult Nina about plans. "Miss Hande is very anxious to go to T'an Chüeh Ssu— do you think to-morrow or Sunday would be the better day?"

Derek had risen too, and while Mrs. Nevile was engaged with La Touche, he took Laura gently but firmly by the elbow. "Come on, come and stroll, wise lily!" he said in her ear.

For some time they walked in silence, arm-in-arm. It was almost dark now—the shapes of the great trees on the terrace were just deeper darknesses with a pattern in them; colour had deserted the buildings, leaving them invisible except for a glimmer of white marble at the base, or an outline of fantastic roof blocked in against the faint grey star-shine of the sky. They went up some steps into one of the courtyards above the terrace. It was just possible to make out the dark shapes of the huge bronze incense-burners which rose here and there from the pavement, higher than their heads, strange formal symbols of worship; pale and insubstantial as water at dawn, groups of almond trees bloomed shadowy in the dark. Laura paused to smell their faint freshness, holding her face close to the clustering boughs—Derek did the same, and she heard him draw a deep breath.

"Well?" she said.

He did not answer at once, except to press her arm gently. She waited without impatience. Something was working in him, born of the spring, urged by the stars and the flowering trees towards expression; held back perhaps by the formality of shape, of restrained carven symmetry which surrounded them on all sides, stylised within rigid bounds. No one has yet measured the pressure exercised on our moods and impulses in moments of tension by external things, though every one has at some time been forced to recognise its existence, if only by the way in which particular emotional states remain linked in our minds with some irrelevant object which was before the eyes at the time. Laura was always aware, at Chieh T'ai Ssu, of these dual influences pressing on her, but she had not yet seen Derek subject to them. He had been there before, but never in the company of a young woman with whom he was beginning to be in love; nor, so far as Laura knew, had he ever yet begun to be in love with anyone who was, so to speak, in earnest about life. She realised this new ferment working in him now, but when he did speak, it was in the light coaxing tones he often used.

"Tell me about her, wise one," he said.

"I expect you know more than I do, by now."

"No—women have their own ways of knowing one another, and their own things to know, that we don't get at."

"What do you want to know?" Laura asked.

But he didn't ask a question at once—he pondered in silence as they strolled along.

"I think she probably has a temper," he said at length, rather unexpectedly. "I like what that stands for, but I don't like it shown." Laura laughed. He gave her arm a little shake in rebuke. "She's got a sort of strength," he went on, thinking aloud, "and that can be a bad thing. She looks sometimes as if she might be ferocious."

"Why do you like her?" Laura asked.

"Her eyebrows!" he said at once. "And she's very alive, Laura—so honest and quick. She asks the most amazing questions, and gives the most amazing answers.

There's none of the usual fencing with her. It's rather refreshing. But I wonder if she'd ever learn any *savoir-faire*."

Laura rather wondered this too. "It wouldn't come very natural to her," she said.

"Do you think she likes me?" he asked, turning round on her suddenly.

"Ask her—she'll tell you."

"Ooh"—he made a long sound—"that's being so crucial. I wish she'd show one a bit, in the ordinary way. She gives one no lead—you know, shoulders and all that."

"No, I don't suppose she will give you that. You mustn't expect those manners from her. You'll have to meet her on her own ground."

"But what *is* her own ground?" he asked. "That's just what I want to know."

"Well, I suppose her own ground is really my ground, more or less," said Laura. "You know what that is well enough."

"Oh, *you!*" he put an indescribable note of affection into the word. "Your ground, blessed Laura, is all background—you never ram it down anyone's throat."

"What a mixed metaphor!" said a high merry voice out of the darkness close by—Touchy's voice, they knew it at once. They had wandered down on to the terrace again as they talked, and were nearly at the further end. "Ramming a background down somebody's throat!" went on the voice, and through the gloom they saw La Touche, strolling with Mrs. Nevile. The sound of drums at intervals, and of a strange continuous chanting, which had been faintly in their ears for some time, rose loudly ahead of them. "We're going to see what all the noise is about—there's some sort of jamboree going on," said Touchy. "Come along."

All four together walked to the end of the terrace and out into the confusion of courtyards beyond, following the sound in the darkness. They found themselves at length in a sort of broad paved lane, with small buildings on the right and one large one on the left. A yellowish light streamed out through the open doors, round which a small crowd of servants and donkey-boys had gathered; the near resonance of the music told them that they had reached its source. Making their way gently through the crowd, which gave them passage with ready courtesy, they mounted a few steps to the doors and looked in.

They saw a hall, long and high—so long and so high that the further end and the open space under the roof were lost in shadows. Almost opposite the door, close to but not touching the further wall, stood a sort of altar, lit up with painted horn lanterns; red columns at the four corners supported a baldaquin over it. Touchy whispered that it looked like a very high four-poster bed, as indeed it did. Round this erection sat seven figures on tall wooden stools, two at a side and one at the further end, between the altar and the wall. The six at the sides were dressed in robes of pale blue and pale pink satin, worn and faded to the most dream-like delicacy of tone, and smothered in silver embroidery of an inconceivable richness. But at the further end the strangest figure of all sat alone. They could only see him as low as the breast, the altar hid the rest. His robe and sleeves were of white satin, so covered with silver thread that the stuff was barely visible—and on his head was a great lotus flower in satin and silver, with lace-like silver edges to the big curved petals. With eyes half-closed, his ivory-coloured face as sealed and expressionless as a mask, he intoned, at regular intervals, some chanted phrase; as he ceased, the six others, without pause, joined in an antiphon, sustained for a couple of minutes; they ceased, the lotus figure resumed, paused, and their antiphon followed his voice as before. Regular as the recurring beat and fall of waves on a shore, the strange chant rose and fell, rose and fell—nasal, impersonal, prolonged—in an Eastern mode quite unlike any European music. Down against the wall to the right of the altar, in the shadows, an old man in a black cap and a tattered black cotton robe crouched on a low stool near a brazier; now and then he put out one hand and beat a few strokes on a drum beside him. A pan of water stood on the brazier, and a tea-pot in a padded wicker cover beside it; while they watched, the old man took off the pan and refreshed the tea-pot with the contents; then he rose, tea-pot in hand, and walked round the altar, pausing by each figure in turn to fill the small porcelain bowls which stood before them with steaming tea.

"What *are* they doing?" whispered Nina.

"I believe it must be some sort of ordination service," Laura whispered back; "I've heard of them, but I've never seen one before. These will be the postulants for ordination, I expect."

"Judith must hear this," said Derek. "Music's in her line."

"Yes, and fetch the others too—especially the Professor and Miss Hande," whispered Mrs. Nevile urgently. Derek nodded and slipped out through the crowd.

The crowd, however, was not whispering. Smoking and conversing, not noisily, but normally and pleasantly, they thronged round the door, leaning aside occasionally to spit with a loud hawking sound. One or two strolled into the building, and then strolled out again, casually. There was a complete absence of any outward sign of awe or reverence. On the other hand, the fumes of garlic were very strong. "Could we go in, do you think?" Nina whispered.

"Yes, come on," said Touchy.

They went in. Low wooden benches stood against the plastered walls on both sides of the doors, and they sat down on one of these. A figure shifted to give them room, and looking round Mrs. Nevile saw the Iberian Minister, his yellow boots thrust out in front of him, sitting beside her.

"How long will it last, do you think, Excellency?" she asked him in French.

"Unfortunately I ignore completely the length of these ceremonies, Madame," he replied. "I would wish to know, for I count to sleep here." He pointed to the shadowy further end of the hall. "*Mes boys ont installé mon lit là-bas*," he explained. He pulled out an enamelled watch and looked at it—the hands pointed to ten o'clock. "I wait still an hour," he said firmly. "If they have not finished then, I walk with my bed, like the gentleman in the Saint Évangile." Touchy laughed softly. "I wish we could smoke," he said.

"But of course one can smoke! *Regardez donc ces messieurs là-bas!*" The Iberian pointed to the benches to the left of the door, where they now saw that several Chinese sat smoking quietly. "It makes absolutely nothing to them, that one should smoke in their church!" he chuckled. And, indeed, when Touchy took out his cigarette-case and handed it to the ladies, the old man who attended to the drum and tea part of the service shuffled up nimbly, bringing a live coal from his brazier in a pair of tongs to light their cigarettes—having done so, he begged one for himself and lit it in the same way.

"Do ask him what it's all about," said Nina. But the old man had gone back to his seat. Unmoved, as if asleep, the figures at the altar continued to intone their rhythmic alternating chant, oblivious of their surroundings—a sound so ancient, so remote from the twentieth century that it was like the past made audible. Presently there was a little stir round the door, and the rest of the party looked in. Nina beckoned, and they too entered and sat down on the benches. Vinstead took a seat by Laura. "This is most interesting," he murmured; "do tell me what's going on."

Laura explained. She believed the figure with the lotus crown to be the ordaining priest, "the lotus is the symbol of Buddha, as you know," and the six others to be postulants for ordination, who were probably in the early stages of becoming bonzes. "Later on they have pastilles of incense burned on their heads, till it burns into the skin," she said, "but I'm not sure if that happens at this service or at a later one."

"Not really? How grim!" said the Professor, scanning the faces of the candidates. "There's our friend," he said suddenly. "Look—the end one on the far side." Laura looked, and recognised the young monk whose beads they had rescued on the way up. Above his pink embroideries his face wore a look of dreamy ecstasy as he chanted with the rest.

"What do they say?" Vinstead asked. "Can you make it out?"

"Hardly a word—they drone it so. And I believe the language of these chants is very archaic; I shouldn't understand it if I did hear. My husband would."

At this point a noise rose from the entrance, where some disturbance seemed to be taking place. Voices were raised outside; heads were popped in and withdrawn; the word "*Li-t'ou*" (within) was heard several times. Then up the steps and through the crowd strode a tall figure in blue, leading a small donkey by the

halter; right into the hall of ordination he came, leaving
his ass among the bystanders at the entrance—the small
grey noses of other donkeys were visible, pressing in at
the doorway behind him. He came to a stand before
the group of foreigners.

"Why, it's Shang!" said Mrs. Nevile.

Shang it was, in an agony of contrition and despair,
with all his ten asses and their drivers. He poured out a
flood of anguished explanation, his charming deeply
wrinkled face twisted with emotion. He had been at
Mo-yu Ferry—from twelve o'clock he had been there,
with his best donkeys, "*teng-cho pen chin*" (waiting long
time) till seven-thirty, when he had learned from some
peasants that the *Ying-Kuo-jen* had crossed by the Mo-
shih-k'ou Ferry and gone on to Chieh T'ai Ssu with other
lü (donkeys). So he had come to explain—and here he
was, with his men and animals; ready, he said, to take
the *T'ai-t'ais* back to the ferry, or to T'an-Chüeh Ssu—
anywhere! It was to Mrs. Nevile that he addressed
himself, but the General answered. He explained that
the donkeys had been ordered for Mo-shih-k'ou Ferry;
the party had found none, had had to order others, to
wait, to pay other men—what was done was done.
Shang's protests grew passionate. It was for *Mo-yu*
Ferry that Lin had ordered the *lü*, "he tell me *this*
place!" The money was nothing—Shang had lost face.
Nina and Laura both intervened; it was really possible
that Lin had made a mistake; Shang should not be condemned out of hand. In the end he was given seven
dollars, a dollar a day being the rate for one ass and
his attendant man—there were ten men and ten donkeys,
but the three dollars were a sort of fine for failure. Shang
pocketed the money, beaming; this restored his face.
Smiling, bowing, he withdrew; a satisfied murmur of
"*Hao!*" (well) arose from the crowd without—showing

clearly, as Touchy remarked, that they had given him at least three times as much as he deserved.

Unmoved, even by the presence of donkeys and the voices of bargaining, the singers continued to sing, rapt and immobile. Judith was trying to note down the tune on the back of a visiting-card, but the rest of the party became a little bored. Touchy suggested an adjournment to the terrace. Quietly they all slipped out, leaving the Iberian Minister patiently invigilating his bed. His enamelled watch still showed half an hour to go. "Bon repos, Excellence!" mocked Nina softly as she left him. "You have a lovely serenade!"

"*Mon Dieu, Madame, quelle religion!*" he groaned resignedly, recomposing himself to wait after his bow of farewell. Vinstead, pausing for a last look from the door, saw him take out a long cheroot, and the old tea-maker shuffle across to light it; the latter scrounged a cheroot too, and the fumes of Manila tobacco mingled for a time with those of incense at the ordination of the six priests.

Chapter Twelve

IT was Touchy who suggested some singing when they were back again on the terrace. Touchy had quite a good tenor, General Nevile a fine bass; and these two, with Mrs. Leroy as alto and Mrs. Nevile as soprano, were in the habit of doing a good deal of solid and conscientious part-singing. They were all sufficiently good and sufficiently keen to sing for their own pleasure at all sorts of odd times and in all sorts of odd places, and struck now without fuss or preamble into "The Silver Swan." Vinstead, leaning back on a cushion against the balustrade, listened with surprise and pleasure to the excellence of their rendering of one song after another. The moon was just rising behind the little bell pagoda, and filled the sky on that side with a golden glow, against which the shapely massed boughs of the white pine stood out black and distinct—the light, not powerful as yet, was just beginning to bring the terrace and the buildings behind it back to life. The songs rang out with the peculiar and penetrating charm of harmonised voices in the open air, and as the growing light touched out the strange shapes of roof and shrine and carved marble stairway, Vinstead thought how odd it was to be listening to Elizabethan madrigals and English folk-songs in such a setting. His mind savoured fastidiously the contrast between the English voices and the well-known time and words, and the strange and ancient chanting to which he had been listening just before.

Then Judith sang. The effect on her hearers was instantaneous, especially on Vinstead and Henri Delache, both in their way connoisseurs. This was the real thing, not an amateur show; effortless, steady, strong, the girl placed note after note with an assurance, a purity, a control which, with her flawless enunciation of vowels and consonants, lifted her singing almost on to the impersonal plane of instrumental music. Laura saw Henri stiffen up with attention, almost visibly cock his ears like a terrier, and then remain poised, delighted, the critic suspended in appreciation; in the ever-strengthening light she saw the Professor, too, rouse himself, arrested by the quality of the singing—examine it, as it were, critically, and then sink back, satisfied, on his face the expression of pained beatitude so familiar among English music-lovers. Something in his attitude of deliberate surrender reminded her of Aubrey listening to music. So he, when the opening bars had satisfied him, used to sink back with closed eyes, on an uncomfortable seat in the Queen's Hall or, more often, in an arm-chair in his room at Christ Church, his immensely expensive gramophone carefully adjusted, to listen. How well she remembered those evenings in his room—the firelight playing on the pale panelling and the tea-things on the hearth; the little bronze horse on the mantelpiece in front of the ·cloudy background of the Hebridean sketch; the books; the sense of ease and warmth and deep satisfaction. How rare it was, the mutuality that existed between her and Aubrey—the easy interchange of outside shots in the way of ideas, the quick come-back of his mind at hers, the ready appreciation of each other's best. She used to sit in that room, watching him, while the music spoke its impersonal version of life. The Schubert seemed to be summing it all up, in its own universal and eternal way—making the place and the time, her and Aubrey, and the bronze horse and the firelight on the panels, part of all achieved understanding and mutual pleasure in all minds at all times. Long moments, out of succession—most serene when she had been, as at first, still free enough to feel no need to grasp them, to press their essence out, but was content to let them flow over her, under the spell of the music's timeless peace.

Perhaps the strangest quality of that strange thing, music, is this power it has of translating the personal and immediate for us into the universal and eternal; or, working backwards, as it were, of bringing the universal, the whole meaning of things, with arrowy immediacy and certainty into our personal knowledge. And as we thus see our own problems and experience, our immediate apprehensions of life, clothed with the aspect of eternal truth, they take on for us a different importance, a new weight; they are re-valued in the serene terms of a celestial currency—they look otherwise than did our old defaced personal coinage of silver and copper. And this change of values is effected in us by music so swiftly and smoothly; the solvent slips into our being without friction of argument or dogma to arouse our irritable wills. No prose, no preacher, could so drive these certainties home.

Something of this change, this vision, reaches every one when music speaks. And when Judith Milne sang on the terrace at Chieh T'ai Ssu, Laura was faintly aware of this influence, disturbing yet serene, at work about her as well as in her. Judith stood easily by the leaning pine, one hand resting lightly on its trunk; her shadowed face was barely visible, but her voice poured out beyond the shadows, into the moonlight and up among the shrines, carrying truths beyond her speech. It was a soprano, with that untouched perfect purity of tone so seldom found, and still more rarely left by teachers in girls' voices; cool, impersonal, clear as the high voice

of a boy. The skilful training which had placed the
voice so perfectly, and given it power and control, had
for a wonder left this precious quality untouched. "Mais
c'est formi*dable!*" Henri whispered, leaning across to
Laura. "She must be professional." "She is—but
don't talk," Laura whispered back.

She sang two or three folk-songs, first, and then Lilah
asked for "Bright is the Ring of Words." "You know it
doesn't go well without accompaniment," said Judith, but
sang it nevertheless. As her voice drew to the lovely close—

> "The lover lingers and sings
> And the maid remembers,"

Laura looked across at Annette Ingersoll, and thought
she knew why Lilah had asked for that particular one.
The girl was listening with parted lips, stirred, troubled,
and yet soothed—there was a look as of dawn breaking
in her face. Oh yes, the maid remembers all right—
she would remember, poor maid, that shadowed scene,
and Henri whispering beside her. Henri asked for something French. Unhesitatingly Judith broke into, "*Bon-
jour, Suzon!*" with its delicious infection of happiness and
light-hearted love. Derek was smiling appreciatively at
the close. But she went on to "*Rose et Blanche,*" and his
face changed a little as she sang:

> "*Pourquoi mon âme est rêveuse
> Me demandez-vous encore?
> Elle a glané, la glaneuse,
> Mon cœur dans sa gerbe d'or.*"

She went on with some Gounod and Fauré, old-fashioned
stuff, but very singable; the enchanting pure quality of
her voice twirled round the flowery phrases, somehow
redeeming their sentimentality. Henri was ravished.
"*Dame, quelle virtuosité!*" he muttered. At Touchy's

request she went back after that to English. "Do you know this one, from the Appalachians?" she asked, and began "The Dear Companion."

The little plaintive melody, with its curious hesitation in the middle of the line, its unexpected lift and fall, floated out into the air, hauntingly sweet, carrying the artless sadness of the words straight into the heart—it flowed on to the last verse:

> " Oh when I see—your babe a-laughing
>   It makes me think—of your sweet face
>   But when I see—your babe a-crying
>   It makes me think—of my disgrace."

Laura watched Derek's face. It told its own tale, for a brief moment. Something was taking hold of him, some fresh influence joining its force to those she had already felt at work in the darkness under the almond trees. A sudden impulse moved her to deal him another stroke through the music, or rather to let Judith, the happy warrior, strike a resounding blow for herself and her way of life.

"Now sing 'Fain would I change that note,' Judith," she said imperatively; she meant to jump the girl into it without giving her time to think, and the abrupt and imperious tone succeeded. With a half-startled glance at her aunt, Judith obeyed. Up rose the glorious voice, steady, strong and full, gathering power as the song proceeded, carrying the noble words out into the night with superb assurance.

Judith lost herself now in the music—triumphant, grave, her voice rose in the second verse.

> " O Love, they wrong thee much
>   That say thy sweet is bitter,
>   When thy rich fruit is such
>   As nothing can be sweeter.

Fair house of joy and bliss
Where truest pleasure is
    I do adore thee.
I know thee, what thou art,
I serve thee with my heart
    And fall before thee."

As the solemn *sostenuto* of the last words died away
there was silence among Judith's listeners. Derek had
turned his head aside into the shadow, and was tracing
the cracks between the flag-stones with his fingers.
"That's all," said Judith abruptly, and with her swift
strong step she walked away from the thanks and
applause which broke out. A little group of Europeans
from the other party had collected some distance off to
listen—with subdued "Bravas" they melted away. As
though some band which held them still had suddenly
broken, the Neviles' party began to shift and disperse.

"By Jove, some singing Kuniang!" said Touchy,
getting up from his cushion and stretching his cramped
limbs. "She's a wonder, Laura."

"*Mais écoutez, Laura, c'est magnifique, cette voix,*" Henri
exclaimed; "she should give a—'ow do you say?—
repetition."

"Concert," said Touchy.

"Ao yes, concert. We 'ave so little music in Peking.
She sings very very well—she 'as sung this Gounod
marvellously."

"Who trained her, do you know?" Vinstead asked of
Laura. She felt almost like the proprietor of some per-
forming animal. "I should say Hengel, at a rough
guess."

"Yes, she has worked with him," she answered.

"She has a great future before her," he said, almost
solemnly.

Praising and discussing, every one drifted off towards

bed. Back in their own courtyard—"Who's for a drink?" said Touchy. "All that singing has given me a Sahara thirst."

A few were for drinks, and whisky and soda and barley water were produced. They sat on the marble steps leading up to the main pavilion. The proximity of their sleeping-quarters reminded Delache of the rats, and he insisted on having his camp bed carried out into the courtyard.

"This is *convenable, n'est-ce pas*?" he inquired; "since the ladies sleep indoors?"

He was told not to be a goose—of course he could have his bed out. Touchy decided to follow his example. "It's a divine night—much too good to spend behind paper. Why don't you sleep out too?" he asked, turning to Vinstead. Vinstead thought he would.

"The War made me comparatively indifferent to rats," he observed, "but I have rather a fancy for seeing the dawn."

So presently three camp beds stood out under the peach trees near the well-head. But they were not at once inhabited. Vinstead wandered off to take a last look at the terrace by moonlight, and Touchy and Laura sat on with Henri, too idle to go to bed at first, and afterwards too much amused. For Henri, after a couple of whiskies, became animated. He talked with even greater freedom than usual, and Touchy and Laura were kept laughing, half at his efficient but curiously placed English, half at his point of view. He was consumed with the ambition to behave and speak correctly in an English way, especially where the proprieties were concerned; he had many English and American friends, and he wished, quite sincerely, to adapt himself to their attitude and to respect their conventions. But our island point of view was altogether

too much for him. He could not understand it, could
never be sure what was proper and what was not. With
Mrs. Leroy and La Touche he was quite at his ease, and
put his troubles before them with comic freedom. His
latest was in the matter of a story he had told to Miss
Hande on the terrace after dinner; "I think this is quite
correc', but she look at me as if I was a serpent."

"What was the story, Henri?" Touchy inquired,
giggling.

"'Ow, it was nothing," but he told it, and it was
sufficiently hair-raising; Laura laughed to think of the
effect on poor Miss Hande.

"You should be more careful, Henri!" she said; "that
was a very improper story."

"Improper? *Comment?* You mean not *correc*'? But
I am very careful—I did not tell her this one because I
think it is not *correc*'. You see, I was in the Train Bleu—
I 'ave a sleeper, of course——" There followed a completely innocuous tale of a confusion in sleeping-cars, in
which all the parties had behaved in the most *correc*'
manner possible.

"But that was all right, Henri, old man—you could
have told her that one and she wouldn't have turned a
hair," said Touchy, stifling his mirth as well as he could.

"*Non—vous blaguez!*" said Henri, with conviction.
"My dear Touchi, I knoh one thing—for Americans
wagons-lits are always shocking!"

Presently the moonlight, flooding the further side of the
court, made him reflective. "This is what you call
romantic, *n'est-ce pas?*" he observed, waving his hand
at it.

"Quite right, my lad," said Touchy; "you've got it
in one."

"Now the romantic, for you, it promotes kissing, isn't
it?" pursued Henri.

"Rather crudely put, but broadly speaking, yes," Touchy replied.

"*Mais c'est vrai*," Henri went on. "I 'ave noticed this. For English people, moonlight makes them wish to kiss—it is romantic. *C'est curieux*," he pursued, in his monotonous voice. "I—I am not romantic. I do not wish to kiss *simplement à cause du clair de lune*. When there is moonlight, I will admire the moonlight—I will not kiss."

Laura could not help laughing.

"*Non, mais écoutez, Laura, c'est vrai, ce que je dis là. Vous autres Anglais, vous confondez*—mix up—two things. There are the beauties of Nature, and there are the pleasures of Love. *Tous deux sont bons*, but I will not mix them. Love goes better indoors."

Touchy exploded with laughter.

"But why is it, then, that you will mix them up?" Henri persisted, quite unperturbed; he was accustomed to being laughed at by Touchy. "*C'est idiot!*"

"I'll tell you," said Touchy, pulling himself together. "You're quite right; we have a romantic idea of love, and we like to bring all beautiful things, like nature and music and so on, into it."

"*Mais ça ne donne jamais rien de bon*," said Henri emphatically. "You forgive me, my dear Touchi, but the English are not good lovers. You make yourselves a fine theory of love and moonlight, yes, but your—'ow do you say?—practice, *ça fait pitié! En somme*, there are exceptions"—he nodded amicably at Touchy, to indicate that he was one, and no doubt an admirable lover—"*mais en fin de compte, toute femme française vous dira que c'est rasant, l'amour anglais!*"

"Sorry about that, old man," said Touchy amiably.

Henri, with his quick courtesy, was instantly apologetic. "My dear Touchi, you do not mind what I say? You knoh 'ow I talk! *Mais, admettons, c'est la théorie*

qui cloche! You see, I read your English books, and I
knoh what it is, the theory. You will 'ave the impossible; you will love only one woman, and marry 'er,
and be faithful to 'er always, and live 'appy ever after.
N'est-ce pas?"

"That's about the idea," said Touchy, lighting
another cigarette.

"*Mais je vous assure que c'est impossible!"* said Henri
vigorously. "And you pretend to possess 'er 'eart and
mind; you will be like one person. *Cela n'arrive jamais,
mon ami.* 'Ow will you possess a woman's mind? 'Er
body, yes, but 'er mind? *Vous confondez toujours les choses.*
Women 'ave the intelligence very delicate, *on peut bien
s'en réjouir, et c'est par la conversation qu'il convient de com-
mencer—mais ce n'est pourtant pas l'amour, avouez-le!* And
when you will love a woman, you think always about 'er
mind, 'er 'eart—*mais vous ignorez l'essentiel, la façon de
s'y prendre, et la chose est râtée!"*

At this point Vinstead's tall, rather precise figure
entered the courtyard through the gate opposite and
crossed the moonlit square, his black shadow following
him over the pavement towards them. It broke up the
little party. "Midnight, by Jove!" said Touchy, looking
at his watch.

As Laura went off to bed she was turning Henri's
words over in her mind. She remembered her talk with
the Professor on the way up, and how she had failed to
find a precise expression for the world the French do
not enter. Was it, perhaps, just the kingdom of romance?
Delache had thrown some light on the subject. She saw
the French attitude more clearly than ever as deliberate,
the fruit of an intellectual decision, and even containing
a certain rather arid wisdom. They refuse to mix
themselves up with the tears of things, she thought;
there are certain satisfactions which they value—good

food, good wine, conversation, women, intellectual activity—but they keep them all distinct, and they don't go chasing the impossible. It was clear to her also that Delache was right in this—the English do. "We want the impossible even when we know it to be the impossible; we go on being disappointed because we don't get it; in the midst of our disillusionment we hug our dreams." She thought of Derek. His trouble at the moment was just that he too had begun to want the impossible. Irish as he was, but with an English mother, he took, on the whole, very much the French point of view about life and the satisfactions it affords, especially women; but this carefully cultivated attitude was breaking down before a stronger emotional impulse, which worked on him in the way traditional to his race, and he was in the first throes of a struggle between the two. "It will probably beat him in the end," she thought; "if not with Judith, with someone else. The English can only love in one way, really. It's true that they can't love with complete success even in *that* way, but they can't be happy unless they are trying to. We would rather fail on our own lines than succeed on any others; we can never really get away from our traditions and our racial make-up." And because her mind was like that, she began to think about the difference between Venetian and Florentine painting as a parallel. Everything that the Venetians had in them to express, they expressed to perfection, a complete and consummate achievement. But the Florentine artists never finished with a subject—there is always about their pictures a sense of the "yet more," of some idea too great for them, striving for expression behind their finished work. "Yet shall there hover in their restless heads, some thought, some grace, some wonder at the least, which into words no virtue can digest," she muttered to herself. It was one of her outside shots in the way of ideas which Aubrey took up so readily, but hardly anyone else—she had learnt to suppress them in conversation as a rule. But it led her on to Aubrey. Curious, how the Professor had brought him to life in her thoughts—he had made her, to-day, meet Aubrey, so to speak, at every step her mind took. There was already between them, after one walk together, the beginnings of the same easy interchange of ideas.

On entering her pavilion she went to her bare chamber and lit the candle, passing as quietly as she could through the darkness of the central hall. A moment later Judith came tiptoeing in in her pyjamas, her hair in a cloud round her head.

"Laura, I simply *won't* sleep indoors to-night! What ages you've been! Can't we take our beds out?"

"The men are all over the courtyard," said Laura.

"The terrace, then—let's go on to the terrace!"

Laura was aware of a certain urgency in Judith's voice, and realised that this was one of the nights when youth must have its way—to thwart it in the interests of middle-aged comfort would be almost criminal.

"We must take our beds ourselves, then," she said resignedly. "The servants will have gone to bed."

But they had only got a few yards with Judith's bed when a figure in white came slippering softly across the courtyard—the ever-watchful Niu had observed their proceedings. He fetched a coolie, and their two beds were carried out and placed on the inner terrace under the white pine. Laura went back and undressed, then she went out to them.

Having once got their camp beds out of doors, it was impossible not to feel that it was worth while. The inner terrace lay utterly quiet under the moon, marked by sharp black pictures of the turret, the tablet, and the twisted yellow fir—even the bells of the little pagoda, silhouetted against the luminous sky, dangled a second time on the moonlit pavement. In under the white pine, where their beds were, the shadows were deep—only a fleck or two of white light lay like rags on the flag-stones; overhead, through the cold grey-white interlacing of the shadowed lower boughs, they could see the topmost branches shining golden in the strong moonlight.

"Golly, what a place!" breathed Judith unpoetically. "It was *divine* of you to bring us here."

"There's nowhere like Chieh T'ai Ssu," said Mrs. Leroy contentedly.

There was silence for a little while—then, "Laura, are you very sleepy?" inquired Judith's voice.

"No, not particularly," Laura replied, still under the compulsion of her feeling that this was Youth's Night Out.

"Then may I talk to you for a bit?"

"Yes, rather, do." And to emphasise her conversational mood she lit a cigarette. "Carry on!" she said. But the beginning was unexpected.

"What *exactly* did you mean when you said the other day that sincerity was rather over-rated?" Judith asked.

"Did I say so?"

"Oh yes—don't you remember? The day the picnic was arranged, when we'd been to the Summer Palace. We were talking about entertaining and people and all that, and then the Minister rang up, and you went away, and never finished."

Laura delved back into her memory with an effort, and did remember their talk to some extent. There had been—oh yes—some question of the sincerity or otherwise of entertaining people who bored one.

"I think I probably meant that in those anyhow

very superficial social relationships, it was a mistake to make such a fetish of sincerity as to let it cramp one's style," she said, choosing her words rather carefully.

"But you don't think it a mistake in more—*personal* relationships?" the girl pursued.

"No—I think it enormously important. But you know sincerity isn't a matter of words only."

"Oh no, I *know!*" said Judith, with conviction. "That's what's so difficult, partly. It's about Derek, of course. You've guessed that."

"More or less. Well, tell me about him."

"Well, you see, things are getting to a stage where almost everything one says or does seems to *count*; they're not just bricks in a heap any more—each thing is either building up or pulling down. Do you know?"

Laura did know. She recognised the mood of suspense fraught with a sort of exaltation—the sense of trivial words and actions being weighted with an almost terrifying significance.

"Are you finding sincerity difficult?" she asked.

"Not exactly—well yes, in a way. You see, *I'm* accustomed to it!" said Judith quaintly. "It's more. . . . Oh, Laura, I want to be *wise!*"

"Yes?" Laura waited for more.

"You see," the girl went on, "I think I understand now pretty well what he *is*—I mean I know he's accustomed to hareing round after various women all the time. But now there's *me*—and I have a sort of feeling that that is rather different, even for him—and even already. And that it might become *quite* different."

Laura thought this too, but she did not say so. She must keep the ring only—the girl must settle it alone.

"Yes, go on."

"Well, I think in a way I might rather *like* it to," Judith brought out in a burst. "But there are some

snags. I don't really want to—oh, reform him, as they
call it; he's so fearfully nice as he is, in lots of ways.
Only——" she paused. "Oh, surely, Laura, there *are*
more important things than sleeping with people? And
surely there's something in—well, in love itself that you
miss by just doing that, on and on? You see, when he
talks of love, he means *making* love, and to comparative
strangers at that—and that isn't what I mean by it a
bit."

"Yes, I see," said Laura. Judith needed very little
help, she felt. She had apparently only to show that she
was awake at intervals for it all to come pouring out.

"But then, I must be *wise*, somehow, to—oh, you *do*
see what I mean? If we——" she hesitated. "Well, if
we do go on, I should need to be *hideously* wise later,
because it will be a fearful job, obviously, for one woman
to satisfy him after so many. But you see, if I love him, I
shall *mind* if he goes after other women. And if I don't
love him, the whole thing's a wash-out. And if I love
him, I don't want him to be *satisfied* with a greedy sort
of love—and besides, he *isn't*, really."

Laura was struck by the last words. Judith had
managed to hit on the essential thing, Derek's dawning
comprehension of a way of love different to his own,
and his first stirrings of desire for it. This was the key
to the situation for her, if there was a key. She was
impressed, too, with the girl's courage in facing the
facts. Out of the jumble of italics and broken sentences
there emerged an attitude so valiant, so sensible and so
responsible as to command her respect. And Judith
had made no sort of inquiry as to Derek's attitude, she
noted with admiration. Her heart warmed to her
niece.

"Do you want it to go on?" she asked gently.

"Yes, I think so," said Judith thoughtfully. "I

believe I could take it on, really. If only I can be wise
enough. What I've been wondering is whether it would
be insincere to—well, to give him a certain amount of
rope just now; I mean, not always tell him how utterly
dud I think lots of his goings-on are. What do you
think?"

Laura found this rather difficult to answer. "Could
you tell me a little more what you mean?" she asked.

"Oh yes," said Judith readily. "Well, for instance,
he was telling me only yesterday about how amusing
someone was—that terrible little Miller creature we see
dancing at the hotel sometimes; how at one party she
held her dress and let them pour champagne into her
cami-knickers at the top and catch it in a wineglass
when it came out at the bottom. And I said I really
didn't know whether it was *more* silly or more disgusting.
Because *really*, Laura!" She paused for a moment, "We
can't go on quarrelling *all* the time," she wound up.

"Aren't you ever at peace?" Laura asked.

"Oh yes—sometimes it's quite heavenly; mostly when
we just sit and don't talk much. But you see he wants
to do it all by—by touch, as it were—no, not as it were,
as it is," said the girl, with a little nervous laugh that
came out with the effect of a sob. "He says, if only I
would stay quiet and not keep on thinking and fidgeting,
we should find out all about one another that way. But
I *can't* learn about people only through my body; some
of it I *must* do by talking and thinking. He says——"
She stopped, and when she spoke again Laura could
hear in her voice the strain of the compulsion she was
putting on herself to get it all out. "He says people
neglect much too much letting their bodies make friends,
and I expect he's right. Only that isn't *all* of it. So what
do you think?" she said again.

There were few things that Laura liked less than

acting as mentor. However, in this case the position was thrust on her, and she saw that there was no escape. Judith's extreme honesty and courage made her wish to help her if she could, and the tones of the girl's voice warned her that no superficial counsels would do—it had got to be first principles and the real thing.

"I am sure you are right to try to be as wise as you can," she said; "but you see already that no amount of wisdom will altogether resolve your difficulties with Derek, because they're there and they're genuine." She stopped and considered. "Something in him is fighting on your side—you've seen that too. Well, you must back that up."

"How do you mean?" Judith asked.

"Like this—don't think so much about picking holes in *his* point of view, but go on putting your own as well as you can. I don't only mean in words—just hold it in your mind." She paused, seeking the word that would give Judith what she needed, and then murmured, half to herself:

> "Love is swift of foot,
> Love's a man of war
> And can shoot
> And can hit from far."

"Say that again, will you?" said Judith as she ended. Laura did so, and there was silence from the other bed for a few minutes. Then she heard the girl say, on a deep breath, "Yes—that's what will do it, if anything will."

There was a longish pause, after that, before the girl's voice came again. "Laura!"

"Yes?"

"Suppose I do, and then in the end it's all a wash-out?"

"It won't matter," said Laura confidently.

"But I—what *do* you mean?"

"I mean your effort won't have been wasted. Love never is wasted—it's out of its nature to be wasted."

"Are you *sure*?"

"Absolutely. You aren't really afraid of it either. You aren't a miser."

"No-o-o—only it would be a little like having put one's shirt on an also-ran," said Judith a little hesitatingly.

"Never mind——" She sought for some way of expressing her strong conviction that the sacrifice of the shirt was at once all-important, and of no importance whatever, and fell back once more on words older and better than her own. "Listen—

> "That I spent, I had,
> That I gave, I have,
> That I kept, I lost."

She lay back, then, staring up at the illuminated topmost boughs of the white pine, wondering if she had found the right words after all. No sound came from Judith's bed for some time. But at last there was a sort of light creaking and shuffling, and Judith's figure stood over her.

"Good night!" she said quickly, gave her aunt a light kiss, and slipped back to bed. The cheek that had touched Laura's was wet.

Chapter Thirteen

SOME hours later Mrs. Leroy woke up, and looked, as the human habit is, at her watch. It was a quarter-past three. The moon, lower now, had swung round behind the shoulder of the hill, and the terrace lay in darkness, yet it was not quite dark—the sky looked as if flood-lighted from below by the hidden planet, and had lost the small stars; only the big ones burned like huge steady jewels in the illuminated heavens. There was as yet no sign of the dawn. She lay in the warm freshness of the late end of the night, listening to the complete and utter stillness. Suddenly across this stillness came the distant resonance of a drum—it stopped, and after an interval was repeated.

"Good heavens! They can't still be going on with that business," she thought lazily to herself; but as the drum sounded again and yet again, curiosity overcame her. Slipping quietly out of bed, she set off to see what was happening. In the dim light from the moon-washed sky she passed along the great terrace and out through the straggling courts beyond; but long before she reached the hall of ordination itself the sea-like alternating rise and fall of chanting, beating with the monotony of waves on the silence, told her that the ceremony was still in progress. On coming to the doorway she went quietly in and sat down on one of the benches as before, aware that according to Chinese ideas she was much more modestly and decorously dressed in her long nightgown and coat (or for the matter of that in jodhpurs) than in any short-skirted European dress.

She saw the seven richly robed figures still sitting round the altar, precisely as they had done five hours previously, chanting in their curious rhythm. In his shadowed corner the old black-robed tea-maker crouched by his brazier, beating at intervals on his drum. The crowd had disappeared, and Mrs. Leroy was the only onlooker. Leaning her head against the plastered wall she sat with half-closed eyes, listening. Old as time, regular as the alternation of night and day, incomprehensible as eternity, the music flowed round her, bearing her out into a strange impersonal region where ceremonies, religions, sacraments, all the ancient formalisations of human experience were seen in their true relation to little brittle human life, with its capricious individuality— at once its sum and its support. If the singers had been also in this remote world, she mused, for eight hours, they should indeed know their task, and be priests for ever after their own strange order.

A touch on her arm roused her. The old tea-maker stood at her side, and asked her the time. She showed him her watch—the hands marked five minutes to four. Indicating the hour on the tiny dial with a yellow finger, "*Tou wan-la!*" (All finish) he said. Mrs. Leroy took the hint, and left the pavilion. A change had come over the light since she went in—the stars were fewer and fainter, and a creeping greyness was mixing with the dying moonshine. A light fresh wind had sprung up, heralding the invisible dawn—she shivered, felt cold and small, chilled within by the bleak immensities into which her mind had been borne by the music, chilled without by the unearthly light and the cold breath of daybreak. Muffling herself closely in her coat she hurried back along the terrace, and crept into bed again.

When she next woke the day was fully come. The

first thing she saw as she opened her eyes was the brilliant sunlight splintering off the long needles of the white pine overhead, and glowing warm and golden on the chalky upper branches. Lying on her back, staring idly up at it, she became aware of a sensation of pleasure, like a warmth, stealing through her; a sensation which somehow reminded her of Oxford. Curious! Her half-awakened mind rested lightly on this association, and so captured without destroying it. Yes!—the sunlight in the pine-needles reminded her of the way in which the low rays used to shoot level through the curtain-fringes above the window in those ugly rooms in Oxford where she stayed in the early days when she went to see Aubrey, and the faint sensation of pleasure to come which clung to that memory resembled her morning feelings with a day of Aubrey in prospect. And rousing herself to search her mind further, she found the Professor in it! She was looking forward, if ever so little, to a day which held opportunities of talking to him again. Smiling with an amused impatience at her folly she decided to get up and go for a walk. The time, her watch showed her, was nearly six. In the next bed Judith was still fast asleep, her cloud of fair hair gilded by the level sunlight, her face, tucked into the pillow like a child's, wearing that disarmed, rather innocent look, which sleep brings to maturer faces than hers. Mrs. Leroy stood looking down at her for a moment, and then slipped away to her own pavilion to dress.

In the courtyard the low sun, striking through a gap in the buildings, touched the group of peach trees about the well-head till the blossom burned with a fiery rose, as if incandescent. She stood still to look at it, in a sort of wonder; then her eye fell on the three sleeping figures, still hunched log-like under the trees in their camp beds, and with a little laugh she went into her own room.

The pavilion, with its non-conducting paper lattices, still held the stuffy warmth of yesterday's heat, and she was glad after a rapid toilet to escape again into the freshness outside. Cool without chill, shot with sunlight, strong and delicately heady as a fine white wine, the air bathed her body through her thin clothes as she walked along the terrace, and thrilled her nerves with a quickening intoxication. The air of North China has this peculiar quality of causing nervous stimulation, which produces quite definite results—the unfortunate social phenomenon known throughout China as "Peking quarrels" is one. Newcomers are particularly affected by it. There comes a lightness, a nimbleness of mind and body, and a sort of emotional exaltation in which the most unusual behaviour seems possible, normal, and delightful. Old hands know this, and are prepared for it and for the depressing reactions which follow, but they feel it nevertheless.

Mrs. Leroy was aware of it now as she left the monastery by the main gateway and followed a small path which led up towards the crest of the ridge behind it. Spring morning though it was, the hill-side was wintry in aspect, once she had risen above the level of the fruit trees; the coarse tufts of last year's grass, yellow against the black shaly soil, left no pattern of dew on her shoes (there is no dew in North China), and the sere leaves of autumn still clung to the low scrub of dwarf oaks and crataegus, making a dry metallic rustling as the light air stirred them. Reaching the ridge, she turned and looked back. Chieh T'ai Ssu lay below her now, visible only as a collection of fantastic roofs: jade-green roofs, golden ones, roofs of amber and plum-colour; square, round, oblong; fluted, convoluted, tiered—but each lifting its edges to the sky in delicate curves, like skirts swung by the wind or by swift movement. And these roofs with their dancing eaves, jewel-like in colour, fantastic as a ballet in shape, stood up out of a sea of fruit-blossom, out of a pink and white foam which eddied like spindrift among and between their fluted curves. She had left spring behind in the temple.

She wandered on up the bare ridge, and sat down on a rock at a high point of it. Below her the Peking plain was spread out in the morning light, an expanse of fawn-colour fading into blue—the city itself lay under the sun, and invisible, its position only indicated by the curious outline of the great Dagoba, which stood up like an immense scent-bottle, white as a peppermint, from the dusty dazzle of the plain. So she might sit, so she had often sat, looking down on Oxford. Oxford!—the very name, out here, was like a chime of its own bells, pealing out into the blue mist that hangs forever over the spired city in the plain, pencilled with the outline of tower and dome, as one sees it from above—from Shotover, from Horsepath Hill, from Cumnor or Headington or Sto-wood. Oxford was haunting her mind that morning, after her curious waking memory of it, and she began to think of all her friends there, and then of all the friend-ships Oxford had ever known, from the great classical ones that got into the books, like those of Colet and More and Erasmus, right down to to-day—eager friend-ships of undergraduates; sober friendships, mellow as vintages with age and wisdom, of dons and learned men. And the gay friendships, spiced with amusement, of men and women together. Her fancy, picturing the visible city of stone as she had so often seen it, saw also for a moment a second city, built of these insubstantial yet enduring relationships, these airy edifices of the affec-tions—as varied, rich, and beautiful as the other, and as ancient. Lovely and permanent, it would stand for ever. She sighed, thinking of the ease and integrity, in

that city, of the meeting of friend with friend, and contrasting with it the artificiality of so many social encounters in Peking—the farce of calling, of receiving
cards left in a box at your gate; the long dull dinners,
the fuss over precedence, looking up people's correct
order at table in a book, as you might look up trains in a
Bradshaw. She was lucky, she lived in a little oasis of
amiable affectionate people, Touchy and Derek and the
Neviles; but compared with the riches and variety of
intercourse at home it was so little. Something—Judith's
talk the other day, partly, perhaps, and perhaps partly
the Professor's conversation, had suddenly made her
homesick for her own friends; she realised afresh how
that side of her went always half-starved, out here.

An isolated dwarf oak tree stood just below her—its
shapely dead leaves, each nearly a foot long, cut a curious
brown pattern on the view, threw singular elongated
patterns of blue shadow on her very feet, in their white
string-soled shoes. As she stared at it with idle concentration something in the strangeness of those leaves, so
impossible in England, roused her to a peculiarly sharp
sense of the division in her life. The next time she
looked down on Oxford from Shotover, she would
remember that oak tree! And *this* would seem reality,
this and no other, and England would be the dream;
and for this she would then be homesick. She knew it
well. She would be suffocated again by England's
smallness and muffling greenness, maddened by its
petty irrational humps and hollows, after the masterly
geometrical flatness of the China plain; oppressed by
its grey dripping skies, after that high light firmament
in which the sun glitters like a burnished shield from
dawn till evening for nine months of the year. The very
people in the streets and lanes would vex her eye by their
ugly parti-coloured ungraceful clothes, after the beauti-

ful universal blue garments of the Chinese country-side, the dignified grey and black robes of the towns. And her friends even, her best and dearest, after asking inquisitively whether she knew Wang or Tu personally, and whether China wasn't very "dangerous," having listened politely to her replies would presently go on to tell her what a good round of golf they had had at Walton last week. No—it was too difficult, it was impossible; she could never make the two halves of her life fuse and fit properly. People should live only one life, and not two—otherwise, in both one was divided, uncertain, incomplete. And in a flash of understanding she realised suddenly *why* Anglo-Indians congregate in places like Cheltenham, and old China hands frequent the Thatched House Club—it is in a forlorn attempt to keep their most important reality alive and intact.

Restless, she rose and wandered on, till she reached an isolated spur that stood out into the plain, separated from the main ridge by a narrow saddle. From here she could see the line of mountains swinging round to the north-west, shading away into infinite distance. You must go three hundred miles through those mountains to find plains again, and then they are the rolling uplands fringing the Gobi Desert. Feeling in her pocket for her cigarette-case, she pulled out a letter—it was from Aubrey, left there accidentally from yesterday. She read it again. Aubrey rebuked her, gloomily if kindly, for not writing enough, for writing trivially when she did write; and she remembered that other letters of yesterday's mail, now lying in the pavilion, complained in various ways of the same thing. It was true—she had written little lately, and badly; she had felt oppressed and discouraged by the hopelessness of trying to keep in touch with people by letter, over ten thousand miles of distance. And standing there, on her hill-top, regarding the shadowy mountains, she had a sudden vision of those leagues beyond leagues dividing her from those she loved best. Her mind flew in the sky like a bird—over the Central Asian wastes, empty and silent, over mountains, over the bare Persian uplands, and the green shores of the Caspian; over Europe, murmurous with population and smoky with manufactures, to the narrow ribbon of the Channel, with little England a dark speck on the silver ocean beyond. Over England the smoke was thicker, and the murmur rose to a roar, in which single voices could be heard clearly, raised in complaint: Tim's and Sarah's, high and shrill, Aubrey's deep and gloomy, Grand-mère's piping faintly, Rachel's and Richard's flat and definite—all rebuking her, the distant Laura; loved, but careless, inadequate, forgetful.

The line of mountains grew more shadowy, wavered, and swam before her, as the tears of depression started to her eyes. And at that moment a near living voice hailed her cheerfully with, "Good morning, Mrs. Leroy." She looked round, and there on the narrow saddle stood the Professor, as much like Bond Street as ever in his neat suit.

> "'Margery Brown on the top of the hill,
>   Why are you standing, idle still?'"

he declaimed as he came up to her. "Do you know that?" he went on, after a glance at her face. "I always think it stamps Kate Greenaway as one of our better poets. You remember how it goes on?

> "'Oh, the night is come, but I can't go down,
>   For the bells ring strangely in London Town.'

There's a marvellous sense of mystery in that. You put me in mind of Margery Brown when I saw you standing here."

Laura smiled. In spite of her natural irritation at being found in tears (which would have been even greater if she had known that it was for the second time) Vinstead brought her a curious feeling of relief; she had a sudden sense that in a way he rather combined her two worlds, bringing the "home-side" fashion of easy intercourse out on to this Chinese hill.

"I think I was really listening to the bells of London Town," she said, falling in with his whim.

"You looked as though you were listening to something. You very often do, do you know? I have noticed you several times; you look as though you were hearing something a long way off, and were quite unaware of us all about you. Is it always the bells of London Town you are listening to?" he asked her, as they strolled back along the saddle towards the ridge. "Are you very homesick?"

The simple question, the direct tone of kindness, increased Laura's sense of comfort.

"It isn't really homesickness," she said; "it's being one person in two lives. You see I go home fairly often—the children are there." He noticed that her voice sank a tone or two on the last words. "So I can't really settle down in this life, though I love it in a way—and of course I can't settle down in the other, because I live mostly in this one. So I am in two halves all the time." It sounded extraordinarily lame and foolish to her as she said it, and she wished she hadn't tried—she felt suddenly tired, and more than ever inclined to cry.

"Did you have anything to eat before you came out?" Vinstead asked abruptly.

"No."

"Well, have some chocolate now." He produced some from his pocket. "Let's sit on this rock." They sat. "Your admirable servant brought me some tea when he saw me stirring," he went on. "Why didn't you have some?"

"I came out at six," said Mrs. Leroy.

"Good heavens! It's eight o'clock now. You must be fainting. I wish you would tell me more about your in-halfness," he went on, as he plied her with chocolate. "I think I can understand it. It struck me as I walked out this morning that the mere physical and visual strangeness of all one's surroundings out here, though it is stimulating, must in a way put an unconscious strain on Europeans who are sensitive to such things. And most of us are sensitive to them to some extent. Do you feel that? Or does one get over it after years?"

"I did at first, tremendously," said Laura, startled at his comprehension; she remembered how only the day before, on the bluff above the river, she had been thinking of this very thing.

"That oak tree!" he went on, pointing to another of the dwarf oaks which stood in front of them. "Look at those leaves! They're so portentous as to be almost sinister. There isn't a single familiar thing here for the eye to rest on, or the mind to anchor by. I find it very tiring; I feel like a specimen suspended in a bottle, cut off from everything that is my natural habitat. But you get over that, do you, in time?"

"Yes, I think one does—I have even got to love all this, and to—oh, live on it, you know." He nodded. "In fact, when I do go home——" She went on to tell him how in England China seemed the reality, and she became homesick for that, irrational as it must seem. But to the Professor it appeared that it did not seem irrational, but quite normal, and to her surprise she found herself telling him about all the aspects of this duality in her life, including the aridity of social inter-course and how she missed her friends. He was so sympathetic, and the relief of expressing herself was so great that it was some time before the thought darted into her mind that he might be studying her as a "case." When it did, she had recovered her tone, and turned round on him merrily with, "As a psychologist, you ought to be able to suggest a cure!"

"I don't think there is a full cure," he said, smiling back at her, but his voice was sober. "Of course to sit lightly to life always helps, and in your case you have to sit lightly to two lives—but I rather think you do that."

Too lightly, Laura said—one of her complaints was that she tended to become absent-minded about her daily occupations.

"Yes, perhaps, but never about essentials, I feel sure," he said. "You see," he went on, "the only unifying point in your two lives is you yourself. That is inevitable. And the more you can—do you know what I mean by integrate?—well, the more you can *unify* yourself, the nearer you bring your two lives together, and the easier it becomes to live them both harmoniously. There is no other way." He stopped, and lit for her the cigarette she had taken from her case. "Of course," he went on, "some overwhelming compulsion, either of emotion or conviction, will sometimes do the unifying trick completely—a great faith or a great passion. But in any case, the point where the stresses of contending forces meet will always be in yourself, like the point in a building where two opposite thrusts meet. And like a good architect, you must just make that point strong." He rose, and stood looking down at her with a very pleasant expression on his face. "I am sure it is pretty strong," he said. "But in the interests of strength I think you ought to come and have some breakfast," he added. "It's after half-past eight."

As they walked back to the temple they caught sight,

on the terrace below them, of Derek and Judith strolling along together.

"I don't think that young man is so deeply asleep but what he might wake up one of these days," observed Vinstead, indicating Derek with his walking-stick. "I was looking at him last night, and thinking of what you said. Did you notice him while Miss Milne was singing?"

"No—I mean yes," said Laura vaguely—she had been thinking of the Professor's words on her own problem, and was now too startled by this fresh instance of his noticing exactly the things she noticed to pay attention at once to what he was saying.

He looked at her with amusement. "Mrs. Leroy, this is getting serious! I am sure you did notice."

"Yes, I did, and I agree," said Laura laughing.

"I am not at all sure that the same applies to the little American girl, though," he continued. "I very much doubt whether she has the capacity for living any but the most instinctive sort of life."

"Oh, do you really think so? You don't think perhaps circumstances might wake her up?"

"I am not sure that it would be good for her even if they did," he said thoughtfully. "There are people, you know, who can live quite satisfactorily on what is practically the instinctive plane, but if they are roused to that fuller consciousness of which we were speaking yesterday, they may be almost maimed in the process, and go halt ever afterwards. In such cases to attempt to 'wake them up,' as you call it, is cruel as well as useless."

"But would it be wrong to try to wake up the half-and-halfs, like Mr. Fitzmaurice?" Laura asked, thinking of her talk with Judith overnight.

"Interfering with other people's characters or souls is always a very dubious business, I think," he answered, "except of course by interested parties like wives and husbands, who can't help doing it to some extent. But if anyone is a suitable subject for it I should say that young man is! And I should say he was likely to get it, from what I have seen of your niece!" he added, with the quick grin which Laura had liked from the outset. "But I am not so happy about Miss Ingersoll. I should be afraid of her getting more rousing than is good for her from the Frenchman."

They had reached the terrace now, and saw the party, including Henri and Miss Ingersoll, gathering round the tables under the leaning pine at the further end.

"Poor Annette!" said Laura, as they approached, and the girl, radiant in her summer frock, waved to them. "I wonder what the way out for her will be."

"There always is a way out, though not always an agreeable one," said the Professor.

Chapter Fourteen

THE first breakfast of any party in any Chinese Temple is always spent in comparing notes of the night. The party at Chieh T'ai Ssu was no exception. While they ate their grape-fruit, the General inquired politely of Miss Hande whether she had slept well.

"Why, I *have* slept more profoundly in my time," replied that lady, "but I didn't feel any way disagreeably. I would say there isn't a great deal of ventilation in those pavilions."

"No, it was horribly stuffy," said Mrs. Nevile. "It was really a mercy you three went to the other pavilion," nodding at Laura and the two Milnes.

"Air at night is quite unnecessary," said the General firmly. "The Chinese are perfectly right about that."

"Did you 'ave any rats in your room?" Henri asked Laura.

"I slept out there," she said, pointing to the inner terrace door behind the tables.

"Ow, you were outside too! Well, I 'ave not slept well outside. I do not think it is the air," to General Nevile, "I think it is the camp bed."

Sleeping in a camp bed was a trick, Touchy declared— he for his part slept better in one than in anything else.

Vinstead turned to Lilah, who as usual was eating in complete silence, and asked her how she had passed the night.

"Oh, all right," she answered. "There were a few rats, but I don't mind them."

"*Comment?* You 'ave 'ad rats in your room?" exclaimed Henri. "Nina! Laura!—listen! She 'as 'ad rats—your boy is quite right."

"Oh no, Miss Milne, surely not!" said Nina. "What makes you think there were rats?"

"Because I heard a scrabbling on the matting, and switched on my torch, and there were five of them sitting eating biscuits on the *k'ang* by me," said Lilah tranquilly.

"Heavens! What did you do?" asked Derek.

"Threw a slipper at them and went to sleep again," said Lilah, and returned unconcernedly to her kidney omelette.

After breakfast Laura and Nina and Miss Hande strolled along the inner terrace and sat in the little turret at the end. It was already warm, and the sun brought out the aromatic resinous smell of the white pine, and the faint nutty scent of the fruit-blossom below the terrace wall. They chatted idly, with that pleasant sense of independence which older women have when they draw together from the younger elements of a mixed party.

"Well, Anna, are our two couples providing you with plenty of material for your next book?" asked Mrs. Nevile presently, with her engaging wide smile.

"Why no, I wouldn't say they are," replied Miss Hande. "I find young people's love affairs a most difficult subject for treatment."

"Are older people's easier?" Laura asked.

"Oh, surely—incomparably so."

"But why, Anna?" Nina inquired.

"I can hardly tell you," replied Miss Hande honestly. "But I would say it's because young people's love is too simplified to be interesting, perhaps."

"What do you mean?" asked Laura, interested.

"Why, when young things are in love, they're just plain crazy about one another, and that's all there is to it, as a rule," said the novelist, fixing her lorgnette on Mrs. Leroy. "It's all new to them, and it fills the world, but to outsiders they're just as alike as birds in spring. But when older people fall in love there are all sorts of cahmplicated forces and elements in the situation, and it makes a much richer material."

"Go on, Anna; this is rather thrilling," said Mrs. Nevile. "What sort of forces?"

"Why, it's like this," said Miss Hande, turning her lorgnette now on Nina. "Take our two couples here. They're just being drawn together by some instinct, and there's nothing to hinder it. But if you, or Mrs. Leroy here, were to fall in love, you'd be pulled two ways, or three, by extraneous considerations, and so there would be some drama to the situation."

"Indeed there *would*!" said Nina gaily. Laura said nothing.

"Even when older men and women who aren't married fall in love," pursued Miss Hande, "they have much richer natures and a wider experience than the young folk have, and so you get emotional reactions of intrinsic value."

"I wonder how often older people *do* fall in love," said Laura thoughtfully.

"Freely, I should say," said Miss Hande.

"They say round about forty is the dangerous age," laughed Nina. "You're nearly there, my dear"—she nodded at Laura—"you must look out!"

"I don't believe that is universal by any means," said Laura. "I think women round about forty tend to go in for one of two things, lovers or detachment—but quite as often detachment as the other. What do you think?" she asked Miss Hande.

"Well, that's an entirely new viewpoint," said the novelist. "You may be right. And what would you say determines the *direction* of their interest?"

"Oh, how they have spent their thirties!" said Mrs. Leroy, with a little wintry smile of irony. She got up. "I am interested in detachment," she added.

Nina pealed with laughter, like a run of little bells. Miss Hande hadn't quite got there, and before she did Mrs. Leroy had wandered away towards the outer terrace.

"Why has she gone off?" Miss Hande asked, looking after her tall figure rather regretfully.

"Oh, Laura's always slipping through one's fingers like that," said Nina airily.

"*Has* she had many lovers?" the novelist inquired, her lorgnette still fixed on Laura's retreating figure.

"None that one ever heard of," said Mrs. Nevile. "Lots of people have been devoted to her—she has that sweet lovely way with her, and she's a marvellous friend— but she has always seemed too fastidious for anything of the sort. I can always imagine her, when anyone makes her a declaration, telling them it's so nice of them to mention it, but she happens to have an engagement!" The silvery peal of laughter came again. "And of course she's terribly absorbed in her children."

"How old is she, actually?"

"Thirty-seven."

"You surprise me! I wouldn't have thought her much more than thirty. Of course her mind is very mature, but the mind is immortal, I guess," said Miss Hande blandly. "I would like to know her history," was her final comment.

Meanwhile Laura had been annexed by Touchy for a stroll. Touchy had so far seen very little of her on the picnic, and was inclined to feel slightly defrauded. He was not therefore overpleased when Professor Vinstead after a short time joined them, and asked whether, if they were looking at the temple, he might be shown it too? The three of them wandered about, visiting various shrines where the images of Buddha sat solemnly in front of formal flat curtains of yellow brocade. Priests in grey thrust little aromatic sticks of incense into their hands, which they obediently stood in the powdery sweet-smelling ashes of the incense-burners and lit with a taper. These burners, mostly shallow bowls on three feet, stood on long narrow tables before the images, between superb vases and ornaments; here and there little offerings of painted cakes, which looked like marzipan, were piled among them. These caught the Professor's eye, and he asked if they were edible.

"Oh yes," Laura told him.

"Who does in point of fact eat them, Laura—do you know?" Touchy asked. "One often sees other food offered too—what becomes of it all?"

"The priests eat it," Laura answered. "The Abbot at T'ien T'ai Shan told me all about it once. He said that Buddha took the spiritual essence of the food, and then the priests ate the material remainder. And he said that one must never give such offerings to children, because to nourish them properly they need the spiritual essence of the food as well as the other. Isn't that rather nice?"

"Yes, it's what Miss Hande would call a 'beautiful idea,'" said Touchy, as he felt in his pockets for a small coin to give to the attendant priest. Laura was a little chilled, and on leaving the shrine they walked for a time in silence. At the Professor's suggestion they went up one of the broad flights of steps towards the upper levels of the monastery, treading interminable shallow marble stairs splashed with shade. They found themselves presently on another terrace, flanked by an imposing shrine with a richly-carved latticed front. Henri and Little Annette were sitting on the steps of this shrine, deeply engaged in conversation—the girl, Laura thought, looked a little puzzled and strained, as if disturbed by something. Laura and her two companions leant on the balustrade, and looked down at the scene below—the roofs, peeps of the great terrace between the trees, and their own courtyard spread out like a plan beneath them. The balustrade was warm to the touch—it was getting hot, and they were glad to rest after the ascent; they were silent, slightly embarrassed at having unwittingly intruded on the seated pair, but unable to leave forthwith, slightly ill-assorted as a trio.

A voice from behind disturbed them—Judith's clear voice. "We *must* find someone! Oh, there's Laura! Splendid! She'll be able to talk to him."

They turned round. From the opened doors of the shrine they saw Judith and Derek emerging, followed by a priest, who pursued them with earnest gestures of explanation.

"He wants something, and we *can't* find out what it is," said the girl as she approached. "Come on, Laura." She gave her aunt's arm a little tug.

Laura spoke to the priest, and then turned to the others.

"It's the shrine where they do a sort of fortune-telling," she said. "He only wants to know if you wish to have your fortunes told."

"Oh yes, come on, do let's!" said Judith. Henri and Annette joined them, and the whole party entered the shrine. The bonze carefully closed the doors behind them, and they stood in the cool gloom, heavy with the smell of incense, before a small and rather unimposing

Buddha, seated as usual behind a long narrow table full of incense-burners and ornaments.

Judith was first. The bonze, having extracted fifty cents from her, handed her some sticks of incense, which she lit and placed at his direction in the central burner. From the table he then took a tall bronze vase full of narrow slips of bamboo, whose ends only projected an inch above the rim, and holding it almost horizontally, waved it round in a circle till one of the slips fell out. He replaced the slip and handed it out to her.

"You must do it yourself," Laura murmured. The girl did so. The slips were about fifteen inches long, and though the projecting ends were exactly alike, lower down they were inscribed with characters. The bonze took the one which fell out and read it out to her. "What does he say?" Judith inquired.

"He says, 'Many children bring wealth,'" said Laura. She took the slip from the bonze and examined the characters, in the dim light. "It isn't the usual word for children," she said. "It really says, 'Offspring of your creation,' as near as I can make it out." She handed it back to the bonze. "Those will be your songs, perhaps," she said, smiling at Judith.

"Certainly ordinary children are more apt to consume wealth than to bring it," observed Vinstead.

"Now who's for truth at fifty cents?" said Touchy. Henri stepped forward with his coin. "I 'ope 'e does not refer always to children, this Boudha," he murmured in an aside to Touchy, who giggled. But when Henri's slip was read out it appeared that he did. "The children of the virtuous bring no anxiety." Derek and Touchy burst out laughing.

"Now who?" said Laura, laughing too. "You, Derek?"

"Not I!" said Derek firmly, amid general mirth. "That fellow"—he indicated the impassive Buddha—"seems to have an *idée fixe* about the rising generation; I won't trust him with my private life."

Annette, however, was eager to know her fortune. She burned her incense, and rather hesitatingly shook out her slip. "Go on—perhaps you'll keep a crèche!" Derek urged her. The priest's face seemed to deepen in inscrutability as he read it—slowly, with a barely perceptible gesture of negation, he handed it to her, and let his eyes rest on her in a long strange stare.

"What is it, Mrs. Leroy?" the girl asked.

"It's a curious one—it tells you very little," said Laura, examining the slip. "This is as near as I can get to it—'Enlightenment shall escape her'—or him, of course—'but Death enlightens all men.'" Her eyes met Vinstead's as she handed back the slip, and a quick gleam of intelligence passed between them; she knew that he was thinking of the same thing as she was—their conversation about Annette before breakfast.

"Another glimpse of the obvious!" was Touchy's comment.

"Oh, they're nearly always these moralising saws and proverbs," said Laura lightly. She saw that Annette was a little dissatisfied with her fortune, and could not herself help being struck rather disagreeably by its appositeness. "Does anyone else want theirs done? It's very stuffy in here."

"Yes. I must see whether he knows what my bad joss is to be," said Vinstead. "He ought to, as it's all in his line of business." He lit the joss-sticks and shook his slip out briskly.

But his fortune was also rather uninformative. "The wise shall find wisdom, but the traveller will journey with a heavy heart," Laura read out.

"Well, he's spotted your profession, anyhow," remarked Derek.

"Is that *exactly* what it says?" Vinstead asked, peering first at the slip and then at Laura.

"It's the best translation I can make," she said. "Of course they have no tenses in Chinese, as you know. As a matter of fact, I think I've heard that one before—the real meaning is that wisdom, or too much of it, may be rather a burden, I suppose."

"Aren't you going to hear yours?" he asked her.

"I? No!" she said emphatically.

"Why not, Laura?" Judith asked.

"When you have given hostages to Fortune you don't want to hear her views," said Mrs. Leroy lightly—but Vinstead saw a fleeting expression cross her face, as of one who winces from some hidden pain. As they left the pavilion, "The image was rather on the spot about our little friend, wasn't he?" he murmured in her ear.

Outside, the party dispersed, vaguely. Mrs. Leroy wished to read, and allowed Touchy to fetch her a cushion and a book; when they were brought, declining all offers of company, she climbed higher still to a tiny courtyard where one deeply-coloured double cherry bloomed between two memorial tablets. She settled herself down in the shade behind one of these, her back against the cool marble, and rested. A troop of black ants was crossing and re-crossing the pavement within a few inches of her, treading busily over the pitted surfaces of the paving-stones, laden with mysterious burdens of eggs, grubs, and unknown substances; she watched them idly, sure that while intent on their house-moving they would not leave their high-road to molest her. She was a little tired after her disturbed night and early walk—it was pleasant to be quiet, and alone, in the hot sunny stillness of the little courtyard, lulled by the soft

industrious murmur of the bees in the flowering cherry,
amused by the industrious activities of the sturdy ant
community. The great thing about Chieh T'ai Ssu was
that you could always get away from people—it was so
intricate, and so big. Perfect for love-making, she
thought with a smile, and began to wonder how Judith
was getting on with the practice of wisdom.

An hour later she was still sitting there, contented and
rested—her mind half on Judith, she was singing "Fain
would I change that note" softly to herself. As the song
ended, a shadow fell on the pavement in front of her,
and looking round she saw Derek. He plumped himself
down unceremoniously beside her in the narrow patch
of shade.

"Sing that again, will you?" was his only salutation.

Laura did so. When it was over he sat silent for a few
minutes. She saw that he was in a restless worried state.
Suddenly he whipped round on her with one of his
brusque movements. "Laura, do you believe all that?"

"I know it," she said.

"She sang it like a prophetess last night," he murmured. "She made it sound true. 'Where truest
pleasure is'—hm?" he said interrogatively, cocking his
head at her.

"Yes, truest pleasure is there, Derek dear."

"Have *you* found it, yourself? You and Henry?"
His voice was urgent.

"Yes, I and Henry—and others," she added
honestly. There are times, and she knew this to be
one, when only an extremity of honesty will serve.

"Oh, so you have known change then?" he said, looking at her curiously. "I've always wondered about you
—and about people like you altogether. But they never
will tell one the truth, so how is one to know? There's
always this pretence about marriage and the great love

of a lifetime being one and the same thing," he said irritably. "Is Henry the great love of your lifetime?" he asked her abruptly, but not ungently.

"He's one of the three," said Laura. Something in the quaint moderation of the tone and statement made Derek laugh.

"Oh, Laura darling, you are priceless! Tell me about the other two, and how you made it all work, will you? Were they before Henry, or after?"

"One was before. We were engaged, and he was drowned yachting." She spoke in the same even tone. "Then three years later I married Henry. The other one was after."

"Well, what about him? He's the one that matters. Were you faithful to Henry, technically, when he came along?" he said, turning to look at her. His black spaniel's hair was rumpled up, his blue eyes inquiring, insistent. Again the thought of Tim darted unbidden into Laura's mind. She would want anyone to tell Tim the truth, if he should ever feel obliged to ask such a question.

"No, I wasn't, for a time," she answered slowly, meeting his eyes steadily.

"Oh, bless you!" said Derek. "I knew you'd be honest. Did Henry know?"

"No!" she said emphatically. "That would have been the most senseless cruelty."

"And then you chucked it?" he said thoughtfully.

"Then I chucked being his mistress," she said; her voice grew cold and hard on the ugly word. "I didn't chuck him."

Derek pondered over it. "Well, there you are," he said at length. "Even you haven't stuck to one person."

"I don't know why you should say 'even' me," said Laura rather sadly; "lots of people might."

"I say 'even' you because you're the most honourable person I've ever met, and the most unselfish," he said, turning to her again. And suddenly he lifted one of her hands and kissed it. The quick gesture brought the tears to Laura's eyes.

"Rubbish!" she said, nevertheless. "That's because you hardly know any nice people. But, Derek, 'even' I"—she gave a little unsteady laugh—"though I've loved three people, I've been—well, *permanent* with them."

"What do you mean?" he asked.

"I haven't been promiscuous." Again her voice hardened on the word. "I've never stopped loving any of them. I think that's the important thing. There must be what lawyers call the *animus manendi*—the intention of permanence."

"Even if it's bound to fail?"

"Yes, even if it's bound to fail. It's an essential condition, somehow or other; you can't get the real thing without making your surrender to that." Her voice grew dreamy—it was extraordinary, he thought involuntarily, how her voice changed with her thought; really a conversation with her was almost like listening to a piece of music. "It's the key to the 'fair house of joy and bliss,'" she murmured, half to herself.

They sat silent, then, for some time, but Derek's frowning face and irritable twiddling of Laura's cigarette-case, which he had picked up off the pavement, showed that he was deep in difficult thought.

"My God, I *do* wish I knew if it would work!" he burst out at last. "I see it's real enough to you, but would it ever be for me? You've got to have that *animus manendi*, I suppose, before you propose? I half want to marry her, and yet I'm terrified of the idea."

"Why don't you talk to her about it?" said Laura.

"Tell her how you've been accustomed to live and what you're afraid of, and see what you make of it together. I think you'll find she'll understand."

"Propose, you mean?"

"No, certainly not. You must learn to love before you try to marry. Tell her why you're afraid to propose."

"Would that be fair to her?" he said doubtfully.

"Much fairer than dawdling on making love to her, as you've been doing, without any explanation," said Laura, with decision.

"It seems a damnably odd thing to do," he observed slowly, still unconvinced. "And bloodily difficult. Do you really mean *tell* her about my life? And argue it all out? She might never look at me again."

"Try it on," Laura reiterated. "My dear, she *knows* most of it—she isn't an imbecile. You needn't be luridly detailed, but the one thing you *must* be is honest."

"H'm. Well, you've set me an example of that, wisest of lilies," he said, getting up. He stood looking down at her. "I'll try it on, since you say so. Bless you!" He held out his hand to pull her up. "Come on—there's Touchy's whistle. That's lunch."

Chapter Fifteen

AT lunch Derek did not sit by Judith, according to what was becoming a custom, but by Mrs. Leroy, making himself very agreeable—a piece of insight and courtesy which touched her considerably. Judith sat between Touchy and the Professor, and Laura was again struck by her curious air of strength and assurance, which seemed to deepen from hour to hour. She was talking to the Professor about psychology—catechising him, rather, as to how one set about being a psychologist. "But what's the *main* thing? Is it spinning theories out of your own inside like a spider, or collecting little lumps of facts about people like a magpie?" Vinstead laughed heartily at this rather unflattering comparison, but proceeded nevertheless to explain at some length what one actually *did* do. Laura noticed how, in spite of her rather ingenuous way of expressing herself, the girl succeeded in really making him talk, and talk well, on his own subject, by the sheer force of her spontaneous interest. It was the same thing, later on, with La Touche, who sat on her other side. From psychology the talk swung round to music, of which Touchy, for all his rather Guardee appearance, was passionately fond; and here again Judith, on her own ground this time, drew out his interest and his contribution to the subject till he talked in a way not unknown to Laura, but sufficiently unusual to make Nina raise her pretty eyebrows, and the General to fix his eyeglass on him in a long amused stare. What a sure touch on people the girl had, she thought, in spite of her youth. It was her *actuality*, of course, and her own quite violent interest in people and things that was the key to it. And glancing round the table she suddenly noticed Annette Ingersoll also watching Judith, with a curiously wistful expression on her pretty inexpressive face—so much prettier than the English girl's, but so wholly without the life, the shooting play of expression from feature to feature which put Laura in mind of the flight of a swallow, sometimes, as she watched her niece.

After lunch General Nevile decreed a universal "shut-eye." "You won't get one if you go to Tan Chüeh Ssu to-morrow, and you'll only get sunstroke if you go walking about in this heat. Yesterday was bad enough." The heat had, indeed, become considerable— Touchy averred that his little travelling thermometer registered ninety in the shade before lunch, and the party were glad enough to betake themselves, some to their pavilions, some to camp beds on the shady side of the courtyard. Laura carried a heap of cushions through the little door and prepared herself a couch under the white pine.

"May I come and rest here too, Mrs. Leroy?" Little Annette asked. "I won't say a word!"

Of course, Laura told her—she remembered the girl's rather strained look as she sat outside the upper shrine, and guessed that she might wish to be away from Henri for a bit. They spread their cushions in the shadiest corner, and lay down. The resinous smell of the great tree was strong as apples in the heat; the shadows of the bell pagoda and the yellow fir lay close and fore-shortened on the hot pavement, where the minute specks of mica in the stone sparkled like tiny diamonds in the sun; the bees droned sleepily in the fruit trees under the terrace wall. Only the long whistling note of some bird, repeated at regular intervals, broke the perfumed

humming silence. The cushions were stuffy and hot to
the body—they perspired as they lay; Annette turned
from side to side. "Lie perfectly still, and count icicles
with your eyes shut," Laura adjured her, "you'll forget
the heat then and go to sleep."

"That bird!" Annette complained. "I just hate the
sound of it."

"Bother the bird!" Mrs. Leroy said unsympathetically.
"Forget him too." And lying relaxed on her cushions she
was soon asleep. But Miss Ingersoll, untrained in the
particular trick of self-control which enables anyone to
sleep in discomfort, whether mental or physical, lay
awake, fidgeting, staring at the black glittering pattern
of pine-needles against the sky, changing her position
continually—till at last she gave it up, and propping
herself cautiously against the wall, took a book and tried
to read. From time to time she glanced enviously and
half-curiously at her companion. Asleep, Mrs. Leroy
looked older than when awake; her dark thin face,
unlit by the play of expression and by her brilliant eyes,
was like a fine worn cameo, profiled against the cushions;
Annette was moved to a vague wonder as to what tools
life had used to cut it so fine. She did not express it to
herself quite like that; what she thought was, "She
looks like Anna Karenina."

The study of anyone's face in sleep produces a curious
effect on the beholder. It makes for the moment a new
relationship, one-sided, tinged with the involuntary
sense of superiority of the waking over the sleeper, and
issuing always in a slight movement either of repulsion
or of sympathy. In Annette's case the result of an hour's
scrutiny of Mrs. Leroy's sleeping countenance was an
increased sympathy. Anna Karenina was perhaps her
favourite heroine. She was, however, delighted when
her living prototype woke up; she was getting bored.

Mrs. Leroy woke, as she did most things, leisurely, and said, "Did you sleep?"

"No, I read—I guess I wasn't sleepy. Mrs. Leroy," the girl went on, "are you tired, or would you take a little walk?"

"Where to?" said Laura, without moving.

"Why, I'd just love to see that view of the monastery from the hill at the back, that the Professor was talking about at breakfast—where you see all the roofs."

"All right—come on," said Laura. "But you must get a hat."

"Oh no, honestly, Mrs. Leroy, I never wear one."

"You must wear one here," said Laura firmly, "you don't know this sun."

The hat fetched, they strolled out of the main gate and up the little path on to the hill, and stood looking down at the fantastic collection of roofs, rising out of the drift of blossom which covered the hill-side below.

"It *is* very like a ballet," murmured Mrs. Leroy.

"What wonderful things you say!" Annette exclaimed admiringly.

"That's not very wonderful, surely?" expostulated Laura, half-amused and half-irritated.

"Why yes, it is—and you do, you all do," said Annette earnestly. "I was noticing Miss Judith at tiffin—the way she was talking with the Professor and Major La Touche. She was getting right ahead with them—making them say remarkable things."

"They were interested, that was all," said Laura, turning away and moving on up the hill. She had spied a rock in the shade of a dwarf oak, and on reaching it sat down. Annette followed and seated herself beside her.

"I wish I knew how it was done, to make people all that interested," she pursued half-wistfully.

"Isn't it by being interested oneself?" said Laura lightly.

Annette did not answer. She sat staring at the roofs below her, her pretty brows drawn together. Presently she turned to her companion with a sudden movement.

"Mrs. Leroy, do you think there's anything *in* those fortunes?"

"No, not much—I think they're a very hit-or-miss business," Laura replied.

"I just *hated* mine!" said the girl, with surprising energy in her tone. "What is enlightenment, anyway? Is it the same as learning? I guess I know quite a lot."

"No, I don't think it's quite the same as learning," said Laura.

"I've been wondering if it was just that—knowing how to know people, as you do, and Miss Judith."

"I think that's only part of it—enlightenment must mean knowing altogether about the nature of Life, mustn't it?"

"Yes, but that would be no use to you when you're dead," said Annette, "it's now you want it. I wish I'd never gone near that old shrine!"

Laura urged her not to worry about it, "They're only ancient proverbs, and it's just chance which you pull out."

Annette was silent. When she spoke again she did not look at her companion, but at the toe of her brown and white shoe, which she scraped to and fro in the shady dust.

"I guess there's something queer happening to me," she said slowly. "Since I came up here I feel, somehow, that I'm almost nothing." She hesitated. "I can't seem to get near people, the way you all do. I feel like a child playing blind-man's-buff. I know people are there, but when I put out my hand I can't touch them. I feel *alone*," she said, turning now to Laura with wide astonished eyes. "It seems to me I've never really known anyone—but that's just silly."

Not so silly, Laura thought to herself—it's reality she's missing at last. And she fell to wondering just what had prompted the realisation. Was it Henri? Was it Judith? Or was it Chieh T'ai Ssu and its ancient wisdom, and the magic of the blossoming tree?

"Do you think I'm crazy to talk to you this way?" the girl went on. "I never have before, to anyone—but then I've never felt this way before. I've always been quite satisfied with things. What is it I haven't got? It's not religion—I *am* religious," she said quaintly. "It seems just crazily foolish to want something and not know what it is. Do *you* know? I thought possibly you might."

"Why did you think that?" Laura asked, to gain time. Vinstead's words before breakfast about the dangers of rousing the unawakened were ringing like bells in her head—and here was the unawakened, poor child, stirring in her sleep and muttering uneasily.

"Why, I always feel you're terribly wise," said the girl. "I guess you are, too. I heard the Professor telling Miss Hande before lunch that you had 'extraordinary virtuosity in your touch on life.'"

"Oh glory!" said Laura, with a comical lift of the brows. "He doesn't know much about me, you know, Annette." She was secretly pleased by the remark all the same. "Tell me," she went on, "did no one ever tell you at home how to talk to people—no, not exactly that, but how to *think* about them, and try to understand them?"

"Why, no," said Annette, looking a little surprised. Laura was struck afresh by the doll-like charm of her face; the small, rather vacuous mouth, now open in astonishment, was just like the formal rosebuds on the expensive waxen Claras and Angelas of her youth—the large, slightly piteous eyes and brows might have been beautifully and carefully painted on some inexpressive china visage.

"No," Annette went on; "but I was very carefully brought up—we were taught to dress properly, and my mother was tremendously particular about our manners. Is that what you mean?"

"No, not altogether. Manners are like clothes—you can't go into society without them; but your clothes don't make friends, and manners alone won't. Had you friends when you were growing up? Intimate friends? Girls you chattered to at night, or boys you rode and sailed with?"

"Why no, not a great many. I went to parties," said Annette, looking puzzled. "But before I came out my mother didn't much like our having *beaux*. We were with her a good deal. We read French Memoirs to form our manners," she said, with a rather naïve air of self-satisfaction. "And my mother felt that gentlewomen ought to have really cultivated minds, so we studied a lot."

"I am sure she was most successful," said Laura warmly. She could visualise this cultivated upbringing with painful clearness—every virtue and accomplishment sedulously fostered, while the capacity to live was wholly overlooked. She tried another tack—there was something else she must know.

"Does Henri come into this?" she asked abruptly.

"Why, Mrs. Leroy!" Annette looked at her, staggered; then the swift colour flooded her face, and she looked away.

"Yes, but he does, doesn't he?" Laura pursued gently. "It would be odd if he didn't, you know."

To her extreme surprise the girl burst into tears. "Oh, I can't see any of it!" she sobbed, "I just can't make it out."

Laura was a good deal distressed. She put an arm round the girl; against her shoulder Annette cried more quietly. The tears would probably relieve her, Laura thought, and she let her have her cry out. Henri clearly did come into it—no doubt he had helped to show her that she *was* alone, that she had not learned to be any-one's "dear companion." But he was not an ideal teacher—and more than ever she felt convinced that Nina was wrong, and that while Judith might well take on Derek with a possibility of success, a marriage between Henri and Annette could only lead to tragic failure.

At length Annette's sobs ceased, and she raised a woe-begone face. "Don't apologise," the older woman said, smiling at her. "It's not so long since I was young, you know—you needn't tell me about it. Come on, powder your nose and let's go and have tea."

"But won't you try and explain to me what it is that's the matter with me?" said Annette, with a curious insistence.

"You must let me think about it, and tell you to-morrow," said Mrs. Leroy. She felt she would like to consult someone—Nina, or better still Lilah—before she embarked on a diagnosis of Annette's complaint.

As they strolled down the hill the path led round above a little hollow, screened rather thickly with oaks in front. Looking down into it they saw two figures seated there, those of Derek and Judith; even at a distance their attitude suggested some painful contro-versy—and Judith too was in tears. Laura could not help smiling as she turned away and walked on. Poor Youth—Love put it properly through the hoops! Still for all that, how much simpler the love of youth, she thought, with its eager resilience through any ups and downs, than the slow, painful, and consuming love of middle age. Miss Hande was quite right—not a doubt of it.

A little way further on they came on Lilah, sitting under her painted parasol, doing nothing at all. Laura was beginning to wonder sometimes whether Lilah's wisdom, which she so much respected, might not be due partly to her immense conservation of energy in all other things. She rarely read, never sewed, moved as seldom and as little as possible, and was incredibly economical of her speech. She simply ate, slept, sat, and observed. Her blue eyes, under their white sleepy lids, took in Annette's recently restored countenance now with one calm glance. When she heard that they were going in to tea, "Come this way—I'll show you a short cut," she said. They followed her along one of the little winding goat-paths to the foot of the monastery wall, at a point higher up than the main gateway. There was no door, but a heap of rocks against the masonry made a way up. Inside, however, the drop was considerable, into a sort of narrow alley between some building and the wall. Not without difficulty they swung themselves down. "How did you find this?" Laura inquired.

"I came out this way," said Lilah.

"But how on earth did you get up?" Laura asked. There were no stones on the inside, and the wall was six feet high at least.

"Like this," said Lilah. Placing her back to the wall she put her feet against the building opposite, bridging the gap—and bracing herself, regardless of her frock, she shuffled steadily upwards by what climbers call "the back and foot method." When she reached the top she swung half round, took hold of the tiled coping and hauled herself on to the top of the wall, where she sat swinging her feet and looking down at them with calm amusement.

"Well, isn't that just marvellous!" said Annette. Laura stared in stupefaction. It was a considerable muscular feat, and the last thing in the world that one would have expected of Lilah.

"I'd no idea you were a gymnast," she said as her niece dropped down again.

"Oh, I used to be, at school," said Lilah, as she led them on towards the terrace. "Rather fun."

Tea was rather a scratch meal, taken as and when people came for it. Judith and Derek were absent altogether—Professor Vinstead and his camera turned up very late. Nina and General Nevile presided, and endeavoured to get the plans for the expedition to T'an Chüeh Ssu on the morrow cut and dried. "Whoever goes, must start early," the General pronounced.

"What is your notion of early?" Miss Hande asked.

"Leaving here at latest at nine o'clock," he told her, "and we must order as many donkeys as we need this evening."

Miss Hande was most anxious to see T'an Chüeh Ssu, the other great temple some miles away in the hills, with its famous gingko tree. Little Annette had seen it, and did not want to go again; nor did the Neviles, nor Henri. "It will be fearfully 'ot," he observed. Touchy was lukewarm on the subject. Lilah, when sounded, said that Judith was certain to want to go, "She always wants to do everything."

"And you?" Nina asked her.

"I may as well," she said indifferently.

"Well, that is you, and Miss Hande, and Judith—and Mr. Fitzmaurice, I suppose," Nina counted on her pretty beringed fingers. "And the Professor, of course,

I know he wants to go. Five. What about you, Laura?"

"Oh, I hope Mrs. Leroy is coming!" said Miss Hande. "I'm sure she'll be a wonderful cicerone."

"Someone who can speak the language had better go," said General Nevile.

"Yes, I'll go," said Laura.

"Then what about donkeys?" Nina wanted to know.

"*I* shan't want a donkey," said Laura, getting up; she strolled across to the balustrade, leant on it and gazed out at the view. Annette troubled her—at tea the girl's face, under its mask of little smiles and gesturings, had still worn something of the rather piteous look of strain and bewilderment that she had shown so openly on the hill. Mrs. Leroy waited impatiently for Lilah to have finished the large meal which she was making as usual; she wanted to talk to her. But before Lilah had nearly done, Henri Delache got up and joined her.

"Laura, I 'ave found something just priceless! You must come and see it."

"What is it?" said Laura without stirring.

"Ow, it is most funny. Come on—I shall show you."

From Henri, anyhow, she probably need not fear any more confidences, Laura reflected with relief, as he marched her off—she was pretty well sated with confidences for the moment. As they strolled through various courtyards she wondered whether she, on the other hand, ought not to drop him a hint about Annette; but what could she say? No, it was really Nina's business, and she must talk to her first.

Henri led her to the extreme eastern end of the monastery, into a small court where she had never been before, and opened a door in the building which surrounded it as usual on three sides. Within, what was

indeed a curious sight met their eyes. A broad shelf
several feet in depth ran round the whole length of the
building, and this shelf was covered as thickly as they
would stand with hundreds of coloured images of
Buddha in all his manifestations, and of Kwan-yin, the
Goddess of Mercy. It looked like one of those Catholic
shops near the Brompton Oratory, only on a much
vaster scale, and with a strange composed remoteness
about the faces, very different from the over-emphasised
humanity of Christian images. Henri wandered about,
drawing her attention to the peculiarities of this one and
that. "'Ow odd it is," he said, pausing before a group
of Kwan-yins, "*Cette dame-là n'a presque pas de seins!*"
"'Ow do you say this in English, '*sein*'?" he went on.
"I am never sure. You say breast? or boosum?"

"Probably bosom," Laura said. She could not help
laughing a little, and wondering to what use Henri
would put the word; if it was to tell another story to poor
Miss Hande she hoped she might be there to hear it.

"They should not make Mme Kwan-yin without
boosums," pursued Henri meditatively, "they are most
attractive in the figure. *Savez-vous*, Laura, this is what
first please me in Miss Ingersoll, 'er boosums," he said,
leaving the Kwan-yins and turning round to her, with
a communicative stare of his large pale eyes. "We
were at a peecnic, and ride donkeys—she makes me
ride in front, and says I am not to look round, because 'er
skirt is so short. I do not look round—*les jambes, ça me
dit peu de chose, du reste*," said Henri, with fine detachment.
"But when we get off I look at 'er; *il faisait du vent*, and
'er jersey *se plaquait contre son corps*, so that I 'ave seen 'er
boosums. They are very pretty, Laura, *n'est-ce pas?*"

"She is most charming in every way," said Laura
evasively.

"Yes, but in particular 'er boosums. *Je n'ai jamais*

rien vu de pareil. And she is *très-intelligente.* Do you knoh, I think per'aps I want to marry 'er?"

"Because you like her figure?" said Laura mockingly.

"Now, Laura, *ne soyez pas embêtante!* I like 'er very, very much. *Mais il faut être raisonnable.* With Americans, much more than with Englishwomen, *il est indispensable de remplir ses devoirs de mari.* And for that—*enfin, il faut que la femme soit jolie.*"

"My dear Henri, the American idea of *les devoirs du mari* is much more comprehensive than you think. You would be expected to give up your mistresses, you know."

"Ow yes, *bien sûr,* for some years," said Henri easily. "But this is just what I say—she 'as great charm, she 'as *du tempérament; je crois que cela pourrait marcher. Qu'en pensez-vous?*"

"I disapprove of international marriages altogether," said Laura. She felt herself in some difficulty, between her knowledge that Nina wished for the match and her own sense that it would not *marcher,* as Henry called it.

"*Mais pourquoi donc?* Very often they 'ave a great success."

"And very often they are a miserable failure. Our idea of marriage is quite different to yours, Henri—you said so yourself last night."

"*C'est entendu*—but, my dear Laura, I think you see things *trop en noir.*"

"Oh, well, you must do as you think best," said Laura, turning to go.

"*Non, restez encore un instant!*" he said, catching her arm. "You disapprove—*pourquoi? Dites donc!*"

"You should talk to the Neviles about it," said Laura. "It's no business of mine."

"*Non!* 'E is too English! 'E would understand nothing. You do understand more."

"Talk to Nina, then."

"*Non!* It becomes then a *conseil de famille*, and I 'ave not yet decided. *Je ne pourrais évidemment pas aborder le sujet avant de me décider*," said Henri firmly. "But you 'ave good judgment—*en somme, vous donnez des conseils.*"

"I can't give you any in this case," said Laura, getting cross, as she always did when driven into a corner.

"*Enfin*, you can tell me why you disapprove? *Dans ce cas particulier?*"

Could she? Laura wondered. What was the use of saying to a Frenchman, "You don't love her enough?" She and Henri meant different things by the very word "love." And did anyone ever love anyone enough for happiness?

"How fond are you of her?" she asked reluctantly.

"*Rien que de lui toucher la main m'excite!*" he said triumphantly. "*Et quand je la rencontre soudainement, ça me fait battre le cœur.*" He threw out this announcement with a naïve self-satisfaction which made Laura laugh.

"*Vous vous moquez de moi!*" he said reproachfully. "You are not nice, Laura!"

"Yes, I am," she said. "Tell me, what do you talk about?"

"Ow, Love; of course—and literature. She 'as pretty good taste for literature," he said. "*Elle est très calée sur les écrivains modernes. Une jeune fille française* would be less amusing."

"Yes, it's all very well now, but afterwards you wouldn't find her as accommodating as a *jeune fille française*," said Laura. "You must see that."

"Per'aps you are right. *Comme il est difficile de se décider!*" he said, turning to her with a comically frank air of doubt. "I wish you would tell me truly what you think, Laura—you 'ave something up your sleeve."

For a moment Laura dallied again with the idea of

having it all out with him there and then. She stood
silent among the crowding images, vaguely aware of
their quiet painted faces regarding her with cold detachment, Oriental, incomprehensible. Should she try to
make him understand the situation as she saw it—
Annette's youth and pathetic ignorance, the complete
superficiality of her literary experience, the enchanted
unconsciousness in which she still walked through life?
And the possibilities of tragedy if she were roused from
it too suddenly? Unconsciously she turned towards the
group representing Kwan-yin, the Goddess of Mercy,
the undefiled princess, who turned back from the gates
of Paradise, so the legend goes, at the sound of a child's
crying—Kwan-yin, whose thousand mystic hands are
for ever stretched out to console human distress. Still,
serene, beautiful in the pure flow of the lines of hands
and drapery, carrying, modern as they were, the traditional grace of an ancient symbolic perfection, the
Kwan-yins stood there, a score or more of them, regarding her with cool gracious composure. Remote,
remote from human trouble they seemed; their antique
serenity relegated present distresses to an infinite
distance. All had been the same a thousand years
before, said their grave almond eyes—and a thousand
years hence, again all would be the same. The quality
of Mercy is oblivion, Time's great gift—and we who
stand with Time above the tides of human struggle, as
the moon above the sea, with a thousand hands bestow
this gift on men.

Was that the Kwan-yins' message? Laura wondered,
staring at them, troubled. Depressed, weakened by their
impassive faces, her impulse wavered and failed. She
must have time to think—she would procrastinate,
compromise.

"Let's talk about it to-morrow, when we get back

from T'an Chüeh Ssu," she said, turning to Delache once more. "And in the meantime, don't make love to her too much, Henri; you know you wouldn't be allowed to with your own *jeunes filles*—you wouldn't get the chance."

"*Non, non—c'est entendu*—I knoh this very well," he said, with the ready sincerity which was so engaging in him. "*Enfin, ma chère, je connais un peu les usages anglais!* I am most careful. *Voyons*, I never kiss 'er. *Je le voudrais bien—avez-vous remarqué comme elle a les lèvres fraîches?* Like flowers, which 'ave dew on them!—but I 'ave not done this. *Je ne ferai pas de bêtises, parole d'honneur!*" he said, as they left the pavilion of the images.

Chapter Sixteen

LILAH was not in the pavilion when Laura went before dinner to wash and put on a clean shirt— the normal temple toilet. She had hoped to find her there, and when she was ready she strolled out, took a cocktail from Niu and wandered with it on to the inner terrace. Lilah was not there either, but the Professor's lean pale length rose up from a chair in the little turret and greeted her. The evening light laid beauty over hill and plain, stretched out before them—Mrs. Leroy leaned on the parapet and gazed, and the Professor studied her face.

"I saw you out walking with our Undine on the hill this afternoon," he presently observed, "and you had a talk with her young man this evening too, didn't you?"

"Yes," said Laura, uncertain whether she was grateful for the lead or not. "It's all rather difficult," she said slowly, wondering whether failing Lilah she had better perhaps get such light as Vinstead could throw. "She *is* coming awake, or at least stirring in her sleep, poor child, and I am not sure how far the young man is the cause of it."

"He is certain to be partly the cause, with that type," said Vinstead.

"Yes—but you see I'm not her natural guardian, and I can't very well interfere with both of them on the spot," said Laura disconnectedly. "And it isn't an easy thing to make people see. It is all so tenuous—like a maze of silk threads. And yet it is perfectly real."

"Of course it is real—those are the realities," he said,

coming over to the balustrade beside her. He was trying
to guess at the nature of her difficulties with the guardians,
and the nature of the confidences which she might have
received. But she made no answer. She was not telling
him much—he had no right to complain of that, of
course, stranger as he was; but, contrasting it with her
openness about her own feelings that morning on the
hill, he was slightly disappointed. She had clearly
learned something more. As they stood leaning their
elbows on the parapet, side by side, their common
attitude suggested an intimacy that was for the moment
denied him, and he was aware of a sense of frustration
which surprised him by its sharpness. It was ludicrous
to attach so much importance to a refusal of intimacy
from a person he had only met two days before! With a
curious impulse to try to account for his own feelings he
twisted his head sideways to look at his companion. Her
long figure leaned beside him in an attitude of easy
grace; she was so near to him that he could note the
precise modelling of every line of her clear profile, the
fine dark brushwork of brow and eyelash on the delicate
texture of the skin, so warm and golden-white at the
temples and neck, where the thick hair swept away in
heavy curves; so near that he could not escape the faint
perfume which made her presence flower-like. As he
looked at her, the mood of detached curiosity which had
prompted him to turn his head vanished, swallowed up
by a sudden rush of an emotion stronger and simpler
than any he had experienced for years. He had a perfectly plain and almost overmastering desire to take in
his arms that slight figure over which the thin shirt
rose and fell with the light breathing, to touch with
hands and lips the softness of that golden-white skin.
He drew in his breath, sharply, and turning away, lit a
cigarette. His impulse to study his own feelings and the

cause of them had been a mistake. God! what a fool he was, he thought angrily to himself, finding that his hands actually trembled as he held the match. At his age, in his profession, to be a victim still to simple physical desire, of such a strength! To admire and enjoy a delightful and intelligent woman was one thing —and Mrs. Leroy *was* delightful and intelligent, there was no doubt about it. But if he had derided his own folly in being faintly hurt by her reticence, how he now scourged himself for the sudden feeling which had surprised him. He moved a step or two away, and threw the match over the parapet. From this distance he looked at her again, covertly. Had she noticed anything? She was still staring at the view, but now turned her head to him with the air of one who has come to a decision.

"I rather want to talk to you about it all," she said, "but I think I must talk to Mrs. Nevile first, as she is her aunt. I am sure it will help me to clear my mind to talk to you. May I, later on?"

Oh, but of course, Vinstead told her. He was entirely at her service. The explanation, trivial as it was, helped to soothe him and to restore his self-control. As they walked back along the inner terrace they met Mrs. Nevile. Vinstead took Laura's glass and carried it back, leaving the ladies to stroll together.

Nothing escapes notice in temple picnics. "Well, did you have a nice talk with Little Annette?" was Nina's opening.

Laura used it to plunge at once into the subject. She urged Mrs. Nevile to keep an eye on her niece for a few days, to give her a chance to find out where she stood.

"Her feelings for Henri, do you mean?"

"More than that. She's going through a phase that is partly independent of him, I think, and she needs time for it."

"What sort of phase?" Nina wanted to know.

"Growing up—waking up. She's always lived in a sort of dream about people, and she's beginning to wonder if it's enough."

"My dear, she's perfectly practical. I don't see what you mean. Did she tell you this?"

"As well as she could. She doesn't understand it herself."

"Did she speak to you of her feelings for Henri? That's probably at the root of it."

"Not directly—of course that must come into it. But it's more fundamental than a love-affair, I feel sure," said Laura seriously.

Nina was inclined to doubt whether anything could be more fundamental than a love-affair. "Once she gets engaged to him comfortably she'll be all right," she said complacently. "I don't really see what there is to be in a fuss about. Of course she's all wrought up just now."

"Yes, of course she is—but she shouldn't be wrought up more, that's the point," said Laura, feeling nevertheless that she was making no headway. "An engagement is no cure for a psychological crisis." "Even if it comes to an engagement," she thought, but did not say so; the *conseil de famille* came into her mind, and she felt that she could not give Henri away. Nina's practical mind would pounce with terrible certainty on any indication of the state of his feelings.

What it pounced on now, however, was the word psychological.

"My dear, what in all the earth is a psychological crisis?" She took her friend's arm, and looked up at her, her gay face sparkling with arch rebuke. "You've been letting that old Professor of ours stuff your head with all sorts of maggots," she said, shaking her head at her. "All these *tête-à-têtes* you and he have had! I'm not sure he's so wise after all! I wouldn't wonder if *he* was heading for a 'psychological crisis,' if that's the latest word for it!" she said, with her pealing laugh, and a significant glance which drove the point of her remark home.

"What *utter* nonsense, Nina," said Mrs. Leroy coldly— but the ready blush which she always felt to be so humiliating and ridiculous, and which Mrs. Nevile found most engaging and loved to provoke, leapt into her face. "I can't think how you can bear to be so *banal*," she said, turning to her friend with a burst of impatience. "That's *the* joke again—you're always making it, and it *is* so boring."

"Oh well, it's the oldest joke in the world, and I guess it's a rather good one," said Nina Nevile impenitently. "Come on," she pursued coaxingly, turning her companion round with an affectionate pressure of the arm she held, "don't be vexed with me, but stop worrying about Annette, and come and have some dinner."

To stop worrying about Annette was sooner advised than performed, as Laura found during the meal. Nina had found her own friendly means of silencing her, but the interior voice of her concern would not be silenced. It might be fancy, or some effect of the faint late night, reflected off the glowing distant surfaces of hill and plain, but she thought the girl's face paler than usual, her light laugh a little less frequent, her pretty rather empty smile more mechanical than ever. Judith and Derek, too, were both somewhat abstracted—Derek noticeably so; he crumbled his French roll with little irritable gestures, and was moodily unresponsive to some well-meant ragging on Touchy's part. The burden of entertainment fell mostly on Touchy and Nina that evening, as Laura had long ago foreseen that it would, though Henri, apparently in his usual spirits, seconded them well. Love-affairs were love-affairs, but food was food—there was no danger of Henri's "confounding two things," as he called it. Lilah sat eating and observing, her immense blue eyes moving slow and inexpressive from face to face, but as usual making an absolutely minimal contribution to the conversation; watching her, Laura could have laughed to think that the thing she wanted most at the moment was an opinion from this apparently vacant loveliness. She hoped to get it too—but the moment that the advent of coffee caused a general movement to rookhi chairs and cushions, Derek sprang up, thrust his black spaniel's head over her shoulder, and with his mouth at her ear insisted in an urgent undertone that she should bring her coffee on to the inner terrace with him.

They sat in the turret. The dusk was deepening rapidly, making the fruit-blossom below the terrace ghostly; the roofs of the temple stood up, black fanciful silhouettes, against the last yellow glow in the western sky behind the hill. The long note of the bird which had troubled Annette's siesta was still repeated with monotonous persistency, mournful and somehow mechanical—a sinister sound to Laura's mind.

"Well?" she said, lighting a cigarette.

Derek sat with his elbows on his knees, his hands plunged in his hair, in an attitude of profound and dejected meditation.

"Well, I did as you said," he remarked at last gloomily, raising his head and staring at her.

"Good," said Laura.

"I'm not sure that it was so jolly good," he said, relapsing into his former position. Laura said nothing. "I love her damnably!" he burst out suddenly, with a curious accent of surprise. "And Laura, she *cried*!"

"She might well cry," said Laura.

"Why do you say that?" he asked, looking up again at her curiously. "I thought she might turn me down, and that would have been beastly enough, but I never dreamt she would cry. Oh, blast it all!" "Laura, do *you* mind it?—my goings on?" he asked after a pause.

"Yes, a little."

"You've kept very quiet about it," he said, half resentfully. "You never let on that you minded."

"It was none of my business, and I thought enough people disapproved of you as it was," she said, smiling.

"Damn them!" he said irritably. "But, Laura, *why* do you mind? Tell me, please."

"Oh, the waste, really."

"Waste of what?"

"Time—no, emotion. Waste of a personality. One hates to see anyone one's fond of cherishing a fake and missing the real thing," said Laura rather hurriedly. "It must blunt the taste, too."

"But you've had lovers—or one, at any rate," he said, in a sort of doubtful tone.

"Yes, but I loved them," she said with energy. "It was all blood and tears, anyhow—not a meal or a movie. I'm not taking the high moral line, Derek—I'm not in a position to. It's the—the *flippancy* of promiscuity that I hate. And I imagine that's what Judith minds too. It *is* ugly, say what you like," she said decidedly.

"Why on earth didn't you tell me before that you minded so much?" he asked, roused by her tone.

"Would you have paid the smallest attention if I had?"

"No, I don't suppose I should, at the start," he said thoughtfully. "I should probably just have lumped you in with the usual run of C. of E. hags. No, it's just because you've never been a Pharisee, Laura darling, that I'm talking to you about it now."

"Not even that," said Laura. "You're listening to me now because Judith minds, my dear."

"Funnily enough, in a way I mind *your* minding almost more," he said, rumpling up his hair and looking at her. "It's so damned unexpected. Has she talked to you about it?" he asked after a moment's pause.

"Not since you had a go at her to-day—she did before."

"Girls' minds are extraordinary," he said. "I can't follow them. In a way she was so awfully sensible, and tried to be completely slap-dash about the whole thing, but she couldn't carry it off. It simply made her miserable."

"Have you settled anything?"

"Lord, no! How could we? Heaven knows what X does next!" said Derek gloomily.

Laura made no reply, and for some time they sat in silence. The dusk had deepened rapidly—more and more stars came out and hung like lamps in the sky; the outline of the hill running down into the plain was merely a line below which lay starlessness. It was very still— the distant drumming and booming of the ordinary evening rites was over, and only the long isolated note of the bird, or whatever it was, broke the silence. Suddenly, out of the darkness, there burst a scatter of silver notes, high and clear, fresh as dew, fresh as a lark at dawn—a girl's voice singing—Judith's voice. Heard so through the dark and from a distance, unexpectedly, the effect was magical, transporting—Laura felt a little shiver run through her; she heard Derek catch his breath.

"There she goes!" he muttered; "the Singing Kuni- ang!"

"Let's go back," Laura whispered. They walked softly along the inner terrace towards the invisible voice.

She was singing that lovely early song of Somervell's, his setting of Christina Rossetti's "Young Love lies sleeping"—now they were near enough to hear the words clearly, and by unspoken consent stood still to listen to the second verse. Derek suddenly slipped his hand through Laura's arm and squeezed it against his side. She stood stirred, moved, in a soft glow of emotion; thinking of him, of Tim, of Aubrey and Henry—Young Love past, present, and to come, Young Love with its ardours and ecstasies in all springtimes everywhere.

"Young Love lies sleeping——"

the voice rang down towards the beautiful close:

"And round about him, the may bushes are white."

It ended—ended, for Laura, in a rush of visions of the blossoming tree. Not here, not here, bringing its magic into the ancient courts of temples, or painted incredibly on a brown-paper background, but of the English hawthorn, springing in free fountains of white on the slopes of green downs, topping the banks with wreaths against the blue above the dust of chalky roads, sheltering the hidden nightingale whose voice out-bubbled the bubbling spring, up in the hollow behind Garsover. She could see it, smell it; for the moment it obliterated the present, and in a sort of dream she followed Derek through the little door which he held open for her, and under cover of the applause settled down among the listening group.

She found herself seated between Vinstead and La Touche, who had both shifted a little to make room for her. Vinstead had joined in the general clamour for a further performance from the Singing Kuniang, hoping perhaps for some distraction from his thoughts, which he was not enjoying. His mind, naturally honest, and

trained to the analysis of human reactions, played like a
searchlight over his moment of folly, trying to account
for this sudden irruption of the emotional into his carefully regulated and rational life. He honestly could not
think how it had happened. He had, of course, studied
the faces of the group of strangers presented to him at
the Legation when the expedition started, and had
been struck by Mrs. Leroy's; his curiosity had been
aroused by her strange concentration when she had
failed to see him on the rocks by the ferry, and by the
casual remarks of the others about her; a string of
minute accidents had thrown him specially into her
company, and her conversation had frankly delighted
him. It was his habit to enjoy and appreciate delightful
people, and he had hitherto done so without disquieting
results. Then why—why, in heaven's name, in this
particular instance, was his peace disturbed, and his
very body shaken by emotion? Professor Vinstead, of
course, was new to China, and left out of account the
peculiar quality of Peking air; he fell back on the
strangeness of the circumstances, on the heat, on strain
after a journey, to account for his trouble. He struggled
with his mind, which would interpolate little pictures of
her as arguments—a graceful movement, the ironic lift
of the brows, the quite peculiar beauty of her voice in
speech. He diagnosed the whole thing, and became very
cool and rational. He would see to it that it did not
happen again—and in the meantime he would, like a
sensible man, enjoy the company of an agreeable woman;
to shun her would be absurd. Also he might really help
her with the problem of Miss Ingersoll, which intrigued
him professionally. And at that moment Mrs. Leroy
herself, beckoned to by La Touche, came and sat down
beside him in the dark, and Judith Milne began to sing
Brahms's "Nachtwandler."

There are those who think Brahms's "Nachtwandler" the greatest song in the world. Laura Leroy knew it well, and Vinstead heard her give a little sigh of contentment as she leaned back to listen. Judith sang it in German, and the strange words, so closely matched by the haunting subtlety of the intervals, poured out into the night, carrying to at least two of the listeners an intensity of meaning they had never borne before. Yes, Laura thought, as she listened to the opening lines, that was the very picture of the simple, the unawakened, wrapped, as little Annette was wrapped, in a sort of enchantment, a wistful dream. She half turned to Vinstead, and he nodded at her in the gloom. He knew what was in her mind. "There you are!" he murmured in her ear at the close of the second verse. "What did I tell you this morning?"

Vibrant on the lower notes of the register, Judith's voice took the altered melody of the third verse, with its shivering hint of menace; it rose magnificently into the glorious intoxication of the fourth line, and poised on the sharp note of warning in the fifth, sinking away into the pitying cadences of the last.

In the moment of silence before the applause broke out Vinstead leant over to Laura.

"What an amazing piece of writing that is," he murmured. "You can hear him walking the tight-rope on the first line of that last verse, can't you?—keeping level on those two notes."

There was a general appeal for an encore. "But can't we have it in English?" said Miss Hande. "It's such a glorious thing, but I can't quite follow the German."

"Yes, *do* sing it in English, Miss Judith," urged Nina. "I'm dying to know what it's all about. You can tell it's something fearfully dramatic."

"Can you, Judith?" Laura asked, as the girl hesitated. "Is there a decent translation?"

"Yes, moderate, I think," said Judith.

"Go ahead then," she was urged. A snort of disapproval from Derek, who disliked translations, passed unnoticed. Effortless and clear, the lovely melody flowed out again from the shadows under the leaning pine, carrying this time words accessible to all.

> "Rouse him not, whose simple spirit
> Walks in slumber, dream-enchanted,
> Let his heart the night inherit
> In its peace, desire-haunted.
>
> "Menaced now by storm and danger
> On he moves, serene, unshaken—
> Come you not, a careless stranger
> Him with reckless words to waken.
>
> "Deep in sleep's enchantment sunken
> Passing now o'er depths unsounded,
> With the full moon's glory drunken—
> With the full moon's glory drunken—
> Leave, oh leave his peace unwounded,
> Oh leave his peace unwounded."

There it was, set forth for all to see, the problem of the somnambulist in life, the sleeper whose only safety is in his sleep—whose sudden awakening will plunge him into those perils over which, wrapt in his dream, he does indeed pass serenely. The music was as usual summing up the immediate and personal into the timeless and universal, carrying its truth with final certainty into the very heart. Laura as she listened would have given worlds to be sitting beside Nina, to watch her face and to whisper in her ear, "Now do you see?"

But Nina was at the other side of the group. Vinstead, close beside her, did see, she knew, and she turned towards him. But Vinstead was sitting in a curious abstraction, with a remote look, almost of pain, on his face. Ah, music has a way of getting back at us, of searching out the secret places of the heart—it is no good going to music for distraction. The Professor had then a swift vision of the sleep-walker who lies hidden in all men's hearts, below the rationality of consciousness and intellect; the dreamer who stirs sometimes and walks abroad, intoxicate with golden visions, over the giddiest abysses; the sleeper whom we dare not waken.

He jerked his shoulders impatiently. This was worse than ever! And turning to Mrs. Leroy with his most Cambridge voice, at the close, he asked if she knew whose the translation was. "It's extraordinarily good."

Every one wanted to know this. "What beautiful words!" Miss Hande ejaculated; and Touchy leant across to Laura with, "Yes, by Jove! And absolutely right for the music. Whose is it?"

Mrs. Leroy did not know, and Judith was applied to. She hesitated a good deal, and when pressed, "Lilah made it for me," she said at last, reluctantly—it was evident that she had promised not to mention the fact.

But Lilah accepted the congratulations which poured in on her with calm gratification. "I'm glad you like it!" she said to Touchy.

"It's an absolute gem!" Touchy declared roundly.

But Mrs. Leroy went off to bed an hour later more astonished than ever at her eldest niece. To be calmly wise was one thing, but to write a song like that was quite another. Lilah! Well, well!

Chapter Seventeen

THE T'an Chüeh Ssu party set off next morning at 8.30 a.m. in considerable spirits. Miss Hande during breakfast had been positively chatty, so exhilarated was she by the prospect of adding yet another famous temple to her collection; even Lilah showed a frame of mind a degree removed from resignation, and when mildly rallied by Touchy on her unusual energy in going somewhere that she needn't, hazarded the opinion that she "had an idea it might be going to be rather fun." The nature of the fun she kept to herself—only her eyes slid slowly round, first to the Professor's face and then to Laura's. Derek had thrown off his dejection of the night before, apparently, and was trying to get Miss Hande to listen to his account of the private lives of bonzes. General Nevile was supervising the feet of the party. As a soldier of experience, he attached importance to suitable footgear. The Professor's feet were adorned with stout brogues, heavily nailed, which called forth his condemnation.

"Haven't you got any tennis shoes?" he asked, fixing a gloomy eyeglass on these objects. "You'll be sorry you ever saw those things before the day is out."

"What's wrong with them?" asked Vinstead in surprise. His shoes were walking shoes, and he was going to walk—in mountains, moreover.

"Those nails will slip on these cobbled paths at every step," said the General. "And that leather will make your feet sweat till you can't stand. You want shoes like Mrs. Leroy's here, or Fitzmaurice's."

Vinstead glanced at Laura's feet. She was wearing shorts and knee-stockings; her white canvas shoes had thick string soles, such as the Chinese wear. Derek and Judith had the same, and even Lilah wore tennis shoes. But the Professor had no tennis shoes. Touchy offered a pair which were, however, too small for him, and in the condemned brogues he finally set off, feeling slightly foolish. But how the devil was one to know, he reflected gloomily, as he walked up the cobbled path above the temple, his hobnails screaming on the stones, *what* to do or expect in this damned country? He realised by now that his suit was too thick for comfort on such an expedition; that a collar was a mistake, and braces intolerable. His topi was all right, only it was so difficult to keep it on—it slithered about on his head, and he envied Derek his double-felt. He had not slept well either. While he was broad awake he could force his thoughts to remain rational, but so soon as he slipped off into the border-lands of sleep, they behaved intolerably, crowding images of Laura Leroy before him in the most impracticable fantasies. And when he jerked himself awake, and opened his eyes, there was the peach-blossom above his head, between him and the stars, to remind him of her grave face as she stood in the turret with the flowering spray in her hands, on the first evening. In the warm stillness of the moonlit night he had lain and cursed the fruit-blossom, the temple, the picnic, the whole enraging business. The middle-aged do not welcome emotion, bathe in it, swim gloriously on the strong tide as youth does; they jib, wrestle, struggle in an agony of self-preservation. Late love is apt to be not a joyous irradiation, a heavenly suffusion of the whole of life— but a slow painful consuming of habit, reason and will in deep-smouldering combustion. Among the self-contained, anyhow, this is so—self-respect, even, resists with all its might. Professor Vinstead was extremely self-contained, and he was in the first throes of this resistance. At such moments a man wants all his armour, even that of a normal appearance. This had been denied to the Professor, and scorning himself for minding such things, he yet did mind—minded his condemned shoes, his collar which would presently wilt, his topi which kept canting tipsily sideways, his indecently tidy suit. He surveyed the latter with an expression of sour grieving which was not lost on Lilah. From her ass she called to him, "What's wrong with your suit?"

Vinstead started guiltily, and looked at her. What an odd observant creature she was! But somehow the sleepy mockery in her face was not irritating.

"It's too hot and too tidy," he said truthfully.

"Take off your coat then, and hang it on my saddle."

Vinstead did so, remarking, "Even that won't keep my collar alive."

"Take that off too—horrible tight thing! You can wear this." She produced from a pocket a soft gaudy silk 'kerchief. Vinstead looked at it doubtfully, but finally removed his collar, and knotted the thing round his neck. It was certainly more comfortable. And when Laura, happening to look back, called out, "Oh, how sensible you look!" his comfort was increased.

There are two ways of reaching T'an Chüeh Ssu from the direction of Peking—up from Men-t'ou-kou, the coal-mining village near the railway, down in the valley of the Hun-ho, or by a hill-track from Chieh T'ai Ssu, which dips up and down along the ridges, and finally joins the valley track at a sort of stony col on the lip of the cup in which T'an Chüeh Ssu lies. There is a third road to it, little used by foreigners as a rule, coming over the hills behind from the direction of the Ch'ing Shui Tien, or Clear Water Peak, the lovely Chinese name for the shapely summit which Europeans, seeing it from the city wall, call Mount Conolly—a sort of back entrance leading down through groves of oaks and thujas to the great courts.

In its way the Temple of the Oak Pool is almost more impressive than Chieh T'ai Ssu. It lacks its wonderful terrace, wide view, and steep-pitched situation on the hill-side, but it is on an even vaster scale, and it has running water. The great walled enclosure fills the bottom of the hollow in which it lies, and straggles gently up the northern slopes of it; there are spread the mighty courts, acres and acres of flagged pavement, surrounded by the gay colours of painted eaves and scarlet pillars; freshened by the runnels of bright water which flow in open stone conduits through every court-yard, great or small; chattering beside the flag-stones in the shadowed passages between buildings, racing down inclined shoots past flights of marble steps, or lingering with lazy tinklings and soft murmurs in pools below the grottoes, where goldfish swim mysteriously. The whole temple is full of the light gentle voice of water; the formality of stone and shrine and symbol is made gay with its shining freedom, brought in, like the blossoming tree, to worship within the holy places. The Chinese do deeply love and honour the things of nature—air, water, flowers and trees; more deeply than almost any other people; not with a vague poetic yearning, as northern races do, but with a practical recognition, a visible universal allegiance. These things are, as it were, part of the Established Church, not lovely pagans or shy dissenters. At the great entrance gate of T'an Chüeh Ssu are several large inscriptions in painted characters. "Purple Hills and Red Springs," says one; "Fragrant Groves and Clean Earth," another. To such things is the pilgrim invited, as well as to shrines and ceremonies. And within, in the largest court of all, stands a gingko

tree of unknown age and immense size, tall as the tallest
English elm and of a mighty circumference, which a few
casual centuries back was canonised as a saint, and
also elevated to the peerage with a title corresponding
to that of marquess. At the foot of its great silvery-
yellowish trunk stands a little altar where the pious may
burn joss-sticks in its honour; close by a carved tablet
bears its patent of nobility. No one knows exactly how
old it is, but like its parent temple it has outlived many
dynasties. The written records of T'an Chüeh Ssu are
said to go back to the year 400 A.D., and an old country
proverb declares, "First there was T'an Chüeh, and
after there was Yu Chou." Yu Chou is an old name for
Peking; a name so ancient that it had already fallen
into disuse in the days of Kublai Khan.

After nearly three hours' going the party found themselves looking down on T'an Chüeh Ssu from the col
where their track joined the shorter way up from Men-
t'ou-kou, and they paused for a breather, perching on
the hot slabby rocks, whence the lizards scooted swiftly
away into the still-withered yellow bents and scrubby
herbs. A hot walk they had had, up hill and down,
along the narrow stony or cobbled tracks, and the
temple, lying below them in its cup in the hills, em-
bowered in thujas, looked marvellously cool and in-
viting. They had passed more than one group of soldiers
on their way—obvious T'ao-pings, without armlets and
without officers; and now as they rested on the col yet
another company appeared, straggling up a small by-
path. They seemed in poor case; their uniforms were
soiled and worn, their slippers in some cases dropping to
bits, and their faces wore a look of sullen weariness as
they stared with sulky curiosity at the group of foreigners;
but they were all fully armed, each man with a rifle and a
bandolier of cartridges, and many with revolvers as well.

"I say, Laura, there are a hell of a lot of them about," said Derek, half-aside. "I wonder what the devil they're all up to."

"Goodness knows!" said Mrs. Leroy indifferently. "Peking may have fallen by this time for aught we know, and Li legged it off somewhere. We shouldn't have heard anything out here, and it's two days since we left."

"They do look a ruffianly lot, I must say," said Derek, fixing his eyeglass on the soldiers with much distaste. More and more of the grey-clad figures were coming up and crowding round the party on the col, filling the air with the fumes of garlic; he was aware of the vague mental discomfort which is generally induced by the presence of numbers of armed men of another race. "Don't you think we might move on?" he said.

They moved on, then, down the broad paved road into the hollow, the group of soldiers staring curiously after them as they went. At the entrance to the monastery they were met by Niu; he had preceded them with the asses and food, and now led them to the pavilion where he was preparing lunch. They followed him across court after court, where the shadows of curved roofs fell short and black on the hot dazzling pavement; past high carved fronts of shrines, loggiaed with scarlet pillars; feeling a cold chill as they passed into the shadow of a building and trod damp stone, feeling a rush of heat as they emerged again into the glare of sunshine, till at last they reached their quarters for the day.

Right up in the north-east corner of the enclosure, jammed in under the monastery wall, lies a little oblong courtyard, reached only by a narrow entry-way, with a small two-roomed pavilion at the back. Just within the entry-way stands a curious erection, one of the small architectural fantasies in which the Chinese so much delight—a little cupola supported on slender pillars, shading a tiny island of stone pavement, on all sides of which water flows in open channels. Here a table was spread invitingly for lunch; Niu informed Laura that the rice would be opened at one o'clock. Miss Hande and Judith exclaimed with delight at such a luncheon-place, and while the two men paused at the table for drinks after their hot walk, the ladies went on into the pavilion to wash and titivate before exploring the temple till lunch-time.

One of the lesser complications of visiting a Chinese temple is the question of sanitary arrangements. Few Europeans will willingly pay a second visit to a Chinese lavatory, the open pit between paving-stones, with two bricks for the feet to stand upon and generally without a door of any sort, where the effluvium from the accumulations below has been known to produce a fainting-fit. In private temples, and in the better-arranged apartments of the big ones, a series of *cabinets-de-toilette* gets over the difficulty. But in such places as the corner pavilion of T'an Chüeh Ssu it becomes necessary to explore. Accordingly they explored. The two ends and the back of the courtyard were enclosed by the outer wall of the monastery itself, which was here a sort of rampart against the actual slope of the hill, from which the courtyard had been scooped out—a wall of large uneven bricks or stones with a slight batter which took it barely off the vertical, and overgrown with moss. It was possible, they found, to squeeze round one end of the pavilion into the long narrow chasm behind, between it and the wall. This particular exploration produced some notable results later in the day, and is therefore recorded.

Vinstead was astonished, later, to remember the peaceable casual way in which they strolled about the temple after that. They went and admired the giant gingko tree and his smaller wife, in the greatest court of all; Miss Hande was intrigued by their curious fern-like foliage, and deeply interested to learn that the gingko is really a tree of the Coal Epoch, geologically, and no longer found wild anywhere in the world.

"How *like* the Chinese, isn't it?" said Derek, "to preserve a tree from the Coal Age in their temples till now. Just the sort of thing they would do."

"Why, that certainly adds to the sense of their anti-quity," said Miss Hande, turning to him with a startled gleam behind her lorgnette, as happened when a new idea struck her.

"I suppose that's why they used coal before anyone else did," said Judith, with the thoughtless inanity which overtakes us all sometimes, when most of our mind is concentrated on something else.

"Do you suggest that they were there when it was laid down, and never forgot the place?" said Vinstead, eyeing her with benevolent amusement.

Judith blushed furiously then, conscious, too late, of her folly. But the party wandered on to the shrine of Kwan-yin, and stared in the dim light at the portrait of Miao Yen, the daughter of Kublai Khan, who left the pleasure-domes of Xanadu to become a nun at T'an Chüeh Ssu, worshipping, with shaven head, night and day at the shrine of the Goddess of Mercy. One or two priests came and talked to them, standing restrained and still, their delicate hands tucked into their wide grey sleeves, their discreet eyes gravely scanning the strangers; but they saw no other Europeans.

At 12.30—Vinstead remembered the time because Derek looked at his watch and said they would have to wait for lunch—the heat and glare off the white pave-ments decided them to return to their pavilion. Vinstead fell a little behind with Laura on the way and inquired how Judith and Derek were getting on?

"Being rather sensible, I think," Laura replied. "They're thrashing it all out. It troubles her rather."

"His past?"

"Yes, and his present." They both laughed.

"She doesn't approve of the theory of sowing one's wild oats before marriage, then?" said Vinstead.

"It's more that she mistrusts it, I think. She doubts whether the dog Sex, even after being given such a prodigious run in the garden beforehand, will settle down quietly in his kennel for ever afterwards."

"A very prudent doubt. And does he think it will?"

"Oh, Derek's too feckless to think sensibly of the future at all. So far he's entirely taken up with the novelty of his own sensations. If he's ever been seriously in love before it's so long ago that he's forgotten about it. What engrosses him at the moment is really the discovery that someone else has the power to cause him pain."

Her words gave Vinstead a sharp small prick. Actually that was really, he realised, what had been engrossing him for the last twelve hours. And it had taken away the completeness of his ease and freedom in discussing with Mrs. Leroy the amusing peculiarities of sex. With a certain stubbornness he forced himself to go on, nevertheless.

"It's idle to suppose that anyone can take out an all-risks insurance policy against emotion by any means whatever," he said, with a curious bitter pleasure in the personal truth of his words. "The dog Sex, as you call it, is a long-lived animal, and a wild one."

"With a tendency to bark at a stranger's step," said Mrs. Leroy merrily.

Vinstead winced, and glanced at her. No, she was quite

unaware, but for some reason the words hurt him, almost as if she had been addressing them to him with full knowledge of his state. Involuntarily, in his sudden pain, half-forgotten phrases floated to the surface of his mind. "Tread softly, for you tread on my dreams"— where had he heard that? "A careless stranger, him with reckless words to waken." That was from the song last night, and he had struggled at the time against the thought that she, the stranger, should awaken the sleeper hidden in his heart. With a sudden movement of resentment at her gaiety, her unawareness, he looked at her walking beside him, in her shorts and shirt—the length and strength of her body, the ease of her movements, her face as usual with a far-away expression; and with something of his former stubbornness mingling with his irritation he repeated the lines aloud:

> "Come you not, a careless stranger,
> Him with reckless words to waken."

She turned towards him, then, with a look of amused inquiry, clearly pondering the precise apropos of the quotation—one of the things he had so liked in her was the way she visibly took up a remark, turned it over and examined it, before replying. But now he saw her face change, and a startled look come for a fleeting second into her eyes. Something in his tone, something in his face, had struck her. She half paused—but they were already within a dozen yards of the island pavilion, and Derek called out to her, "Laura, can't you ginger up the lunch a little?"

She went forward then, sat down at the table under the cupola, and called, "*Lai!*" Niu fluttered out from some building close by. "*K'ai fan!*" (Open the rice!) said Laura —the phrase always used when ordering a meal to be served. Niu vanished, and they sat about the table, waiting.

From where they sat they could look down, past a green octagonal roof and the tops of a lesser pair of ginkgo trees, into one of the great courtyards below, which had a large isolated shrine standing like an island in the middle of it, the back towards them; beyond the shrine, in the further corner, a little dark bolt-hole of a passage led away out of sight. The main entrance into the court was hidden from them by the shrine itself; its huge bulk, shadowed by the immense eaves, stood dark and almost colourless under the blazing flood of the noonday light. As they sat looking idly down into this courtyard, sipping their cocktails, they saw a curious thing. A couple of priests emerged from the little dark passage, stood for a moment in the shadow, looking right and left, and then ran like hares across the open space to the back of the great shrine. One of them pulled out a large key and opened a small door in the lattice; and then both nipped in with the alacrity of frightened animals. Bonzes usually move with the utmost slowness and dignity, and it was astonishing, and somehow sinister, to see these two men run—they were so far off that their slippered feet made no sound, and the watchers had a curious impression of looking on at the silent drama in a shadow-show, set on some strange architectural stage, as they saw the doll-like grey figures dart from shade into light, and then into shade again, and disappear, minute specks, into the great shrine.

"What the devil are they up to?" said Derek, his eye-glass fixed on the door. "Can they be thieves?"

"They're frightened men, whoever they are," said Vinstead, who had also observed the small scene.

For some moments past a vague noise of commotion and shouting had been audible from somewhere far below, in the direction of the monastery entrance; but, watching the scene in the courtyard, none of the party paid any attention to it. They continued to watch the shrine. A sound of banging, and dull clangings as of the shooting of bolts, came up to their ears. Then the little door opened again, and the two priests peeped cautiously out. Seeing no one, they swiftly locked the door. Still with hurried sideways glances, the one who held the key ran along in the shadow of the shrine for some distance, darted across the open to one of the small goldfish-pools which ornamented the court, and stooping down, slipped the key into the water. Then he ran back to his companion, and together, still in complete silence, they scuttled back across the blazing pavement, darted like rabbits into the little passage, and disappeared.

"Why, I believe they have been locking it up! Now why in the world would they do that?" asked Miss Hande, turning as usual to Laura for information.

Before she could answer, "Hullo! Listen!" said Derek.

A sharp dry crack, like the crack of a whip, broke lightly across the hot sun-washed air that filled the temple courts—and then another, and another. Snap, snap, snap—rather like someone breaking tough sticks for firewood. Such a little harmless sound across the blazing afternoon; to Judith, Lilah and Miss Hande it conveyed nothing at all. But the two men looked at one another with faces positively luminous with a common intelligence. Involuntarily Vinstead glanced quickly at Mrs. Leroy. Snap, snap—two more whips were cracked across the glittering roofs, away down by the gate.

"Those damned T'ao-pings!" she said, rather resentfully.

"Why, what is it?" Judith asked.

As if in answer, a loud and terrible screaming rang up for a moment from below, and as suddenly fell silent.

"It's rifle-fire," said Mrs. Leroy.

Chapter Eighteen

OUT to the island pavilion Niu came slippering in his white coat. His pale-green skin was paler and greener than ever; his teeth chattered as he addressed his mistress, gesticulating and pointing first downwards in the direction of the gate, and then up towards the hill behind them.

"What does he say?" asked Derek and Vinstead together.

"He wants us to go, by the upper gate. He says there are lots of bandits, and that they've shot two monks already down by the entrance."

"I bet he's exaggerating," said Derek. "Niu's a frightful old funk-stick. Remember him on that trip in the hills, when Touchy christened him Æolus because he got the wind up so often? They won't touch us. I think we'd much better have lunch first, anyhow."

"I rather think so too," said Laura. "But, Derek, we'd better see about the donkeys. If the T'ao-pings do get in they'll almost certainly collar them."

"Yes, that's true. What a damned nuisance they are!" grumbled Derek. "Well, tell him to send that chap of Nina's down to bring the mokes up here; he'll be too frightened to go himself."

"I'll tell him myself," said Laura. She spoke to Niu, who presently reappeared with a fat jolly-faced house-coolie in blue clothes. Laura told him in Chinese to go down and find the donkeys, and bring them up to the pavilion. He bowed over his clasped hands and went. "*K'ai fan!*" (Open the rice!) said Laura to Niu again.

Miss Hande put up her lorgnette now, and gazed at her deputy hostess. "Do you really consider it prudent to remain here, if the temple is just full of bandits?" she inquired, with her usual flat mildness.

"Oh, I think so," replied Mrs. Leroy, beginning to drink the soup which Niu brought in little cups. "They very rarely bother Europeans. It would be the most extraordinary bad luck if they were to interfere with us."

"You and the Professor are due for some bad joss," observed Lilah casually.

Vinstead frowned at this inopportune remark, and the soup was consumed in a rather uneasy silence. The knowledge that men were shooting to kill within a few hundred yards of him produced in the Professor that particular stimulus to the nervous system which is usual to civilised man in such circumstances. He could not judge, stranger as he was, what was the proper course to take. Given the presence of that most inconvenient adjunct to trouble known to Englishmen as "women in the party," his normal instinct would have been to get away, as far and as fast as possible. But he might well be mistaken. What he could judge of to some extent was the attitude of those who were taking the decision. And he was clear of this—Mrs. Leroy and Derek might be careless, but they were sincere. Vinstead had been through the war on three fronts, and he was familiar with fear, and with every form of bravado which men used to mask fear. And he recognised that these two people, if they *were* being criminally casual, were at least being so in good faith, with the simplicity of those to whom wars and rumours of wars have become such a commonplace as to cause no particular excitement.

They finished their soup, but there was no sign of the donkeys. "What a time he is! I hope nothing's happened to him," said Laura presently, rather anxiously.

"Well, let's have the next course, anyhow," said Derek. "*Lai!*" he called loudly.

No one came.

"*Lai!*" be bellowed again. Still no one either came or answered. "Damn them! What are they up to? I'll go and see," he said, jumping up.

He reappeared in a couple of minutes looking a good deal disturbed.

"They've gone!" he said.

"What, the servants? Oh, nonsense, Derek—you can't have found the right place."

"Yes, I did—they'd left this," he held out a little saucer which Laura recognised as belonging to Nina's coffee-set. "But they've done a clean bunk with everything else."

"Goodness! How monstrous of Niu," said Mrs. Leroy.

"Might we not perhaps go ourselves?" suggested Vinstead, "since we can't have any more lunch."

"We must wait till Nina's chap—what's-his-name—who went for the donkeys, comes back," said Derek. "We can't very well leave him behind, and besides, we want the beasts."

"The servants may have met him and taken him along, mayn't they?" said Lilah, lighting a cigarette.

"Yes, they may—but then we don't know," said Derek impatiently.

They decided to wait a few more minutes, and waited, now in considerable discomfort. Nothing is more trying than uncertainty as to the right thing to do, in a position of possible danger; the suspense and inaction weigh on the spirits, and apply nettle-stings to the nerves. Miss Hande, after her one protest, sat silent, gazing about her; Lilah smoked, and Vinstead also lit a cigarette; Judith, declaring—"This is rather fun," went over to a balustrade and stared down into the court below.

"Which way would he come up with the donkeys?" she called.

"Oh, a hundred ways!" said Derek irritably, "these places are perfect rabbit-warrens," and then turned back to discussing with Laura the way out by the upper gate. "Do you know how one gets to it?" he asked.

"Yes—you go down on to that long narrow terrace just below here, and along it, and then through a few more small courts, up into the corner. It's almost in the same position as we are, but the opposite side of the temple."

"There's no other way out, is there?"

"Not that I ever heard of."

"And what do you come out to?"

"The track over from the temple of the Jade Emperor. But I think there's a small side-track that brings you down towards Men-t'ou-kou. I've never actually been along it. Henry showed the start of it to me once."

"Look—oh, look!"

Judith's voice, on a soft breath of excitement, made them turn their eyes where she pointed.

Down in the courtyard, which since the departure of the two priests had lain empty except for the black shadows on the pale pavement—empty, and perfectly still, with a complete architectural stillness which gardens never know—there was a movement. A little black shadow, like that of a monkey with a cap and stick, was suddenly projected round the corner of the great shrine, silently. Then a small figure, rather monkey-like in grey uniform, followed his shadow round the shrine— a soldier with a rifle. Two followed him, and then three more. They stood a moment or two, uncertainly, and then with the purposeless inquisitiveness of monkeys they scattered over the court, poking and peering here and there. They spat into the goldfish ponds, and rattled the lock of the door in the shrine. Gathered there, in the shadow, they were out of sight of the exit from the little dark passage by which the two priests had come and gone—and a lay-brother who now emerged from it did not see them. He had some object clasped to his blue bosom, and peering out, started to run swiftly up the side of the court. As he came abreast of the shrine, he saw the soldiers and they saw him, at the same moment. He turned back, scuttling for his life towards the passage, but they were too quick for him. A pack of grey monkeys, with the high if awkward turn of speed of apes, they streamed across the court, and intercepted him just as he reached the bolt-hole. One of them made a grab at the thing he held clasped to his chest; the monk resisted, protesting; clutched it more desperately than ever. Grinning and jabbering, they scuffled with him; one of them inserted a rifle-butt under his left arm, and while the others held him, prised it free of his body and twisted it cruelly. The monk writhed and screamed, and at last, suddenly, let the object go. A porcelain vase, it fell with a crash on the pavement—the bright splinters flew in all directions. The soldiers pounced with insane acquisitiveness on the fragments, handled them, and then tossed them aside. Defrauded of their booty, a gust of senseless fury seemed to overtake the group. Before the sickened eyes of the onlookers, one snatched up the rifle which he had used before, and while two more held his victim by the arms, he plunged the bayonet into his body—once, twice, a third time. The blue figure turned limp, and sank down between the hands of his tormentors—they loosed their hold, and it rolled over, with a horrible boneless collapse, on to the pavement, among the shards of the broken vase. A dark patch appeared beside it, under the pitiless light, spreading over the flag-stones. But the soldiers were now bored—casually they kicked the corpse, and then turned to seek fresh amusement elsewhere—chattering and grinning, they entered the little passage and disappeared.

When modern civilised people see such a thing take place in front of them, it has a curiously paralysing effect. Judith and Miss Hande each made a little moaning sound, surprisingly alike—but except for that, for some moments the whole party remained quite still, staring down at the courtyard, empty again now save for the two patches on the pavement—the shapeless blue one and the darker one which spread and spread, slowly, over the paving-stones. In the glaring heat they felt chilly, and a little sick. Vinstead was the first to throw off the numbness of the shock.

"I suggest that we go, now," he said—rather temperately, in the circumstances, he thought. "Can we do any good by waiting?"

"No," said Laura decidedly. "Now that they've got inside, the coolie will never get the donkeys up here. They've very likely been pinched already. We'd better go at once." As she spoke she took off her pearls and slipped them into her pocket. "You'd better take off your brooches and things," she said to Miss Hande and Lilah.

"Why?" asked Miss Hande.

"Because they might tempt the T'ao-pings, if we meet any. They covet what they see, like magpies."

Action of any sort was a relief after that silent paralysis.

"Where shall I put these?" asked Lilah, who ran rather to jewellery and was encumbered with pearl-and-coral chains and long fringed ear-rings to match.

"Oh, in your pockets—anywhere out of sight," said Mrs. Leroy briefly. Miss Hande was pinning her handsome rings carefully into the lining of her neat jacket, and Lilah finally disposed of her trinkets in her vanity-bag.

"Lead away, Laura," Derek urged.

To reach the long terrace which led across the upper levels of the monastery towards the exit on the further side, they had to descend a few steps into a small court, and then follow a broad marble staircase which led down in a series of sharp right-angled turns, sunk deep between high banks covered with flowering shrubs. All close together, and in silence, the party moved swiftly down this staircase, up which, straggling and chattering, they had come less than an hour before, on their way to the lunch that they had never eaten. The last abrupt turn was only a few steps above the terrace itself—as they rounded it they came on a group of T'ao-pings, gathered in a bunch a few yards ahead, disputing over some trivial piece of loot which they had picked up.

"Come on, walk straight past them as though you didn't see them," said Mrs. Leroy low and urgently.

But the party was too large and undisciplined to obey. Besides herself not one of them, except Derek, knew the strange virtue of an appearance of resolved and purpose-ful action on the vacillating and inconsequent Chinese mind. Involuntarily they paused. "Can't we go round some other way?" Miss Hande asked. She was shaken by the horrible scene she had just witnessed; and these men, too, had bayonets, and were quarrelling loudly, menacing one another with yellow fists. Her hesitation was natural enough, but it was fatal.

"Nonsense, come on," said Laura firmly, and con-tinued to walk forward. After another second's hesita-tion Miss Hande and the others followed. It was too late. The T'ao-pings had seen the check, the argument; they had smelt irresolution, fear perhaps—the things by which they live. With the idle instinct for terrorising which they love to exercise, they sprang up and barred the way, brandishing their rifles. And then someone gave a little scream.

But for that scream they might still have got through. Derek and Mrs. Leroy, accustomed to this sort of thing, were walking steadily forward; a very remarkable expression of ostentatious good humour, mingled with determination, which Vinstead had never seen before, set like a mask on both their faces. It is an expression which those who live much among the Chinese in troubled times come to know well, and to dislike the sight of most heartily. But at the sound of that slight scream a still more noticeable expression appeared on the faces of their opponents—the delighted grin of armed power in the face of helplessness; silly, cruel, half-animal. When they saw that grin Derek and Mrs. Leroy knew that they were done. She stood still, murderous hate in her heart against the unknown emitter of that fatal little cry. "We must go back," she said over her shoulder, without turning her head; "turn round and walk slowly back up the steps." And to the grinning T'ao-pings before her she observed, smiling pleasantly, "*Pu yao chin; tsai-chien*" (It doesn't matter—good-bye), and turned and walked slowly after the others.

For some moments the soldiers remained nonplussed by this sudden change of front, and the party reached the top of the steps undisturbed. A horseshoe-shaped door led off out of the small court at the top, on the opposite side to the entrance to their own pavilion. "Shall we try that?" said Derek, pointing to it. "We may be able to get through up here, and drop down on to the terrace further on."

"All right, let's try," said Mrs. Leroy.

"I've forgotten my camera!" said Vinstead suddenly.

"I'll follow you," he called as he darted back to the island pavilion.

"Damn the fellow!" said Derek. "Come on, Laura— he'll catch us up."

"No—I really think we had better keep together," said Laura. Her mind caught a sudden flashlight picture of the Professor's tall lean figure in the hands of a group of grey monkeys. "We'll wait," she said stubbornly. She had no time to analyse her feelings about this picture, but acted on them decisively. The little party stood still, uncertain and impatient, in the small court at the top of the steps, watching for Vinstead's reappearance. "Let's go and hurry him up—I saw his wretched camera under the table in the lunch place," said Lilah rather contemptuously, and moved off towards the corner court. The others followed her. Perhaps if Laura's mind had not been obsessed by that picture, she might have considered the unwisdom of their all reassembling in a dead end, from which there was no other exit, but she went with the rest. Vinstead was groping and peering round the inner court—the camera lay where Lilah had said. She picked it up and called to him, "Here you are."

"Oh, thanks!" he said; "stupid of me."

"Very!" said Derek under his breath. "*Now* come on," he said aloud.

"Oh, look!" That soft breathing note of Judith's came for the second time that day, and it was ominous in Laura's ears. Before she turned her head she really knew what she would see. The narrow entry-passage beyond the island pavilion was full of grey uniforms, blocking it from wall to wall. They were fairly trapped.

Derek's explosive, "Oh, dam*n*ation!" was the first sound made by any of the party. To Vinstead's amazement, the next moment he turned to Mrs. Leroy with

an apology; he had not hitherto shown any special care
for niceness of language in her presence.

"Never mind, *this* time," she said. Then she turned
to the rest and spoke low and rapidly, but with a tone of
authority which he had not heard since he left the army.
"Listen, all of you. Whatever happens, no one must
show alarm or resentment. Do you understand? *Whatever* they do. Look cheerful and polite. Don't talk much
among yourselves, and *don't laugh*. Just keep quiet and
look unconcerned. Now I'll talk to them. Have you
got a card, Derek?"

From a note-case in the breast pocket of his shirt Derek
produced a card. On one side was written:

M. Derek Fitzmaurice,
    Premier Secrétaire à la Légation de Grande Bretagne.

Laura turned it over. On the back a single line of
curious characters stretched across it from side to side—
his style and title in Chinese. "Good," she said, and
holding it in her hand she advanced upon the grey
group in the entry-way. Derek went with her.

In a parley even with bandits, in China, certain for-
malities are to be observed. Mrs. Leroy, again with
that disturbing and disagreeable expression of good
temper on her face, asked for their general. It appeared
that they had no general. An officer, then—her tone was
equable, but a little haughty. They had no officer.
Then, their Number One. She was, she explained, from
the *Ying-kuo-fu* (British Legation) and this Great Man
(indicating Derek) was the *San-ch'in-ch'ai*, or Third
Envoy. Obviously, therefore, they could only profitably
speak with the Number One. The T'ao-pings indicated
that the Number One was elsewhere—they pointed
down towards the lower courts. Then, let him be
fetched, said Mrs. Leroy. Holding Derek's card ver-

tically, she showed it to the gang. Here was the *p'ien-tzu*, which showed his rank. They all peered at it curiously, but it was clear that only one or two could understand it —these read it aloud, several times over, to their companions.

A slight uncertainty now showed itself among the T'ao-pings. They jabbered among themselves, while Mrs. Leroy returned, still with her air of good-tempered *hauteur*, to the rest. Eventually they came up to the group, and counted them over on their fingers—six. Then four or five of them went on into the inner court, where the pavilion was, and examined it thoroughly. Finding nothing to interest them, and walls at least fifteen feet high all round, with no means of exit, they returned to their comrades, and after further discussion several went off, and the rest, to the number of seven or eight, sat down in the entry-passage on guard. For the moment the foreign party were left to themselves.

Chapter Nineteen

WHEN anything so legendary as being briganded does actually happen to ordinary people in real life, the first feeling is almost always one of quite flat surprise. "This has happened to *us*!" Fear comes later. It comes all right, but not at first. On the contrary the surprise, especially in the young, may be not untinged with a certain adventurous satisfaction. And then the further reflection follows, "What *will* happen to us?"

It was so with the party at T'an Chüeh Ssu. Since the moment of their first seeing the soldiers enter the court below, the whole thing had passed so rapidly that when they finally found themselves boxed up in the corner courtyard they had to adjust their minds to the astounding fact that they really were prisoners, and that their own volition no longer completely controlled their actions. That group of under-sized yellow-faced men in the dirty uniforms, who now squatted in the entry-way, some examining the sores on their feet, while others rather ostentatiously cleaned their rifles, could prevent them from leaving if they tried to walk out—could, and certainly would. Those same rifles gave them complete power to enforce their will. And the question then rose to the surface of each mind, "What else will they do, or make us do?"

Accordingly, they began to question Mrs. Leroy. Her knowledge of the language and long experience of the country naturally placed her to some extent in the position of leader, and to her they looked for information. "What did they say?" "What will they do?" "What happens now?"

Laura could not give them much satisfaction. The Number One was being sought for. As to what would happen when he came, Heaven knew! You never did know, with T'ao-pings. The only constant factor about them, the inevitable certainty, was that they always wanted money. "They may be content with robbing us, or they may hold us to ransom, if they don't think the risk too big."

"But I thought you said they never interfered with foreigners," protested Miss Hande.

"*Almost* never. It isn't usual. Especially so near Peking. But this seems a very large gang, and they're in pretty desperate straits, by the look of them. I haven't asked yet, but I'm fairly sure they're some of Wang's three battalions who've recently been disbanded, and if so they're probably almost starving."

"But surely they won't dare to interfere seriously with you? They know you come from the Legation. It would be madness," said Vinstead.

"It would have been madness a few years ago to touch any British national," said Laura gloomily, "but is it now? Look at the murders they've got away with lately—Captain Briggs, the Gowers, Miss Angus."

"What happened about them? I'm afraid I don't know," said Vinstead.

"Feeble protests to the Chinese Government on our side, and insolently hypocritical replies on theirs," said Derek bitterly. "And there it ends. Your life depends now out here on your own ingenuity, not on any protection you get from your Government."

"I wish Henri were here," said Laura fervently.

"By Jove, yes!" said Derek.

"Why on earth Henri?" Judith asked, and Vinstead, who was wondering exactly the same thing, waited with interest for the reply.

"Oh, because the French won't stand for this sort of thing, and the Chinese blooming well know it," replied Derek. "If old La Roche were to get some fingers sent in to jog him up over a ransom his answer would probably be a couple of aeroplanes or something of that sort. But in point of fact he doesn't get them. When did anyone last hear of a French national being shot up? Except missionaries, of course, who come at their own risk?"

"And just why is that?" Miss Hande inquired, putting up her lorgnette.

"What I say—the French make it too jolly uncomfortable for the Chinese. Kidnapping Frenchmen is simply too unremunerative for words, whereas we're a perfect gold-mine, safe as houses."

Vinstead was surprised at the bitterness of this outburst. And a certain emphasis was lent to Fitzmaurice's remarks by the fact that he, Vinstead, was himself at the moment in the position of the kidnapped. It was very different to reading about someone else in *The Times*. He felt that his views of Government policy would probably undergo considerable modification if it lasted very long. But his profound English instinct for treating serious matters lightly triumphed for the moment.

"Well, I shall insist on having *my* fingers sent direct to the Foreign Office," he said. "I hope you'll be able to arrange that for me," turning to Laura. "I'd like the Secretary of State to open them himself."

"He wouldn't do that," said Derek, giggling, "they'd come to him in a nice red box, with a neat memorandum from someone like me explaining how improbable it was that they really *were* your fingers—or fingers at all, in fact. Laura," he went on, "what about taking a nose round and seeing if there's any way out of this blooming place."

"All right," said Mrs. Leroy. "You go, and we'll sit

here and show ourselves, otherwise they may come with you."

Vinstead and Derek accordingly nosed for some time, while the ladies sat in the outer court by the island pavilion, in full view of the guard—but the operation produced no result. There were no doors in the back walls of the buildings which enclosed the inner court in front, and they reported the monastery wall behind as impossible to climb; it was far too high and steep to get up.

"Well, now, you sit here," said Laura. "I want to go and dodge my pearls. Have you got a knife, Derek?"

Taking his knife, she and Miss Hande repaired to the inner pavilion. There she slit open the stitches of the hem of the right leg of her shorts for an inch or so, and using a safety-pin as a bodkin, threaded her pearls through the hem and fastened the snap. The string exactly fitted the shorts. Miss Hande observed the operation with the deepest interest. "Well, isn't that smart?" she remarked at length.

"I always put them there," said Mrs. Leroy. "I advise you to pin your rings inside your lining, too."

Miss Hande thought this smart also. A portion of the sewing of her jacket lining was cut, and Laura helped her to pin her rings to the inside of it, under the breast-pocket, where the pins would not show. "They'll hardly find them now, even if they search you," she said, with satisfaction.

"Why, you don't say they will *search* us?" exclaimed Miss Hande.

"I shouldn't wonder," said Laura. "And remember, if they do, you have got to treat it as a joke, and make no resistance. It's your one chance."

"Why, for mercy's sake! But I'm an American citizen! Surely, if you tell them that they won't touch me? Our relations with the Chinese are so marvellous—

they've always been perfectly cordial; quite different to other nations."

"I'll tell them gladly," said Laura, "but I'm afraid you won't find that international cordiality helps much with bandits. Wholesome dread is the only consideration which affects them. Now if you were French there would be something in it, as Mr. Fitzmaurice says. By the way, was it you who screamed a little, when we first met them, down on the terrace?"

"No—I vurry rarely scream," said Miss Hande, with most convincing flatness.

"Mmm—then it must have been Judith," said Mrs. Leroy. "Well, don't scream, anyhow—not even if they threaten to shoot."

"Why not?" inquired Miss Hande, with impartial interest.

"Oh, they like it," said Mrs. Leroy, "and it pokes them up. Come on, we'd better go back."

On their return to the outer courtyard Lilah announced her intention of going to the pavilion and disposing of *her* trinkets, which bulged and chinked rather in her vanity-bag. "I shall find a crack in the wall or something," she observed, "and leave them there till we go," and wandered off, very coolly, to look for a suitable place.

The rest made themselves as comfortable as they could on the small wicker chairs and stools from round the lunch-table, which they placed in a patch of shade in one corner of the court. There, rather huddled together, because the patch was small, they discussed the next move in low tones. Since they could not get out themselves, the obvious thing was, if possible, to get word out. The only chance of this was to bribe one of the guards to take a note to Chieh T'ai Ssu—supposing he knew the way, which, as Laura pointed out, was very doubtful. Their total funds, they ascertained, amounted to twenty-three dollars between them. No one had any paper, but Vinstead produced a minute copy of Housman's *Last Poems*, and on the fly-leaf of this, Laura wrote:

"For Touchy. All six impounded at T.C.S.—B.s' intentions uncertain. Jump alive. L.L."

"I think that will do," she said, after reading it over. "Even if an English-speaking T'ao-ping lights on it, it won't help him much."

"I shouldn't put 'all six,'" said Derek, "numbers are just the one thing they might understand."

"Yes, you're right. That won't do. What shall I put?"

"Whole bunch," suggested Judith. This was accepted, and the correction made. Vinstead reluctantly agreed to part with his little book, on Mrs. Leroy's pointing out to him that a book was so much less like a note than a note.

But it was no good. The most careful procedure in bribery was observed; one T'ao-ping was detached from the rest by Laura, much as a dog cuts out a sheep from the flock; and Derek was told off to offer him ten dollars to carry the book to Chieh T'ai Ssu and give it to Nei, the English Great-Man, it being thought that Derek's limited knowledge of Chinese would avoid awkward explanations. The T'ao-ping selected, however (who had ring-worm of the scalp, but whose feet and slippers had appeared sound to Laura, who chose him on those grounds) was either deaf or mentally deficient. He seemed quite unable to take in what was required of him, even when Laura, rather reluctantly, joined in the explanations. He merely reiterated, "You from where come?" over and over again, and had obviously never heard of Chieh T'ai Ssu. When in desperation they showed him a five-dollar note, hoping that this would stimulate his intellect, his simian screech of rapture brought all the others crowding round. The note was rescued with some trouble, but the attempt had to be abandoned.

So there they were, no better off than before. There was no sign of the appearance of the Number One. Once or twice some more grey-clad figures came up and exchanged remarks with the group in the entry-way, and then moved off, aimless and shiftless, after staring curiously at the foreigners. And once Judith, who was sitting on the outside of the group, and could therefore see furthest down the passage, vowed that she saw Niu appear for a moment and signal to her. He was not in his white coat, she said, but in black trousers and "a sort of jacket," but she was sure it was Niu. Derek had sprung up and moved out from behind the wall, to get a view—but the figure had gone. "He nipped off at once, when the T'ao-pings turned round," Judith said. Derek looked at his watch, "Two o'clock—no wonder I'm hungry," he observed. "Damned old brute—he might at least have left the lunch behind, and we could have had something to eat. What sort of signal did he make?"

"He waved his hand about, and tapped his chest with his fingers."

"That might mean anything," said Derek.

"It *might* mean that he was going to do something," said Judith doubtfully, "it was just like what he does when he says, 'I fix.'"

Laura could not help smiling. "I fix" represented Niu's principal stock of the English language, and it always amused her to hear him using it to Hubbard in those curious bi-lingual colloquies of theirs, which were somehow so effectual. He did, she remembered, on such occasions tap his chest importantly with the middle and first fingers of his right hand. It might well be that he intended to "fix" something, somehow, now. She found it hard to believe that Niu, cowardly and tyrannical as he was, would abandon his *T'ai-t'ai* permanently in such an emergency. But she was too prudent to raise false hopes, and kept her ideas to herself.

The time dragged on. Occasionally the sound of shots or screams from somewhere below broke the hot silence, otherwise only punctuated by the hawking and belching of their captors—a cheerless interruption, showing that the bandits were getting on with the good work in other parts of the temple. In this period of inaction the party had leisure for the first time to become aware of fear; and (those of them who were so minded) to observe their reactions to it. Vinstead, watching the others, decided that so far as it was possible to judge it manifested itself, in them as in him, as a sort of dull excitement. There was also of course that peculiar sensation round the diaphragm, which always accompanies suspense—he was too familiar with this to allow himself to put it down to hunger, as pride suggested. No—hungry he was, but without the presence of those dirty yellow men with the rifles his hunger would have produced different physical symptoms. He was frightened too, and below all his other sensations was the gnawing of this dull excitement, and a sense of exasperation at the futility of fate, in subjecting them to such an experience.

About them all, of course, was that curious unspoken determination to behave very *normally*. Sound enough, thought Vinstead—the more normally you behave, the more normal you will feel. He noticed with approval that Fitzmaurice had begun telling Judith Milne an interminable series of Irish stories connected with hunting; and, feeling a bit of a fool, he was nevertheless constrained to support Miss Hande's spirits by starting a conversation about Freud's Theory of Laughter. It was, he felt, a poor choice, but he couldn't think of anything else on the spur of the moment; and there was something about the uncompromising flatness of the novelist's attitude which reminded him vaguely of the incredibly un-funny stories with which the great Viennese illustrates *Die Komik* and *Der Humor*.

Mrs. Leroy, meanwhile, was not making the smallest effort to talk to anyone. Sitting on a stool, her back propped against the wall, with her feet stretched out in front of her and her hat tilted over her eyes, she was smoking dreamily—as much absorbed, to Vinstead's watchful observation, as she had been on the rocks above the ferry at Mo-shih-k'ou three days—was it *really* only three days?—ago. Her mind however was busily at work. From wondering what, if anything, she could possibly do next to extricate the party from their predicament, she passed—finding nothing at all—to the circumstances which had led them into it. She was responsible, of course, for the lot of them, and she was wondering whether it was just pure bad luck that they had been briganded, or whether she had somehow, in Derek's favourite phrase, "bogged it." She ran rapidly over the sequence of events, from the moment of their arrival at the temple, questioning her action at each one. They might, of course, have left when Niu first suggested it, but then there were the donkeys, and they had not lunched—she knew how strenuously opposed Henry always was to launching any party on an expedition unfed. When they met the T'ao-pings down on the terrace—well, that was not her fault; that miserable Judith had screamed, and torn it. It was a succession of small chances lost by inches, and the last was when they waited in the upper court for Vinstead to fetch his camera. *No*—she had been right then, at least; you could not leave anyone behind at such a moment.

The recollection of that pause for Vinstead, however,

led her on to a number of other considerations, which she now had leisure to examine. She recalled his curious look and tone, just before they went to lunch, when he quoted at her, "Come you not, a careless stranger, Him with reckless words to waken." There had been pain and bitterness, or something very like them, in his face and voice—and going over the context of their conversation, pain and bitterness, with the words he used to her, then, could only point to one rather surprising conclusion. Mm'm—she wondered where he stood? Mrs. Leroy, for all her absent-mindedness, was not such a fool as not to realise perfectly well when men were beginning to be interested in her; but till that moment before lunch she could honestly say that she had not observed any signs of a feeling for herself in the Professor—indeed, it would have been more than ridiculous to look for them, "Bless my soul, I only *met* the man two days ago!" Now, however, she could not say that she had noticed nothing. Moreover, that lightning picture of Vinstead among the T'ao-pings which had flashed so decisively across her inner vision had given a sort of jab to her own consciousness—she was forced to realise that he had made rather a big hole for himself in her mind, even in this short time.

Her thoughts, however, did not stay long with Vinstead. They ran on to Henry. How angry Henry would be—and how anxious! How completely all his objections to the picnic were being justified—and how he would enjoy *not* telling them all that he had told them so, when they got back. *When they got back*—the words left a horrid little creeping question in the mind, like a nasty taste. When *would* they get back? Impossible to say. They might merely be *dévalisés*, little as they had to steal; or, more probably, held to ransom. Ransoming was a lengthy process—two months, or three, or even more—if you survived. Mrs. Leroy knew a good deal about the slow cautious negotiations, conducted at long range through some more or less competent consul or missionary, when a ransom was in question; she knew how often, if the business dragged on too long and the ransom finally offered were too small, the object of it quietly disappeared. The brigands said the person had died—it was more than likely! And she remembered how Henry, on more than one such occasion, sickened by the timidity and belated caution of the authorities, had suggested telegraphing through the intermediary the terse advice, "Commit suicide immediately"—a suggestion which discomposed Sir James Boggit, and moved him, uncomfortable and incensed, to refer to his Commercial and Oriental Attaché as "a fantastical felloh." Three months—but she was due to start home in just over two! The children would be so disappointed if she didn't come. With the thought a sudden passion to escape and live awoke in Mrs. Leroy. Tim and Sarah needed her still—not for many years more, but a few. Sarah must be steered through her teens, over those difficult awkwardnesses which her ruthless sincerity and her scorching tongue would make more marked than usual; Tim ought to be shown—but ever so lightly and casually—a vision of life which would save him alike from a timid and Wykehamical rigidity and from Derek's Gallic and irresponsible excesses. At least she must try—and there was no one to do it but herself— no one! Who else would have the patience? Or *see* just where the need lay, and the delicate roundabout remedy? No, you couldn't delegate those things. Fear had taken on for Mrs. Leroy the sharpest edge of all—the fear for the beloved child. She thought of those two dear heads, the rough brown and the furry brown, bent together over some important task—the skinning of a mole, or the painting of a flower in Bentham—in the school-

room at Garsover. She could see the big light shabby
room with the glossy magnolia-leaves framing the high
windows, the enormous table and the ancient comfortable chairs; all in a complete litter now, of course—
Sarah was so dreadfully untidy. With that vision of the
massive security of English life, the present faded
gradually out of her consciousness. The sun crept round
and scorched her knees, unnoticed; the others moved
their chairs, the T'ao-pings hawked and spat, but Laura
Leroy never stirred. Those things had become unreal—
her other world had swallowed her up. Judith observed
her absorption and thought, rather resentfully, "Even
when we're all briganded, she can't concentrate on it";
she knew that far-away look. And suddenly she glanced
round her and said aloud, "Where's Lilah?"

No one knew. No one had seen Lilah since she went
to hide her jewellery. They looked for her in the inner
court, and then in the pavilion, where they expected
confidently to find her, but there was no sign of her.
She had vanished as completely as if an eagle had carried
her off.

"But it isn't *possible!*" said Laura, roused at last.
"Even if they'd let her go, we should have seen her walk
past us, and there's no other way out."

"*You* wouldn't have seen her," said Derek, "but we
should—for certain. She must be somewhere."

They looked again. She wasn't anywhere. There was
not cover for a mouse in the pavilion, let alone for
Lilah, who was no mouse. Suddenly Judith, who had
been roaming about, came up to Laura, her eyebrows
positively lambent with intelligence. "I know," she
murmured, putting her mouth to her aunt's ear, "she's
got out at the back."

"How? The back? What do you mean?" asked
Laura in the same tone.

"Round here—look!" she led Mrs. Leroy to the chasm behind the pavilion. "Don't you remember how she got up the wall at Chieh T'ai Ssu—she told me she'd shown you yesterday—with her back and feet? I'm sure she's got out like that. You can see where she's scraped the moss."

Sure enough, in the middle of the long narrow space a sort of broken line showed on the monastery wall, where something had recently rubbed the bricks free of moss—it ended where the roots of an oak tree hung down in loops from the hill-side, some fifteen feet above where they stood. Laura looked at the height in amazement. "But, good heavens, she could never have got right up there!" she said.

"Oh yes she could—I bet she has!" said Judith triumphantly.

"Laura!" Derek's voice came sharp and urgent. "Where are you? Come here!"

"All right," said Mrs. Leroy, squeezing back round the end of the pavilion, "what is it?" But she soon saw what it was. The outer courtyard was full of soldiers, fifty or sixty of them, all talking loudly and at once— the original guard were pointing at the foreigners and giving explanations to an individual who appeared to be the long-awaited Number One; for some reason they seemed to be angry, and one soldier was holding Vinstead by the elbow and giving him a shake now and then.

"I think they thought you'd gone off," said Derek as she came forward. "For heaven's sake come and talk to them. They look rather nasty."

They did look very nasty, especially the Number One. He was small and stoutly built, and short of one eye; his yellow face was deeply pitted with smallpox, and his hands between the fingers were roughened and pocked with scabies. Their mere numbers somehow made the bandits all at once more menacing than the first party had been.

"Keep quite still," Laura said to Vinstead. "He'll let go presently." And she asked some of the men if they had got or not-got the Number One?

"Got, got," they replied in chorus, indicating the one-eyed individual. "Got, got!"

To him Mrs. Leroy addressed herself, rather formally. He wanted to speak-talk? Apparently he did. "That man wants what?" she said, indicating the soldier who held Vinstead. "He let go, can talk." The bandit dropped Vinstead's arm. "You want what?" Mrs. Leroy then asked. She spoke with a curious slow deliberation, and that impervious friendliness was again on her face.

What the Number One wanted first was to count his bag. The prisoners were marshalled in a row and counted over—*i-kō, lian-kō, san-kō, ssu-kō, wu-kō*—five-piece. Then a terrific argument began. There should have been *liu-kō*—six-piece. "Still one," said the guards. They searched noisily and frantically through the inner court and pavilion, as our party had themselves searched a few moments before, but the six-piece was nowhere to be found.

And then suddenly, swift as the blowing-up of a summer storm, the bandits turned dangerous. Enraged by the loss of the sixth captive, they seized all the others by the arms and shoulders and shook them roughly to and fro, shouting and shaking their fists in their faces. "Keep quiet—do keep perfectly quiet," Laura gasped out, the breath nearly shaken out of her. "Smile."

This last piece of advice Vinstead and Derek found it impossible to follow, with yellow soldiers handling Laura and Judith with brutal roughness. Never in their lives, probably, had they experienced such violent emotions of murderous hatred and helpless impotence.

Miss Hande, though her lorgnette was knocked off and broken, and her neat dark bun of hair shaken down, obediently preserved a gallant smirk all the time. In a lull Laura managed to make herself heard by the Number One. "What plan?" she asked, still with that almost drawling deliberation. She tried rather ingeniously to throw the onus for Lilah's loss on the guards. "We know nothing—you ask-ask these men; we all-time sit-sit; they all-time here sit—*they* know."

She was listened to, but her words did not produce quite the effect she intended. Vinstead could only think afterwards of what followed as a sort of typhoon which burst over them. A frightful quarrel broke out between the newcomers and the men on guard; bayonets and rifle-butts were freely used; one man was shot, and lay under the courtyard wall, jerking his legs up and down. No one paid any attention to him, except that while he still moved another T'ao-ping quietly helped himself to his bandolier. Released for the moment, Vinstead moved quickly over to Laura. "Are you hurt?" he asked.

"No, not a bit; but you really must keep steady. You were making awful faces just now."

"Faces! My God!" said Vinstead. "If you knew——"

He had no chance to tell her what she didn't know. The T'ao-pings had a fresh plan, possibly inspired by the guards out of revenge. The hands of the five prisoners were tied roughly behind their backs, and they were stood up in a row against the courtyard wall. A file of soldiers loaded their rifles and stood opposite, with weapons pointed at them.

"Oh, Christ, the swine!" ejaculated Derek.

"It's all right—they won't hit us. You can see they're aiming high," said Vinstead. The words came out in a voice whose careful normality made it sound quite unreal. For a fraction of a second he stood, hoping to God that those crazy yellow fiends wouldn't change their minds, or shoot crooked. Then the volley came. He was right —it splintered the plaster above their heads, and the dust drifted down into their eyes, but they were not hurt. Blinking through the dust, he peered anxiously along the row to see how the women had stood it—his own knees were unsteady, and the blood kept racing in waves over his body and then draining sickeningly back to the heart. Judith and Laura were both very white. Miss Hande, however, with superb composure, blew a speck of plaster off her nose and observed that, "She guessed she didn't think Oriental humour so vurry subtle after all." The T'ao-pings, grinning and chattering, swarmed round them, again with the question, "Six-piece what place?"

"We don't know," Laura told them, with the same weary deliberation. "Gone, *wai-t'ou* (outside)." She felt suddenly immensely tired, and quite unable to think of anything to say or do to mend matters. Then a burst of laughter drew her attention. The bandits had started a new game. One of them advanced towards Vinstead with a fixed bayonet. Her heart turned over horribly in her body as he came close to him, paused, drew back, and lunged forward. The steel struck the wall just between them, within a couple of inches of his arm—if Vinstead had moved he must have been hit. Amid roars of applause the soldier moved on towards Judith. Suddenly Laura had an inspiration.

"*Chê-li Lai!*" (come here!) she called loudly to the man with the bayonet. Startled, the soldier paused, and with the ingrained Chinese habit of obedience came towards her; the others, astonished, were silent. "More near," she told him, and then in the sudden quiet, loud, slow, and clear, she made an oration. If that man, she told the bandits, holds his fire-stick there till I count ten, I jump on it. Then I die. I from the *Ying-kuo-fu*—that man *Ying-kuo-fu* Third Envoy; this man—nodding at Vinstead—*Ying-kuo Ta Shuai*. (Why she chose the title of Commander-in-Chief for Vinstead she couldn't think, but it was heard with silent respect.) This, she proceeded, was a *hu-tu-ti fah-tzu*—an idiot-plan. "I die—English Emperor very angry; afterwards you all extreme regret this plan. Now!"—she paused dramatically—"one, two, three, four——"

In China such speechifying is quite in order. The commonest affairs of daily life are there conducted with an amount of oratory inconceivable to us. The difficulty is to catch the attention of the audience. On this occasion Laura's speech and manœuvre succeeded beyond hope. Abashed, discomfited, before she reached "five," the small soldier stepped back—Mrs. Leroy, tall, menacing, and still slowly counting, walked after him, till he lowered his weapon and shrank away into the crowd, whose laughter broke out tumultuously. Pursuing her advantage, she strode up to the Number One, and standing sideways before him, indicated her bound hands. "What plan? Not-good plan," she said loftily, and expatiated further and with considerable detail on the exact means that would be used to avenge any injury to English Commanders-in-Chief and people from the British Legation.

The supreme characteristic of the Chinese is their inconsequence. As rapidly as it had arisen, the storm subsided. Something like friendliness succeeded to hostility and bullying. Her hands were freed, and she showed Derek's card. The others were also released, and the Number One, impressed by the *p'ien-tzu*, even offered some kind of apology. He retired into a corner to take counsel with a sort of Soviet of six or seven other T'ao-pings, while the little party, rubbing their wrists, sat down again on their stools and lit much-needed cigarettes.

They all had rather the sleepy confused sensations of relief with which one comes to after an anæsthetic. The stools were occupied by soldiers, but Laura, determined to hold the ground momentarily gained, quietly turned them off with the single word, "Ours."

"Phew! That was a go!" said Derek, wiping the dust off his face. "What did you tell them, Laura?"

"Have you any brandy?" Laura asked, ignoring his question. Judith was sitting in a rather crumpled attitude on her stool, her head against the wall, her eyes shut again—a case for brandy, if ever there was one; she herself felt that she could do with some very well indeed. She felt cold too, but most of all she wanted something normal to do, like drinking, to shake off the sense of nightmare which kept surging sickly over her whenever she looked in the direction of the grey figures with rifles just across the little court.

However, Derek had no brandy. They had to make do with cigarettes as a restorative, and conversation. Laura translated her speech for the benefit of the rest, and Vinstead began discussing this last episode with Miss Hande. He was no doubt right to try, but it was not a great success; their nerves were too stunned, the suspense as to what was to come next was still too acute. Presently the Number One and the Soviet approached. They were clearly rather undecided, but Mrs. Leroy gathered that a search would be made for Lilah. Rather cautiously the Soviet opened the subject of a ransom. Laura, still on the haughty line, said that she must discuss this at great length with the Commander-in-Chief and the Third Envoy. Time was, of course, now their object, since Lilah *had* got out—if she got back to Chieh T'ai Ssu, help would presumably be forthcoming sometime. So she temporised, and asked to be left to consider it quietly—also they would like some tea. This the

Soviet undertook to produce, and retired. Laura looked
at her watch. It was five minutes to four. No one, of
course, knew *when* Lilah had got out—but she had left
them, ostensibly to hide her trinkets, some time before
Judith had seen Niu; and that was at two o'clock, as
Derek had remarked. By now she ought to be well on
her way, they reckoned.

"Anyone got a cigarette?" Derek asked presently.
"Mine are done."

A census produced a gloomy result. Judith had two,
Vinstead four, Laura one. Miss Hande did not smoke.
They were all rather shaken by their recent experiences,
and they were, moreover, beginning to feel the lack of
food—except for a cocktail and a cup of soup, none of
them had had anything to eat since breakfast, eight
hours before. Tobacco was their one resource, and
there was very little of it—seven cigarettes between the
four of them. Vinstead had a slab of chocolate, which
he offered to Miss Hande; at her instance they had a
piece all round, and felt better.

"Hullo, *now* what's up?" Derek exclaimed suddenly.
A fresh commotion was taking place in the passage. The
soldiers crowded together, jabbering and pointing—
shouts of *Liu-kō* (the sixth), came to their ears.

"Goodness, surely they haven't got Lilah!" Laura
exclaimed in dismay, catching a glimpse of a figure in
European dress among the crowding grey uniforms.
But as they parted to allow the newcomer passage, she
fairly gasped with astonishment. No, they hadn't got
Lilah—with a simper of respectful triumph on her ugly
little face, a flask of eau-de-Cologne grasped firmly in
one hand, and her small brown handbag in the other,
into the corner courtyard walked Hubbard, the maid.

Chapter Twenty

"WELL, madam, this is a proper do, as you might say," was Hubbard's first observation, when the exclamations of astonishment had begun to subside.

"But how on earth did you get here?" Laura repeated; she had asked this before. "Where did they capture you?"

"They didn't capture me, madam," said Hubbard firmly; "I *came* in. When I heard from Miss Lilah that you was in here, among these brutes, I thought, 'Well, my mistress must have *someone* to see after her,' so I made that Niu bring me in."

"But, Hubbard," Laura interrupted, "where did you meet Miss Lilah? And how did you come to be here at all?"

"Why, madam, you said I could take the week-end if I wanted, and I came out yesterday to this hotel place —Barter Jew, they call it—such names!"—said Hubbard, with her usual discreet giggle—"with some friends, you understand. So to-day, we decided to come over here for a picnic, and a look-see. Of course, I didn't know you was here, *then*, madam," said Hubbard rather deprecatingly. "So when we get to the top of the hill, where you start to come down, who should we meet but Niu. Oh, he was in a stew! '*T'ai-t'ai!*' he kept on, '*T'ai-t'ai*'—and waving down here—but really, he is that dumb, if you'll pardon the word, madam, that not a bit of sense could I get out of him."

"Poor Niu!" said Laura, as Hubbard paused for

255

breath. It was plain that he had not deserted them after all, and no doubt it *was* he whom Judith had seen. "Well, go on, Hubbard. Where did you meet Miss Lilah?"

"Why, madam, as I was talking to him—and really, I could have shaken him for his witlessness!—up comes Miss Lilah. And *she* told me you was all in here, sort of prisoners. Her poor dress!" Hubbard threw in, parenthetically. "Green and ruined! I said to her, 'What*ever* have you been doing to yourself, miss?' 'Oh,' she says, in her way, 'I climbed out.'"

"There!" said Judith. "What did I say, Laura?"

"Well, what next, Hubbard? Where is she now?" asked Laura. She knew that the maid was enjoying her epic, and would not be prevented from telling it in her own way, but she had to poke her on.

"Ah, that I couldn't say, madam. She said she should go on to that Jay Tie Sir, and tell the Major, and straight on she went, without another word, before we could stop her."

"Goodness! I hope she'll be all right," said Laura. "She'll never find the way."

"So I thought, madam—but you know what Miss Lilah is," said Hubbard, with resignation. "I thought to myself—'*That* will take some time, and then the Major will have to send word in to Peking somehow—by the telephone from Barter Jew, most likely—*and* he's got to get there. And it will be pretty well to-morrow before anyone can get here—to do any good, that is.' So I thought perhaps I had better arrange something myself. I hope I did right, madam?"

"What did you do, Hubbard?" Laura asked, with the liveliest possible curiosity for the answer.

"Well, madam, you see my friends and me, we had our donkeys. So they reckoned that they could gallop back to Barter Jew in just under the two hours, down-hill most of the way."

"Yes, they would do that, just about," interjected Derek.

"Yes, sir. So I said they should do that, and get on the telephone to the Legation Guard, and tell them to send out some men and machine-guns, quick, up to Tanjy Sir, because you was all imprisoned here, madam. I gave them the names, wrote down. 'Say it's Major La Touche's orders,' I said, 'and urgent. And *our* Legation, mind—none of your doughboys,' I said to them—you see my friends were from the American Guard," explained Hubbard, with an expression of extreme smugness.

"God bless my soul!" exclaimed Mrs. Leroy, rather staggered by this Napoleonic activity on the part of her servant. "Who was the message to be sent to, Hubbard? Mr. Leroy?"

"Oh, no, madam. Mr. Leroy is out at the Temple to-day—with the new horses, madam. I said the message was to be sent to Lieutenant Jeudwine. He's on duty. Captain Hughes is gone to the Ming Tombs, madam. But the sergeant knows the way here, and he's on duty too. I was here on a picnic with him once," said Hubbard, looking smug again.

Laura nearly laughed. Hubbard's intelligence service was, as usual, perfect—she knew to a hair where every one was, and who to apply to. None of them could have done better, if as well. It was not only a *tour de force*, it was also an immense relief to know that help had been summoned so quickly. Nevertheless, a doubt or two still remained in her mind. Would poor little Harry Jeudwine accept such a message? He would be fright-fully bothered. And if he applied to Sir James, there would certainly be delays and cautions.

"The Minister will be dreadfully worried," she said, uttering part of the last thought aloud.

"Sir James is gone to the races at Nan-something; the Chinese races, madam; with this Lee—the Marshal as they call him, so Mr. Perks said." (Perks was Sir James's valet.) "Sir James was not dressing, I heard—so he would be back late. They'll very likely be here before he commences to worry," said Hubbard primly, but her praeternaturally discreet expression and pinched mouth told more clearly than words that she had her own views of Sir James and his worryings.

"Well, that's one mercy!" said Derek, with his usual lack of discretion. "Thank God *he's* out of the way."

"Nonsense, Derek," said Mrs. Leroy reprovingly. "But I don't quite see," she went on, "how they would get out here, even if Jeudwine acts on the message."

"Lieutenant Jeudwine has his car, madam—and Captain Hughes hasn't taken his out to-day—he went with a party. And there's the Conference car. I mentioned that—cars I said it was to be, madam—or rather I said the Major said so," said Hubbard, looking very self-satisfied.

"Well done, Hubbard! You *are* a champion!" exclaimed Derek.

"Thank you, sir," said Hubbard; but she looked at her mistress.

"Well, thank you, Hubbard. I think you've done very well," said Laura, in a temperate sort of tone, which filled Judith with indignation—she would have liked to crown Hubbard with laurels on the spot. But Hubbard seemed quite content.

"Thank you, madam. And what I was going to say, have you plenty of cigarettes? Because if not, I didn't know if you would care to accept these—if you'll excuse me."

So saying, Hubbard most unexpectedly removed the white felt hat which was perched on her black frizzy hair; the hat was lined with red silk, for the sun, and from the crown, inside the lining, she produced a mass of cigarettes. They were of five or six different sorts, all cheap and all Virginian, but there were nearly fifty of them.

"Crikey! How marvellous! Where on earth did you get these, Hubbard?" said Derek. "We were nearly out."

"My friends, sir. I thought to myself, madam will be nowhere without her cigarettes, and she didn't take all that many with her. And they could get plenty more at Barter Jew, so I took up a collection, like," said Hubbard, smirking demurely. "They're not very good ones, I'm afraid."

This time Laura's response was not temperate. "Hubbard, you're a jewel!"

On the whole the comfort of Hubbard's arrival was immense, and her news astonishingly good. Mrs. Leroy might have some lingering doubts as to how much action the unhappy Lieutenant Jeudwine would take, and some prudent diplomatic ones as to what Henry and the Minister would say about it all, but the broad fact remained that the alarm had been given, and given thoroughly, much more quickly than it could have been by Lilah, going back to Chieh T'ai Ssu. They had already experienced relief when the T'ao-pings left off knocking them about, but that was more in the nature of a brief respite—this was likely to be permanent, and their spirits rose. Their position was still not too comfortable—they were hungry, they had only the hard wicker stools to sit on; the T'ao-pings, crowding at one side of the court, filled the air with garlic fumes, and the corpse of the dead guard still lay under the wall; but they had a definite prospect of safety and escape to look forward to, and that was much. Hubbard, with professional zeal, offered to arrange Miss Hande's hair, which since her shaking hung in rather dissipated loops from under her hat, and they retired, with the maid's little brown bag, to the pavilion; while Judith and Laura, with the two men, remained, smoking the good gaspers of which Hubbard had plundered her "doughboys."

"That's a most remarkable woman," observed Vinstead, nodding in the direction of the pavilion.

"What, Miss Hande? Yes, wasn't she splendid?" said Mrs. Leroy.

"Well, she was, but I meant this other person—your maid, is she?"

"Oh, Hubbard!" Laura laughed. "She's a marvel."

"I couldn't quite follow it all—who these friends of hers were, and how she happened to be here," he pursued; the relief inclined even the Professor to chat on rather trivial lines.

"Oh, her friends were men in the American Legation Guard, N.C.O.'s, probably. You wouldn't think it, but Hubbard is a complete vamp," said Mrs. Leroy, laughing again. "They have immense pay, and often take their friends out for week-ends—two or three maids or nurses go together, to chaperone one another, more or less. This time they were all at the hotel at Pa-ta-Ch'u, at the foot of the hills beyond the Hun-ho, and just happened to come over here for a jaunt."

"Oh, *that's* what she meant by Barter Jew—I couldn't think," said Judith.

"Hubbard is so funny about Chinese," said Laura. "She won't attempt to learn it, or pronounce even the names. She's just like the Tommies were in France about that—she uses the nearest English word, and makes that do."

"Talking of Barter Jew," said Derek, "I wonder when these pals of hers will get there. When did they start?"

"She got here just about four," said Judith. "I noticed."

"Yes, but they must have started before that."

"Go and ask if she knows, Judith," said Mrs. Leroy.

"No, here, I'll go—you sit still," said Derek, springing up.

"You may not be too welcome at the toilette, Derek," said Mrs. Leroy.

"Oh, all right." He relapsed a little sulkily, while Judith sped off. "She looks awfully done up," he said reproachfully to Laura. "You shouldn't fag her too much. She's had a pretty good doing."

"I'm sorry, my dear," said Mrs. Leroy tranquilly. She realised what nervous strain and physical violence, and the reaction from them, had probably done to Derek's emotions about Judith, and rather welcomed this evidence of the fact. Indeed she wondered that no one had as yet been particularly cross. That, no doubt, would come.

It did come, and at once.

"Mrs. Leroy has had a pretty good doing too, I think," said Vinstead rather blandly. "After all, she's had all the strain of dealing with these fellows. She's simply carried the lot of us—we've done nothing."

Derek was nettled at once.

"Well, she can talk their cursed lingo," he said. "I can't—or I would like a shot. But she is more or less accustomed to this sort of thing, and it's all new to Judith. It must be a frightful shock to her."

"I'm sure it is, Derek," said Laura quickly, to prevent Vinstead's replying. "And I will look after her. Lilah is really the heroine of this occasion," she went on. "If she hadn't climbed out even the redoubtable Hubbard couldn't have functioned."

"You seem to me to have done a good deal too," said Vinstead, with a certain warmth. "As far as I can see, but for you we might all have been dead before any help came. Do you really feel all right?" he asked her, leaning towards her solicitously.

"No—I'm hungry and cross!" said Mrs. Leroy, with a little smile which belied her words.

"She says they went off at a quarter past two," said Judith, flying back and re-seating herself. "But it took her ages to get in. She made 'that Niu' as she calls him, bring her down here and translate for her and get her up to us. She was so funny. 'I *couldn't* make him understand, miss,' she said. '*Waw*, I said — *waw*, *t'ai-t'ai*.' What does 'waw' mean?"

"Means I," said Derek.

"Oh, that was it. She said, 'He was that stubborn, I could have eaten him, yellow as he is!'" Judith reproduced Hubbard's mincing emphasis so precisely that they all laughed.

"Two-fifteen," said Laura, and looked at her watch. "Well, it's ten-to-five now. They should have got to Pa-ta-Ch'u at least by four-fifteen."

"And then they've got to telephone," said Derek.

They went on reckoning it out. If the line was not cut, and they got a connection quickly, and if Jeudwine acted at once, unhindered, and none of the cars were out of action, the relief party ought to get to Men-t'ou-kou by about seven-fifteen. And then there was the walk up. Laura thought this took an hour and a quarter—Derek said all but cripples would do it in an hour. "Machine-guns are rather crippling," said Vinstead.

"Well, call it eight-thirty, 'at a conservative estimate,'" said Derek. "That gives us three and a half hours to go.

I wish those fellows would bring us that tea! Can't you poke them up, Laura?"

Laura said she would rather not. "The longer everything takes, the better. I'm so afraid of their moving us on somewhere else. Don't look too pleased with yourself, Derek, or you may make them suspect that we have something up our sleeve. If they cart us off somewhere we're done again."

"How am I to look, then? Gloomy and proud?" said Derek. "Curzonian?"

"Depressed," said Mrs. Leroy shortly. Derek at the moment looked anything but depressed. He was sitting beside Judith, lighting her cigarette, arranging his coat as a cushion for her back—there were little questions and answers and touches and undertones passing between them all the time, alongside the other conversation. Vinstead too looked perkier than she had seen him do yet, and in the hours which followed displayed an open interest and solicitude for her welfare which startled not only herself, but, she could see, Miss Hande as well. In spite of his habitual *contenu* manner, there was about him a curious air of a person who has abandoned something—stripped off, as it were, a garment for some plunge. Without being able to define this impression, Laura was aware of and a little disturbed by it, in spite of her other preoccupations.

They were, of course, still in considerable anxiety about Lilah. She would not be able to ask her way, and with the hills swarming with T'ao-pings she might easily get into trouble of a sort that the mind shuddered to contemplate. Laura, however carefully she listened, could not pick up the bandits' intentions, and had no idea whether they were still hunting for Lilah, or had finally accepted Hubbard as a substitute. Hubbard had produced some crochet from her hand-bag, and sat at a respectful distance diligently at work on a lace nightdress top. The Number One and the Soviet had gone off somewhere, and the rest of the gang left them for the time being entirely to their own devices.

They amused themselves as well as they could. Derek suggested a song from Judith, an idea which she repudiated with a wide stare of contempt, and the words "Maniac! Do you realise that I've had no food for *nine hours*?"—a reply which entertained Vinstead highly, and furnished Mrs. Leroy with further illumination as to her niece's state. Three days ago Judith would not have called Derek "maniac" in general company. Vinstead, still with that curious sense of some interior abandonment breathing from him, tackled Miss Hande on the subject of her feelings for America—he wished to compare them with the feelings of Europeans for their countries. "I know about its being God's Own Country, and all that; but does your throat contract when you think of special bits of it, and do you laugh with tears just behind your eyes if someone quotes some very typically countrified, old-fashioned bit of speech from New England or somewhere?"

Miss Hande was puzzled, a little. "I guess Boston people are very fond of Boston," she said at length. "And Southerners make a great to-do about the South."

"Well, do you have poems about it which simply fetch every one when they read or hear them?" the Professor pursued.

Could he give her some English examples of what he meant? Miss Hande asked.

"Oh, I don't know——" he rummaged through his Housman. "No, the best ones are in the other book, and I haven't got it. Can't you say something?" he said, turning to Laura. "I never can remember poetry well enough to repeat it."

"Specially Housman?" she asked.
"Oh, anything—well, yes, that if you can."
She began:

> "'Tis time, I think, by Wenlock Town,
>   The golden broom should blow—"

The beauty of her speaking voice, which had struck
Derek afresh only the day before, was even more noticeable when she spoke verse. Actually, the nostalgia of
that particular poem always "fetched" Laura herself
almost unbearably, and it was only with an effort that
she kept her voice level through the last verse:

> "Oh tarnish late on Wenlock Edge
>   Gold that I never see!
> Lie long, high snowdrifts in the hedge
>   That will not shower on me."

"Why, it nearly makes me cry, the way you say
that!" exclaimed the novelist, at the end.

That, Vinstead explained, was what he meant by
being "fetched." "It almost makes her cry to say it—
doesn't it, out here?" he said, turning to Laura. There
was a curious softening of his voice on the last words,
and Laura noticed the "her." She made no answer, but
lit another of Hubbard's collection of cigarettes. She
was faintly bothered to find how much she liked having
Vinstead speak to her in that tone, even while it embarrassed her. He was forced by her silence to return
to his cross-examination of Miss Hande.

This was presently interrupted, at about 6.30, by
the advent of the Soviet, and some little bowls of tea.
It was the true Chinese tea, milkless and sugarless, the
colour of white wine, strong and yet delicate, and very
stimulating. Over this the Number One and the Soviet
re-opened the question of a ransom Mrs. Leroy con-

trived to occupy an immense amount of time by pro-
moting a long discussion on the ethics of kidnapping in
general, and the practice in *Mei-kuo* (America) and other
countries, as compared with that of China. The bandits,
being Chinese bandits, entered into this with hearty
enjoyment, instead of sending her rudely to the right-
about—and when she told them a funny story about
Chicago they laughed delightedly. When at last they
got back to the point at issue, Laura further delayed
matters by a thousand irrelevant inquiries as to the
T'ao-pings' ages, and families; where they came from,
how the war was doing, and so on; and though she did
not in every case get direct answers, her inquiries, being
thoroughly polite according to the Chinese code, were
met with a corresponding politeness. At last, however,
the matter of the actual ransom could no longer be post-
poned. The T'ao-pings made searching inquiries as to
the precise status of each of their six prisoners, and after
some further discussion among themselves expressed the
desire to keep only three—Mrs. Leroy herself, the Commander-in-Chief, Vinstead, and Miss Hande, because
she was an American. Miss Hande's indignation on
hearing this knew no bounds. "Yes, but they know how
rich Americans are," Derek told her consolingly. "They
see the Rockefeller Institute, and all your Chinese
Missions and Endowments, with marble halls and
money to burn, and of course they consider you all
absolute *plums* to hold to ransom."

"Well, of all the nerve!" was Miss Hande's final
indignant comment.

They discussed it a little. Laura was inclined to
recommend their all sticking together, even if the
rescuers failed them, because a party of six prisoners
would be easier to trace, and unwieldy and embarrassing
to the bandits themselves—harder to feed, slower to

move, in every way more tiresome. However, she felt
they must have their choice, and left it to them. Hubbard, immediately and roundly, declared that she
wouldn't go, but would continue to supervise "my
mistress." Derek, Laura could see, rather liked the idea
of getting Judith into safety, out of it all, there and then,
but clearly felt that he ought to stay himself—and
Judith, her usual appetite for the sensational undimmed
by hunger and danger, light-heartedly plumped for
"seeing it out." So Laura presently informed the
Number One that their suggestion was refused—it must
be all or none.

The reply was unwelcome, they could see. Scowling,
the Soviet once again "went into Committee," as Derek
called it, retiring along the entry-way out of earshot.
Laura and Derek simultaneously looked at their watches.
It was 7.30—they had contrived to spin out the
negotiations for a whole hour. If the relief party really
arrived to time there was only another hour to go.

If! The suspense grew keener, as the time approached.
The sun had set, and the wonderful glittering brilliance
which the sky had held all day was ebbing away, leaving
a tender soft colour, inexpressibly peaceful. Laura sat
looking at it. From their enclosed courtyard they could
see little but walls, and the angle of a roof on which a
series of small tile-ware dogs and dragons sat, black
against the pale sky, mounting guard over the little clay
hen who sits at the lowest corner, with the Pong, the
most nefarious of China's evil spirits, bound to her back.
But Laura was not looking at the Pong. Staring at the
sky, she thought of all the prisoners of all time, whose
one freedom had lain in that sight. A sentence of
Richard Jefferies' came into her mind, "The unattain-
able blue flower of the sky"—and she remembered that
he went on to say that "pure colour is rest of heart."

Marvellous phrase! But for her, she found, it was not then, rest of heart. Her anxiety was too urgent. Would they come? She was almost appalled at the intensity of her longing that they should. She looked again at her watch; 7.45—another quarter of an hour had gone.

Voices and the shuffle of feet roused her. She turned. The Soviet had come back, and the Number One, with a menacing look of determination on his ugly pock-marked visage, stood before her. He brought the gang's decision. Very well—if all wished to go, all should go —and *now*! The soldiers were collecting their effects and slinging their rifles on their backs in preparation for departure; the Soviet roughly motioned the prisoners to their feet. They were to start at once.

It was ten minutes to eight.

Chapter Twenty-one

THIS last blow was almost unbearably sharp. To have their chance of rescue snatched from them by a margin of forty miserable minutes was too wretched. They stared at one another in helpless despair. The bitter thought darted into Laura's mind, as she watched Hubbard collectedly stuffing her crochet into her bag, with a good-tempered, "All right! All right! Time for all things, I suppose," to the soldier who pulled at her arm, that in vain now had been the maid's intelligent promptitude, in vain Lilah's wonderful climb and escape. And with the thought of Lilah's escape came a sudden idea; she remembered the excuse her niece had given for going off—to hide her jewellery. The Professor saw Mrs. Leroy's face tighten with a sudden resolution. Wriggling herself free of the soldier who held her by the arm, she darted towards the inner pavilion. The soldier ran after her and pulled her back. With an admirable appearance of breathless agitation, Mrs. Leroy struggled from him, calling out something in Chinese over and over again. Drawn by the fuss, the soldiers turned to watch—the Number One came up; the Soviet came up. Mrs. Leroy poured out a flood of Chinese to them, pointing towards the pavilion; then to the astonishment and dismay of the others, she was marched into the inner courtyard. The rest, staring, followed. There, she began to feel in the cracks among the moss-grown brickwork of the wall, looking into hole after hole, as if in search of something.

An amazing scene followed. The T'ao-pings joined in

the search for whatever it was, swarming about and fumbling in the cracks, for all the world like grey apes hunting for fleas. As the search went on they grew more frenzied in their efforts; they poked, peered, and pulled in all directions, levering out loose bricks with their bayonets, and pulling down whole stretches of the wall in their mad haste. Mrs. Leroy continued to seek with them, lamenting loudly in Chinese all the time. Vinstead, watching with the rest in a sort of dismal astonishment, really began to think that the strain of the day had been too much for her reason, till he heard Fitzmaurice break into a delighted chuckle beside him. "By Jove! She's put them on to hunt for Lilah's necklaces and things."

"What on earth for?"

"Time, of course. They'll pull that place to bits before they give up."

Vinstead glanced furtively at his watch. Yes, it was already ten past eight, and still the search went on. "What will they do to her if they don't find them?" he asked presently, rather anxiously. "Miss Milne might have taken them with her."

"Probably did," said Derek. "But it's no good crossing bridges before you come to them. She's gaining time, at any rate. I wonder where they mean to take us at this hour of night, anyhow."

Vinstead wondered this too. "What do you imagine?" he asked.

"They generally shift on a bit from the place where they pinch you, I believe," said Derek. "And this is pretty close home for them. But *where*, Heaven knows."

In the failing light the search, growing always more violent and desperate, went on for a few more minutes. Then there was an interruption. Two or three soldiers, running fast and silently on slippered feet, their rapid breathing the only sound they made, dashed into the inner courtyard, panting out some message. Instantly confusion reigned. With sullen fury the T'ao-pings abandoned their search—orders were called out—the words, "Foreign soldiers! Foreign devils!" ran from mouth to mouth. "What is it?" "What's happening?" Judith and Miss Hande asked of Laura as she came back to them, wiping her hands, which were green and stained with moss.

"They've come!" she said. "They're at the lower gate now."

"Why, how marvellous! Then we're rescued!" exclaimed Miss Hande. "Isn't that just——"

The rest of her words were lost. The bandits had no intention of allowing their captives to be rescued. With clumsy haste the prisoners' hands were once more tied behind their backs, and they were led swiftly out of the corner courtyard, down the flight of steps, and along the terrace where they had first met the T'ao-pings. "Where are they taking us?" Judith asked Laura in a whisper as they marched along. To Mrs. Leroy and Derek it was only too plain where they were being taken. While their rescuers battered at the main gateway, and searched the endless courts and pavilions, the bandits were going to get them out of the temple by that same upper gate through which they had themselves hoped to escape—out into the hills and the tangled wild country, where rescue would be difficult, if not hopeless. As they stumbled along in the dusk, hustled, cursed, and prodded with rifle-butts, till they reached the upper gate and were marched out through it, they savoured the bitter irony of the fact that it had become for them a gateway, not to freedom, but into a further imprisonment. It was, indeed, very bitter. Something like despair fell on Laura.

Outside the gate the path, still paved, passed under

oaks and thujas. Here, in the deep dusk, it was almost
dark. They pushed up it, not in any particular order,
but in the usual go-as-you-please draggle-tailed fashion
of Chinese troops on the march—bandits ahead, bandits
behind, the prisoners strung out along the line with more
bandits beside them. Miss Hande, bereft of her lorgnette,
really found it hard to see, and stumbled more than
once, only to be brutally cuffed by the soldier nearest
her. Laura, with her hands tied, could do nothing to
help, but she cursed the soldier sharply and told him to
lead Miss Hande by the arm—which surprisingly, he
did. Otherwise they walked in silence.

Presently they entered a patch of deeper darkness
still, where the track passed for a hundred yards or so
between high banks. When the straggling file was well
into it, a voice ahead cried, "*Chan-choh!*" (Stop!) with
startling suddenness.

The head of the column recoiled in astonishment,
throwing the already disorderly mass behind into confusion. The voice, loud and rough, proceeded in coolie
Chinese of the richest description to inquire of the
T'ao-pings who they were, and where they were going.
From the darkness figures emerged shadowily, descend-
ing the banks before them, behind them, all round them;
bayonets gleamed in the dusk. "Oh, what is it now?"
came from Judith in a little gasping moan. But Mrs.
Leroy, straining her eyes, had seen that the dim figures
had buttons which *shone*, and she broke into the nervous
laughter of relief. "It's Jamieson!" she said, "the
Constable! Do listen to him!" None of this conveyed
anything to Vinstead, least of all the Legation Constable's
vigorous Chinese periods—he and Miss Hande stood
completely mystified till an English voice called out,
"Here they are, sir! One of 'em, anyhow." "Ah,
would you? Hands off, there!" "And here's another,"

and then they heard a familiar voice, Touchy's voice, calling, "Laura? Derek? Are you all there?"

"Yes, all here but Lilah," Derek called back.

"Lilah's all right. Miss Judith? Miss Hande? Vinstead?"

"Yes, all here—and Hubbard," Laura answered.

"And all O.K.?"

"More or less—if we could get our hands untied."

Professor Vinstead called the book which he subsequently published on China, *The Psychology of Anticlimax*. And to the end of his life he declared that he first got an insight into the key-quality of that strangest of races on the occasion of his rescue from the bandits at T'an Chüeh Ssu. Anything more unemphatic, undramatic, and generally speaking flat than the scene which followed it would be hard to imagine. While some of the Tommies untied the prisoners' hands, and others tried to hem in such T'ao-pings as began unobtrusively to melt away, with an occasional firm "Now, Daniels, come off it!" Jamieson, the Constable, continued to harangue the gang on "What*ever* do you think you've been up to?" lines, regardless of every one else. He asked for the Number One, but the Number One had faded out. Such bandits as remained, seeing men with bayonets, and hearing the voice of authority scolding them, assumed the sheepish and abject attitude of small boys caught stealing apples. There was no attempt at resistance, no violence, no sensation of any sort; those who could, quietly wriggled away—those who were forced to stay, stayed, grinning foolishly.

A prolonged discussion then took place between Jamieson, La Touche and Derek as to what should be done with them. Three members of the Soviet, whom Derek had identified by the wavering light of the sergeant's torch, were held firmly by as many Tommies.

Jamieson was all for taking these back to Peking and handing them over to the Chinese authorities for justice; Derek agreed. La Touche, however, had doubts. He pointed out that no member of the party had suffered serious physical injury, that no property had been stolen; and if, as was very possible in these circumstances, the Chinese did nothing, the Legation would lose face. Mrs. Leroy here took a hand in the discussion, in support of La Touche's views; mindful of Henry's probable feelings, her one desire was to have the unlucky episode terminate with as little publicity as possible. Why not disarm them, she contended, and let them go? Exhausted, strained, she wanted the matter done with. Her words had nearly turned the scale when a new voice was uplifted.

"Why, for gracious sake!" exclaimed Miss Hande suddenly, "do you mean to tell *me* that you're all proposing to let these bandits go scot free? After we saw them murder that poor harmless bonze? I call it monstrous. Surely you'll have some of them punished?"

The murder of the bonze was news to La Touche and Jamieson. Since murder had been committed, and under the eyes of witnesses, there was nothing for it but to hand over some of the gang, they agreed. It was accordingly arranged that Jamieson and the sergeant should disarm such brigands as remained, and take the three members of the Soviet back to Peking with the rest of the troops. Jamieson conveyed this decision to the now diminished gang. There were some protests then, but he flashed the light of the torch on two wicked little cylinders, which stood on iron legs on the paved pathway—the Lewis guns; and the protests died. Some thirty rifles and bandoliers were removed, Jamieson all the while pointing out to the disarmed bandits how great was their folly and wickedness in attempting to kidnap

Ying-kuo-jen. Had not the *Ying-kuo-ping* men, as they saw, at every place, ready to strike-shoot? How could they hope to succeed? How great was their good fortune, and undeserved, merely to lose their *lai-fus* (rifles) and not their lives. And so on in the same strain, till he gave them leave to go, and they shuffled off, grey ape-like shapes melting into the darkness of the trees.

During this oration the ex-prisoners sat quietly on the path, sipping brandy, the only form of sustenance he had thought to bring with him, from Touchy's flask. Both parties, rescuers and rescued, were still not a little bewildered as to the course of events, and as they started homeward explanations began. Touchy's appearance was quite unexpected, and in answer to questions he told his tale. The indomitable Lilah had actually found her way back to Chieh T'ai Ssu, and had arrived between five and half-past, just when vague rumours of a large foreign party having been "mopped up" at T'an Chüeh Ssu had begun to filter in through the servants and donkey boys, carried by the usual semaphore system of the Chinese countryside—news which had greatly disturbed the General and himself. On Lilah's arrival their worst fears were confirmed; and he, Touchy, had at once (like Hubbard) decided to telephone to the Legation for help. He set off "full bat," as he said, for Men-t'ou-kou, hoping either to telephone from the office at the coal depot there, and failing that to go on to the hotel at Pa-ta-Ch'u. He lost his way once or twice, and the coal depot was shut when he arrived at about a quarter to seven—pushing on along the road to Pa-ta-Ch'u, what was his astonishment to meet three carloads of his own men, with rifles and Lewis guns! "I had the surprise of my life!" said Touchy, "and I still don't know who sent the message. Lilah—Miss

Milne—said nothing about it. It was sent in my name too, apparently."

"Ah, that was Hubbard," said Derek, "we'll tell you about that later. Go on, Touchy."

"*Hubbard!*" said Major La Touche, peering round uselessly to look for the maid in the dark. "Oh yes, Lilah said she met her, but how on earth——"

"Oh, never mind that now, Touchy—do go on," said Laura. She realised that a faint sense of *lèse-majesté* might be awakening even in his unmilitary mind, and didn't want the whole story dragged out there and then, in front of both Hubbard and La Touche's own men.

La Touche, always quick as a weasel at a hint, proceeded with his tale. Finding the forces he was in quest of miraculously brought to the spot, he hurried on with them towards T'an Chüeh Ssu, in considerable fear lest he might find his birds flown when he got there. ("And so you would have, but for Laura," from Derek.) It occurred to him almost at once that even if the bandits and their captives were still there, he might have considerable difficulty in finding them in such a rabbit-warren, especially in the dark; and pondering over this problem as he marched—for the cars had to be left behind at Men-t'ou-kou—he remembered, by good luck, the little-known back gateway into the temple. "I knew they'd probably bolt if they *were* there, so I settled to put Jeudwine in at the bottom, like a ferret, so to speak, and stop the earth at the other side myself."

"Well, wasn't that smart!" exclaimed Miss Hande.

As they passed through the temple on their return journey an effort was made to secure a donkey for this poor lady, who was not accustomed, and had never expected to do more walking than the usual strolling through temple courts incidental to sight-seeing; but

none was to be had. With the advent of local troops,
regular or otherwise, in China, donkeys, and camels too,
are wont to vanish, like shadows in a total eclipse—
suddenly they simply are not. Miss Hande, with the
gallantry which she had shown all day, declared that she
did not mind, and could get along "just splendidly"
with the arm which La Touche offered her. In the
temple also they met Jeudwine. Relieved and thankful
to be well through with what he described as "the most
outré expedition I ever undertook, Mrs. Leroy," he again
assumed charge of the rest of his men for the return to
Peking, with the exception of the sergeant and six
Tommies, whom Touchy decided to take on to Chieh
T'ai Ssu in case of accident. Jeudwine was further
bound over by La Touche to make no sort of report on
his proceedings till his superior officer should return
next day.

The party then continued on their long trudge homewards, talking as they went. It might be supposed that
they would have been silent from hunger and fatigue,
but not at all—the reaction from nervous strain produced
an almost hysterical chattiness. The moon was not yet
up, and in the darkness they had constantly to stop at
crossways of the small rough paths for Touchy and
Laura to peer about and make sure of the way, with
argument—delays almost intolerable to the exhausted
party. But as soon as each of these checks was over, the
conversation flowed on again, unceasing. To the rear
the rescuing sergeant was clearly making a good deal of
running with Hubbard, as shrill giggles and high-pitched
protests testified. "Well, Miss 'Ubbard, you see you *are*
takin' a walk with me this Sunday after all! Ain't it
nice? Comin' again next?" "Ow, get on!" from
Hubbard. In front, Derek walked with Judith. He had
made her take his arm at first, but as they passed through

a faint dusty glare of yellow light from the open doorway of a house beside the path, it was evident that his arm was "more fully in support," as Touchy murmured to Miss Hande. Neither of them appeared to mind in the least whether this arrangement were patent to the rest or not; they continued on their way with the supreme carelessness of a strong emotional exaltation. Vinstead walked with Mrs. Leroy. Like him, the Tommies had hobnails in their heavy British boots, which screamed on the stones, so that the party walked to a following accompaniment as of a fife band. Thus piped on their way, weary and overwrought, but in a perfect gale of conversation, they marched off into the night.

Chapter Twenty-two

IT was close on 11.30 when the party, dirty, dishevelled and exhausted, at last stumbled into Chieh T'ai Ssu. The moon had risen, and as they walked along the great terrace a figure in white came to meet them, slipping silently in and out of the patterned pools of shadow thrown by the great trees on the pavement—it was Niu, immaculate as ever and quite unperturbed. The only sign of emotion he gave was that he kow-tow-ed deeply to his mistress, using the formal rever- ence usually reserved for such occasions as China New Year, or for announcing the death of a relation. Under the leaning pine a table waited, fully spread for dinner, and another with an array of drinks; as they approached them Mrs. Nevile sprang up out of the shadows, and ran to meet the weary party with a little fluttering cry, "Thank Heaven, it's them at last!" The General limped after her, but though Nina kissed every one except Touchy and Vinstead and Hubbard, and he didn't even shake hands with anybody, his relief and pleasure were not less evident, and expressed themselves practically in forcing whiskies-and-sodas on every one before they attempted to eat. Lilah drifted up out of the darkness, lovely and com- posed, smoking a cigarette in a long holder—she took the congratulations on her feat in climbing out very coolly. "*Did* you leave your corals in a crack?" Judith asked her.

"Of course not."

Derek passed this on to Laura. "Laura, Lilah'd got her jewellery with her all the while, so those lads had their digging party for nothing."

"But I never told them her things were there," said Mrs. Leroy, turning from her conversation with Nina Nevile, and looking at him with amusement over her whisky-and-soda.

"What were they after, then?" Derek asked in amazement.

"My pearls."

"But I thought you'd got those in your hem!" objected Miss Hande, staring at her.

"So I had." She turned back to Nina.

"Well of all things!" murmured Miss Hande.

To Vinstead, perhaps the most fantastic part of that fantastic day was the meal which followed. His perceptions, sharpened by fatigue, want of food, and nervous exhaustion, made him peculiarly awake to the strangeness of eating a regular four-course dinner, at midnight, on a moon-lit terrace in a Chinese temple; of drinking wine in a buzz of European conversation, with shapes as odd as the shapes of those fluted roofs cutting the star-filled sky behind him; himself and most of his companions fresh from the hands of bandits, his wrists still raw from over-tight bonds, his shoulders still aching from blows with rifle-butts. Once, by accident, he put up a hand (which he had washed, the total of his hasty toilet) to his head, and found it gritty—his hair still held the fallen plaster from the wall under which they had stood when the T'ao-pings fired at them. In his strung-up mood he felt these contrasts as strange to the point of madness; he could not watch Mrs. Leroy, answering the General's questions so sensibly, without also seeing her body held and shaken almost senseless by yellow hands; he could not look at Judith Milne, gradually restored by food and drink to her usual enthusiasm, without seeing her white face and piteous horrified eyes when she stood bound against the wall, and the soldier prepared to jab at her with his bayonet. Above the hum of civilised voices he kept on hearing the sound of those first rifle-shots, tearing the sunny midday silence like a piece of silk; as he watched the competent noiseless movements of Niu and his underling waiting at table, he saw again the grey ape-like figures—also with yellow hands and faces—who had come stealing so silently into the courtyard down by the great shrine, and murdered the lay-brother there.

With all this, he was increasingly aware of an overwhelming, if confused and helpless, feeling about Laura Leroy—that she might somehow soothe this whirling disturbance of his mind and imagination, if only she would. He recognised vaguely that to a great extent she was herself the cause of it. Something in him was clamouring for expression—he did not, or dare not, as yet know it very precisely for what it was. It is possible, and indeed usual for people to live through such an experience as Vinstead had just undergone with, as it were, the top layer of the mind only, passing from moment to moment, from emergency to emergency, with complete matter-of-factness, concentrated wholly on practical details. But the depths of personality are ravaged all the same, and when the immediate tension is removed the violently disturbed emotions surge up, insisting on some form of release; and then, and then only, do we begin to realise what the experience has done to us. It was so with the Professor now. His surface preoccupation was a miserable certainty that, exhausted as he was, he would nevertheless not sleep— but he longed passionately to lie awake, since lie awake he must, in some sort of assurance such as he felt Mrs. Leroy might give him, if only he could talk to her. And mixed in with all this was a strange feeling of exaltation in this new emotional disturbance—a sense of rivers long frostbound breaking into flood, of buds on boughs long bare, of bird-song in the blood.

All the time, of course, the general conversation was flowing past him. Sometimes he was addressed, and jerked himself into full attention at the sound of his own name. "The first thing that made me pretty sure we'd got the right lot," he heard Touchy saying at one point, "was your boots, Vinstead. I heard your nails screeching in the dark—of course I couldn't see a thing—and I guessed there weren't two pairs of hobnailed boots in the hills on the same day, so I told Jamieson to carry on."

"Jamieson's oration was a masterpiece," said Laura. "I didn't recognise his voice at first—he does talk exactly like a Chinese when he chooses."

Mrs. Leroy had not passed such a meditative meal as the Professor, at least not at first. It was from her and Derek that the General and La Touche expected to get a coherent story of the incident with the bandits, and she was kept busy explaining and answering questions. She gave her account as well as she could; but when the fire of questions slackened she made no further effort to talk. The hysterically conversational stage was over, for her— she sat relaxed, relieved, conscious of exhaustion and yet at peace, and in a sort of trance watched the others. Derek and Judith had the first share of her dreamy attention, and looking at them she was quite satisfied— there was a silent air of security and achieved under- standing about the pair which boded well for the future. In a vague sort of way, looking at Henri, who sat twirling a glass of liqueur brandy, thoughtfully, in his fingers, she speculated about Little Annette. Annette had gone to bed with a slight headache, it was reported; but before dinner Nina Nevile had already found time to tell Mrs. Leroy that she was not over-happy about that pair—she had an idea that something had "gone wrong" with them during the day. "They sort of hung about, looking awkwardly—*I* don't know what's amiss!" It might, of course, have been the headache.

At Vinstead Laura hardly looked. They had had a long talk on the way home, and the result was a sense of intimacy much more pronounced than anything which had gone before. She recalled his charming tired unguarded voice in the dark, which gave him away with every question about what they'd said or done or felt, at this moment or that, as they went over the events of the day. Oh well, she thought, stealing a glance at his composed face, and hearing his voice at its most Cambridge-y as he answered the General—he was overwrought and so was I. He'll be different to-morrow. She remembered his firm tones on the first day, when he spoke of manifestations of emotion later in life— "They should be dealt with drastically." He would be more than equal to dealing with this sudden burst of emotion in himself, she felt. She had liked it, mind you —it had been soothing, warming, after the acute strain and violent unpleasantness of the day, bringing a glow and a sense of *soulagement*. But it wouldn't last, of course— it was one of the delicate fragrant things that you put away in a drawer in your mind, and it smelt sweet for a while, and then faded and got lost, somehow.

Her thoughts ran on, dreamily—really she was half-asleep as she sat! She was roused by hearing Vinstead's voice say with energy, "Coffee? Good Heavens, no! I shan't sleep as it is." Mechanically, as they rose from the table, she took a cup from the servant, and then heard him beside her asking, "Can I carry your coffee somewhere for you?"

"Where?" she asked, in almost stupid surprise, letting him take the cup.

"Anywhere—through here," he said, holding open

the door on to the inner terrace for her to pass through. "You must drink it somewhere, you know."

Too dulled by fatigue to resist, she followed him passively, half her mind protesting feebly that she ought to be going to bed. However, one must drink coffee somewhere, as he said, and the buzz of voices was still loud behind them under the leaning pine as they walked along the inner terrace.

They sat in the turret. The moon was behind it, on the side without openings; and within the small circle of the parapet it was very dark. The long whistling note —they had still never found out if it was a bird or not, Laura thought idly—was repeated at intervals, mechanical, insistent. She lit a cigarette, and began to drink her coffee; but still the Professor said nothing. His silence lasted till even in the dreamy passive state of her consciousness it produced a sense of tension, of suspense, that was almost ludicrously familiar. How often one had sat like this, waiting for a man to speak! Sometimes the prisoner of courtesy, sometimes inwardly trembling with secret ardent expectation. Which are you *this* time? her mind asked her, suddenly. Oh, she was so deadly, deadly tired and sleepy, she really *didn't* know. And then Vinstead spoke.

"I can't see you, now," he said, in a curious tone, half meditative and half surprised; "and yet I can—I'm afraid I always shall. Standing here, as you stood the first evening."

Laura said nothing at all—the only words which came with maddening persistence into her head were, "Dealt with drastically." He waited a moment, and then asked, "Does that anger you?"

"Of course not—why should it? Only——" she wanted to tell him why, really, she felt it probably wasn't any good, as her experience with Aubrey had

taught her; but it was such a long story, and difficult—
oh, tired out as she was, impossible! Before she could
think of anything to say he was speaking again, still in
that curious meditative tone which had yet a sort of
appeal. "You seem so free—I don't think you can be
afraid of love in any form."

What an odd way to put it, Laura thought. "I don't
think I am," she said slowly. "It can only be all to the
good."

"All to the good?" he echoed, surprise now in his
voice.

"That there should be a little more affection in the
world, I mean—it's such a divine commodity." Oh,
that was a silly thing to say! She roused herself and
went on, "But look here—do you think we might talk
in the morning? I rather fancy we may have quite a
lot to say to each other, that we oughtn't to miss, but I
really am not quite up to it to-night. Do you mind?"

Again his answer surprised her. "I don't mind anything, so long as you *know*."

"Then I'll say good-night," she said, getting up.

He rose too; took her hand, and kissed it with surprising efficiency. "Good night!" he said.

She left him and walked away. But half-way along
the terrace she called back, "By the way, would you like
some allonal? I've got some. *I'm* going to have a
couple."

"Oh, thanks very much. Yes, I think I would," said
Vinstead, rejoining her. The prospect of getting some
sleep was marvellous. It ought of course to have spoilt
their little situation completely, he felt, to join forces
again the moment it was over—but somehow it didn't.
Without any sense of embarrassment he walked back
with her to the courtyard and got his tablets and some
soda to drink them down with. And then he went to

bed. He lay again under the peach trees by the well-head, looking up at the moonlit blossom between him and the stars—but to-night he was not fretting. The thing was out. He had been right—to speak to Laura had brought him the assurance he craved. Just what distillation of peace had dropped on him he could not say, but the sense of it was cool as dew. He lay still, allowing himself the idiotic happiness merely of knowing her only twenty yards away, in the pavilion whose lattice glowed a dull yellow from her single candle. In peace now he closed his eyes on the blossoming tree, undisturbed by the strange flowering within him; to dream—for contrary to expectation he slept—of having plunged into cold dark waters which suddenly turned warm and buoyant, bearing him out serenely on a shining sea. He woke thinking of Virgil's shipwrecked swimmer, who saw Italy from the top of a wave.

Chapter Twenty-three

MRS. LEROY did not sleep well, in spite of the allonal. Her right arm had been badly twisted by the bandits at some point or other, and hurt her when she lay on that side; she had had a blow with a rifle-butt on her left shoulder-blade which as soon as she got into bed hurt whatever she did. She lay turning about, seeking a comfortable position. And of course she thought of the Professor. She *did* like him so much! was the drowsy sum-total of her thought at first, but there was more to it than that—that experienced kiss of his on her hand had left a small tingling thrill in her nerves. The longer she lay awake, the clearer, to her despair, her mind became. She found herself beginning to examine him, using all the indications she had gathered in the past three days, and continued in this exercise till at last she thought she had a fair idea of the sort of person he was and what had happened to him. Clearly he was not a misogynist, but framed by nature for the best, the most valuable and amusing sort of man-woman relationship. But either something had gone wrong with him in connection with some woman, or else the deadly clarity of his professional analysis of emotion had put him off the whole thing. Or both. Anyhow, he'd been put off, and now he was—reluctantly, she could see—put on again. And she had put him on. And being, for a woman, reasonably honest, "What about it?" she asked herself.

Mrs. Leroy was no psychologist, but she had seen enough of things to know how badly wrong late love can go, if it does go wrong, and what dire damage it can do to the whole personality. It was all rather unlucky, but having happened, it must just be dealt with as well as possible. "I can't have him all rotted up a *second* time," was how she thought of it. In a way it was a good thing that she liked him so very much; "a bit more, my girl, and you'd be head over ears," she told herself, lighting a cigarette to help thought, in despair of sleeping. She had a fairly strong sense that this might not be the best plan for *her*. Wedlock held one mysteriously by some subtle bond; there it was!—the most important job in life, and the best worth doing, without doubt, for her as for most people; and in the long run, quite the most interesting. Laura had never found marriage and maternity in the least dull. But she was aware too of a strong temptation to take this offered affection, this companionship which she had seen could be very good indeed. Her life in China was rather lonely and rather empty, with Henry absorbed in his own occupations, and the children away. And—no getting over it, and no good blinking the fact, she said, with stubborn honesty— the hunger for love and affection was still strong in her; the lingering effect of that kiss on her hand showed her how strong. She felt already the faint beginning of that heightening of all perception and intensifying of all mental activity which accompanies emotion. Oh, she knew that so terribly well! Heavenly in itself, until it reached the point where only the one person had any meaning or reality; when only the hours spent with them were alive, and the rest of the time, the rest of the world, was just a grey ash-heap across which one passed, weighted with an intolerable languor. Was she ready for all that again?

She put that aside, for the moment. What would work best for him? After all, that was really the point. Any fresh frustration ought to be avoided at all costs, even if it evolved a completed relation between them, with all its "pains and penalties," as Aubrey called them. Goodness, how difficult this love business was! It meant tearing misery sooner or later, nearly always. But it was fatal to try to cut it out. Her own view was that the great thing about sex was to accept it, pains and penalties and all—to realise, however you got there, the relative unimportance of the physical side, inevitable as that was, compared with the essential thing—to love, and to be willing to be hurt because you loved. Once you had reached that position, however painful the process, sex and emotion became, she said to herself, a straight line that you could walk along—no fears and no muddles; any other way it was all knots and tangles, in which you struggled, helpless and disabled. But often people seemed to see all that much better after a completed relation than before! She had, with Aubrey. Vinstead was very clever—perhaps he would see it anyhow. Or not! She couldn't tell! Her thoughts ran round in circles—now to Vinstead, now to the emotion just stirring in her for him. There was a moment—there nearly always *is* a moment—when one could stamp on it; this was that moment for her. But had she better? What about him, if it meant battening down the hatches again on what was visibly struggling with difficulty to life?

The hardest decisions of all are those where the head and the heart, the duty to one's neighbour and the pleasure for oneself, seem to lie in the same direction. Mrs. Leroy failed to reach one that night. She must wait on events, she murmured to herself, beginning at last to get sleepy. If they had to see it out—well, there it was! On which at last she fell asleep. To wake, strangely enough, with a settled mind, not at war with a certain absurd dancing in the blood. That was all part of the game, and there was no need to worry over it.

It was late when she woke. The sun was making the air inside the paper lattice a dull powdery gold, and a tray of morning tea steamed beside her. She poured herself a cup, and immediately afterwards Judith came in, in her pyjamas, her hair a golden cloud, and curled herself up cross-legged on the *k'ang*, near the tea-tray.

"I heard your spoon chinking, so I knew you were awake," the girl remarked, taking one of Laura's cigarettes.

"How did you sleep?" Laura asked.

"In*credi*bly! Wow, I am stiff, though," she stretched her arms out and twisted her trunk first to one side and then to the other. There didn't seem much wrong with Judith, Laura thought—the girl looked brilliantly well except for faint shadows under her eyes, and her whole being seemed to breathe a radiant contentment as she sat smoking on the *k'ang* in the dimmed dusty sunshine.

"I say, Laura," Judith went on—and then stopped.

"Well, what?"

"You talked to Derek about me, didn't you?"

"Yes,—or rather mostly he came and catechised me," said Laura, smiling.

"I know—I mean I thought so. Laura!"

"Yes?"

"I believe you're going to be right."

"What about?"

"About the shirt!" said Judith unexpectedly. "We had a *fearful* doing on Saturday," she went on, rather disconnectedly. "We had it all out. Of course, I haven't really seen you since then, have I? He told me all about—oh, *them*, and all that, and it seemed so horrible, just going on and on, from one to another, with no—no *life* in it!" said Judith, with a curious note of indignant pain in her voice. "I was a fool, and cried, it was so beastly—and then he got cross, or crossish; and I told him how I loathed it, and he said people *were* like

that, and I was a fool not to know it, practically." She
paused.

"Well, and then?" Laura asked.

"Oh, just hopeless. I felt we should never get anywhere, and the whole thing was a complete failure. I
could see I hadn't been wise, or not wise enough," said
Judith. She meditated for a time, trying ineffectually to
blow smoke rings. "How funny it is," she resumed,
"that what matters is the way you're *feeling* when you
talk about a thing Do you know? Now last night,
coming home—I suppose it was because we'd both been
frightened, and all that—but we were feeling *kind* to one
another. I mean that sort of pride one has, and keeping
one's end up, and scoring points, was simply *gone*. And
another thing—though he had his arm round me, *that*
didn't mean anything either—I mean not in the ordinary
way. It was more like a very kind nurse is to a child—
that, oh, just *absolute* kindness and being loving. Do
you know?" she said again.

"Yes, rather. That's the unassailable part of love.
Well, go on," said Laura.

"Unassailable!" Judith repeated. "That's a good
word! That's just what it was. Because after a time we got
on to talking about ourselves again, but somehow this time
it was all *right*. We could both understand what the other
said, and I felt it was all *possible*—to let it go on, I mean.
And that however difficult it was—because, of course, it
will be; no one's idiot enough to think it won't!" said
Judith emphatically—"that—that there would be a part
of it that would be indestructible. And yet we were up
against just the same things, really. Wasn't it odd?"

"Yes—no, not a bit. Judith dear, I am very glad.
Derek is really valuable, and he wanted someone like
you to make this possible for him. And *I* wanted it
before he knew he did," said Laura, smiling.

The girl looked at her oddly, with no answering smile, for a moment. Then she left the *k'ang* and went and stood behind the camp bed, out of Laura's field of vision. "Now what's up?" Laura wondered—but she held her peace.

"I was a bit of a hell-hound," came presently from behind her, in rather a strangled voice.

"Were you? Why?"

"On Saturday. I—I hated his having talked to you about it."

"But my dear, what's the matter with that? It's only natural that you should," expostulated Laura. "That isn't being a hell-hound." "I couldn't really avoid it, you know, either," she added after a moment.

"I *know*!—and I talked to you about him! It was so *damnable* of me," said Judith; and coming up from behind she suddenly thrust her head into Laura's shoulder. "I had to tell you, now that it's all right," she said, in a voice rather muffled from her face being hidden.

Laura twisted her stiff arm free, so that she could put it round the girl. She pulled her niece in front of her. "Boodle! Give me a kiss," she said. Judith lifted her face then and gave the older woman, not a kiss, but a long hug. "I *am* happy," she murmured. And then she began her delightful gurgling chuckle. "Boodle!" she repeated. "Such a word! as Hubbard would say. Laura, we *must* dress!" And still chuckling, she went off to her own room.

The rest of the party were all assembled when Mrs. Leroy joined them on the terrace for breakfast. Every one seemed in fair order, in spite of their various experiences, except Annette Ingersoll. She looked very unwell. There were deep rings under her eyes, and her face had a blotchy yellowish pallor; about her forehead and eyebrows was the curious indefinable tight-drawn look which tells unmistakably of severe headache.

Inquiries revealed the fact that she had slept badly and had been sick in the night; she was eating next to nothing, and spoke very little, turning with a visible effort when addressed, as though to speak involved the lifting of some heavy weight. Mrs. Leroy was shocked by her appearance, and when they left the table she confided her concern to Nina Nevile. "I think she looks ill; the sooner we get her home the better."

"Why yes, but you know what a business getting off is!" said Mrs. Nevile. "I don't think there's really a lot the matter with her. Something must have upset her stomach."

The business of "getting off" from a temple week-end is indeed always considerable. What the servants do is done efficiently enough, but the supervision and combination of the activities of the Europeans and the donkey - boys require generalship of a high order. Touchy excelled at this. Mrs. Leroy, who loathed fuss of any sort, confined her activities to telling Hubbard to pack for Miss Ingersoll as well as for herself, and then took her book and strolled off along the terrace, well out of reach of consultation, and sitting down on a marble bench began to read. Touchy came by, hastening to a consultation with Shang about the donkeys. "Vinstead's asking for you," he called to her as he passed.

"Tell him I'm here, there's an angel—*now*," said Laura.

Touchy obediently turned back, and presently reappeared with the Professor. "Did you think of taking a walk?" the latter asked, seating himself beside her. "I gather we don't start for another hour. I should like to look down on these roofs again."

"Yes, let's," said Mrs. Leroy.

They walked along to the main gate. In the sloping courtyard just within it the little grey shapes of the donkeys were disappearing under burdens of every sort as they stood tied to the trees. They were being loaded, unloaded, re-loaded under Touchy's supervision.

"You're not starting?" he called to Vinstead and Laura.

"No, going for a stroll."

"Are you packed?"

"Yes, Hubbard's seeing to it."

"Well, for pity's sake be back in an hour!" he adjured them.

They strolled up the ridge till they could look down on the ballet of the roofs in its *décor* of fruit-blossom, and by common consent sat down on the very rock on which Laura and Annette had sat two days before. Both were of an age which felt no necessity to make excuses for coming out— but neither was wholly without self-consciousness.

"I feel that perhaps I ought to apologise for last night," Vinstead began at length with an abruptness which showed this feeling.

"Wouldn't that be just a little ungracious?" said Mrs. Leroy slowly. She was holding an oak-leaf to her eye and looking at the roofs through a hole in it, but lowered it as she spoke.

He turned fully to her, then, with a quick relieved smile.

"Thank you!" he said. "I half hoped you'd feel that. I don't really want to apologise, but I should rather like to explain. I'm still so surprised at myself!" he said.

"At the suddenness? Because that's the air, largely," said Laura. "We get to expect that here."

"Oh, really? Do you?" He was professionally interested at once, to Laura's secret amusement. "Well, I don't think it's *only* the air," he pursued after a moment, with a curious wry face. "And it is not only the suddenness that is startling to me in myself—the whole thing is so—well, so wholly out of my line."

Would he tell her why anything so normal as falling in love had come to be out of his line? Laura asked.

He would—and did. It was not a long story, but not even his deliberately dry and scientific presentation could make it anything but painful to a degree. He had been wildly—and seriously—in love with a beautiful and not unintelligent girl, and engaged to her; poverty had put marriage out of the question for about a year and a half. He had had scruples against living with her before marriage; scruples which, he realised too late, she did not share. They had ultimately married—only to find, in his case, that she was unfaithful to him—freely, continuously, scandalously; that she had been, as she had at last told him casually, unfaithful to him even during the period of their engagement. There was no question of turning from him to someone she loved better—she had le goût pour l'homme to a point which made normal life impossible for her. "It was a genuine case of nymphomania," he said. "Actually that is a comparatively rare thing in Northern Europe, in spite of the free way in which people throw the word about." He could not bring himself to divorce her, and the last thing she wished was to divorce him—a home, an income, the protection of a respectable name were just what she wanted. So he had gone on, in a misery which he did not mention, but which Laura shivered with pity to guess at, till at length she ran away with somebody richer and died of typhoid in Naples. The Professor told his tale without rancour and quite impersonally, but Mrs. Leroy could see with hideous clearness the wretched and piteous accompaniment—every natural feeling, every tradition, every eager hope and tender or sacred association trampled in the mud, degraded and ruined, till sex had become for him an obsession, a horror, the slow murderer of all the things by which he lived.

"So you see," he ended up, "why I have become rather abnormal. Only I didn't really realise it—at least, if I did, I felt my abnormality to be the greater wisdom. Of course, my job makes me look at all emotion professionally; Love has become an exhibit, and not always an amusing one. And what you have done for me here has been to turn me into an exhibit myself," he said, turning again to her with a half-rueful smile.

To his astonishment she turned her head away from him quickly, but not before he had seen the tears on her face. "You're not crying?" he said incredulously. "Not for me? My dear," he took her hand and pulled her round towards him, "you're not crying for me?"

"Oh yes," she said, nodding at him with a curious helpless gesture. "Oh yes." The pity of it had taken her by surprise, and jerked her completely off her rather careful, if sincere attitude of frankness and sympathy. He had been hurt hideously, and it made her cry; she was nearly as much surprised as he, but there it was.

"Don't cry, please," he said, still holding her hand. "There is no need to worry about it, you know—it was all so long ago. I've hardly thought of it for years—it is certainly years since I *felt* it at all. Please don't cry for me." And suddenly he put his arm round her and kissed her—gently, like an older person comforting a child.

Laura, who had begun to dab at her eyes, was completely taken aback by this. "Oh, wait a bit," she said, in a startled voice. "We—we haven't got there yet!"

Vinstead burst out laughing. "*I* have!" he said. "When did you expect to get there?"

Laura began to laugh too. Her tears, his kiss, had suddenly put the whole thing on a fresh and perfectly natural basis, where none of the usual gambits were needed or even possible. There was no "situation" any more between them; they began to talk like two human beings, and not like a professor and a married woman with whom he has fallen in love. What to do about it all would have to be faced and settled sooner or later, but the immediate concern was simply to understand. In this new blessed ease they fairly got down to it, coming to grips with the question of how you look at love, which is one of the two or three things that make a life sane or otherwise, civilised or otherwise. Their points of view were not the same, but they were in a state where human communication is at its best; where words are used and used well, but where the meaning flows through them and along with them, unhampered by submerged emotions or conventional reticences. *On vit plus ou moins à travers des mots*, as a rule, but sometimes these moments do come when words and thought are one, and one with the receptive understanding. And in such moments the individual reality of two lives—for reality is subjective, personal to each one of us, held in by the crystal walls of our own experience—can be fully understood; the crystal walls are broken down for a space, and two realities mingle and become one. There is little better. The physical falls away, almost irrelevant, when naked spirits meet in kindness.

So, though they sat side by side on the rock, the Professor was not even holding Mrs. Leroy's hand when Annette Ingersoll suddenly appeared on the path below them. Even at a distance her figure suggested some serious disorder; she was bare-headed, and broke now and then into a little stumbling run.

"Good heavens!" said Laura, starting to her feet, "how mad of her to come out with no hat, with that head! What *is* the matter with her?"

"Go gently with her—I'm afraid she's very ill," said Vinstead in a low voice, as she started down the path towards the girl. She checked at his words, and went on more slowly. As she approached she saw that Annette looked even worse than at breakfast, barely an hour ago

—the circles under her eyes had deepened, and were almost purple; the pallor of her face was more marked, and she made little nervous movements with her hands as she walked. When she saw Mrs. Leroy she ran up to her with, "Oh *there* you are, Mrs. Leroy."

"Am I wanted? Are you all starting?" asked Laura.

"No, but I just *had* to find you," said the girl. She spoke with little short breaths. "We'll be going in no time, and you haven't told me. You promised——" she said, catching at Laura's hand; the heat of her touch was startling.

"Told you what?" said Laura—and then she remembered. Annette's appearance had bumped her out of that world of serene communication so suddenly that for a moment she was at a loss.

"About enlightenment—and what's wrong with me; why I don't *know* people. I *have* to know!" She spoke with the same feverish haste that showed in her movements, and though her voice was not raised, her tones had almost the frantic urgency of a scream. "You just *must* tell me."

"I will," said Mrs. Leroy. "Come on down, and we'll talk as we go. Here, put this on," she said, taking off her hat. "Yes, you must, in this sun—or I can't talk to you." Annette submitted, looking at her with childish relief and obedience. Her small unformed mouth, so like a doll's mouth, smiled vaguely; Laura noticed that her lips were no longer like dewy petals, as Henri had said, but dry and cracked.

"Are you thirsty?" she asked.

"Yes, terribly, Mrs. Leroy."

"Would you go on down and tell Niu to get out some soda-water?" said Laura to Vinstead.

"Right!"

"Annette, why do you worry so much about enlightenment?" Mrs. Leroy said then, her eyes on his swift

striding figure below them. Her thoughts were clamour‚
ing to follow her eyes—what was that he had said about
love showing us both our weakness and our strength
more clearly than any other experience? But she forced
them on to the girl. "How old are you?"

"I'm twenty-three, Mrs. Leroy."

"Well, don't you think enlightenment—or knowing
people, whichever it is you want—is largely a matter of
age and experience?"

"Why maybe it is—but I guess the kind of experience
makes a whole heap of difference," said Annette, with
unexpected penetration. "Just running around with
people, and laughing, doesn't teach you much. I'm
just standing outside people all the time, looking at them.
There must be a way to learn—*you* do it, I can see you
do. I want—oh, mercy, how my head aches!" she said,
putting her hand up and then dropping it again with a
sort of hopeless gesture. She began to talk once more,
speaking very fast. "Why did that bonze shake his head
at me, when he read my fortune? Oh yes, he did—I
saw him. I guess *he* knew I was a dud at people! Why
won't you tell me?" she said again.

"Annette dear, I will—everything I can that will
help you, or that's helped me," said Laura. "But I really
don't think you are fit to talk *or* listen now, while your
head is so bad." She spoke very composedly, hoping to
quiet Annette's feverish distress; she was exceedingly
alarmed by the girl's state. "Sit down here," she said as
they reached the courtyard, and sitting beside Annette she
took her hand, in such a way that she could feel the bumping pulse. Heavens! she must have a terrific temperature.
"Now listen to me," she went on, "if I promise to tell
you all I can as soon as your head is better, will you
promise me not to worry about it till I do? Then we'll
take our time and have a good go at it. Shall we?"

"Oh yes—how good you are, Mrs. Leroy!"

"All right—that's a bargain. Tell me, did you go out without your hat yesterday too?" she asked.

"Only just a little while, just up the hill here."

"What time?"

"Why, we got in just before tiffin."

How mad of Nina, to allow such a thing, thought Laura angrily. Vinstead now appeared with Niu, bringing soda-water, and Laura went in search of Mrs. Nevile, leaving him with Annette. Just beyond the first court she met General Nevile, limping hastily towards the gate.

"Vinstead says he thinks that child's really ill," he said abruptly. "What do you say?"

"I'm afraid she may be—she has a tremendous pulse, and she's inclined to be hysterical," said Laura. "I think perhaps she has a touch of the sun. She went out with no hat yesterday, she tells me, just before lunch."

The General frowned at this intelligence, but kept characteristically to the practical side.

"What are we to do? Keep her here till it's cooler, or get her down?"

"Have we any ice up here?"

"No—the coolies went off with all the food and stuff nearly an hour ago."

"*I* don't know," said Laura. "I should be almost inclined to get her down if we've no ice."

"She ought to be all right if she rides, and has a topi and an umbrella," said the General, pulling worriedly at his blond moustache. "Hope she won't be bad, poor little thing. She looked seedy enough at breakfast."

"If she's going, oughtn't she to start at once?" said Laura, "and not wait for the rest?"

"Certainly she ought," said the General. "We'll get her off."

Chapter Twenty-four

THE journey down to the cars was rather a nightmare. As it turned out, there was no question of waiting for the others—they were all ready, and the caravan set off as soon as Annette had been provided with a topi, Miss Hande's painted paper parasol, and a big handkerchief of Touchy's soaked in water and draped over her head and neck. Henri at first volunteered to walk beside her and hold the parasol over her head, but he chattered, and his presence seemed to cause her a vague distress. She kept turning round and asking for Laura, who at last felt obliged to come and take Henri's place—this arrangement seemed to soothe the girl, who consented to sit still on her donkey and not talk. It involved some sacrifice on Laura's part, nevertheless. She had counted a good deal on spending at least a part of the two hours' walk in Vinstead's company. But the sense of security and comfort persisted, and she had plenty to think about—the whole lay-out of his attitude, as he had begun to make it clear to her, and his response to the point of view which she had expressed. If they could keep the generosity of understanding which they had once achieved, nothing else mattered—whether they ultimately became lovers or not, was almost irrelevant, she thought to herself.

Alongside these meditations, she kept a watchful eye on Annette Ingersoll. At first the girl seemed to stand the ride well enough, but after they left the smallpox village and began to cross the open plain she wilted almost visibly under the increasing heat. A hot wind was blowing down out of the funnel-shaped valley of the Hun-ho, tossing and bending the round fluffy tops of the poplars, and raising nasty little choking whirlwinds and eddies of dust along the path. As they proceeded across the plain towards the river the sky behind them took on a dull menacing yellow glare. Touchy moved up and down the line, urging the donkey-boys to greater speed. "I'm afraid we're in for a dust-storm if we don't hurry," he said to Laura as he passed her. She nodded—she feared it too, late in the season as it was; she knew that yellow glare which betokened a sky full of fine particles of Gobi dust, whirled up off the bare desert flats and carried three hundred miles, to drop when the wind dropped. They hurried on. "*T'za! t'za!*" cried the donkey-boys, hastening the small beasts; and trip-trip-trip went the little neat feet on the earthen path. As they approached the shallow branch of the Hun-ho Vinstead came and walked beside her, taking the umbrella which she found it hard to keep vertical against the increasing force of the wind, and himself holding it over Annette; when they reached the ford he simply splashed through it, this time, regardless of his trousers. Something in Laura's heart warmed to him for this small action—it seemed to her somehow important, indicative of a new freedom and a capacity for extravagance. That after all was what he most needed—just moral extravagance—after his years of cautious self-regulation.

The storm hit them as they reached the river bank by the ferry. For the last few minutes the wind had been thrashing the poplar-heads till they looked like green balls tossed loose in the air, their slim boles lost in a luminous haze of dust. Now, with a shriek, it fell on them. "Down! Down! Cover your heads!" Touchy yelled above the screaming wind. "Your coat off!" he shouted at Vinstead. Laura had pulled Annette off the donkey and cowered down with her where they were on the path, wrapping the damp handkerchief over the girl's face, and tying her coloured neck scarf round her own—she knew that in a dust-storm it is madness to attempt to move into shelter—literally madness, for the blind confusion of flying particles, the torture of dust in eyes, ears, mouth and lungs, drive one demented in a few seconds. "There! Over all of you!" she heard Touchy's voice, and found Vinstead beside her and Annette, his coat and a donkey-blanket flung over all their heads. They crouched there in the semi-darkness, listening to the shrieking wind, to the patter of sand on the cloth over their heads, to shouts and cries in the distance, and—in the lulls—to one another's breathing. Annette's was short and irregular—her shoulder, which touched Laura's, seemed almost to burn through the two thin sleeves. Oh, maddening delay! Just when it was so urgent to get her home quickly. For what seemed ages they crouched there, breathing uncomfortably through the wrappings on their faces, feeling their teeth nevertheless gritty and their lips dry, as the fine eddying dust searched into every fold and cranny. Actually it was barely half an hour before the worst of it was over, and Touchy came round, uncovering the huddled groups, whose corpse-like appearance moved him to laughter, and telling them that the ferry-boat was at the shore.

They rose then and went on board, every one beating and shaking the sand out of their clothes, and wiping their necks, their ears and the hollows of their faces with handkerchiefs to get rid of the fine film of yellowish dust which covered them. They could see the tail of the storm moving off across the sandy flats by the river towards Peking, black at the heart, with flying luminous

yellow fringes. Again they landed on the sloping shore,
and followed the narrow and discoloured track round
the foot of the bluff to where the cars waited on the
river-bank. Deadly familiar those features had become
during their long wait four days ago—identical they now
greeted their return, even to the single patch of shade
under the stunted thuja, up on the rocks. But not all of
those who returned brought back with them an equal
identity. Human lives develop at unequal speeds at
different times. Those four days had been a period of
accelerated growth, of swift subtle modification, for
several of the week-enders who set out so light-heartedly
on their picnic. Derek, Judith, Annette, Laura, Vinstead
—even Miss Hande perhaps, as to her theories about the
Chinese—had been confronted, not fruitlessly, up at
Chieh T'ai Ssu, with the ancient wisdom and the
blossoming tree. Vinstead in particular looked about
him as he stepped ashore, almost aghast at the strangeness, the swift movement of reality. Here on this path,
four days ago, Laura had stood near him; an interesting
face and a name—Mrs. Leroy!—she who had now
mixed herself so integrally with his thoughts, his emotions, his very life; up on those slabs he had looked her
straight in the face, and failed to make an entrance for
himself into her absorbed eyes—he who this morning on
the hill had seen his own miserable past realities come
back to life in her pitying gaze, in her sudden tears.

It was arranged that Annette should go in Laura's
car, which was the fastest and the best sprung, and with
Derek and Judith as well it set off first, bumping and
crawling over the fields towards Mo-shih-k'ou. Once on
the road it went faster, but still not fast enough to
satisfy Laura's desire to get Annette safely home. The
girl lay back in the corner, with closed eyes most of the
time—sometimes she turned her head from side to side,

as if seeking a position that would lessen the pain. "Is
your head very bad?" Laura asked her, arranging the
freshly soaked handkerchief on her forehead, and sprink-
ling it with Hubbard's eau-de-Cologne. "Oh my, *yes!*"
the girl answered in a sort of moan; "and my legs, too—
and my back. It seems just everywhere." There was
nothing to be done but to sit and watch the familiar
landmarks on the road, as they reached and passed them
one by one—Pa Pao Shan, the golden hill on the brown-
paper-coloured landscape; the little walled town astride
the road; the empty bed of the old Imperial Canal; God-
damn Britishers, painted on the roadside wall. Every
small hindrance—a file of camels crossing from a side
road, a cart upset—seemed intolerable to Laura, whose
anxiety was increasing all the time. If this were sunstroke, it was a severe case; and now at intervals Annette
gave a curious little sharp cry, not loud, but of a painful
and striking intensity. At last the grey outline of the
city wall rose ahead of them, and the mighty bulk of the
gate-tower; they swung through, and bumped and raced
along the wide sordid streets of tumble-down one-storey
houses, vertical signs, and teeming commercial activity
on the side-walks. As they turned into the Jade Canal
Road and approached the Legation, Laura gave an
order to the chauffeur in Chinese; at the Legation gate
the car stopped.

"You two get out here," said Laura abruptly to
Judith and Derek, and sprang out after them. "I'm
going to take her to the German Hospital at once," she
said in a low tone. "You, Judith, go to Nina's house and
wait, and tell her when she comes—send her on there
immediately; the doctor may want to know things I
can't tell him. Derek, ring up Doctor Hertz's house and
find out where he is; if he's at the hospital, all right—if
not, you must get hold of him and send him there at

once. Oh, and Judith—send the amah round in a ricksha with a nightgown of Annette's and some handkerchiefs—she talks English." She stepped back into the car and was gone.

Judith and Derek were left standing on the path under the locust trees. For a moment they remained almost benumbed, while the ricksha coolies who hung about the gate sprang up and shuffled towards them, proffering their services with loud cries. *"Pu yao"* (Don't want), said Derek mechanically, and turned towards the gate.

"Do you think she's really *ill?*" Judith asked incredulously, as they walked in.

"Laura evidently thinks so," he said gravely. "Poor kid. Well, come on, Juno—we must do our jobs." And suddenly, regardless of the sentry, he gave her elbow a quick squeeze. "If it had been *you!*" he said, "where should I be now?"—and hurried off to his own house.

In the polished concreted hall, smelling of ether and disinfectants, of the big white building off Legation Street, Mrs. Leroy asked for Schwester Johanna. Small, stout, motherly, comely in her wide-folded white head-dress, the sister superintended the removal of Annette from the car to a room upstairs with swift competence. Dr. Hertz was operating, but would be free in a few minutes. Meanwhile, the sister took the girl's temperature, and handed the thermometer to Laura with grave eyes. It was over 105°. An ice pack was being prepared —the Schwester knew her job—when Dr. Hertz came in, still wiping disinfectant from his hands with a little towel. He made a brief examination—touched the pulse, raised the head from the pillow and let it lie back again, and removing the sheet, gently first lifted and then lowered the right leg. "This hurts?" he asked.

"No—oh, I can't bear the light!" moaned Annette. He half drew the curtain, and then stood in a characteristic attitude at the foot of the bed, watching the patient intently, as if to draw in information from her general aspect—a trick of his that Laura knew well. So he had stood, gazing from the foot of the bed at Sarah, when she had nearly died of scarlet fever three years before. After a prolonged survey of the now flushed face, the nervous movements of the hands, the uncertain breathing, with a brusque gesture he beckoned Mrs. Leroy from the room.

"It is grave," he said when they stood in the passage, where the greenery from the great trees outside almost brushed the high windows. "Unless this temperature shall come down! But we pack her with ice—perhaps it comes down. She has been in the sun, yes?"

Laura gave him, briefly, the history of the picnic; the long hot wait on Friday, in the full heat of the day, beside the ferry; the hot walk up to Chieh T'ai Ssu—the fact that Annette had gone out, hatless, before lunch on Sunday. At this last detail he gave an impatient little shrug, and almost a moan of distress. "So they do! So they do! And she has headache—when?"

Last night, Laura said—and was sick; she had seemed listless in the afternoon, she heard. "I wasn't there myself—some of us went to T'an Chüeh Ssu."

"Ah, yes—you have an episode with bandits, I hear!" said the doctor, with an amused glance. The bandit-ing of one's friends and acquaintances is an invariable source of rather malicious entertainment in China. But he returned at once to the point. "She is how old?"

"Twenty-three."

He made a note. "And is in Peking how long?"

Barely two months, Laura told him—she was Mrs. Nevile's niece, and staying with her.

"Ah, I see her. Do you know, has she any illness since she comes here? Any shock?"

"Not that I know of," said Laura. She hesitated, and then said: "It is sunstroke, is it?"

"But yes, it has that look. Hyper-pyrexia she has certainly, and it shall be from the sun, most probably. There can be also some septic condition, but I do not see the signs of it. She is exposed to the sun all these hours on Friday—and yesterday without the hat!—this suffices!" He turned to go. "*Na, auf wiedersehen, gnädige Frau! Es kann schon gehen!* But I cannot promise. You stay here?"

"I shall stay till Mrs. Nevile comes," said Laura.

"*Schön! Schön!* I see her when she comes." He went off, with his heavy hurried step.

Twenty minutes later Mrs. Nevile arrived, rather breathless. "Oh yes, much better bring her here, if she's really ill," was her reply to Laura's explanations. "Has Doctor Hertz seen her yet?" Laura told her what had passed. "Hertz always thinks it's death!" said Nina, with the petulance of extreme worry. "Where is she?"

"Here," said Laura, opening the door—and treading softly they went in. In the darkened room the nurses were still plying their task with damp cloths and ice-bags; Annette lay with closed eyes, moaning a little, her small mouth open, her hair showing dark and flattened with moisture under the pads on her brow. The sister held up a warning hand—Laura, whispering, "Let me hear how she goes on," slipped out and went back to the Legation.

In the hall she met Lilah. "How is she?" Miss Milne asked at once.

"Baddish, I'm afraid," Laura answered, her foot on the bottom step of the stairs. "But Hertz is always frightfully pessimistic." Small wonder, she thought to herself, as she went on up to her room and ordered a bath, if he was—*she* would be, if she followed the profession of medicine in Peking! People were always going off like flies, at a few hours' notice, and half the time no one ever really knew what *was* the matter with them— not even Hertz, whom she, like many other people, considered to be the best doctor from Harbin to Singapore. However, Annette was young and strong—she might throw it off, she said to herself, wrestling with these gloomy thoughts as she lay in her bath. And then she heard her husband's voice in her bedroom, "Laura?"

"Yes—I'm in my bath—I'll be out in a moment," she called back.

"Don't hurry—I've got to be off in two minutes. I only came in to hear how you'd enjoyed your picnic," boomed Henry jovially through the door. "I gather you had a lovely time—bandits and all! I've just seen La Touche for a moment in the compound. Where are the girls? Were they frightened? He said Lilah had done something rather plucky, but I was in a hurry, and I couldn't wait to hear."

"Didn't he tell you about Annette Ingersoll?"

"No—what about her?"

"She's down with sunstroke—I've just dropped her at the German Hospital."

"Oh Lord! Bad?"

"Nearly a hundred-and-six."

"That's high enough! What's Hertz say? '*Ich kann nichts versprechen,*' I suppose?"

"Yes—but I'm afraid he's worried about her."

"So he may be. Poor little thing. Well, I shall be back to dinner—the Professor chap's coming, isn't he? I'm off to the temple now. That banana-coloured griffin is showing remarkable form, Laura—I shouldn't wonder if he's fit to put in for the Counsellor's Plate." She heard her door bang, and Henry's heavy departing step along the passage.

Downstairs tea was laid on the verandah. Mrs. Leroy and her nieces sat among the stocks and oleanders, all rather silent. Judith's expression reminded Laura forcibly of a boiling kettle with the lid bouncing on it, her inner effervescence was so evident under her quite sincere concern for Annette Ingersoll. "But she'll get *well*, won't she, Laura?" she burst out at length. "It would be too—too *bloody* for her to die just now. Though she's miles too good for that little worm Henri!" she added.

"Poor Henri! Why is he a worm?" asked Laura, amused in spite of her anxiety by the girl's train of thought.

"Oh, I don't know! He's so—so *accurate*; I'm sure he makes love like a dancing-master!" said Judith impatiently. She jumped up. "I shall go for a turn on the wall," she said. "One can't just sit still here and think ——" and disappeared into the house.

For some moments after her departure Mrs. Leroy and her elder niece said nothing to one another. Then Lilah lit a cigarette, and blowing out a cloud of smoke, "I don't think Little Annette is at all well qualified to live," she observed.

"What makes you think so? Did General Nevile say anything?" Laura asked quickly, startled.

"No—I don't mean her chances of recovery," said Lilah. "I can't judge of those, poor little beast—though I should think a brain-storm was a pretty poor foundation for sunstroke. I meant generally."

"How did you know about her brain-storm?" Laura asked, remembering with something of a shock how badly she had wanted to discuss this with Lilah at Chieh T'ai Ssu. She had never got the chance, and now the need was over, for the time.

"It was pretty obvious, wasn't it?" said Lilah. "I

know she talked to you, but it stuck out of her a foot, without talking."

"What did you make of it? I should really like to know," said Laura.

"She simply wasn't up to having a love-affair with anyone, as far as I could see, any more than a child of eleven would be," said Lilah; "she hadn't developed the capacity. And she was just beginning to find it out —but by that time she'd got herself somehow tied up with Master Henri, I imagine, and didn't know what on earth to do about it. Really this illness will be a perfect godsend if Mrs. N. has any wits at all, because it will make a break. She can take her to the sea or something afterwards, and keep him off."

"Do you think she ever will develop the capacity for having love-affairs? The Professor wasn't at all sure that she would," said Laura.

Lilah looked at her aunt a little curiously. "He ought to know," she said bluntly. "I shouldn't have thought so, I must say. I think she's quite half-baked about people. The only thing for girls like her is to marry some hundred-per-cent. he-man, or whatever they call them, who's as simple as she is, and be perfectly happy in a perfectly prep-school way for ever after. It's no good her taking on a hyper-civilised European like Henri. That's her way out, if only Nina Nevile could see it."

"Vinstead says there always *is* a way out, but not always a good one," said Laura meditatively, remembering his remark on the terrace.

"*What* a bromide!" said Lilah. "By the way, what's his Christian name, Laura?"

"I've no idea," said Mrs. Leroy. She was amused and surprised to realise that this was so. Lilah was doing her good; her blunt matter-of-factness, which was not in the least unkind, had insensibly relieved the anxiety which hung over her. She forgave her the bromide—it was true, of course.

"I gather from Judith that Master Fitzmaurice has more or less decided to chuck his ladies and become a respectable citizen," said Lilah, changing the subject with her usual abruptness. She looked amused and non-committal.

"Oh, it's as definite as that, is it?" said Laura. "Well, do you approve?"

"I don't think anything else would satisfy her—or him either, at the moment," said Lilah judicially. "It may work. She's a pretty stiff proposition, you know," she said, turning on Laura her slow amused stare. "She'll either make a man of him, or send him flying. But it won't kill either of them. Hullo, there they are! That's Judith's idea of walking on the wall!"

Across the lawn, among the flowering trees of the upper garden, the figures of Derek and Judith came into view, walking rather more than arm-in-arm. The on-lookers on the verandah saw them stop, and the girl look up into the man's face with a happy confident gesture, before he took her by the shoulders and gave her a slight shake. It was the very diagram of a good-tempered disagreement. They moved on and were lost to sight among the trees. Laura smiled. "They look all right," she said.

"Yes, they're all right—for the moment," said Lilah. "Hullo, here's His Excellency. I rather think I'll leave you to it." She rose and trailed indoors through the french window of the drawing-room, as Niu announced "Big Envoy!" at the glass door leading from the hall.

Neat and dapper, Sir James stepped through on to the verandah. His manner expressed a mixture of gallantry and disapproval, unique to himself.

"Well, Mrs. Henry, I'm afraid you've had a disagreeable experience," he began. "Bit unwise, of course, these expeditions, when the country's disturbed and all that. However, you're *looking* none the worse! That's an admirable frock!"

"Let me make you a cocktail, Sir James," said Laura, as Niu and Li removed the tea-things and put the cocktail tray in their place. "Yes—it's after six, so it's quite in order! Tell me," she went on, as she mixed the drinks, "what's been happening here? We've heard nothing, of course." She thought it would be safer to ask for information than to give it, if possible.

"Oh, Li's all right. He and Tu really seem to be going to stand together, and freeze old Wang out," said Sir James. "In fact, the Marshal's in great form—I was at Nan-yuan with him yesterday. Thank you—— Ladies whose bright eyes——!" he raised the glass she handed to him. But he was not to be put off. "These brigands you fell in with—know whose men they were?"

"Yes, Wang's—luckily, as things stand," said Laura. "They were some of those three battalions he disbanded the other day, and of course they were down and out— no officers, no pay, and no food."

"Hm! Most unfortunate, the whole thing," said Sir James, beginning to gnaw his moustache. "Most unfortunate! Tiresome if these fellohs start kicking up a fuss about the three chaps you brought back. Don't quite see what La Touche wanted to bring them for."

"They'd knocked us about a good deal," said Laura. "But the real reason was because we saw them murder a monk. I think the Yamen will want to have them for that, you know." She began to laugh. "Sir James, you can have some fun with Doctor Schuyler over this! We'd half decided to let them go, to save a fuss, and it was Miss Hande who insisted on having them brought to justice—a full-blown hundred-per-cent. American citizen!"

"Miss Hande? Who's she? That writing woman at the M.A.'s?"

"Yes—but the writing woman, as you call her, is a famous novelist," said Laura. "She's a quite enormous noise! You tell Doctor Schuyler it was her doing. It's a lovely situation!"

Sir James was tickled. "Quite good! Quite good! You'll bear witness, dear lady?"

"*Six* of us will bear witness," said Laura, laughing again.

But Sir James was not mollified for long.

"Unlucky, though, our fellohs going out! Armed forces operating on Chinese soil! Most irregular! Can't think what they'll say about it at home. I don't know what La Touche was thinking of."

"I expect he *would* have been thinking of saving our lives," said Laura rather coldly. "But in point of fact it wasn't he who sent for them."

"Who did, then? Jeudwine said he had a message from La Touche."

"Sir James, it's rather awful, and you must help me if you can," said Laura, suddenly looking very troubled. "It was really my fault, and what Henry will say I can't think. Will you help me?"

"My dear lady, of course, of course. But how on earth do *you* come into it?" said Sir James, gallantry visibly overcoming disapproval—his real kindness, Laura knew, was seldom appealed to in vain. She knew quite well what Henry would say when she told him the story of Hubbard's performance—he would guffaw till the furniture shook, and give Hubbard ten dollars. But it really *was* important to get the Minister well set on blanketing the whole affair, and making no scapegoats—

the most obvious animals in this category being Jeudwine and Derek, neither of whom was in any way in fault. So she told Sir James of Hubbard's false message with a considerable appearance of distress, and of anxiety for the results to herself and Henry if there were any sort of official fuss over the matter. Sir James rose to the occasion—he was shrewd enough to see that Li Ch'ing-hui, the Marshal, would be very unlikely to make any trouble over the decapitation of three of his rival's common soldiers; and as for Peking gossip—always a factor, though a minor one—Miss Hande's action put the Americans in the hollow of his hand, if they should try to make capital out of the episode. He was encouraging and kind. There need be no official commotion. "No, no—don't you worry, Mrs. Henry—your maid's little game shan't get you into trouble."

At this point Niu entered with a chit-book and two notes, for which Laura signed. The book was Nina's, and one of the notes was from her, asking Laura to go round as soon as she could. "The packs have not been very successful yet, but the Schwester is still hopeful." The other note was in a strange handwriting, and Laura's pulse gave a little jump as she guessed whose script it was that she was seeing for the first time. She was right—it was from Vinstead, to excuse himself from dining with them. "I cannot imagine that you will want a guest in the circumstances. Mrs. Nevile remains optimistic, but personally I have little hope." The signature was A. Vinstead. She made her excuses to Sir James and went off to Nina.

Late that night Professor Vinstead was in his room at the Neviles'. He was in bed, but he was neither sleeping nor reading, though a book lay open on the quilt near his hand. The mental discomfort of acute anxiety lay over the whole house. Mrs. Nevile had been fetched back at half-past eight by her husband from the hospital, where her presence was of no use—but a telephone message had been received at ten o'clock to say that Annette Ingersoll was now unconscious. Vinstead had taken himself off to his room early, anxious to relieve them of his presence, and equally anxious to be alone. He had been doing some pretty hard thinking all day, and had travelled a considerable distance from his position of even twenty-four hours ago. He saw at last in its true perspective, or so he thought, his long-cherished attitude of aloof avoidance of sex and emotion—no longer as something wise and lofty, but as a thing in itself crippling and deforming; saw at last that the secret of life is to abandon all our own inner pretensions to superiority. Man cannot be a god; he must accept the normal human lot, with all the humiliations it imposes—the ardours, the pangs, the butterfly joys and the long cold sorrows; the small things with the great. This he had come to see; and lying half in the narrow circle of the light from the bedside lamp, staring into the shadows of the room, he was endeavouring to make a rational application of it to his own case—embracing the spears of a new torment, making his surrender to a suffering he had avoided for years, which yet held, for him as for every one, the vital springs of life.

Suddenly there was a knock at his door.

"Come in!" he called, and there entered, longer and leaner than ever in a dressing-gown, the long lean figure of his host. General Nevile limped across the room; he was carrying a small box in one hand, and a bottle in the other.

"You'd better have one of these," he said, setting down the bottle, and opening the box, which contained several large white cachets.

"What is it?" Vinstead asked.

"Santonin," replied the General briefly.

Vinstead had never kept dogs, and the reply conveyed nothing to him. "What's that?" he asked.

The General explained what Santonin was. "We always take it after a spell in the hills or anywhere—as a precautionary measure," he said, with his gloomy grin. "This is Epsom salts"—he touched the bottle—"take a good tot of that to-morrow morning, and castor oil to-morrow night, and you ought to be all right. Good night," and he limped out again.

Vinstead took his cachet, as he was bidden, and lay back in bed again. The current of his thoughts had been changed by the General's entrance—his mind was fetched up with a jerk by this last episode, and from thinking of his own emotions and problems, he fell to brooding on the oddity of the whole week-end. He had been on a picnic with a number of total strangers; they had been captured by brigands, and rescued again; a girl had got sunstroke and lay at the point of death; he himself had fallen in love more violently and completely than ever before; and finally his host had come to him and administered a worm-powder. "I suppose that *is* *Peking*," he murmured to himself, and fell asleep.

Chapter Twenty-five

ON the following morning Mrs. Leroy was sitting on the verandah, finishing her breakfast alone. Letters, in England such an accessory of the breakfast-table, are absent from it in Peking—the daily flight of chits round the city does not begin much before 11 a.m., and the rather uncertain mail comes in, when it does come, towards midday. She was reading the typed Reuter's sheets with the latest news, which are distributed in the Legation. A couple of flower-sellers had set down their round flat wicker trays, full of pots of small monthly roses in full bloom, at the foot of the verandah steps, and with loud and persistent shouts drew her attention to the beauty and value of their wares—at intervals Mrs. Leroy, without looking up, mentioned a lower price, and then went on with her reading. Presently Niu announced *"Ha Kuniang!"* Laura rose and went indoors, followed by screams from the flower-sellers, who on seeing her disappear immediately dropped their price by another third—she paid no attention to them, but walked into the drawing-room, where she found Miss Hande.

"Well?" she said.

"She's passed over," said Miss Hande briefly.

"Oh Lord! When?"

"About one o'clock this morning. We heard late last night that she had relapsed into this sort of coma, and she was never conscious after that. They couldn't get the temperature down. It ran up to a hundred-and-nine degrees, and she died then."

"Was Nina there?" Laura asked.

"No—they telephoned, and she and the General went round, but it was too late."

"Poor child!" said Laura, sitting down sadly on the sofa. "Poor Little Annette."

"Why yes, it's a great tragedy," said the novelist. "So much brilliance and promise just cut right off! And for nothing! Mrs. Leroy, I think this is a terrible place. Do you recall what Mr. Fitzmaurice said when we were driving out to the picnic?"

"No, what?"

"Why, when I asked if there wasn't a great deal of illness here, he said, 'There's a good deal of death!' I thought he was just exaggerating, but it seems that it's true!"

"Oh, Lord, yes, it's true enough. Poor Little Annette," said Laura again. "How's Nina? I must go and see her."

"Oh, she's all to pieces over it," said Miss Hande. "The doctor has given her a sedative and put her to bed."

"Has Monsieur Delache been told?"

"Why, they say at the hospital that he was telephoning at all hours and heard right away. I've been round there just now—he's sent the most marvellous flowers. I just wonder," Miss Hande went on, peering at Laura, without her lorgnette, with a rather blind intentness, "if that would have come to anything if she hadn't died?"

"I don't know," said Laura.

"Nina seemed to think it wasn't going quite so well on Sunday," pursued Miss Hande. "She seemed out of sorts with him somehow, she said. But then I daresay she was feeling wretchedly already, poor child. Well, I guess we shall never know, now."

"No, we shall never know now," said Laura. She felt suddenly the tremendous finality of death; the cutting-off of the knowledge of other lives which is so inadequate, but is all we have. She would never know now whether the girl's feeling for Henri had gone beyond mere sense-enchantment, nor how far he was at the root of her spiritual disturbance. And there was so much that Annette would never know, now. "Buddha was quite right about her," she said suddenly.

"What do you mean?" asked Miss Hande.

"Her fortune in the shrine—oh, you weren't there. It said, 'Enlightenment shall escape her, but Death enlightens all men.'"

"Indeed! That's vurry striking," said Miss Hande. She rose to go. "Well, Buddha may say so, but I guess that's a pretty speculative proposition," she observed, in a tone whose sadness robbed the words of all insensitiveness, and took her leave.

Laura sat still among the freesias in her drawing-room. There were numbers of things to be done after her absence, but she made no attempt to do them. She sat with her hands in her lap, thinking about Annette, especially as she had last seen her, lying in the darkened room at the hospital. It was curious that the last thing she had heard her say should have been, "I can't bear the light." No—she couldn't bear the light—a waking life was not, mysteriously, for her. At Chieh T'ai Ssu she had stirred in her sleep, and muttered uneasily; but she had never wakened, and now she would sleep for good.

Mrs. Leroy was roused by the entrance of Hubbard, her arms full of clean linen, with some question about the wash-man. The matter liquidated, "Hubbard, Miss Ingersoll is dead," Laura said.

"Never!" exclaimed Hubbard, putting down her

linen. "What a misfortune, madam. Poor young lady. Well, I always *did* think she was too tall, if I may say so."

"Too tall, Hubbard?" said Laura, in a sort of dreary surprise.

"Yes, madam—too tall for health. Those tall pretty ones, and dreamy-like with it, they can't stand up to illness. There's no fight in them. Miss Judith wouldn't have died, madam—*nor* Miss Lilah. Well, I'll tell Chang to wash these drills again, then, madam," said Hubbard, and picking up her linen, departed.

Laura was just thinking that she really must begin to tackle her accumulation of notes and tasks when Niu announced, "*Wei Hsien-Sheng!*" and in walked the Professor.

They began by talking about Annette Ingersoll, of course—that was inevitable. Her death had been a good deal of a shock to Vinstead too, in spite of the serious view he had taken of her illness from the first; he was unused to the violence and suddenness of everything in Peking—life, death, love, all banging at you with the force of high explosive. "Well, she has found her way out," he said at length.

"You said there always was a way out," said Laura, meditatively and rather inanely—she was so much occupied at the moment just in watching his face and his hands, and taking fresh stock of his whole person, that she paid little attention to her words.

"Well, it would be hard to call this a good way," he answered, "and yet it might be even harder to think of a better. If she had lived she must have suffered, up to the limit of her capacity, anyhow."

Laura said nothing. She was thinking that perhaps Annette's real tragedy lay just in the fact that she *hadn't* suffered up to the limit of her capacity—that that would be anyone's tragedy. But Vinstead began to speak again.

"I've really come to say good-bye," he said. "I'm going to Nanking this evening."

Laura was aware, almost with astonishment, of the jump of pain that her mind gave at his words. "Oh," she said. "Why?"

"Well, the Neviles can't possibly want me in their house now—if they ever did," he said, with a ghost of his grin, "and I've got to put in a month or three weeks in the Schulz-Otway Institute down there anyhow, so I thought I would go at once. They can't very well let me go to an hotel here, you see, and it will suit me just as well to come back later. There's another reason too," he said, looking directly at her, "which you can probably surmise."

"Yes, I expect I can," said Laura rather faintly. There was that funny familiar difficulty about breathing, which belongs to these occasions. However, perhaps those five words which she had got out were enough, for the moment.

"I think it may be a good plan for us to take a little time to look at all this," said Vinstead. "It wouldn't be easy for me to stay here just now and see a lot of you, without—well, without wanting to see a lot more of you! That's obvious, isn't it?"

"Oh yes," said Laura.

"Well, I don't know how much more of you you'd let me see," pursued Vinstead. "And there's the question of fairness too. I don't *want* to be fair, particularly—but you are married, after all."

"Yes," said Laura again. This was practical politics, and all much more difficult than their easy meeting of minds on the hill—she could see, and still more hear, that Vinstead was in a nervous *froissé* mood, as a result of attempting to work it all out.

He went on, still in the rather staccato accents that she had never heard before:

"Then there's another thing. Even if you'd take a
lover, and I don't know if you would, I don't know
whether I should make a very good one. You know that
I've got a complex about the whole business, and you
know why. Well, that might rot it all up, at any moment;
I might fly completely off the handle and let you down
frightfully. I can't tell till I try—and yet I can't possibly
try"—he seemed almost to shiver, and the look on his
face reminded Laura of a frightened horse—"unless I'm
in love with the person. So it would be subjecting you
to an experiment, even if you agreed."

"I don't think that would matter much," said Laura.
"I'm not a young person."

"No, thank God! Only don't you see that you're just
the one person in the world that I couldn't bear to have
it go wrong with"—he dropped his voice, and the last
two words were barely audible—"my darling?"

Laura was more moved than she had expected by this.
But she spoke as off-handly as Vinstead.

"Well, there are one or two things I can tell you,"
she said. "I shouldn't go off with anybody, ever,
because to begin with there are the children, and there's
my husband. We are rather fond of one another, and I
shouldn't hurt him. But neither of those things would
prevent me from taking a lover, if it seemed a good thing
to do otherwise, and if I wanted to." She paused, and
looked meditatively in front of her, with the expression
which Vinstead remembered noticing when she sat in
the boat trailing her fingers in the water, and General
Nevile said that she specialised in rips. "Really just
that one thing," she went on, "seems so small, compared
to the rest of loving. I know it's there, and it's delightful—but it isn't in the least enduring, so it can't be
so enormously important, after all."

"No, but it seems very important indeed sometimes,"

said Vinstead, speaking rather more naturally. "It does to me now."

"Yes, I daresay. And I expect you're wise to go away and see if it still looks so important a month hence," said Laura. "As to your complex," she continued, "I don't know about them. And I don't know what makes a good lover, really. But I suppose it must always help the thing on a bit if both parties love one another, mustn't it?" "What *are* you staring at?" she asked, for Vinstead was fixing her with a gaze of extraordinary intensity.

"Do you mean to say you really do care about me at all?" he said—the staccato accents had entirely gone now.

"Yes—I believe I do, rather a lot."

He got up, and walked up and down the room.

"You know that makes it quite easy to go," he said at length, stopping in front of her. "But I shall come back. I forgot to ask you—you'll be here, won't you?"

"Yes, I shall be here," Laura said. She, too, got up and moved over to the window; bent to smell one of the bowls of freesias, and then turned back to him again. "If you find you do want to come back, after a month, we can see how we feel about it then. But remember, if you *don't* want to come back, in two months I shall have gone home for the summer, so the coast will be clear up here."

"You are very good to me," he said—something in his voice made the flat words completely adequate. "But I shall come back," he repeated. He picked up a book, turned it over absently, and put it down. "I am not sure that I shall write to you," he said unexpectedly. "I am rather afraid of that."

Laura had not thought of this. "Ot course not, unless you want to," she said. "Only——"

"Only what?" he asked, as she hesitated.

"Only if it were a case of *more* bottling yourself up—not writing, I mean—I should advise you to write. Anything to be a little extravagant!" she said lightly.

"I'll remember," he said. "But whether we write or not, we shall be all right, shan't we? I shall think gently of you—and you will think gently of me, won't you?"

"Of course I will," she said.

There was a moment's silence, and then Vinstead spoke again.

"It's the security that is so marvellous," he said. "That we should suddenly have that in one another. We all want it—like the French!" He came over and stood beside her. "I must go now," he said. "I've got things to see to. But I take the certainty of your kindness. Good-bye." Rather gently, rather hesitatingly, he kissed her—and with a simple gravity that was almost like a child's she kissed him in return.

At the door he paused suddenly, and turned back to her.

"That Buddha was very wise," he said; "for some of us, anyhow. That poor child, and now me."

For the moment Laura had forgotten the Professor's fortune. It darted back into her mind, as he repeated it, "'The wise find wisdom'—well, if I ever was wise," he said, "I have found more wisdom." He took her hand, and kissed it once more. "But the traveller will journey with a heavy heart," he said, and went out.

When the door had shut after him Laura Leroy walked slowly over to a small table. She took up from it the book which Vinstead had picked up and laid down, when he said that he should not write to her. For a moment she held it in her hands, and then raised it slowly towards her face. But she did nothing else. Presently she put it down again, gently, on the table from which she had taken it, and stood looking at it with a curious expression on her face, as of a person who is lost and for the moment cannot find their way. Then she smiled, and went over and rang the bell; when Niu answered it, "I speak with the son of the kitchen," she said. Niu held open the door for her, as she passed out to the ordering of her household.

Before dinner on that same evening Laura was sitting on the seat under the group of tamarisks in the upper garden. Their boughs of filmy green were less pale and tenuous than a week before, and the blossoms on the bushes of flowering cherry and plum were almost over-blown. But the scent of the lilacs and of the yellow briars round the house still filled the air, and the smells of the city—wood-smoke and Chinese sanitation and Chinese cooking and donkey-dung—came stronger than ever in the warm dusk. Again she sat idle, her hands in her lap, thinking of the week that had passed since she last sat there, and what it had brought—the strange un-expected ripening of her acquaintance with Little Annette, just at the girl's moment of crisis, and the cutting-short of that lovable and unawakened life; the development, which had an air of finality, in the relation between Judith and Derek; the sudden flowering of love between herself and Vinstead. She held his face in her mind—the curious sweetness of his eyes when he smiled, the mixture of humour and grimness round his mouth. The noises of the city came to her as she sat—the soft hum of unshod traffic, the hoot of motor-horns, the clanging of tram-bells, the hoarse strange cries. Sud-denly a steam-whistle screamed from the station just outside the Tartar wall, followed by the heavy puffing of an engine and the rumbling of coaches moving. She looked at her watch. Yes, it was the seven-thirty going out, rather late, as usual, and Vinstead was on it. He was sitting, lean and pale, in one of those first-class coaches, with his neat luggage—she was sure it was neat—his tired eyes, and the heavy heart that he said he should journey with. And suddenly Laura put her head down on her arms on the end of the bench. "It isn't only the traveller," she murmured to herself.

She lifted her head, after a moment or two, as a sudden question, a doubt, came into her mind—would he come back? She had a curious instinctive wondering whether, for them, the most intimate, the securest, the most perfect moment had not been reached on the previous day, out on the hill, before Little Annette's interruption. The passage of time, opportunities for intercourse, do not always develop a relationship, she knew—it may often happen that at an early stage a point is reached, a zenith of truth and understanding, which is never achieved again. Had it been so with herself and Vinstead, she wondered? Would it prove so? Then, indeed, he would do better not to come back.

Suddenly, out of the pale evening sky, there came again the winging of music. She looked up, and saw the flight of pigeons wheeling over the house. Watching them, catching at any distraction from the doubt and pain in her heart and mind, she noticed a solitary white bird a little behind the rest. For some reason this single white pigeon attracted her attention; he reminded her of the white fantails who cooed and preened above the heavy pale cornice, who strutted and quarrelled among the geraniums on the terrace at Garsover. And with the picture she remembered the terrible episode of Tim and the fantails, years ago now—the catapult presented to the still blue-smocked little boy by a worshipping under-gardener; the havoc wrought; Grandpère's wrath. She could see the child's flushed tear-stained face, the hair damp with the perspiration of emotion round the white brow, the poor angry little voice actually strangled with the sense of injustice and innocent intention. Her funny foolish Tim! Always in hot water of one sort or another. Actually the tears started to her eyes at the thought of him. What was he doing? He was there—the pigeons cooed about him now, the wagtails tripped and ran; in no time the fly-catchers would be perching on the tennis-poles and the bare stem of the tree-paeony.

Slowly the tumult died down in her. The pain of uncertainty, of parting, ebbed away out of her heart. She was back again at Garsover, with her children, with her parents—where in three months' time her body would be, as well as her spirit. A look of musing peace and happiness came gradually into her face, as she sat under the tamarisks in the Legation garden in Peking. Her other world had gathered her into it once more.